Printing Statement:

Due to the very old age and scarcity of this book,
many of the pages may be hard to read due to the
blurring of the original text, possible missing pages,
missing text, dark backgrounds and other issues
beyond our control.

Because this is such an important and rare work, we
believe it is best to reproduce this book regardless of
its original condition.

Thank you for your understanding.

CONTENTS.

WILLING TO DIE.

TO THE READER.

IRST, I must tell you how I intend to relate my story. Having never before undertaken to write a long narrative, I have considered and laid down a few rules which I shall observe. Some of these are unquestionably good; others, I daresay, offend against the canons of composition; but I adopt them, because they will enable me to tell my story better than, with my imperfect experience, better rules possibly would. In the first place, I shall represent the people with whom I had to deal quite fairly. I have met some bad people, some indifferent, and some who at this distance of time seem to me like angels in the unchanging light of heaven.

My narrative shall be arranged in the order of the events; I shall not recapitulate or anticipate.

What I have learned from others, and did not witness, that which I narrate, in part, from the hints of living witnesses, and, in part, conjecturally, I shall record in the historic third person; and I shall write it down with as much confidence and particularity as if I had actually seen it; in that respect imitating, I believe, all great historians, modern and ancient. But the scenes in which I have been an actor, that which my eyes have seen, and

B

my ears heard, I will relate accordingly. If I can be clear and true, my clumsiness and irregularity, I hope, will be forgiven me.

My name is Ethel Ware.

I am not an interesting person by any means. You shall judge. I shall be forty-two my next birthday. That anniversary will occur on the first of May, 1873; and I am unmarried.

I don't look quite the old maid I am, they tell me. They say I don't look five-and-thirty, and I am conscious, sitting before the glass, that there is nothing sour or peevish in my features. What does it matter, even to me? I shall, of course, never marry; and, honestly, I don't care to please any one. If I cared twopence how I looked, I should probably look worse than I do.

I wish to be honest. I have looked in the glass since I wrote that sentence. I have just seen the faded picture of what may have been a pretty, at least what is called a piquant face; a forehead broad and well-formed, over which the still dark-brown hair grows low; large and rather good grey eyes and features, with nothing tragic, nothing classic—just fairly good.

I think there was always energy in my face! I think I remember, long ago, something at times comic; at times, also, something sad and tender, and even dreamy, as I fixed flowers in my hair or talked to my image in the glass. All that has been knocked out of me pretty well. What I do see there now is resolution.

There are processes of artificial hatching in use, if I remember rightly, in Egypt, by which you may, at your discretion, make the bird all beak, or all claw, all head, or all drumstick, as you please to develope it, before the shell breaks, by a special application of heat. It is a chick, no doubt, but a monstrous chick; and something like such a chick was I. Circumstances, in my very early days, hatched my character altogether out of equilibrium.

The caloric had been applied quite different in my mother's case, and produced a prodigy of quite another sort.

I loved my mother with a very warm, but, I am now

conscious, with a somewhat contemptuous affection. It never was an angry nor an arrogant contempt; a very tender one, on the contrary. She loved me, I am sure, as well as she was capable of loving a child—better than she ever loved my sister—and I would have laid down my life for her; but, with all my love, I looked down upon her, although I did not know it, till I thought my life over in the melancholy honesty of solitude.

I am not romantic. If I ever was it is time I should be cured of all that. I can laugh heartily, but I think I sigh more than most people.

I am not a bit shy, but I like solitude; partly because I regard my kind with not unjust suspicion.

I am speaking very frankly. I enjoy, perhaps you think cynically, this hard-featured self-delineation. I don't spare myself; I need not spare any one else. But I am not a cynic. There is vacillation and timidity in that ironical egotism. It is something deeper with me. I don't delight in that sordid philosophy. I have encountered magnanimity and self-devotion on earth. It is not true that there is neither nobility nor beauty in human nature, that is not also more or less shabby and grotesque.

I have an odd story to tell. On my father's side I am the grand-daughter of a viscount; on my mother's, the grand-daughter of a baronet. I have had my early glimpses of the great world, and a wondrous long stare round the dark world beneath it.

When I lower my hand, and in one of the momentary reveries that tempt a desultory writer tickle my cheek slowly with the feathered end of my pen—for I don't incise my sentences with a point of steel, but, in the old fashion, wing my words with a possibly too appropriate grey-goose plume—I look through a tall window in an old house on the scenery I have loved best and earliest in the world. The noble Welsh mountains are on my right, the purple headlands stooping grandly into the waves; I look upon the sea, the enchanted element, my first love and my last! How often I lean upon my hand and smile back upon the waters that silently smile on me, rejoicing under the summer heavens; and in wintry moonlights, when the north wind drives the awful waves upon the rocks, and

I see the foam shooting cloud after cloud into the air, I have found myself, after long hours, still gazing, as if my breath were frozen, on the one peaked black rock, thinking what the storm and foam once gave me up there, until, with a sudden terror, and a gasp, I wake from the spell, and recoil from the white image, as if a spirit had been talking with me all the time.

From this same window, in the fore-ground, I see, in morning light or melancholy sunset, with very perfect and friendly trust, the shadowy old churchyard, where I have arranged my narrow bed shall be. There my mother-earth, at last, shall hold me in her bosom, and I shall find my anodyne and rest. There over me shall hover through the old church windows faintly the sweet hymns and the voices in prayer I heard long ago; there the shadow of tower and tree shall slowly move over the grass above me, from dawn till night, and there, within the fresh and solemn sound of its waves, I shall lie near the ceaseless fall and flow of the sea I loved so well.

I am not sorry, as I sit here, with my vain recollections and my direful knowledge, that my life has been what it

A member of the upper ten thousand, I should have known nothing. I have bought my knowledge dear. But truth is a priceless jewel. Would you part with it, fellow-mourner, and return to the simplicities and illusions of early days? Consider the question truly; be honest; and you will answer " No." In the volume of memory, every page of which, like " Cornelius Agrippa's bloody book," has power to evoke a spectre, would you yet erase a line? We can willingly part with nothing that ever was part of mind, or memory, or self. The lamentable past is our own for ever.

Thank Heaven, my childhood was passed in a tranquil nook, where the roar of the world's traffic is not so much as heard; among scenery, where there lurks little capital, and no enterprise; where the good people are asleep; and where, therefore, the irreparable improvements that in other places carry on their pitiless work of obliteration are undreamed of. I am looking out on scenes that remain unchanged as heaven itself. The summer comes and goes; the autumn drifts of leaves, and winter snows;

and all things here remain as 'my round childish eyes beheld them in stupid wonder and delight when first the world was opening upon them. The trees, the tower, the stile, the very gravestones, are my earliest friends; I stretch my arms to the mountains, as if I could fold them to my heart. And in the opening through the ancient trees, the great estuary stretches northward, wider and wider, into the grey horizon of the open sea.

> The sinking sun askance,
>   Spreads a dull glare,
>   Through evening air;
> And, in a happy trance,
>   Forest and wave, and white cliff stand,
>   Like an enchanted sea and land.
>
> The sea-breeze wakens clear and cold,
>   Over the azure wide;
> Before whose breath, in threads of gold,
>   The ruddy ripples glide,
> And chasing, break and mingle;
>   While clear as bells,
>   Each wavelet tells,
> O'er the stones on the hollow shingle.
>
> The rising of winds and the fall of the waves!
> I love the music of shingle and caves,
> And the billows that travel so far to die,
> In foam, on the loved shore where they lie.
> I lean my cold cheek on my hand;
>   And as a child, with open eyes,
>   Listens, in a dim surprise,
>   To some high story
>   Of grief and glory,
> It cannot understand;
> So, like that child,
> To meanings of a music wild,
> I listen, in a rapture lonely,
> Not understanding, listening only,
> To a story not for me;
>   And let my fancies come and go,
>   And fall and flow,
> With the eternal sea.

And so, to leave rhyme, and return to prose, I end my preface, and begin my story here.

CHAPTER I.

AN ARRIVAL.

ONE of the earliest scenes I can remember with perfect distinctness is this. My sister and I, still denizens of the nursery, had come down to take our tea with good old Rebecca Torkhill, the Malory housekeeper, in the room we called the cedar parlour. It is a long and rather sombre room, with two tall windows looking out upon the shadowy court-yard. There are on the wall some dingy portraits, whose pale faces peep out, as it were, through a background of black fog, from the canvas; and there is one, in better order than the others, of a grave man in the stately costume of James the First, which hangs over the mantel-piece. As a child I loved this room; I loved the half-decipherable pictures; it was solemn and even gloomy, but it was with the delightful gloom and solemnity of one of Rebecca Torkill's stories of castles, giants, and goblins.

It was evening now, with a stormy, red sky in the west. Rebecca and we two children were seated round the table, sipping our tea, eating hot cake, and listening to her oft-told tale, entitled the Knight of the Black Castle.

This knight, habited in black, lived in his black castle, in the centre of a dark wood, and being a giant, and an ogre, and something of a magician besides, he used to ride out at nightfall with a couple of great black bags, to stow his prey in, at his saddle-bow, for the purpose of visiting such houses as had their nurseries well-stocked with children. His tall black horse, when he dismounted, waited at the hall-door, which, however mighty its bars and bolts, could not resist certain magical words which he uttered in a sepulchral voice—

> " Yoke, yoke,
> Iron and oak ;
> One, two, and three,
> Open to me."

At this charmed summons the door turned instantly on its hinges, without warning of creak or rattle, and the black knight mounted the stairs to the nursery, and was drawing the children softly out of their beds, by their feet, before any one knew he was near.

As this story, which with childish love of iteration we were listening to now for the fiftieth time, went on, I, whose chair faced the window, saw a tall man on a tall horse—both looked black enough against the red sky— ride by at a walk.

I thought it was the gaunt old vicar, who used to ride up now and then to visit our gardener's mother, who was sick and weak, and troubling my head no more about him, was instantly as much absorbed as ever in the predatory prowlings of the Knight of the Black Castle.

It was not until I saw Rebecca's face, in which I was staring with the steadiness of an eager interest, undergo a sudden and uncomfortable change, that I discovered my error. She stopped in the middle of a sentence, and her eyes were fixed on the door. Mine followed hers thither. I was more than startled. In the very crisis of a tale of terror, ready to believe any horror, I thought, for a moment, that I actually beheld the Black Knight, and felt that his horse, no doubt, and his saddle-bags, were waiting at the hall-door to receive me and my sister.

What I did see was a man who looked to me gigantic. He seemed to fill the tall door-case. His dress was dark, and he had a pair of leather overalls, I believe they called them, which had very much the effect of jack-boots, and he had a low-crowned hat on. His hair was long and black, his prominent black eyes were fixed on us, his face was long, but handsome, and deadly pale, as it seemed to me, from intense anger. A child's instinctive reading of countenance is seldom at fault. The ideas of power and

mystery surround grown persons in the eyes of children.
A gloomy or forbidding face upon a person of great
stature inspires something like panic ; and if that person
is a stranger, and evidently transported with anger, his
mere appearance in the same room will, I can answer for
it, frighten a child half into hysterics. This alarming
face, with its black knit brows, and very blue shorn chin,
was to me all the more fearful that it was that of a man
no longer young. He advanced to the table with two
strides, and said, in resonant, deep tones, to which my
very heart seemed to vibrate :

"Mr. Ware's not here, but he will be, soon enough ;
you give him that ;" and he hammered down a letter on
the table, with a thump of his huge fist. "That's my answer ; and tell him, moreover, that I took his letter,"—
and he plucked an open letter deliberately from his great-
coat pocket—"and tore it, this way and that way, across
and across," and he suited the action fiercely to the words,
"and left it for him, there !"

So saying, he slapped down the pieces with his big
hand, and made our tea-spoons jump and jingle in our
cups, and turned and strode again to the door.

"And tell him this," he added, in a tone of calmer
hatred, turning his awful face on us again, "that there's
a God above us, who judges righteously."

The door shut, and we saw him no more. I and my
sister burst into clamorous tears, and roared and cried for
a full half hour, from sheer fright—a demonstration
which, for a time, gave Rebecca Torkill ample occupation
for all her energies and adroitness.

This recollection remains, with all the colouring and
exaggeration of a horrible impression received in childhood, fixed in my imagination. I and dear Nelly long
remembered the apparition, and in our plays used to call
him, after the goblin hero of the romance to which we had
been listening when he entered, the Knight of the
Black Castle.

The adventure made, indeed, a profound impression
upon our nerves, and I have related it, with more detail
than it seems to deserve, because it was, in truth, connected with my story ; and I afterwards, unexpectedly,

saw a good deal more of the awful man in whose presence
my heart had quaked, and after whose visit I and my
sister seemed for days to have drunk of "the cup of
trembling."

I must take up my story now at a point a great many
years later.

Let the reader fancy me and my sister Helen; I dark-
haired, and a few months past sixteen; she, with flaxen,
or rather golden hair and large blue eyes, and only fifteen,
standing in the hall at Malory, lighted with two candles;
one in the old-fashioned glass bell that swings by three
chains from the ceiling, the other carried out hastily from
the housekeeper's room, and flaming on the table, in the
foggy puffs of the February night air that entered at the
wide-open hall-door.

Old Rebecca Torkill stood on the steps, with her broad
hand shading her eyes, as if the moon dazzled them.

"There's nothing, dear; no, Miss Helen, it mustn't a'
bin the gate. There's no sign o' nothin' comin' up, and
no sound nor nothing at all; come in, dear; you shouldn't
a' come out to the open door, with your cough in this
fog."

So in she stumped, and shut the door; and we saw no
more of the dark trunks and boughs of the elms at the
other side of the courtyard, with the smoky mist between;
and we three trooped together to the housekeeper's room,
where we had taken up our temporary quarters.

This was the second false alarm that night, sounded, in
Helen's fancy, by the quavering scream of the old iron
gate. We had to wait and watch in the fever of expectation for some time longer.

Our old house of Malory was, at the best, in the forlorn
condition of a ship of war out of commission. Old Rebecca
and two rustic maids, and Thomas Jones, who was boots,
gardener, hen-wife, and farmer, were all the hands we
could boast; and at least three-fourths of the rooms were
locked up, with shutters closed; and many of them, from
year to year, never saw the light, and lay in perennial
dust.

The truth is, my father and mother seldom visited
Malory. They had a house in London, and led a very gay

life; were very "good people," immensely in request, and everywhere. Their rural life was not at Malory, but spent in making visits at one country-house after another. Helen and I, their only children, saw very little of them. We sometimes were summoned up to town for a month or two for lessons in dancing, music, and other things, but there we saw little more of them than at home. The being in society, judging by its effects upon them, appeared to me a very harassing and laborious profession. I always felt that we were half in the way and half out of sight in town, and was immensely relieved when we were dismissed again to our holland frocks, and to the beloved solitudes of Malory.

This was a momentous night. We were expecting the arrival of a new governess, or rather companion.

Laura Grey—we knew no more than her name, for in his hurried note we could not read whether she was Miss or Mrs.—my father had told us, was to arrive this night at about nine o'clock. I had asked him, when he paid his last visit of a day here, and announced the coming event, whether she was a married lady; to which he answered, laughing:

"You wise little woman! That's a very pertinent question, though I never thought of it, and I have been addressing her as Miss Grey all this time. She certainly is old enough to be married."

"Is she cross, papa, I wonder?" I further inquired.

"Not cross—perhaps a little severe. 'She whipped two female 'prentices to death, and hid them in the coal-hole,' or something of that kind, but she has a very cool temper;" and so he amused himself with my curiosity.

Now, although we knew that all this, including the quotation, was spoken in jest, it left an uncomfortable suspicion. Was this woman old and ill-tempered? A great deal was in the power of a governess here. An artful woman, who liked power, and did not like us, might make us very miserable.

At length the little party in the housekeeper's room did hear sounds at which we all started up with one consent. They were the trot of a horse's hoofs and the roll of wheels, and before we reached the hall-door the bell was ringing.

Rebecca swung open the door, and we saw in the shadow of the house, with the wheels touching the steps, a one-horse conveyance, with some luggage on top, dimly lighted by the candles in the hall.

A little bonnet was turned towards us from the windows; we could not see what the face was like ; a slender hand turned the handle, and a lady, whose figure, though enveloped in a tweed cloak, looked very slight and pretty, came down, and ran up the steps, and hesitated, and being greeted encouragingly by Rebecca Torkill, entered the hall smiling, and showed a very pretty and modest face, rather pale, and very young.

" My name is Grey; I am the new governess," she said, in a pleasant voice, which, with her pretty looks, was very engaging : " and these are the young ladies ?" she continued, glancing at Rebecca and back again at us ; you are Ethel, and you Helen Ware ?" and a little timidly she offered her hand to each.

I liked her already.

" Shall I go with you to your room," I asked, " while Rebecca is making tea for us in the housekeeper's room ? We thought we should be more comfortable there to-night."

" I'm so glad—I shall feel quite at home. It is the very thing I should have liked," she said; and talked on as I led her to her room, which, though very old-fashioned, looked extremely cosy, with a good fire flickering abroad and above on walls and ceiling.

I remember everything about that evening so well. I have reason to remember Miss Laura Grey. Some people would have said that there was not a regular feature in her face, except her eyes, which were very fine ; but she had beautiful little teeth, and a skin wonderfully smooth and clear, and there was refinement and energy in her face, which was pale and spiritual, and indescribably engaging. To my mind, whether according to rule or not, she was nothing short of beautiful.

I have reason to remember that pale, pretty young face. The picture is clear and living before me this moment, as

it was then in the firelight. Standing there, she smiled
on me very kindly—she looked as if she would have kissed
me—and then, suddenly thoughtful, she stretched her
slender hands to the fire, and, in a momentary reverie,
sighed very deeply.

I left her, softly, with her trunks and boxes, which
Thomas Jones had already carried up, and ran downstairs.

I remember the pictures of that night with supernatural
distinctness; for at that point of time fate changed my
life, and with pretty Miss Grey another pale figure entered,
draped in black, and calamity was my mate for many a
day after.

Our tea-party, however, this night in Mrs. Torkill's
room, was very happy. I don't remember what we talked
about, but we were in high good-humour with our young
lady-superioress, and she seemed to like us.

I am going to tell you very shortly my impressions of
this lady. I never met any one in my life who had the
same influence over me ; and, for a time, it puzzled me.
When we were not at French, German, music—our studies,
in fact—she was exactly like one of ourselves, always
ready to do whatever we liked best, always pleasant, gentle,
and, in her way, even merry. When she was alone, or
thinking, she was sad. That seemed the habit of her
mind; but she was naturally gay and sympathetic, as
ready as we for a walk on the strand to pick up shells,
for a ride on the donkeys to Penruthyn Priory, to take
a sail or a row on the estuary, or a drive in our little
pony-carriage anywhere. Sometimes on our rambles we
would cross the stile and go into the pretty little churchyard that lies to the left of Malory, near the sea, and if it
was a sunny day we would read the old inscriptions and
loiter away half an hour among the tombstones.

And when we came home to tea we would sit round the
fire and tell stories, of which she had ever so many,
German, French, Scotch, Irish, Icelandic, and I know not
what ; and sometimes we went to the housekeeper's room,
and, with Rebecca Torkill's leave, made a hot cake, and
baked it on the griddle there, with great delight.

The secret of Laura Grey's power was in her gentle

temper, her inflexible conscience, and her angelic firmness in all matters of duty. 'I never saw her excited, or for a moment impatient ; and at idle times, as I said, she was one of ourselves. The only threat she ever used was to tell us that she could not stay at Malory as our governess if we would not do what she thought right. There is in young people an instinctive perception of motive, and no truer spirit than Laura Grey ever lived on earth. I loved her. I had no fear of her. She was our gentle companion and playmate ; and yet, in a certain sense, I never stood so much in awe of any human being.

Only a few days after Laura Grey had come home, we were sitting in our accustomed room, which was stately, but not uncomfortably spacious, and, like many at the same side of the house, panelled up to the ceiling. I remember, it was just at the hour of the still early sunset, and the ruddy beams were streaming their last through the trunks of the great elms. We were in high chat over Helen's little sparrow, Dickie, a wonderful bird, whose appetite and spirits we were always discussing, when the door opened, and Rebecca said, " Young ladies, please, here's Mr. Carmel ;" and Miss Grey, for the first time, saw a certain person who turns up at intervals and in odd scenes in the course of this autobiography.

The door is at some distance from the window, and through its panes across that space upon the opposite wall the glow of sunset fell mistily, making the clear shadow, in which our visitor stood, deeper. The figure stood out against this background like a pale old portrait, his black dress almost blended with the background ; but, indistinct as it was, it was easy to see that the dress he wore was of some ecclesiastical fashion not in use among Church of England men. The coat came down a good deal lower than his knees. His thin slight figure gave him an effect of height far greater than his real stature ; his fine forehead showed very white in contrast with his close dark hair, and his thin, delicate features, as he stepped slowly in, with an ascetic smile, and his hand extended, accorded well with ideas of abstinence and penance. Gentle as was his manner, there was something of authority also in it, and in the tones of his voice.

"How do you do, Miss Ethel? How do you do, Miss Helen? I am going to write my weekly note to your mamma, and—oh! Miss Grey, I believe?"—he interrupted himself, and bowed rather low to the young governess, disclosing the small tonsure on the top of his head.

Miss Grey acknowledged his bow, but I could see that she was puzzled and surprised.

"I am to tell your mamma, I hope, that you are both quite well?" he said, addressing himself to me, and taking my hand; "and in good spirits, I suppose, Miss Grey?" he said, apparently recollecting that she was to be recognized; "I may say that?"

He turned to her, still holding my hand.

"Yes, they are quite well, and, I believe, happy," she said, still looking at him, I could see, with curiosity.

It was a remarkable countenance, with large earnest eyes, and a mouth small and melancholy, with those brilliant red lips that people associate with early decay. It was a pale face of suffering and decision, which so vaguely indicated his years that he might be any age you please, from six-and-twenty up to six-and-thirty, as you allowed more or less in the account for the afflictions of a mental and bodily discipline.

He stood there for a little while chatting with us. There was something engaging in this man, cold, severe, and melancholy as his manner was. I was conscious that he was agreeable, and, young as I was, I felt that he was a man of unusual learning and ability.

In a little time he left us. It was now twilight, and we saw him, with his slight stoop, pass our window with slow step and downcast eyes.

CHAPTER II.

OUR CURIOSITY IS PIQUED.

AND so that odd vision was gone; and Laura Grey turned to us eagerly for information.

We could not give her much. We were ourselves so familiar with the fact of Mr. Carmel's existence, that it never occurred to us that his appearance could be a surprise to any one.

Mr. Carmel had come about eight months before to reside in the small old house in which the land-steward had once been harboured, and which, built in continuation of the side of the house, forms a sort of retreating wing to it, with a hall-door to itself, but under the same roof.

This Mr. Carmel was, undoubtedly, a Roman Catholic, and an ecclesiastic; of what order I know not. Possibly he was a Jesuit. I never was very learned or very curious upon such points; but some one, I forgot who, told me that he positively was a member of the Society of Jesus.

My poor mother was very High Church, and on very friendly terms with Catholic personages of note. Mr. Carmel had been very ill, and was still in delicate health, and a quiet nook in the country, in the neighbourhood of the sea, had been ordered for him. The vacant house I have described she begged for his use from my father, who did not at all like the idea of lending it, as I could gather from the partly jocular and partly serious discussions which he maintained upon the point, every now and then, at the breakfast-table, when I was last in town.

I remember hearing my father say at last, "You know, my dear Mabel, I'm always ready to do anything you like. I'll be a Catholic myself, if it gives you the least pleasure, only be sure, first, about this thing, that you really do like it. I shouldn't care if the man were hanged—he very likely deserves it—but I'll give him my house if it makes you happy. You must remember, though, the Cardyllion people won't like it, and you'll be talked about, and I daresay he'll make nuns of Ethel and Helen. He won't get a great deal by that, I'm afraid. And I don't see why those pious people—Jesuits, and that sort of persons, who don't know what to do with their money —should not take a house for him if he wants it, or what business they have quartering their friars and rubbish upon poor Protestants like you and me."

The end of it was that about two months later this Mr. Carmel arrived, duly accredited by my father, who told me when he paid us one of his visits of a day, soon after, that he was under promise not to talk to us about religion, and that if he did I was to write to tell him immediately.

When I had told my story to Laura Grey, she was thoughtful for a little time.

"Are his visits only once a week?" she asked.

"Yes," said I.

"And does he stay as short a time always?" she continued.

We both agreed that he usually stayed a little longer.

"And has he never talked on the subject of religion?"

"No, never. He has talked about shells, or flowers, or anything he found us employed about, and always told us something curious or interesting. I had heard papa say that he was engaged upon a work from which great things were expected, and boxes of books were perpetually coming and going between him and his correspondents."

She was not quite satisfied, and in a few days there arrived from London two little books on the great controversy between Luther and the Pope; and out of these, to the best of her poor ability, she drilled us, by way of a prophylactic against Mr. Carmel's possible machinations.

It did not appear, however, to be Mr. Carmel's mission to flutter the little nest of heresy so near him. When he paid his next visit, it so happened that one of these duodecimo disputants lay upon the table. Without thinking, as he talked, he raised it, and read the title on the cover, and smiled gently. Miss Grey blushed. She had not intended disclosing her suspicions.

"In two different regiments, Miss Grey," he said, "but both under the same king;" and he laid the book quietly upon the table again, and talked on of something quite different.

Laura Grey, in a short time, became less suspicious of Mr. Carmel, and rather enjoyed his little visits, and looked forward with pleasure to them.

Could you imagine a quieter or more primitive life than ours, or, on earth, a much happier one?

Malory owns an old-fashioned square pew in the aisle of the pretty church of Cardyllion. In this spacious pew we three sat every Sunday, and on one of these occasions, a few weeks after Miss Grey's arrival, from my corner I thought I saw a stranger in the Verney seat, which is at the opposite side of the aisle, and had not had an occupant for several months. There was certainly a man in it; but the stove that stood nearly between us would not allow me to see more than his elbow, and the corner of an open book, from which I suppose he was reading.

I was not particularly curious about this person. I knew that the Verneys, who were distant cousins of ours, were abroad, and the visitor was not likely to be very interesting.

A long, indistinct sermon interposed, and I did not recollect to look at the Verney pew until the congregation were trooping decorously out, and we had got some way down the aisle. The pew was empty by that time.

"Some one in the Verney's pew," I remarked to our governess, so soon as we were quite out of the shadow of the porch.

"Which is the Verney's pew?" she asked.

I described it.

"Yes, there was. I have got a headache, my dear. Suppose we go home by the Mill Road?"

We agreed.

It is a very pretty, and in places rather a steep road, very narrow, and ascending with a high and wooded bank at its right, and a precipitous and thickly-planted glen to its left. The opposite side is thickly wooded also, and a stream far below splashes and tinkles among the rocks under the darkening foliage.

As we walked up this shadowy road, I saw an old gentleman walking down it, towards us. He was descending at a brisk pace, and wore a chocolate-coloured great-coat, made with a cape, and fitting his figure closely. He wore a hat with a rather wide brim, turned up at the sides. His face was very brown. He had a thin, high nose, with very thin nostrils, rather prominent eyes, and carried his head high. Altogether he struck me as a particularly gentleman-like and ill-tempered looking old man, and his features wore a character of hauteur that was perfectly insolent.

He was pretty near to us by the time I turned to warn our governess, who was beside me, to make way for him to pass. I did not speak; for I was a little startled to see that she was very much flushed, and almost instantly turned deadly pale.

We came nearly to a standstill, and the old gentleman was up to us in a few seconds. As he approached, his prominent eyes were fixed on Laura Grey. He stopped, with the same haughty stare, and, raising his hat, said in a cold, rather high key, "Miss Grey, I think? Miss Laura Grey? You will not object, I dare say, to allow me a very few words?"

The young lady bowed very slightly, and said, in a low tone, "Certainly not."

I saw that she looked pained, and even faint. This old gentleman's manner, and the stern stare of his prominent eyes, embarrassed even me, who did not directly encounter them.

"Perhaps we had better go on, Helen and I, to the seat; we can wait for you there?" I said softly to her.

" Yes, dear, I think it will be as well," she answered gently.

We walked on slowly. The bench was not a hundred steps up the steep. It stands at the side of the road, with its back against the bank. From this seat I could see very well what passed, though, of course, quite out of hearing.

The old gentleman had a black cane in his fingers, which he poked about in the gravel. You would have said from his countenance that at every little stab he punched an enemy's eye out.

First, the gentleman made a little speech, with his head very high, and an air of determination and severity. The young lady seemed to answer, briefly and quietly. Then ensued a colloquy of a minute or more, during which the old gentleman's head nodded often with emphasis, and his gestures became much more decided. The young lady seemed to say little, and very quietly: her eyes were lowered to the ground as she spoke.

She said something, I suppose, which he chose to resent, for he smiled sarcastically, and raised his hat ; then, suddenly resuming his gravity, he seemed to speak with a sharp and hectoring air, as if he were laying down the law upon some point once for all.

Laura Grey looked up sharply, with a brilliant colour, and with her head high, replied rapidly for a minute or more, and turning away, without waiting for his answer, walked slowly, with her head still high, towards us.

The gentleman stood looking after her with his sarcastic smile, but that was gone in a moment, and he continued looking, with an angry face, and muttering to himself, until suddenly he turned away, and walked off at a quick pace down the path towards Cardyllion.

A little uneasily, Helen and I stood up to meet our governess. She was still flushed and breathing quickly, as people do from recent agitation.

" No bad news? Nothing unpleasant ?" I asked, looking very eagerly into her face.

" No ; no bad news, dear."

I took her hand. I felt that she was trembling a little, and she had become again more than usually pale. We walked homeward in silence.

Laura Grey seemed in deep and agitated thought. We did not, of course, disturb her. An unpleasant excitement like that always disposes one to silence. Not a word, I think, was uttered all the way to the steps of Malory. Laura Grey entered the hall, still silent, and when she came down to us, after an hour or two passed in her room, it was plain she had been crying.

CHAPTER III.

THE THIEF IN THE NIGHT.

F what happened next I have a strangely imperfect recollection. I cannot tell you the intervals, or even the order, in which some of the events occurred. It is not that the mist of time obscures it; what I do recollect is dreadfully vivid; but there are spaces of the picture gone. I see faces of angels, and faces that make my heart sink; fragments of scenes. It is like something reflected in the pieces of a smashed looking-glass.

I have told you very little of Helen, my sister, my one darling on earth. There are things which people, after an interval of half a life, have continually present to their minds, but cannot speak of. The idea of opening them to strangers is insupportable. A sense of profanation shuts the door, and we " wake " our dead alone. I could not have told you what I am going to write. I did not intend inscribing here more than the short, bleak result. But I write it as if to myself, and I will get through it.

To you it may seem that I make too much of this, which is, as Hamlet says, " common." But you have not known what it is to be for all your early life shut out from all but one beloved companion, and never after to have found another.

Helen had a cough, and Laura Grey had written to mamma, who was then in Warwickshire, about it. She was referred to the Cardyllion doctor. He came ; he was

a skilful man. There were the hushed, dreadful moments,
while he listened, through his stethoscope, thoughtfully,
to the "still, small voice" of fate, to us inaudible, pro-
nuncing on the dread issues of life or death.

"No sounder lungs in England," said Doctor Mervyn,
looking up with a congratulatory smile.

He told her, only, that she must not go in the way of
cold, and by-and-by sent her two bottles from his surgery;
and so we were happy once more.

But doctors' advices, like the warnings of fate, are
seldom obeyed; least of all by the young. Nelly's little
pet-sparrow was ailing, or we fancied it was. She and I
were up every hour during the night to see after it. Next
evening Nelly had a slight pain in her chest. It became
worse, and by twelve o'clock was so intense that Laura
Grey, in alarm, sent to Cardyllion for the doctor. Thomas
Jones came back without him, after a delay of an hour.
He had been called away to make a visit somewhere, but
the moment he came back he would come to Malory.

It came to be three o'clock; he had not appeared;
darling Nelly was in actual torture. Again Doctor Mervyn
was sent for; and again, after a delay, the messenger
returned with the same dismaying answer. The governess
and Rebecca Torkill exhausted in vain their little list of
remedies. I was growing terrified. Intuitively I perceived
the danger. The doctor was my last earthly hope. Death,
I saw, was drawing nearer and nearer every moment, and
the doctor might be ten miles away. Think what it was
to stand, helpless, by her. Can I ever forget her poor
little face, flushed scarlet, and gasping and catching at
breath, hands, throat, every sinew quivering in the mortal
struggle!

At last a knock and a ring at the hall-door. I rushed
to the window; the first chill grey of winter's dawn hung
sicklily over the landscape. No one was on the steps, or
on the grey gravel of the court. But, yes—I do hear
voices and steps upon the stair approaching. Oh! Heaven
be thanked, the doctor is come at last!

I ran out upon the lobby, just as I was, in my dressing-
gown, with my hair about my shoulders, and slippers on
my bare feet. A candlestick, with the candle burnt low,

was standing on the broad head of the clumsy old bannister, and Mr. Carmel, in a black riding-coat, with his hat in his hand, and that kind of riding-boots that used to be called clerical, on, was talking in a low, earnest tone to our governess.

The faint grey from the low lobby window was lost at this point, and the delicate features of the pale ecclesiastic, and Miss Grey's pretty and anxious face, were lighted, like a fine portrait of Schalken's, by the candle only.

Throughout this time of agony and tumult, the memory of my retina remains unimpaired, and every picture retains its hold upon my brain. And, oh! had the doctor come? Yes, Mr. Carmel had ridden all the way, fourteen miles, to Llwynan, and brought the doctor back with him. He might not have been here for hours otherwise. He was now downstairs making preparations, and would be in the room in a few minutes.

I looked at that fine, melancholy, energetic face as if he had saved me. I could not thank him. I turned and entered our room again, and told Nelly to be of good courage, that the doctor was come. "And, oh! please God, he'll do you good, my own darling, darling—precious darling!"

In a minute more the doctor was in the room. My eyes were fixed upon his face as he talked to his poor little patient; he did not look at all as he had done on his former visit. I see him before me as I write; his bald head shining in the candle-light, his dissatisfied and gloomy face, and his shrewd light blue eyes, reading her looks askance, as his fingers rested on her pulse.

I remember, as if the sick-room had changed into it, finding myself in the small room opposite, with no one there but the doctor and Miss Grey, we three, in the cold morning light, and his saying, "Well all this comes of violating directions. There is very intense inflammation, and her chest is in a most critical state."

Then Miss Grey said, after a moment's hush, the awful words, "Is there any danger?" and he answered shortly, "I wish I could say there wasn't." I felt my ears sing as if a pistol had been fired. No one spoke for another minute or more.

The doctor stayed, I think, for a long time, and he must have returned after, for he mixed up in almost every scene I can remember during that jumbled day of terror.

There was, I know, but one day, and part of a night. But it seems to me as if whole nights intervened, and suns set and rose, and days uncounted and undistinguished passed, in that miserable period.

The pain subsided, but worse followed; a dreadful cough, that never ceased—a long, agonised struggle against a slow drowning of the lungs. The doctor gave her up. They wanted me to leave the room, but I could not.

The hour had come at last, and she was gone. The wild cry—the terrible farewell—nothing can move inexorable death. All was still.

As the ship lies serene in the caverns of the cold sea, and feels no more the fury of the wind, the strain of cable, and the crash of wave, this forlorn wreck lay quiet now. Oh! little Nelly! I could not believe it.

She lay in her nightdress under the white coverlet. Was this whole scene an awful vision, and was my heart breaking in vain? Oh, poor simple little Nelly, to think that you should have changed into anything so sublime and terrible!

I stood dumb by the bedside, staring at the white face that was never to move again. Such a look I had never seen before. The white glory of an angel was upon it.

Rebecca Torkill spoke to me, I think. I remember her kind, sorrowful old face near me, but I did not hear what she said. I was in a stupor, or a trance. I had not shed a tear; I had not said a word. For a time I was all but mad. In the light of that beautiful transfiguration my heart was bursting with the wildest rebellion against the law of death that had murdered my innocent sister before my eyes; against the fate of which humanity is the sport; against the awful Power who made us! What spirit knows, till the hour of temptation, the height or depth of its own impiety?

Oh, gentle, patient little Nelly! The only good thing I can see in myself in those days is my tender love of you, and my deep inward certainty of my immeasurable inferiority. Gentle, humble little Nelly, who thought me so excelling in cleverness, in wisdom, and countless other perfections, how humble in my secret soul I felt myself beside you, although I was too proud to say so! In your presence my fierce earthy nature stood revealed, and wherever I looked my shadow was cast along the ground by the pure light that shone from you.

I don't know what time passed without a word falling from my lips. I suppose people had other things to mind, and I was left to myself. But Laura Grey stole her hand into mine, she kissed me, and I felt her tears on my cheek.

"Ethel, darling, come with me," she said, crying, very gently. "You can come back again. You'll come with me, won't you? Our darling is happier, Ethel, than ever she could have been on earth, and she will never know change or sorrow again."

I began to sob distractedly. I do really believe I was half out of my mind. I began to talk to her volubly, vehemently, crying passionately all the time. I do not remember now a word I uttered; I know its purport only from the pain, and even horror, I remember in Laura Grey's pale face. It has taken a long and terrible discipline to expel that evil spirit. I know what I was in those days. My pilgrimage since than has been by steep and solitary paths, in great dangers, in darkness, in fear; I have eaten the bread of affliction, and my drink has been of the waters of bitterness; I am tired and footsore yet, though through a glass darkly, I think I can now see why it all was, and I thank God with a contrite heart for the terrors and the mercies he has shown me. I begin to discover through the mist who was the one friend who never forsook me through all those stupendous wanderings, and I long for the time when I shall close my tired eyes, all being over, and lie at the feet of my Saviour.

CHAPTER IV.

MY FATHER.

ORTH sped Laura Grey's letter to mamma. She was then at Roydon; papa was with her. The Easter recess had just sent down some distinguished visitors, who were glad to clear their heads for a few days of the hum of the Houses and the smell of the river; and my father, although not in the House, ran down with them. Little Nelly had been his pet, as I was mamma's.

There was an awkwardness in post-office arrangements between the two places then, and letters had to make a considerable circuit. There was a delay of three clear days between the despatch of the letter and the reply.

I must say a word about papa. He was about the most agreeable and careless man on earth. There are men whom no fortune could keep out of debt. A man of that sort seems to me not to have any defined want or enjoyment, but the horizon of his necessities expands in proportion as he rises in fortune, and always exceeds the ring-fence of his estate. What its periphery may be, or his own real wants, signifies very little. His permanent necessity is always to exceed his revenue.

I don't think my father's feelings were very deep. He was a good-natured husband, but, I am afraid, not a good one. I loved him better than I loved mamma. Children are always captivated by gaiety and indulgence. I was not of an age to judge of higher things, and I never missed the article of religion, of which, I believe, he had none. Although he lived so much in society that he might almost be said to have no domestic life whatever, no man could be simpler, less suspicious, or more easily imposed upon.

The answer to Miss Grey's letter was the arrival of my father. He was in passionate grief, and in a state of high excitement. He ran upstairs, without waiting to take off his hat; but at the door of our darling's room he hesitated. I did not know he had arrived till I heard him, some minutes later, walking up and down the room, sobbing. Though he was selfish, he was affectionate. No one liked to go in to disturb him. She lay by this time in her coffin. The tint of clay darkened her pretty features. The angelic beauty that belongs to death is transitory beyond all others. I would not look at her again, to obscure its glory. She lay now in her shroud, a forlorn sunken image of decay.

When he came out he talked wildly and bitterly. His darling had been murdered, he said, by neglect. He upbraided us all round, including Rebecca Torkill, for our cruel carelessness. He blamed the doctor. He had no right, in a country where there was but one physician, to go so far away as fourteen miles, and to stay away so long. He denounced even his treatment. He ought to have bled her. It was, every one knew, the proper way of treating such a case.

Than Laura Grey, no one could have been more scrupulously careful. She could not have prevented, even if she had suspected the possibility of such a thing, her stealing out of bed now and then to look at her sick sparrow. All this injustice was, however, but the raving of his grief.

In poor little Nelly's room my father's affectionate nature was convulsed with sorrow. When he came down I cried with him for a long time. I think this affliction has drawn us nearer. He was more tender to me than I ever remembered him before.

At last the ghastly wait and suspense were ended. I saw no more strange faces in the lobbies; and the strange voices on the stairs and footsteps in the room, and the muffled sounds that made me feel faint, were heard no more. The funeral was over, and pretty Nelly was gone for ever and ever, and I would come in and go out and

read my books, and take my walks alone; and the flowers,
and the long summer evenings, and the song of birds
would come again, and the leaves make their soft shadow
in the nooks where we used to sit together in the wood,
but gentle little Nelly would never come again.

During these terrible days, Laura Grey was a sister to
me, both in affection and in sorrow. Oh, Laura, can I
ever forget your tender, patient sympathy? How often
my thoughts recall your loved face as I lay my head
upon my lonely pillow, and my blessings follow you over
the wide sea to your far-off home!

Papa took a long solitary ride that day through the
warren, and away by Penruthyn Priory, and did not
return till dark.

When he did, he sent for me. I found him in the
room which, in the old-fashioned style, was called the
oak parlour. A log-fire—we were well supplied from the
woods in the rear of the house—lighted the room with a
broad pale flicker. My father was looking ill and tired.
He was leaning with his elbow on the mantel-piece, and
said:

"Ethel, darling, I want to know what you would like
best. We are going abroad for a little time; it is the
only thing for your mamma. This place would kill her.
I shall be leaving this to-morrow afternoon, and you can
make up your mind which you would like best—to come
with us and travel for some months, or to wait here, with
Miss Grey, until our return. You shall do precisely
whatever you like best—I don't wish you to hurry
yourself, darling. I'd rather you thought it over at your
leisure."

Then he sat down and talked about other things; and
turned about to the fire with his decanter of sherry by
him, and drank a good many glasses, and leaned back in
his chair before he had finished it.

My father, I thought, was dozing, but was not sure;
and being a good deal in awe of him—a natural consequence of seeing so little of him—I did not venture either
to waken him, or to leave the room without his permission.

There are two doors in that room. I was standing

irresolutely near that which is next the window, when
the other opened, and the long whiskers and good-
humoured, sensible face of portly Wynne Williams, the
town-clerk and attorney of Cardyllion, entered. My
father awoke, with a start, at the sound, and seeing him,
smiled and extended his hand.

"How d'ye do, Williams? It's so good of you to
come. Sit down. I'm off to-morrow, so I sent you a
note. Try that sherry; it is better than I thought.
And now I must tell you, that old scoundrel, Rokestone,
is going to foreclose the mortgage, and they have served
one of the tenants at Darlip with an ejectment; that's
more serious; I fancy he means mischief there also.
What do you think?"

"I always thought he might give us annoyance there;
but Mandrick's opinion was with us. Do you wish me to
look after that?"

"Certainly. And he's bothering me about that trust."

"I know," said Mr. Wynne Williams, with rather
gloomy rumination.

"That fellow has lost me—I was reckoning it up only
a day or two ago—between five and six thousand pounds
in mere law costs, beside all the direct mischief he has
done me; and he has twice lost me a seat in the House—
first by maintaining that petition at King's Firkins, a
thing that must have dropped but for his money; he had
nothing on earth to do with it, and no motive but his
personal, fiendish feelings; and next by getting up the
contest against me at Shillingsworth, where, you know,
it was ten to one; by Heavens! I should have had a
walk over. There is not an injury that man could do me
he has not done. I can prove that he swore he would
strip me of everything I possessed. It is ever so many
years since I saw him—you know all about it—and the
miscreant pursues me still relentlessly. He swore to old
Dymock, I'm told, and I believe it, that he would never
rest till he had brought me to a prison: I could have
him before a jury for that. There's some remedy, I
suppose, there's some protection? If I had done what I
wished ten years ago, I'd have had him out; it's not too
late yet to try whether pistols can't settle it. I wish I

had not taken advice; in a matter like that, the man who does always does wrong. I daresay, Williams, you think with me, now it's a case for cutting the Gordian knot?"

"I should not advise it, sir; he's an old man, and he's not afraid of what people say, and people know he has fought. He'd have you in the Queen's Bench, and as his feelings are of that nature, I'd not leave him the chance— I wouldn't trust him."

"It's not easy to know what one should do—a miscreant like that. I hope and pray that the curse of——"

My father spoke with a fierce tremble in his voice, and at that moment he saw me. He had forgotten that I was in the room, and said instantly:

"You may as well run away, dear; Mr. Williams and I have some business to talk over—and tiresome business it is. Good night, darling."

So away I went, glad of my escape, and left them talking. My father rang the bell soon, and called for more wine; so I suppose the council sat till late. I joined Laura Grey, to whom I related all that had passed, and my decision on the question, which was, to remain with her at Malory. She kissed me, and said, after a moment's thought:

"But will they think it unkind of you, preferring to remain here?"

"No," I said; "I think I should be rather in the way if I went; and, besides, I know papa is never high with any one, and really means what he says; and I should feel a little strange with them. They are very kind, and love me very much, I know, and so do I love them; but I see them so little, and you are such a friend, and I don't wish to leave this place; I like it better than any other in all the world; and I feel at home with you, more than I could with any one else in the world."

So that point was settled, and next day papa took leave of me very affectionately; and, notwithstanding his excited language, I heard nothing more of pistols and Mr. Rokestone. But many things were to happen before I saw papa again.

I remained, therefore, at Malory, and Laura Grey with

me; and the shadow of Mr. Carmel passed the window every evening, but he did not come in to see us, as he used. He made inquiries at the door instead, and talked, sometimes for five minutes together, with Rebecca Torkill. I was a little hurt at this; I did not pretend to Laura to perceive it; but in our walks, or returning in the evening, if by chance I saw his tall, thin, but graceful figure approaching by the same path, I used to make her turn aside and avoid him by a detour. In so lonely a place as Malory the change was marked; and there was pain in that neglect. I would not let him fancy, however, that I wished, any more than he, to renew our old and near acquaintance.

So weeks passed away, and leafy May had come, and Laura Grey and I were sitting in our accustomed room, in the evening, talking in our desultory way.

"Don't you think papa very handsome?" I asked.

"Yes, he is handsome," she answered; "there is something refined as well as clever in his face; and his eyes are fine; and all that goes a great way. But many people might think him not actually handsome, though very good-looking and prepossessing."

"They must be hard to please," I said.

She smiled good-naturedly.

"Mamma fell in love with him at first sight, Rebecca Torkill says," I persisted, "and mamma was not easily pleased. There was a gentleman who was wildly in love with her; a man of very old family, Rebecca says, and good-looking, but she would not look at him when once she had seen papa."

"I think I heard of that. He is a baronet now; but he was a great deal older than Mr. Ware, I believe."

"Yes, he was; but Rebecca says he did not look ten years older than papa, and *he* was very young indeed then," I answered. "It was well for mamma she did not like him, for I once heard Rebecca say that he was a very bad man."

"Did you ever hear of mamma's aunt Lorrimer?" I resumed, after a little pause.

"Not that I recollect."

"She is very rich, Rebecca says. She has a house in

London, but she is hardly ever there. She's not very old
—not sixty. Rebecca is always wondering whom she will
leave her money to; but that don't much matter, for I
believe we have more than we want. Papa says, about
ten years ago, she lived for nothing but society, and was
everywhere; and now she has quite given up all that, and
wanders about the Continent."

Our conversation subsided; and there was a short
interval in which neither spoke.

"Why is it, Laura," said I, after this little silence,
"that you never tell me anything about yourself, and I
am always telling you everything I think or remember?
Why are you so secret? Why don't you tell me your
story?"

"My story; what does it signify? I suppose it is about
an average story. Some people are educated to be gover-
nesses; and some of us take to it later, or by accident;
and we are amateurs, and do our best. The Jewish custom
was wise; every one should learn a mechanic's business.
Saint Paul was a tent-maker. If fortune upsets the boat,
it is well to have anything to lay hold of—anything rather
than drowning; an hospital matron, a companion, a
governess, there are not many chances, when things go
wrong, between a poor woman and the workhouse."

"All this means, you will tell me nothing," I said.

"I am a governess, darling. What does it matter what
I was? I am happier with you than ever I thought I
could be again. If I had a story that was pleasant to
hear, there is no one on earth I would tell it to so readily;
but my story—— There is no use in thinking over misfortune," she continued; "there is no greater waste of
time than regretting, except wishing. I know, Ethel, you
would not pain me. I can't talk about those things; I
may another time."

"You shan't speak of them, Laura, unless you wish it.
I am ashamed of having bothered you so," I kissed her.
"But, will you tell me one thing, for I am really curious
about it? I have been thinking about that very peculiar-
looking old gentleman, who wore a chocolate-coloured
great-coat, and met us in the Mill Walk, and talked to you,
you remember, on the Sunday we returned from church

that way. Now, I want you to tell me, is that old man's name Rokestone?"

"No, dear, it is not; I don't think he even knows him. But isn't it time for us to have our tea? Will you not make it, while I put our books up in the other room?"

So I undertook this office, and was alone.

The window was raised, the evening was warm, and the sun by this time setting. It was the pensive hour when solitude is pleasant; when grief is mellowed, and even a thoughtless mind, like mine, is tinged with melancholy. I was thinking now of our recluse neighbour. I had seen him pass, as Miss Grey and I were talking. He still despatched those little notes about the inmates of Malory; for mamma always mentioned, when she wrote to me, in her wanderings on the Continent, that she had heard from Mr. Carmel that I was well, and was out every day with my governess, and so on. I wondered why he had quite given up those little weekly visits, and whether I could have unwittingly offended him.

These speculations would recur oftener than perhaps was quite consistent with the disdain I affected on the subject. But people who live in cities have no idea how large a space in one's thoughts, in a solitude like Malory, a neighbour at all agreeable must occupy.

I was ruminating in a great arm-chair, with my hand supporting my head, and my eyes fixed on my foot, which was tapping the carpet, when I heard the cold, clear voice of Mr. Carmel at the window. I looked up, and my eyes met his,

D

CHAPTER V.

THE LITTLE BLACK BOOK.

OUR eyes met, I said; they remained fixed for a moment, and then mine dropped. I had been, as it were, detected, while meditating upon this capricious person. I daresay I even blushed; I certainly was embarrassed. He was repeating his salutation, "How d'ye do, Miss Ware?"

"Oh, I'm very well, thanks, Mr. Carmel," I answered, looking up; "and—and I heard from mamma on Thursday. They are very well; they are at Genoa now. They think of going to Florence in about three weeks."

"I know; yes. And you have no thoughts of joining them?"

"Oh! none. I should not like to leave this. They have not said a word about it lately."

"It is such a time, Miss Ethel, since I had the pleasure of seeing you—I don't mean, of course, at a distance, but near enough to ask you how you are. I dared not ask to see you too soon, and I thought—I fancied—you wished your walks uninterrupted."

I saw that he had observed my strategy; I was not sorry.

"I have often wished to thank you, Mr. Carmel; you were so very kind."

"I had no opportunity, Miss Ethel," he answered, with more feeling than before. "My profession obliges me to be kind—but I had no opportunity—Miss Grey is quite well?"

"She is very well, thanks."

With a softened glory, in level lines, the beams of the setting sun broke, scattered, through the trunks of the old elms, and one touched the head of the pale young man, as he stood at the window, looking in; his delicate and melancholy features were in the shade, and the golden light, through his thick, brown hair, shone softly, like the glory of a saint. As, standing thus, he looked down in a momentary reverie, Laura Grey came in, and paused, in manifest surprise, on seeing Mr. Carmel at the window.

I smiled, in spite of my efforts to look grave, and the governess, advancing, asked the young ecclesiastic how he was? Thus recalled, by a new voice, he smiled and talked with us for a few minutes. I think he saw our tea-equipage, and fancied that he might be, possibly, in the way; for he was taking his leave when I said, "Mr. Carmel, you must take tea before you go."

"Tea!—I find it very hard to resist. Will you allow me to take it, like a beggar-man, at the window? I shall feel less as if I were disturbing you; for you have only to shut the window down, when I grow prosy."

So, laughing, Laura Grey gave him a cup of tea, which he placed on the window-stone, and seating himself a little sideways on the bench that stands outside the window, he leaned in, with his hat off, and sipped his tea and chatted; and sitting as Miss Grey and I did, near the window, we made a very sociable little party of three.

I had quite given up the idea of renewing our speaking acquaintance with Mr. Carmel, and here we were, talking away, on more affable terms than ever! It seemed to me like a dream.

I don't say that Mr. Carmel was chatting with the *insouciance* and gaiety of a French abbé. There was, on the contrary, something very peculiar, both in his countenance and manner, something that suggested the life and sufferings of an ascetic. Something also, not easily defined, of command; I think it was partly in the severe though gentle gravity with which he spoke anything like advice or opinion.

I felt a little awed in his presence, I could not exactly tell why; and yet I was more glad than I would have

D 2

confessed that we were good friends again. He sipped his cup of tea slowly, as he talked, and was easily persuaded to take another.

"I see, Miss Ethel, you are looking at my book with curious eyes."

It was true; the book was a very thick and short volume, bound in black shagreen, with silver clasps, and lay on the window-stone, beside his cup. He took it up in slender fingers, smiling as he looked at me.

"You wish to know what it is; but you are too ceremonious to ask me. I should be curious myself, if I saw it for the first time. I have often picked out a book from a library, simply for its characteristic binding. Some books look interesting. Now what do you take this to be?"

"Haven't you books called breviaries? I think this is one," said I.

"That is your guess; it is not a bad one—but no, it is not a breviary. What do you say, Miss Grey?"

"Well, I say it is a book of the offices of the Church."

"Not a bad guess, either. But it is no such thing. I think I must tell you—it is what you would call a storybook."

"Really!" I exclaimed, and Miss Grey and I simultaneously conceived a longing to borrow it.

"The book is two hundred and seventy years old, and written in very old French. You would call them stories," he said, smiling on the back of the book; "but you must not laugh at them; for I believe them all implicitly. They are legends."

"Legends?" said I, eagerly—"I should so like to hear one. Do, pray, tell one of them."

"I'll read one, if you command me, into English. They are told here as shortly as it is possible to relate them. Here, for instance, is a legend of John of Parma. I think I can read it in about two minutes."

"I'm sorry it is so short; do, pray, begin," I said.

Accordingly, there being still light enough to read by, he translated the legend as follows:—

"John of Parma, general of the order of Friars Minors, travelling one winter's night, with some brothers of the

order, the party went astray in a dense forest, where they
wandered about for several hours, unable to find the right
path. Wearied with their fruitless efforts, they at length
knelt down, and having commended themselves to the
protection of the mother of God, and of their patron,
Saint Francis, began to recite the first nocturn of the Office
of the Blessed Virgin. They had not been long so engaged,
when they heard a bell in the distance, and rising at once,
and following the direction whence the sound proceeded,
soon came to an extensive abbey, at the gate of which
they knocked for admittance. The doors were instantly
thrown open, and within they beheld a number of monks
evidently awaiting their arrival, who, the moment they
appeared, led them to a fire, washed their feet, and then
seated them at a table, where supper stood ready ; and
having attended them during their meal, they conducted
them to their beds. Wearied with their toilsome journey,
the other travellers slept soundly ; but John, rising in the
night to pray, as was his custom, heard the bell ring for
matins, and quitting his cell, followed the monks of the
abbey to the chapel, to join with them in reciting the
divine office.

"Arrived there, one of the monks began with this verse
of the Thirty-fifth Psalm, 'Ibi ceciderunt qui operantur
iniquitatem ;' to which the choir responded, ' Expulsi
sunt nec potuerunt stare.' Startled by the strange despairing tone in which the words were intoned, as well as
by the fact that this is not the manner in which matins
are usually commenced, John's suspicions were aroused,
and addressing the monks, he commanded them, in the
name of the Saviour, to tell him who and what they were.
Thus adjured, he who appeared an abbot replied, that they
were all angels of darkness, who, at the prayer of the
Blessed Virgin, and of Saint Francis, had been sent to
serve him and his brethren in their need. As he spoke,
all disappeared ; and the next moment John found himself
and his companions in a grotto, where they remained,
absorbed in prayer and singing the praises of God, until
the return of day enabled them to resume their journey."

"How picturesque that is !" I said, as he closed the
little book.

He smiled, and answered:

"So it is. Dryden would have transmuted such a legend into noble verse; painters might find great pictures in it—but, to the faithful, it is more. To me, these legends are sweet and holy readings, telling how the goodness, vigilance, and wisdom of God work by miracles for his children, and how these celestial manifestations have never ceased throughout the history of his Church on earth, To you they are, as I said, but stories; as such you may wish to look into them. I believe, Miss Grey, you may read them without danger." He smiled gently, as he looked at the governess.

"Oh! certainly, Laura," cried I. "I am so much obliged."

"It is very kind of you," said Miss Grey. "They are, I am sure, very interesting; but does this little book contain anything more?"

"Nothing, I am afraid, that could possibly interest you: nothing, in fact, but a few litanies, and what we call elevations—you will see in a moment. There is nothing controversial. I am no proselytiser, Miss Grey,"—he laughed a little—"my duty is quite of a different kind. I am collecting authorities, making extracts and precis, and preparing a work, not of my own, for the press, under a greater than I."

"Recollect, Laura, it is lent to me—isn't it, Mr. Carmel?" I pleaded, as I took the little volume and turned over its pages.

"Very well—certainly," he acquiesced, smiling.

He stood up now. The twilight was deepening; he laid his hand on the window sash, and leaned his forehead upon it, as he looked in, and continued to chat for a few minutes longer; and then, with a slight adieu, he left us.

When he was gone, we talked him over a little.

"I wonder what he is?—a priest only or a Jesuit," said I; "or, perhaps, a member of some other order. I should like so much to know."

"You'd not be a bit wiser if you did," said Laura.

"Oh, you mean because I know nothing of these orders; but I could easily make out. I think he would have told us to-night in the twilight, if we had asked him."

"I don't think he would have told us anything he had not determined beforehand to tell. He has told us nothing about himself we did not know already. We know he is a Roman Catholic, and an ecclesiastic—his tonsure proclaims that; and your mamma told you that he is writing a book, so that is no revelation either. I think he is profoundly reserved, cautious, and resolute; and with a kind of exterior gentleness, he seems to me to be really inflexible and imperious."

"I like that unconscious air of command, but I don't perceive those signs of cunning and reserve. He seemed to grow more communicative the longer he stayed." I answered.

"The darker it grew," she replied. "He is one of those persons who become more confident the more effectually their countenances are concealed. There ceases to be any danger of a conflict between looks and language—a danger that embarrasses some people."

"You are suspicious this evening," I said. "I don't think you like him."

"I don't know him; but I fancy that, talk as he may to us, neither you nor I have for one moment a peep into his real mind. His world may be perfectly celestial and serene, or it may be an ambitious, dark, and bad one; but it is an invisible world for us."

The candles were by this time lighted, and Miss Grey was closing the window, when the glitter of the silver clasp of the little book caught her eye.

"Have you found anything?" said I.

"Only the book—I forgot all about it. I am almost sorry we allowed him to lend it."

"We borrowed it; I don't think he wanted to lend it," said I; "but, however it was, I'm very glad we have got it. One would fancy you had lighted on a scorpion. I'm not afraid of it; I know it can't do any one the least harm, for they are only stories."

"Oh, I think so. I don't see myself that they can do any harm; but I am almost sorry we have got into that sort of relation with him."

"What relation, Laura?"

"Borrowing books and discussing them."

"But we need not discuss them; I won't—and you are so well up in the controversy with your two books of theology, that I think he's in more danger of being converted than you. Give me the book, and I'll find out something to read to you."

CHAPTER VI.

EXT day Miss Grey and I were walking on the lonely road towards Penruthyn Priory. The sea lies beneath it on the right, and on the left is an old grass-grown bank, shaggy with brambles. Round a clump of ancient trees that stand at a bend of this green rampart, about a hundred steps before us, came, on a sudden, Mr. Carmel, and a man dressed also in black, slight, but not so tall as he. They were walking at a brisk pace, and the stranger was talking incessantly to his companion.

That did not prevent his observing us, for I saw him slightly touch Mr. Carmel's arm with his elbow as he looked at us. Mr. Carmel evidently answered a question, and, as he did so, glanced at us; and immediately the stranger resumed his conversation. They were quickly up to us, and stopped. Mr. Carmel raised his hat, and asked leave to introduce his friend. We bowed, so did the stranger; but Mr. Carmel did not repeat his name very distinctly.

This friend was far from prepossessing. He was of middle height, and narrow-shouldered, what they call " putty-faced," and closely shorn, the region of the beard and whisker being defined in smooth dark blue. He looked about fifty. His movements were short and quick, and restless; he rather stooped, and his face and forehead inclined as if he were looking on the ground. But his eyes were not upon the ground; they were very fierce, but seldom rested for more than a moment on any one object.

As he made his bow, raising his hat from his massive forehead, first to me, and afterwards to Miss Grey, his eyes, compressed with those wrinkles with which near-sighted people assist their vision, scrutinised us each with a piercing glance under his black eyebrows. It was a face at once intellectual, mean, and intimidating.

"Walking; nothing like walking, in moderation. You have boating here also, and you drive, of course; which do you like best, Miss Ware?" The stranger spoke with a slightly foreign accent, and, though he smiled, with a harsh and rapid utterance.

I forget how I answered this, his first question—rather an odd one. He turned and walked a little way with us.

"Charming country. Heavenly weather. But you must find it rather lonely, living down here. How you must both long for a week in London!"

"For my part, I like this better," I answered. "I don't like London in summer, even in winter I prefer this."

"You have lived here with people you like, I dare say, and for their sakes you love the place?" he mused.

We walked on a little in silence. His words recalled darling Nelly. This was our favourite walk long ago; it led to what we called the blackberry wilderness, rich in its proper fruits in the late autumn, and in May with banks all covered with cowslips and primroses. A sudden thought, that finds simple associations near, is affecting, and my eyes filled with tears. But with an effort I restrained them. The presence of a stranger, the sense of publicity, seals those fountains. How seldom people cry at the funerals of their beloved! They go through the public rite like an execution, pale and collected, and return home to break their hearts alone.

"You have been here some months, Miss Grey. You find Miss Ware a very amenable pupil, I venture to believe. I think I know something of physiognomy, and I may congratulate you on a very sweet and docile pupil, eh?"

Laura Grey, governess as she was, looked a little haughtily at this officious gentleman, who, as he put the question, glanced sharply for a moment at her, and then as rapidly at me, as if to see how it told.

"I think—I hope we are very happy together," said Miss Grey. "I can answer for myself."

"Precisely what I expected," said the stranger, taking a pinch of snuff. "I ought to mention that I am a very particular acquaintance, friend I may say, of Mrs. Ware, and am, therefore, privileged."

Mr. Carmel was walking beside his friend in silence, with his eyes apparently lowered to the ground all this time.

My blood was boiling with indignation at being treated as a mere child by this brusque and impertinent old man. He turned to me.

"I see, by your countenance, young lady, that you respect authority. I think your governess is very fortunate; a dull pupil is a bad bargain, and you are not dull. But a contumacious pupil is utterly intolerable; you are not that, either; you are sweetness and submission itself, eh ?"

I felt my cheeks flushing, and I directed on him a glance which, if the fire of ladies' eyes be not altogether a fable, ought at least to have scorched him.

"I have no need of submission, sir. Miss Grey does not think of exercising authority over me. I shall be eighteen my next birthday. I shall be coming out, papa says, in less than a year. I am not treated like a child any longer, sir. I think, Laura, we have walked far enough. Hadn't we better go home ? We can take a walk another time—any time would be pleasanter than now."

Without waiting for her answer, I turned, holding my head very high, breathing quickly, and feeling my cheeks in a flame.

The odious stranger, nothing daunted by my dignified resentment, smiled shrewdly, turned about quite unconcernedly, and continued to walk by my side. On my other side was Laura Grey, who told me afterwards that she greatly enjoyed my spirited treatment of his ill-breeding.

She walked by my side, looking straight before her, as I did. Out of the corners of my eyes I saw the impudent old man marching on as if quite unconscious, or, at least, careless of having given offence. Beyond him I saw, also, in the same oblique way, Mr. Carmel, walking with down-cast eyes as before.

He ought to be ashamed, I thought, of having intro-duced such a person.

I had not time to think a great deal, before the man of the harsh voice and restless eyes suddenly addressed me again.

"You are coming out, you say, Miss Ware, when you are eighteen?"

I made him no answer.

"You are now seventeen, and a year intervenes," he continued, and turning to Mr. Carmel, "Edwyn, run you down to the house, and tell the man to put my horse to."

So Mr. Carmel crossed the stile at the road-side, and disappeared by the path leading to the stables of Malory. And then turning again to me, the stranger said:

"Suppose your father and mother have placed you in my sole charge, with a direction to remove you from Malory, and take you under my immediate care and super-vision, to-day; you will hold yourself in readiness to depart immediately, attended by a lady appointed to look after you, with the approbation of your parents—eh?"

"No, sir, I'll not go. I'll remain with Miss Grey. I'll not leave Malory," I replied, stopping short, and turning towards him. I felt myself growing very pale, but I spoke with resolution.

"You'll not? what, my good young lady, not if I show you your father"s letter?"

"Certainly not. Nothing but violence shall remove me from Malory, until I see papa himself. He certainly would not do anything so cruel!" I exclaimed, while my heart sank within me.

He studied my face for a moment with his dark and fiery eyes.

"You are a spirited young lady; a will of your own!" he said. "Then you won't obey your parents?"

"I'll do as I have said," I answered, inwardly quaking.

He addressed Miss Grey now.

"You'll make her do as she's ordered?" said this man, whose looks seemed to me more sinister every moment.

" I really can't. Besides, in a matter of so much importance, I think she is right not to act without seeing her father, or, at least, hearing directly from him."

" Well, I must take my leave," said he. " And I may as well tell you it is a mere mystification; I have no authority, and no wish to disturb your stay at Malory ; and we are not particularly likely ever to meet again ; and you'll forgive an old fellow his joke, young ladies ?"

With these brusque and eccentric sentences, he raised his hat, and with the activity of a younger man, ran up the bank at the side of the road; and, on the summit, looked about him for a moment, as if he had forgotten us altogether ; and then, at his leisure, he descended at the other side and was quite lost to view.

Laura Grey and I were both staring in the direction in which he had just disappeared. Each, after a time, looked in her companion's face.

" I almost think he's mad !" said Miss Grey.

" What could have possessed Mr. Carmel to introduce such a person to us ?" I exclaimed. " Did you hear his name ?" I asked, after we had again looked in the direction in which he had gone, without discovering any sign of his return.

" Droqville, I think," she answered.

" Oh ! Laura, I am so frightened ! Do you think papa can really intend any such thing ? He's too kind. I am sure it is a falsehood."

" It is a joke, he says himself," she answered. " I can't help thinking a very odd joke, and very pointless ; and one that did not seem to amuse even himself."

" Then you do not think it is true ?" I urged, my panic returning.

" Well, I can't think it is true, because, if it were, why should he say it was a joke ? We shall soon know. Perhaps Mr. Carmel will enlighten us."

" I thought he seemed in awe of that man," I said.

" So did I," answered Miss Grey. " Perhaps he is his superior."

" I'll write to-day to papa, and tell him all about it ; you shall help me ; and I'll implore of him not to think of anything so horrible and cruel."

Laura Grey stopped short, and laid her hand on my wrist for a moment, thinking.

"Perhaps it would be as well if we were to turn about and walk a little further, so as to give him time to get quite away."

"But if he wants to take me away in that carriage, or whatever it is, he'll wait any time for my return."

"So he would; but the more I think over it, the more persuaded I am that there is nothing in it."

"In any case, I'll go back," I said. "Let us go into the house and lock the doors; and if that odious Mr. Droqville attempts to force his way in, Thomas Jones will knock him down; and we'll send Anne Owen to Cardyllion, for Williams, the policeman. I hate suspense. If there is to be anything unpleasant, it is better to have it decided, one way or other, as soon as possible."

Laura Grey smiled, and spoke merrily of our apprehensions; but I don't think she was quite so much at ease as she assumed to be.

Thus we turned about, I, at least, with a heart thumping very fast; and we walked back towards the old house of Malory, where, as you have this moment heard, we had made up our minds to stand a siege.

CHAPTER VII.

TASSO.

I DARESAY I was a great fool; but if you had seen the peculiar and unpleasant face of Monsieur Droqville, and heard his harsh nasal voice, in which there was something of habitual scorn, you would make excuses. I confess I was in a great fright by the time we had got well into the dark avenue that leads up to the house.

I hesitated a little as we reached that point in the carriage-road, not a long one, which commands a clear view of the hall-door steps. I had heard awful stories of foolish girls spirited away to convents, and never heard of more. I have doubts as to whether, had I seen Monsieur Droqville or his carriage there, I should not have turned about, and ran through the trees. But the courtyard in front of the house was, as usual, empty and still. On its gravel surface reposed the sharp shadows of the pointed gables above, and the tufts of grass on its surface had not been bruised by recent carriage wheels. Instead, therefore, of taking to flight, I hurried forward, accompanied by Laura Grey, to seize the fortress before it was actually threatened.

In we ran, lightly, and locked the hall door, and drew chain and bolt against Monsieur Droqville; and up the great stairs to our room, each infected by the other's panic. Safely in the room, we locked and bolted our door, and stood listening, until we had recovered breath. Then I rang our bell furiously, and up came Anne Owen, or, as her countrymen pronounce it, Anne Wan. There had been, after all, no attack; no human being had attempted to intrude upon our cloistered solitude.

"Where is Mrs. Torkill ?" I asked, through the door.

"In the still-room, please, miss."

"Well, you must lock and bolt the back-door, and don't let any one in, either way."

We passed an hour in this state of preparation, and finally ventured downstairs, and saw Rebecca Torkill. From her we learned that the strange gentleman who had been with Mr. Carmel had driven away more than half an hour before; and Laura Grey and I, looking in one another's faces, could not help laughing a little.

Rebecca had overheard a portion of a conversation, which she related to me; but not for years after. At the time she had no idea that it could refer to any one in whom she was interested; and even at this hour I am not myself absolutely certain, but only conjecture, that I was the subject of their talk. I will tell it to you as nearly as I can recollect.

Rebecca Torkill, nearly an hour before, being in the still-room, heard voices near the window, and quietly peeped out.

You must know that immediately in the angle formed by the junction of the old house, known as the steward's house, which Mr. Carmel had been assigned as a residence, and the rear of the great house of Malory, stand two or three great trees, and a screen of yews, behind which, so embossed in ivy as to have the effect of a background of wood, stands the gable of the still-room. This strip of ground, lying immediately in the rear of the steward's house, was a flower-garden; but a part of it is now carpeted with grass, and lies under the shadow of the great trees, and is walled round with the dark evergreens I have mentioned. The rear of the stable-yard of Malory, also mantled with ivy, runs parallel to the back of the steward's house, and forms the other boundary of this little enclosure, which simulates the seclusion of a cloister; and but for the one well-screened window I have mentioned, would really possess it. Standing near this window she saw Mr. Carmel, whom she always regarded with suspicion, and his visitor, that gentleman in black, whose looks nobody seemed to like.

"I told you, sir," said Mr. Carmel, "through my friend

Ambrose, I had arranged to have prayers twice a week, at the Church in Paris, for that one soul."

"Yes, yes, yes; that is all very well, very good, of course," answered the hard voice; "but there are things we must do for ourselves—the saints won't shave us, you know."

"I am afraid, sir, I did not quite understand your letter," said Mr. Carmel.

"Yes, you did, pretty well. You see she may be, one day, a very valuable acquisition. It is time you put your shoulder to the wheel—d'ye see? Put your shoulder to the wheel. The man who said all that is able to do it. So mind you put your shoulder to the wheel forthwith."

The younger man bowed.

"You have been sleeping," said the harsh, peremptory voice. "You said there was enthusiasm and imagination. I take that for granted. I find there is spirit, courage, a strong will; obstinacy—impracticability—no milksop—a bit of a virago! Why did not you make out all that for yourself? To discover character you must apply tests. You ought in a single conversation to know everything."

The young man bowed again.

"You shall write to me weekly; but don't post your letters at Cardyllion. I'll write to you through Hickman, in the old way."

She could hear no more, for they moved away. The elder man continued talking, and looked up at the back-windows of Malory, which became visible as they moved away. It was one of his fierce, rapid glances; but he was satisfied, and continued his conversation for two or three minutes more. Then he abruptly turned, and entered the steward's house quickly; and, in two or three minutes more, was driving away from Malory at a rapid pace.

A few days after this adventure—for in our life any occurrence that could be talked over for ten minutes was an adventure—I had a letter in mamma's pretty hand, and in it occurred this passage:

"The other day I wrote to Mr. Carmel, and I asked him to do me a kindness. If he would read a little Italian with you, and Miss Grey I am sure would join, I should be so much pleased. He has passed so much of

E

his life in Rome, and is so accomplished in Italian ; simple as people think it, that language is more difficult to pronounce correctly even than French. I forget whether Miss Grey mentioned Italian among the languages she could teach. But however that may be, I think, if Mr. Carmel will take that trouble, it would be very desirable."

Mr. Carmel, however, made no sign. If the injunction to "put his shoulder to the wheel" had been given for my behoof, the promise was but indifferently kept, for I did not see Mr. Carmel again for a fortnight. During the greater part of that interval he was away from Malory, we could not learn where. At the end of that time, one evening, just as unexpectedly as before, he presented himself at the window. Very much the same thing happened. He drank tea with us, and sat on the bench—his bench, he called it—outside the window, and remained, I am sure, two hours, chatting very agreeably. You may be sure we did not lose the opportunity of trying to learn something of the gentleman whom he had introduced to us.

Yes, his name was Droqville.

"We fancied," said Laura, "that he might be an ecclesiastic."

"His being a priest, or not, I am sure you think does not matter much, provided he is a good man, and he is that; and a very clever man, also," answered Mr. Carmel. "He is a great linguist: he has been in almost every country in the world. I don't think Miss Ethel has been a traveller yet, but you have, I dare say." And in that way he led us quietly away from Monsieur Droqville to Antwerp, and I know not where else.

One result, however, did come of this visit. He actually offered his services to read Italian with us. Not, of course, without opening the way for this by directing our talk upon kindred subjects, and thus deviously up to the point. Miss Grey and I, who knew what each expected, were afraid to look at each other ; we should certainly have laughed, while he was leading us up so circuitously and adroitly to his " palpable ambuscade."

We settled Monday, Wednesday, and Friday in each week for our little evening readings. Mr. Carmel did not always now sit outside, upon his bench, as at first. He

was often at our tea-table, like one of ourselves; and sometimes stayed later than he used to do. I thought him
quite delightful. He certainly was clever, and, to me,
appeared a miracle of learning; he was agreeable, fluent,
and very peculiar.

I could not tell whether he was the coldest man on
earth, or the most impassioned. His eyes seemed to me
more enthusiastic and extraordinary the oftener and longer
I beheld them. Their strange effect, instead of losing,
seemed to gain by habit and observation. It seemed to
me that the cold and melancholy serenity that held us
aloof was artificial, and that underneath it could be detected the play and fire of a nature totally different.

I was always fluctuating in my judgment upon this
issue; and the problem occupied me during many an hour
of meditation.

How dull the alternate days had become; and how
pleasant even the look-forward to our little meetings!
Thus, very agreeably, for about a fortnight our readings
proceeded, and, one evening on our return, expecting the
immediate arrival of our "master," as I called Mr.
Carmel, we found, instead, a note addressed to Miss Grey.
It began: "Dear Miss Eth," and across these three letters
a line was drawn, and "Grey" was supplied. I liked
even that evidence that his first thought had been of me.
It went on:

"Duty, I regret, calls me for a time away from Malory,
and our Italian readings, I have but a minute to write
to tell you not to expect me this evening, and to say I
regret I am unable, at this moment, to name the day of
my return.

"In great haste, and with many regrets,
    "Yours very truly,
        "E. CARMEL.

"So he's gone again!" I said, very much vexed.
"What shall we do to-night?"

"Whatever you like best; I don't care—I'm sorry he's
gone."

"How restless he is! I wonder why he could not stay

quietly here; he can't have any real business away. It
may be duty; but it looks very like idleness. I dare say
he began to think it a bore coming to us so often to read
Tasso, and listen to my nonsense; and I think it a very
cool note, don't you?"

"Not cool; a little cold; but not colder than he is,"
said Laura Grey. "He'll come back, when he has done
his business; I'm sure he has business; why should he
tell an untruth about the matter?"

I was huffed at his going, and more at his note. That
pale face, and those large eyes, I thought the handsomest
in the world. I took up one of Laura's manuals of The
Controversy, which had fallen rather into disuse after the
first panic had subsided, and Mr. Carmel had failed to
make any, even the slightest, attack upon our faith. I
was fiddling with its leaves, and I said:

"If I were an inexperienced young priest, Laura, I
should be horribly afraid of those little tea-parties. I dare
say he is afraid—afraid of your eyes, and of falling in love
with you."

"Certainly not with me," she answered. "Perhaps you
mean he is afraid of people talking? I think you and I
should be the persons to object to that, if there was a
possibility of any such thing. But we are talking folly.
These men meet us, and talk to us, and we see them; but
there is a wall between, that is simply impassable. Suppose a sheet of plate glass, through which you see as clearly
as through air, but as thick as the floor of ice on which a
Dutch fair is held. That is what their vow is."

"I wonder whether a girl ever fell in love with a priest.
That would be a tragedy!" I said.

"A ridiculous one," answered Laura; "you remember
the old spinster who fell in love with the Apollo Belvedere?
It could happen only to a madwoman."

I think this was a dull evening to Laura Grey; I know
it was for me.

CHAPTER VIII.

THUNDER.

E saw or heard nothing for a week or more of Mr. Carmel. It was possible that he would never return. I was in low spirits. Laura Grey had been shut up by a cold, and on the day of which I am now speaking she had not yet been out. I therefore took my walk alone towards Penruthyn Priory, and, as dejected people not unfrequently do, I was well enough disposed to indulge and even to nurse my melancholy.

A thunder-storm had been for hours moving upwards from the south-east, among the grand ranges of distant mountains that lie, tier beyond tier, at the other side of the estuary, and now it rested on a wide and lurid canopy of cloud upon the summits of the hills and headlands that overlook the water.

It was evening, later than my usual return to tea. I knew that Laura Grey minded half-an-hour here or there as little as I did, and a thunder-storm seen and heard from the neighbourhood of Malory is one of the grandest spectacles in its way on earth. Attracted by the mighty hills on the other side, these awful elemental battles seldom visit our comparatively level shore, and we see the lightning no nearer than about half-way across the water. Vivid against blackening sky and purple mountain, the lightning flies and shivers. From broad hill-side, through rocky gorges, reflected and returned from precipice to precipice, through the hollow windings of the mountains, the thunder rolls and rattles, dies away, explodes again, and at length subsides in the strangest and grandest of all sounds, spreading through all that mountainous region for minutes after, like the roar and tremble of an enormous seething cauldron.

Suppose these aërial sounds reverberating from cliff to cliff, from peak to peak, and crag to crag, from one hill-side to another, like the cannon in the battles of Milton's angels; suppose the light of the setting sun, through a chink in the black curtain of cloud behind me, touching with misty fire the graves and headstones in the pretty churchyard, where, on the stone bench under the eastern window, I have taken my seat, near the grave of my darling sister; and suppose an uneasy tumult, not a breeze, in the air, sometimes still, and sometimes in moaning gusts, tossing sullenly the boughs of the old trees that darken the churchyard.

For the first time since her death I had now visited this spot without tears. My thoughts of death had ceased to be pathetic, and were, at this moment, simply terrible. "My heart was disquieted within me, and the fear of death had fallen upon me." I sat with my hands clasped together, and my eyes fixed on the thunderous horizon before me, and the grave of my darling under my eyes, and she, in her coffin, but a few feet beneath. The grave, God's prison, as old Rebecca Torkill used to say, and then the Judgment! This new sense of horror and despair was, I dare say, but an unconscious sympathy with the vengeful and melancholy aspect of nature.

I heard a step near me, and turned. It was Mr. Carmel who approached. He was looking more than usually pale, I thought, and ill. I was surprised, and a little confused. I cannot recall our greeting. I said, after that was over, something, I believe, about the thunder-storm.

"And yet," he answered, "you understand these awful phenomena—their causes. You remember our little talk about electricity—here it is! We know all that is but the restoration of an equilibrium. Think what it will be when God restores the moral balance, and settles the equities of eternity! There are moods, times, and situations in which we contemplate justly our tremendous Creator. Fear him who, after he has killed the body, has power to cast into hell. Yea, I say unto you, fear him. Here all suffering is transitory. Weeping may endure for a night, but joy cometh in the morning. This life is the season of time and of mercy; but once in hell, mercy is no more, and eternity opens, and endures, and has no end."

Here he ceased for a time to speak, and looked across the estuary, listening, as it seemed, to the roll and tremble of the thunder. After a little while, he said :

" That you are to die is most certain ; nothing more uncertain than the time and manner ; by a slow or a sudden death ; in a state of grace or sin. Therefore, we are warned to be ready at all hours. Better twenty years too soon than one moment late ; for to perish once is to be lost for ever. Your death depends upon your life ; such as your life is, such will be your death. How can we dare to live in a state that we dare not die in ?"

I sat gazing at this young priest, who, sentence after sentence, was striking the very key-note of the awful thought that seemed to peal and glare in the storm. He stood with his head uncovered, his great earnest eyes sometimes raised, sometimes fixed on me, and the uncertain gusts at fitful intervals tossed his hair this way and that. The light of the setting sun touched his thin hand, and his head, and glimmered on the long grass ; the graves lay around us ; and the voice of God himself seemed to speak in the air.

Mr. Carmel drew nearer, and in the same earnest vein talked on. There was no particle of which is termed the controversial in what he had said. He had not spoken a word that I could not subscribe. He had quoted, also, from our version of the Bible ; but he presented the terrors of revelation with a prominence more tremendous than I was accustomed to, and the tone of his discourse was dismaying.

I will not attempt to recollect and to give you in detail the conversation that followed. He presented, with a savage homeliness of illustration, with the same simplicity and increasing force, the same awful view of Christianity. Beyond the naked strength of the facts, and the terrible brevity with which he stated them in their different aspects, I don't know that there was any special eloquence in his discourse, but in the language of Scripture, his words made "both my ears tingle."

He did not attempt to combat my Protestant tenets directly ; that might have alarmed me ; he had too much tact for that. Anything he said with that tendency was in the way simply of a discourse of the teaching and practice of his own Church.

"In the little volume of legends you were so good as to say you would like to look into," he said, "you will find the prayer of Saint Louis de Gonzaga ; you will also find an anonymous prayer, very pathetic and beautiful. I have drawn a line in red ink down the margin at its side, so it is easily found. These will show you the spirit in which the faithful approach the Blessed Virgin. They may interest you. They will, I am sure, interest your sympathies for those who have suffered, like you, and have found peace and hope in these very prayers."

He then spoke very touchingly of my darling sister, and my tears at last began to flow. It was the strangest half-hour I had ever passed. Religion during that time had appeared in a gigantic and terrible aspect. My grief for my sister was now tinged with terror. Do not we from our Lutheran pulpits too lightly appeal to that protent emotion—fear ?

For awhile this tall thin priest in black, whose pale face and earnest eyes seemed to gleam on me with an intense and almost painful enthusiasm, looked like a spirit in the deepening twilight ; the thunder rattled and rolled on among the echoing mountains, the gleam of the lightning grew colder and wilder as the darkness increased, and the winds rushed mournfully, and tossed the churchyard grass, and bowed the heads of the great trees about us ; and as I walked home, with my head full of awful thoughts, and my heart agitated, I felt as if I had been talking with a messenger from that other world.

CHAPTER IX.

AWAKENED.

E do these proselytising priests great wrong when we fancy them cold-blooded practisers upon our credulity, who seek, for merely selfish ends, to entangle us by sophistries, and inveigle us into those mental and moral catacombs from which there is no escape. We underrate their danger when we deny their sincerity. Mr. Carmel sought to save my soul; nobler or purer motive, I am sure, never animated man. If he acted with caution, and even by stratagem, he believed it was in the direct service of Heaven, and for my eternal weal. I know him better, his strength and his weakness, now—his asceticism, his resolution, his tenderness. That young priest—long dead—stands before me, in the white robe of his purity, king-like. I see him, as I saw him last, his thin, handsome features, the light of patience on his face, the pale smile of suffering and of victory. His tumults and his sorrows are over. Cold and quiet he lies now. My thanks can never reach him; my unavailing blessings and gratitude follow my true and long-lost friend, and tears wrung from a yearning heart.

Laura Grey seemed to have lost her suspicions of this ecclesiastic. We had more of his society than before. Our reading went on, and sometimes he joined us in our walks. I used to see him from an upper window every morning early, busy with spade and trowel, in the tiny flower-garden which belonged to the steward's house. He used to work there for an hour punctually, from before seven till nearly eight: Then he vanished for many hours, and was not seen till nearly evening, and we had, perhaps, our *Gerusalemme Liberata*, or he would walk with us for a mile or more, and talk in his gentle but cold way, pleasantly, on any topic we happened to start. We three grew to be great friends. I liked to see him when he, and, I may add, Laura Grey also, little thought I was looking at his simple garden-work under the shadow of the grey wall from which the old cherry and rose-trees drooped, in picturesque confusion, under overhanging masses of ivy.

He and I talked as opportunity occurred more and more freely upon religion. But these were like lovers' confidences, and, by a sort of tacit consent, never before Laura Grey. Not that I wished to deceive her; but I knew very well what she would think and say of my imprudence. It would have embarrassed me to tell her; but here remonstrances would not have prevailed; I would not have desisted; we should have quarrelled; and yet I was often on the point of telling her, for any reserve with her pained me.

In this quiet life we had glided from summer into autumn, and suddenly, as before, Mr. Carmel vanished, leaving just such a vague little note as before.

I was more wounded, and a great deal more sorry this time. The solitude I had once loved so well was irksome without him. I could not confess to Laura, scarcely to myself, how much I missed him.

About a week after his disappearance, we had planned to drink tea in the housekeeper's room. I had been sitting at the window in the gable that commanded the view of the steward's garden, which had so often shown me my hermit at his morning's work. The roses were already shedding their honours on the mould, and the sear of autumn was mellowing the leaves of the old fruit-trees. The shadow of the ancient stone house fell across the garden, for by this time the sun was low in the west, and I knew that the next morning would come and go, and the next, and bring no sign of his return, and so on, and on, perhaps for ever.

Never was little garden so sad and silent! The fallen

leaves lay undisturbed, and the weeds were already peeping here and there among the flowers.

"Is it part of your religion?" I murmured bitterly to myself, as, with folded hands, I stood a little way back, looking down through the open window, "to leave willing listeners thus half-instructed? Business? What is the business of a good priest? I should have thought the care and culture of human souls was, at least, part of a priest's business. I have no one to answer a question now—no one to talk to. I am, I suppose, forgotten.

I dare say there was some affectation in this. But my dejection was far from affected, and hiding my sorrowful and bitter mood, I left the window and came down the back-stairs to our place of meeting. Rebecca Torkill and Laura Grey were in high chat. Tea being just made, and everything looking so delightfully comfortable, I should have been, at another time, in high spirits.

"Ethel, what do you think? Rebecca has been just telling me that the mystery about Mr. Carmel is quite cleared up. Mr. Prichard, the grocer, in Cardyllion, was visiting his cousin, who has a farm near Plasnwyd, and whom should he see there but our missing friar, in a carriage driving with Mrs. Tredwynyd, of Plasnwyd. She is a beautiful woman still, and one of the richest widows in Wales, Rebecca says; and he has been living there ever since he left this; and his last visit, when we thought he was making a religious sojourn in a monastery, was to the same house and lady! What do you think of that? But it is not near ended yet. Tell the rest of the story, Mrs. Torkill, to Miss Ethel—please do."

"Well, miss, there's nothin' very particular, only they say all round Plasnwyd that she was in love with him, and that he's goin' to turn Protestant, and it's all settled they're to be married. Every one is singin' to the same tune all round Plasnwyd, and what every one says must be true, as I've often heard say."

I laughed, and asked whether our teacake was ready, and looked out of the window. The boughs of the old fruit-trees in the steward's garden hung so near it that the ends of the sprays would tap the glass, if the wind blew. As I leaned against the shutter, drumming a little tune on the window, and looking as careless as any girl could, I felt cold and faint, and my heart was bursting. I don't know what prevented my dropping on the floor in a swoon.

Laura, little dreaming of the effect of this story upon me, was chatting still with Rebecca, and neither perceived that I was moved by the news.

That night I cried for hours in my bed, after Laura Grey was fast asleep. It never occurred to me to canvass the probability of the story. We are so prone to believe what we either greatly desire or greatly fear. The violence of my own emotions startled me. My eyes were opened at last to a part of my danger.

As I whispered, through convulsive sobs, "He's gone, he's gone—I have lost him—he'll never be here any more! Oh! why did you pretend to take an interest in me? Why did I listen to you? Why did I like you?" All this, and as much more girlish lamentation and upbraiding as you please to fancy, dispelled my dream and startled my reason. I had an interval to recover in; happily for me, this wild fancy had not had time to grow into a more impracticable and dangerous feeling. I felt like an awakened somnambulist at the brink of a precipice. Had I become attached to Mr. Carmel, my heart must have broken in silence, and my secret have perished with me.

Some weeks passed, and an advent occurred, which more than my girlish pride and resolutions turned my thoughts into a new channel, and introduced a memorable actor upon the scene of my life.

CHAPTER X.

A SIGHT FROM THE WINDOWS.

WE are now in stormy October; a fierce and melancholy month! August and September touch the greenwood leaves with gold and russet, and gently loosen the hold of every little stalk on forest bough; and then, when all is ready, October comes on in storm, with sounds of trump and rushing charge and fury not to be argued or dallied with, and thoroughly executes the sentence of mortality that was recorded in the first faint yellow of the leaf, in the still sun of declining July.

October is all the more melancholy for the still, golden days that intervene, and show the thinned branches in the sunlight, soft, and clear as summer's, and the boughs cast their skeleton shadows across brown drifts of leaves.

On the evening I am going to speak of, there was a wild, threatening sunset, and the boatmen of Cardyllion foretold a coming storm. Their predictions were verified.

The breeze began to sigh and moan through the trees and chimney-stacks of Malory shortly after sunset, and in another hour it came on to blow a gale from the north-west. From that point the wind sweeps right up the estuary from the open sea; and after it has blown for a time, and the waves have gathered their strength, the sea bursts grandly upon the rocks a little in front of Malory.

We were sitting cosily in our accustomed tea-room.

The rush and strain of the wind on the windows became momentarily more vehement, till the storm reached its highest and most tremendous pitch.

"Don't you think," said Laura, after an awful gust, "that the windows may burst in ? The wind is frightful ! Hadn't we better get to the back of the house ?"

"Not the least danger," I answered ; "these windows have small panes, and immensely strong sashes ; and they have stood so many gales that we may trust them for this."-

"There again !" she exclaimed. "How awful !"

"No danger to us, though. These walls are thick, and as firm as rock ; not like your flimsy brick houses ; and the chimneys are as strong as towers. You must come up with me to the window in the tawny-room ; there is an open space in the trees opposite, and we can see pretty well. It is worth looking at ; you never saw the sea here in a storm."

With very little persuasion, I induced her to run up-stairs with me. Along the corridor, we reached the chamber in question, and placing our candle near the door, and running together to the window, we saw the grand spectacle we had come to witness.

Over the sea and land, rock and wood, a dazzling moon was shining. Tattered bits of cloud, the "scud" I believe they call it, were whirling over us, more swiftly than the flight of a bird, as far as your eye could discern : till the sea was lost in the grey mist of the horizon it was streaked and ridged with white. Nearer to the stooping trees that bowed and quivered in the sustained blast, and the little churchyard dormitory that nothing could disturb, the black peaked rock rose above the turmoil, and a dark causeway of the same jagged stone, sometimes defined enough, sometimes submerged, connected it almost with the mainland. A few hundred yards beyond it, I knew, stretched the awful reef on which the Intrinsic, years before I could remember, had been wrecked. Beyond that again, we could see the waves leaping into sheets of foam, that seemed to fall as slowly and softly as clouds of snow. Nearer, on the dark rock, the waves flew up high into the air, like cannon-smoke.

Within these rocks, which make an awful breakwater, full of mortal peril to ships driving before the storm, the estuary, near the shores of Malory, was comparatively quiet.

At the window, looking on this wild scene, we stood, side by side, in the fascination which the sea in its tumultuous mood never fails to exercise. Thus, not once turning our eyes from the never-flagging variety of the spectacle, we gazed for a full half-hour, when, suddenly, there appeared—was it the hull of a vessel shorn of its masts? No, it was a steamer—a large one, with low chimneys. It seemed to be about a mile and a half away, but was driving on very rapidly. Sometimes the hull was quite lost to sight, and then again rose black and sharp on the crest of the sea. We held our breaths. Perhaps the vessel was trying to made the shelter of the pier of Cardyllion; perhaps she was simply driving before the wind.

To me there seemed something uncertain and staggering in the progress of the ship. Before her lay the ominous reef, on which many a good ship and brave life had perished. There was quite room enough, I knew, with good steering, between the head of the reef and the sandbank at the other side, to make the pier of Cardyllion. But was there any one on board who knew the intricate navigation of our dangerous estuary? Could any steering in such a tempest avail? And, above all, had the ship been crippled? In any case, I knew enough to be well aware that she was in danger.

Reader, if you have never witnessed such a spectacle, you cannot conceive the hysterical excitement of that suspense. All those on board are, for the time, your near friends; your heart is among them—their terrors are yours. A ship driving with just the hand and eye of one man for its only chance, under Heaven, against the fury of sea and wind, and a front of deadly rock, is an unequal battle; the strongest heart sickens as the crisis nears, and the moments pass in an unconscious agony of prayer.

Rebecca Torkill joined us at this moment.

"Oh! Rebecca," I said, "there is a ship coming up the estuary—do you think they can escape?"

" The telescope should be on the shelf at the back stair-head," she answered, as soon as she had taken a long look at the steamer. " Lord ha' mercy on them, poor souls! —that's the very way the Intrinsic drove up before the wind the night she was lost; and I think this will be the worse night of the two."

Mrs. Torkill returned with the long sea telescope, in its worn casing of canvas.

I took the first "look out." After wandering hither and thither over a raging sea, and sometimes catching the tossing head of some tree in the foreground, the glass lighted, at length, upon the vessel. It was a large steamer, pitching and yawing frightfully. Even to my inexperienced eye, it appeared nearly unmanageable. I handed the glass to Laura. I felt faint.

Some of the Cardyllion boatmen came running along the road that passes in front of Malory. I saw that two or three of them had already arrived on the rising ground beside the churchyard, and were watching events from that wind-swept point. I knew all the Cardyllion boatmen, for we often employed them, and I said :

" I can't stay here—I must hear what the boatmen say. Come, Laura, come with me."

Laura was willing enough.

" Nonsense! Miss Ethel," exclaimed the housekeeper. " Why, dear Miss Grey, you could not keep hat or bonnet on in a wind like that ! You could not keep your feet in it !"

Remonstrance, however, was in vain. I tied a handkerchief tight over my head and under my chin—Laura did the same ; and out we both sallied, notwithstanding Rebecca Torkill's protest and entreaty. We had to go by the back door ; it would have been impossible to close the hall-door against such a gale.

Now we were out in the bright moonlight under the partial shelter of the trees, which bent and swayed with the roar of a cataract over our heads. Near us was the hillock we tried to gain ; it was next to impossible to reach it against the storm. Often we were brought to a stand-still, and often forced backward, notwithstanding all our efforts.

At length, in spite of all, we stood on the little platform, from which the view of the rocks and sea beyond was clear. Williams, the boatman, was close to me, at my right hand, holding his low-crowned hat down on his head with his broad, hard hand. Laura was at my other side. Our dresses were slapping and rattling in the storm like the cracking of a thousand whips; and such a roaring was in my ears, although my handkerchief was tied close over them, that I could scarcely hear anything else.

CHAPTER XI.

CATASTROPHE.

THE steamer looked very near now and large. It was plain it had no longer any chance of clearing the rocks. The boatmen were bawling to one another, but I could not understand what they said, nor hear more than a word or two at a time.

The steamer mounted very high, and then seemed to dive headlong into the sea, and was lost to sight. Again, in less than a minute, the black mass was toppling at the summit of the sea, and again it seemed swallowed up.

"Her starboard paddle!" shouted a broad-shouldered sailor in a pilot-coat, with his palm to the side of his mouth.

Thomas Jones was among these men, without a hat, and on seeing me he fell back a little. I was only a step or two behind them.

"Thomas Jones," I screamed, and he inclined his ear to my shrill question, "is there no life-boat in Cardyllion?"

"Not one, miss," he roared; "and it could not make head against that if there was."

"Not an inch," bawled Williams.

"Is there any chance?" I cried.

"An anchor from the starn! A bad hold there—she's draggin' of it!" yelled Williams, whose voice, though little more than two feet away, sounded faint and half smothered in the storm.

Just then the steamer reared, or rather swooped, like the enchanted horse, in the air, and high above its black shape shot a huge canopy of foam; and then it staggered over and down, and nothing but raging sea was there.

"O God! are they all lost?" I shrieked.

"Anchor's fast. All right now," roared the man in the pilot-coat.

In some seconds more the vessel emerged, pitching high into the brilliant moonlight, and nearly the same thing was repeated again and again. The seafaring men who were looking on were shouting their opinions to one another, and from the little I was able to hear and understand, I gathered that she might ride it out if she did not drag her anchor, or "part" or "founder." But the sea was very heavy, and the rocks just under her bows now.

In this state of suspense a quarter of an hour or more must have passed. Suddenly the vessel seemed to rise nearer than before. The men crowded forward to the edge of the bank. It was plain something decisive had happened. Nearer it rose again, and then once more plunged forward and disappeared. I waited breathless. I waited longer than before, and longer. Nothing was there but rolling waves and springing foam beyond the rocks. The ship rose no more!

The first agony of suspense was over. Where she had been the waves were sporting in the ghastly moonlight. In my wild horror I screamed—I wrung my hands. I could not turn for a moment from the scene. I was praying all the time the same short prayer over and over again. Minute after minute passed, and still my eyes were fixed on the point where the ship had vanished; my hands were clasped over my forehead, and tears welled down my cheeks.

What's that? Upon the summit of the bare rock, all on a sudden, the figure of a man appeared; behind this mass of black stone, as each wave burst in succession, the foam leaped in clouds. For a moment the figure was seen sharp against the silvery distance; then he stooped, as if to climb down the near side of the rock, and we lost sight of him. The boatmen shouted, and held up each a hand (their others were holding their hats on) in token of succour near, and three or four of them, with Thomas Jones at their head, ran down the slope, at their utmost speed to

the jetty, under which, in shelter, lay the Malory boat.
Soon it was moving under the bank, four men pulling
might and main against the gale ; though they rowed in
shelter of the reef, on the pinnacle of which we had seen
the figure for a moment, still it was a rough sea, and far
from safe for an open boat, the spray driving like hail
against them, and the boat pitching heavily in the short
cross sea.

No other figure crossed the edge of the rock, or for a
a moment showed upon the bleak reef, all along which
clouds of foam were springing high and wild into the air.

The men who had been watching the event from the
bank, seemed to have abandoned all further hope, and
began to descend the hill to the jetty to await the return
of the boat. It did return, bearing the one rescued man.

Laura Grey and I went homeward. We made our way
into the back-yard, often forced to run, by the storm,
in spite of ourselves. We had hardly reached the house
when we saw the boatmen coming up.

We were now in the yard, about to enter the house at
the back-door, which stood in shelter of the building. I
saw Mrs. Torkill in the steward's house, with one of the
maids, evidently in a fuss. I ran in.

"Oh, Miss Ethel, dear, did you see that ? Lord a'mercy
on us ! A whole shipful gone like that ! I thought the
sight was leaving my eyes.'

I answered very little. I felt ill, I was trembling still,
and ready to burst again into tears.

"Here's bin Thomas Jones, miss, to ask leave for the
drownded man to rest himself for the night, and, as Mr.
Carmel's away, I knew your papa and mamma would not
refuse ; don't you think so, miss ? So I said, ay, bring
him here. Was I right, miss ? And me and Anne Wan
is tidyin' a bed for him."

"Quite right, I'm sure," said I, my interest again
awakened, and almost at the same moment into the
flagged passage came Thomas Jones, followed by several
of the Cardyllion boatmen, their great shoes clattering
over the flags.

In the front rank of these walked the one mortal who
had escaped alive from the ship that was now a wreck on

the fatal reef. You may imagine the interest with which I looked at him. I saw a graceful but manly figure, a young man in a short sailor-like coat, his dress drenched and clinging, his hat gone, his forehead and features finely formed, very energetic, and, I thought, stern— browned by the sun; but, allowing for that tint, no drowned face in the sea that night was paler than his, his long black hair, lank with sea-water, thrown back from his face like a mane. There was blood oozing from under its folds near his temple; there was blood also on his hand, which rested on the breast of his coat; on his finger there was a thick gold ring. I had little more than a moment in which to observe all this. He walked in, holding his head high, very faint and fierce, with a slight stagger in his gait, a sullen and defiant countenance, and eyes fixed and gazing straight before him, as I had heard somnambulists described. I saw him in the candle-light for only a moment as he walked by, with boatmen in thick shoes, as I said, clattering beside him. I felt a strange longing to run and clasp him by the hand!

I got into our own back-door, and found Laura Grey in the room in which we usually had our tea. She was as much excited as I.

" Could you have imagined," she almost cried, " anything so frightful? I wish I had not seen it. It will always be before my eyes.

"That is what I feel also; but we could not help it, we could not have borne the suspense. That is the reason why the people who are least able to bear it sometimes see the most dreadful sights."

As we were talking, and wondering where the steamer came from, and what was her name, and how many people were probably on board, in came Rebecca Torkill.

" I sent them boatmen home, miss, that rowed the boat out to the rock for that poor young man, with a pint o' strong ale, every one round, and no doubt he'll give them and Thomas Jones something in hand for taking him off the rock when he comes to himself a bit. He ought to be thanking the Almighty with a contrite heart."

" He did not look as if he was going to pray when I saw him," I said.

"Nor to thank God, nor no one, for anything," she chimed in. "And he sat down sulky and black as you please, at the side o' the bed, and said never a word, but stuck out his foot to Thomas Jones to unbutton his boot. I had a pint o' mulled port ready, and I asked him if I should send for the doctor, and he only shook his head and shrugged his shoulders, as he might turn up his nose at an ugly physic. And he fell a-thinking while Jones was takin' off the other boot, and in place of prayin' or thanksgiving, I heard him muttering to himself and grumbling; and, Lord forgive me if I wrong him, I think I heard him cursing some one. There was a thing for a man just took alive out o' the jaws o' death by the mercy o' God to do! There's them on earth, miss, that no lesson will teach, nor goodness melt, nor judgment frighten, but the last one, and then all's too late."

It was late by this time, and so we all got to our beds. But I lay long awake in the dark, haunted by the ceaseless rocking of that dreadful sea, and the apparition of that one pale, bleeding messenger from the ship of death. How unlike my idea of the rapture of a mortal just rescued from shipwreck! His face was that of one to whom an atrocious secret has been revealed, who was full of resentment and horror; whose lips were sealed.

In my eyes he was the most striking figure that had ever appeared before me. And the situation and my own dreadful excitement had elevated him into a hero,

CHAPTER XII.

OUR GUEST.

THE first thing I heard of the stranger in the morning was that he had sent off early to the proprietor of the "Verney Arms" a messenger with a note for two large boxes which he had left there, when the yacht Foam Bell was at Cardyllion about a fortnight before. The note was signed with the letters R. M.

The Foam Bell had lain at anchor off the pier of Cardyllion for only two hours, so no one in the town knew much about her. Two or three of her men, with Foam Bell across the breasts of their blue shirts and on the ribbons of their flat glazed hats, had walked about the quaint town, and drunk their beer at the "George and Garter." But there had not been time to make acquaintance with the townspeople. It was only known that the yacht belonged to Sir Dives Wharton, and that the gentleman who left the boxes in charge of the proprietor of the "Verney Arms," was not that baronet.

The handwriting was the same as that in the memorandum he had left with the hotel-keeper, and which simply told him that the big black boxes were left to be called or written for by Edward Hathaway, and mentioned no person whose initials were R. M. So Mr. Hughes, of the "Verney Arms," drove to Malory to see the gentleman at the steward's house, and having there recognised him as the very gentleman who left the boxes in his charge, he sent them to him as directed.

Shortly after, Doctor Mervyn, our old friend walked up the avenue, and saw me and Laura at the window.

It was a calm, bright morning ; the storm had done its awful work, and was at rest, and sea and sky looked glad and gentle in the brilliant sun. Already about fifty drowned persons had been carried up and laid upon the turf in the churchyard in rows, with their faces upward. I was glad it was upon the slope that was hid from us.

How murderous the dancing waves looked in the sunlight ! And the black saw-edged reef I beheld with a start and a shudder. The churchyard, too, had a changed expression. What a spectacle lay behind that familiar grassy curve ! I did not see the incongruous muster of death. Here a Liverpool dandy ; there a white-whiskered City man ; sharp bag-men ; little children—strange companions in the churchyard—hard-handed sailors ; women, too, in silk or serge—no distinction now.

I and Laura could not walk in that direction till all this direful seeking and finding were over.

The doctor, seeing us at the open window, raised his hat. The autumn sun through the thin leaves touched his bald head as he walked over to the window-stool, and placing his knee on the bench on which Mr. Carmel used sometimes to sit, he told us all he knew of the ship and the disaster. It was a Liverpool steamer called the Conway Castle, bound for Bristol. One of her paddles was disabled early in the gale, and thus she drove to leeward, and was wrecked.

"And now," said the doctor, "I'm going to look in upon the luckiest man in the kingdom, the one human being who escaped alive out of that ship. He must have been either the best or the worst man on board—either too good to be drowned or too bad, by Jove ! He is the gentleman you were so kind as to afford shelter to last night in the steward's house there, round the corner, and he sent for me an hour ago. I daresay he feels queer this morning ; and from what Thomas Jones says, I should not be surprised if he had broken a bone somewhere. Nothing of any great consequence, of course ; but he must have got a thund'ring fling on those rocks. When I've seen him—if I find you here—I'll tell you what I think of him."

After this promise, you may be sure we did wait where

we were, and he kept his word. We were in a fever of curiosity; my first question was, " Who is he ?"

" I guessed you'd ask that the first moment you could," said the doctor, a little pettishly.

" Why ?" said I.

"Because it is the very question I can't answer," he replied. " But I'll tell you all I do know," he continued, taking up his old position at the window, and leaning forward with his head in the room.

Every word the oracle spoke we devoured. I won't tell his story in his language, nor with our interruptions. I will give its substance, and in part its details, as I received them. The doctor was at least as curious as we were.

His patient was up, sitting by the fire, in dressing-gown and slippers, which he had taken with other articles of dress from the box which stood open on the floor. The window-curtain was partly drawn, the room rather dark. He saw the young man with his feet on the fender, seated by the wood fire. His features, as they struck the doctor, were handsome and spirited; he looked ill, with pale cheek and lips, speaking low and smiling.

"I'm Doctor Mervyn," said the doctor, making his bow, and eyeing the stranger curiously.

"Oh! Thanks, Doctor Mervyn! I hope it is not a long way from your house. I am here very ridiculously circumstanced. I should not have had any clothes, if it had not been for a very lucky accident, and for a day or two I shall be totally without money—a mere Robinson Crusoe."

"Oh, that don't matter; I shall be very happy to see after you in the meantime, if there should be anything in my way," answered the doctor, bluntly.

"You are very kind, thanks. This place, they tell me, is called Malory. What Mr. Ware is that to whom it belongs ?"

"The Honourable Mr. Ware, brother of Lord H——. He is travelling on the Continent at present with his wife, a great beauty some fifteen years since; and his daughter, his only child, is at present here with her governess."

" Oh, I thought some one said he had two ?"

The doctor re-asserted the fact, and for some seconds the stranger looked on the floor abstractedly.

" You wished a word or two of advice, I understand ?" interrupted the doctor at length. " You have had a narrow escape, sir—a tremendous escape! You must have been awfully shaken. I don't know how you escaped being smashed on those nasty rocks."

"I am pretty well smashed, I fancy," said the young man.

" That's just what I wanted to ascertain."

" From head to foot, I'm covered with bruises," continued the stranger ; "I got off with very few cuts. I have one over my temple, and half-a-dozen here and there, and one here on my wrist ; but you need not take any trouble about them—a cut, when I get one, heals almost of itself. A bit of court-plaster is all I require for them, and Mrs. Something, the housekeeper here, has given me some ; but I'm rather seedy. I must have swallowed a lot of salt water, I fancy. I've got off very well, though, if it's true all the other people were drowned. It was a devil of a fluke ; you'd say I was the luckiest fellow alive, ha, ha, ha! I wish I could think so."

He laughed, a little bitterly.

" There are very few men glad to meet death when it comes," said Doctor Mervyn. " Some think they are fit to die, and some know they are not. You know best, sir, what reason you have to be thankful."

" I'm nothing but bruises and aches all over my body. I'm by no means well, and I've lost all my luggage, and papers, and money, since one o'clock yesterday, when I was flourishing. Two or three such reasons for thankfulness would inevitably finish me."

" All except you were drowned, sir," said the doctor, who was known in Cardyllion as a serious-minded man, a little severely.

" Like so many rats in a trap, poor devils," acquiesced the stranger. " They were hatched down. I was the only passenger on deck. I must have been drowned if I had been among them."

" All those poor fellow-passengers of yours," said Doctor Mervyn, in disgust, "had souls, sir, to be saved."

"I suppose so; but I never saw such an assemblage of snobs in my life. I really think that, except poor Haworth—he insisted it would be ever so much pleasanter than the railway; I did not find it so; he's drowned of course—I assure you, except ourselves, there was not a gentleman among them. And Sparks, he's drowned too, and I've lost the best servant I ever had in my life. But I beg your pardon, I'm wasting your time. Do you think I'm ill?"

He extended his wrist, languidly, to enable the doctor to feel his pulse. The physician suppressed his rising answer with an effort, and made his examination.

"Well, sir, you have had a shock."

"By Jove! I should not wonder," acquiesced the young man, with a sneer.

"And you are a good deal upset, and your contusions are more serious than you seem to fancy. I'll make up a liniment here, and I'll send you down something else that will prevent any tendency to fever; and I suppose you would like to be supplied from the 'Verney Arms.' You must not take any wine stronger than claret for the present, and a light dinner, and if you give me a line, or tell me what name——"

"Oh, they know me there, thanks. I got these boxes from there this morning, and they are to send me everything I require."

The doctor wanted his name. The town of Cardyllion, which was in a ferment, wanted it. Of course he must have the name; a medical practitioner who kept a ledger and sent out accounts, it was part of his business to know his patients' names. How could he stand before the wags of the news-room, if he did not know the name of his own patients—of this one, of all others.

"Oh! put me down as R. M. simply," said the young man.

"But wouldn't it be more—more usual, if you had no objections—a little more at length?" insinuated the doctor.

"Well, yes; put it down a little more at length—say R. R. M. Three letters instead of two.

The doctor, with his head inclined, laughed patiently,

and the stranger, seeing him about to return to the attack, said a little petulantly : " You see, doctor, I'm not going to give my very insignificant name here to any one. If your book-keeper had it, every one in the town would know it ; and Cardyllion is a place at which idle people turn up, and I have no wish to have my stray friends come up to this place to bother me for the two or three days I must stay here. You may suppose me an escaped convict, or anything else you please that will amuse the good people ; but I'm hanged if I give my name, thank you !"

After this little interruption, the strictly professional conversation was resumed, and the doctor ended by directing him to stay quiet that day, and not to walk out out until he had seen him again next morning.

The doctor then began to mix the ingredients of his liniment. The young man in the silk dressing-grown limped to the window, and leaned his arm upon the sash, looking out, and the doctor observed him, in his ruminations, smiling darkly on the ivy that nodded from the opposite wall, as if he saw a confederate eyeing him from its shadow.

" He didn't think I was looking at him," said the doctor ; " but I have great faith in a man's smile when he thinks he is all to himself ; and that smile I did not like ; it was, in my mind, enough to damn him."

All this, when his interview was over, the doctor came round and told us. He was by no means pleased with his patient, and being a religious man, of a quick temper, would very likely have declined the office of physician in this particular case, if he had not thought, judging by his "properties," which were in a certain style that impressed Doctor Mervyn, and his air, and his refined features, and a sort of indescribable superiority which both irritated and awed the doctor, that he might be a " swell."

He went the length, notwithstanding, of calling him, in his conversation with us, an " inhuman puppy," but he remarked that there were certain duties which no Christian could shirk, among which that of visiting the sick held, of course, in the doctor's mind, due rank.

CHAPTER XIII.

MEETING IN THE GARDEN.

I WAS a little shy, as country misses are; and, curious as I was, rather relieved when I heard that the shipwrecked stranger had been ordered to keep his quarters strictly, for that day at least. So, by-and-by, as Laura Grey had a letter to write, I put on my hat, and not caring to walk towards the town, and not daring to take the Penruthyn Road, I ran out to the garden. The garden of Malory is one of those monastic enclosures whose fruit-trees have long grown into venerable timber; whose walls are stained by time, and mantled in some places with ivy; where everything has been allowed, time out of mind, to have its own way; where walks are grass-grown, and weeds choke the intervals between old standard pear, and cherry, and apple-trees, and only a little plot of ground is kept in cultivation by a dawdling, desultory man, who carries in his daily basket of vegetables to the cook. There was a really good Ribston-pippin or two in this untidy, but not unpicturesque garden; and these trees were, I need scarcely tell you, a favourite resort of ours.

The gale had nearly stripped the trees of their ruddy honours, and thrifty Thomas Jones had, no doubt, carried the spoil away to store them in the apple-closet. One pippin only dangled still within reach, and I was whacking at this particularly good-looking apple with a long stick, but as yet in vain, when I suddenly perceived that a young man, whom I recognised as the very hero of the shipwreck, was approaching. He walked slowly and a little lame, and was leaning on a stick. He was smiling, and, detected in my undignified and rather greedy exercise —I had been jumping from the ground—I was ready to sink into the earth with shame. Perhaps, if I had been endowed with presence of mind, I should have walked away. But I was not, on that occasion at least; and I stood my ground, stick in hand, affecting not to see his slow advance.

It was a soft sunny day. He had come out without a hat; he had sent to Cardyllion to procure one, and had not yet got it, as he afterwards told me, with an apology for seeming to make himself so very much at home. How he introduced himself I forget; I was embarrassed and disconcerted; I know that he thanked me very much for my "hospitality," called me his "hostess," smiling, and told me that, although he did not know my father, he yet saw him everywhere during the season. Then he talked of the wreck; he described his own adventures very interestingly, and spoke of the whole thing in terms very different from those reported by Doctor Mervyn, and with a great deal of feeling. He asked me if I had seen anything of it from our house; and then it became my turn to speak. I very soon got over my shyness; he was so perfectly well-bred that it was impossible, even for a rustic such as I was, not to feel very soon quite at her ease in his company.

So I talked away, becoming more animated; and he smiled, looking at me, I thought, with a great deal of sympathy, and very much pleased. I thought him very handsome. He had one point of resemblance to Mr. Carmel. His face was pale, but, unlike his, as dark as a gipsy's. Its tint showed the white of his eyes and his teeth with fierce effect. What was the character of the face I saw now? Very different from the death-like phantom that had crossed my sight the night before. It was a face of passion and daring. A broad, low forehead, and resolute mouth, with that pronounced under-jaw which indicates sternness and decision. I contrasted him secretly with Mr. Carmel. But in his finely-cut features, and dark, fierce eyes, the ascetic and noble interest of the sadder face was wanting; but there was, for so young a person as I, a different and a more powerful fascination in the beauty of this young man of the world.

Before we parted I allowed him to knock down the apple I had been trying at, and this rustic service improved our acquaintance.

I began to think, however, that our interview had lasted quite long enough; so I took my leave, and I am certain he would have accompanied me to the house, had I not taken advantage of his lameness, and walked away very quickly.

As I let myself out at the garden-door, in turning I was able, unsuspected, to steal a parting look, and I saw him watching me intently as he leaned against the stem of a gigantic old pear-tree. It was rather pleasant to my vanity to think that I had made a favourable impression upon the interesting stranger.

Next day our guest met me again, near the gate of the avenue, as I was returning to the house.

"I had a call this morning from your clergyman," he said. "He seems a very kind old gentleman, the rector of Cardyllion; and the day is so beautiful, he proposed a sail upon the estuary, and if you were satisfied with him, by way of escort, and my steering—I'm an old sailor—I'm sure you'd find it just the day to enjoy a little boating."

He looked at me, smiling eagerly.

Laura Grey and I had agreed that nothing would tempt us to go upon the water, until all risk of lighting upon one of those horrible discoveries from the wreck, that were now beginning to come to the surface from hour to hour, was quite over. So I made our excuses as best I could, and told him that since the storm we had a horror of sailing. He looked vexed and gloomy. He walked beside me.

"Oh! I understand—Miss Grey? I was not aware— I ought, of course, to have included her. Perhaps your friend would change her mind and induce you to reconsider your decision. It is such a charming day."

I thanked him again, but our going was quite out of the question. He smiled and bowed a little, but looked very much chagrined. I fancied that he thought I meant to

snub him, for proposing any such thing on so very slight
an acquaintance. I daresay if I had I should have been
quite right; but you must remember how young I was,
and how unlearned in the world's ways. Nothing, in fact,
was further from my intention. To soften matters a
little, I said:

"I am very sorry we can't go. We should have liked
it, I am sure, so much; but it is quite impossible."

He walked all the way to the hall-door with me; and
then he asked if I did not intend continuing my walk a
little. I bid him good-bye, however, and went in, very
full of the agreeable idea that I had made a conquest.

Laura Grey and I, walking to Cardyllion, met Doctor
Mervyn, who stopped to tell us that he had just seen his
Malory patient, "R. R. M.," steering Williams's boat,
with the old vicar on board.

"By Jove! one would have fancied he had got enough
of the water for some time to come," remarked the doctor,
in conclusion. "That is the most restless creature I ever
encountered in all my professional experience! If he had
kept himself quiet yesterday and to-day, he'd have been
pretty nearly right by to-morrow; but if he goes on like
this I should not wonder if he worked himself into a
fever."

CHAPTER XIV.

THE INTRUDER.

NEXT morning, at about nine o'clock, whom do I
see but the restless stranger, to my surprise,
again upon the avenue as I return towards the
house. I had run down to the gate before
breakfast to meet our messenger, and learn whether any
letters had come by the post. He, like myself, has come
out before his breakfast. He turns on meeting me, and
walks towards the house at my side. Never was man
more persistent. He had got Williams's boat again, and
not only the vicar, but the vicar's wife, was coming for a
sail; surely I would venture with her? I was to remember, besides, that they were to sail to the side of the
estuary furthest from the wreck; there could be no possible
danger there of what I feared—and thus he continued to
argue and entreat.

I really wished to go. I said, however, that I must ask
Miss Grey, whom, upon some excuse which I now forget,
he regretted very much he could not invite to come also.
I had given him a conditional promise by the time we
parted at the hall-door, and Laura saw no objection to
my keeping it, provided old Mrs. Jermyn, the vicar's wife,
were there to chaperon me. We were to embark from the
Malory jetty, and she was to call for me at about three
o'clock.

The shipwrecked stranger left me, evidently very well
pleased. When he got into his quarters in the steward's
house and found himself all alone, I dare say his dark
face gleamed with the smile of which Doctor Mervyn had

G

formed so ill an opinion. I had not yet seen that smile. Heaven help me! I have had reason to remember it.

Laura and I were sitting together, when who should enter the room but Mr. Carmel. I stood up and shook hands. I felt very strangely. I was glad the room was a dark one. I was less observed, and therefore less embarrassed.

It was not till he had been in the room some time that I observed how agitated he looked. He seemed also very much dejected, and from time to time sighed heavily. I saw that something had gone strangely wrong. It was a vague suspense. I was secretly very much frightened.

He would not sit down. He said he had not a moment to stay; and yet he lingered on, I fancied, debating something within himself. He was distrait, and, I thought, irresolute.

After a little talk he said:

"I came just to look in on my old quarters and see my old friends for a few minutes, and then I must disappear again for more than a month, and I find a gentleman in possession."

We hastened to assure him that we had not expected him home for some time, and that the stranger was admitted but for a few days. We told him, each contributing something to the narrative, all about the shipwreck, and the reception of the forlorn survivor in the steward's house.

He listened without a word of comment, almost without breathing, and with his eyes fixed in deep attention on the floor.

"Has he made your acquaintance?" he asked, raising them to me.

"He introduced himself to me," I answered, "but Miss Grey has not seen him."

Something seemed to weigh heavily upon his mind.

"What is your father's present address?" he asked.

I told him, and he made a note of it in his pocket-book. He stood up now, and did at length take his leave.

"I am going to ask you to do a very kind thing. You have heard of sealed orders, not to be opened till a certain point has been reached in a voyage or a march? Will you promise, until I shall have left you fully five minutes, not to open this letter?"

I almost thought he was jesting, but I perceived very quickly that he was perfectly serious. Laura Grey looked at him curiously, and gave him the desired promise as she received the note. His carriage was at the door, and in another minute he was driving rapidly down the avenue. What had led to these odd precautions?—and what had they to do with the shipwrecked stranger?

At about eleven o'clock—that is to say, about ten minutes before Mr. Carmel's visit to us—the stranger had been lying on a sofa in his quarters, with two ancient and battered novels from Austin's Library in Cardyllion, when the door opened unceremoniously, and Mr. Carmel, in travelling costume, stepped into the room. The hall-door was standing open, and Mr. Carmel, on alighting from his conveyance, had walked straight in without encountering any one in the hall. On seeing an intruder in possession he stopped short; the gentleman on the sofa, interrupted, turned towards the door. Thus confronted, each stared at the other.

"Ha! Marston," exclaimed the ecclesiastic, with a startled frown, and an almost incredulous stare.

"Edwyn! by Jove!" responded the stranger, with a rather anxious smile, which faded, however, in a moment.

"What on earth brings you here?" said Mr. Carmel, sternly, after a silence of some seconds.

"What the devil brings you here?" inquired the stranger, almost at the same moment. "Who sent you? What is the meaning of it?"

Mr. Carmel did not approach him. He stood where he had first seen him, and his looks darkened.

"You are the last man living I should have looked for here," said he.

"I suppose we shall find out what we mean by-and-by," said Marston, cynically; "at present I can only tell you that when I saw you I honestly thought a certain old gentleman, I don't mean the devil, had sent you in search of me."

Carmel looked hard at him. "I've grown a very dull man since I last saw you, and I don't understand a joke

G 2

as well as I once did," said he; " but if you are serious you cannot have learnt that this house has been lent to me by Mr. Ware, its owner, for some months at least; and these, I suppose, are your things ? There is not room to put you up here."

" I didn't want to come. I am the famous man you may have read of in the papers—quite unique—the man who escaped alive from the Conway Castle. No Christian refuses shelter to the shipwrecked ; and you are a Christian, though an odd one."

Edwyn Carmel looked at him for some seconds in silence.

" I am still puzzled," he said. " I don't know whether you are serious ; but, in any case, there's a good hotel in the town—you can go there."

" Thank you—without a shilling," laughed the young man, a little wickedly.

" A word from me will secure you credit there."

" But I'm in the doctor's hands, don't you see?"

" It is nothing very bad," answered Mr. Carmel; "and you will be nearer the doctor there."

The stranger, sitting up straight, replied :

" I suppose I shall; but the doctor likes a walk, and I don't wish him a bit nearer."

" But this is, for the time being, my house, and you must go," replied Edwyn Carmel, coldly and firmly.

" It is also my house, for the time being; for Miss Ware has given me leave to stay here."

The ecclesiastic's lips trembled, and his pale face grew paler, as he stared on the young man for a second or two in silence.

" Marston," he said, " I don't know, of all men, why you should specially desire to pain me."

" Why, hang it ! Why should I wish to pain you, Edwyn ? I don't. But I have no notion of this sort of hectoring. The idea of your turning me out of the —my house—the house they have lent me ! I told you I didn't want to come here ; and now I don't want to go away, and I won't."

The churchman looked at him, as if he strove to read his inmost thoughts.

"You know that your going to the hotel could involve no imaginable trouble," urged Edwyn Carmel.

"Go to the hotel yourself, if you think it so desirable a place. I am satisfied with this, and I shall stay here."

"What can be the motive of your obstinacy?"

"Ask that question of yourself, Mr. Carmel, and you may possibly obtain an answer," replied the stranger.

The priest looked again at him, in stern doubt.

"I don't understand your meaning," he said, at last.

"I thought my meaning pretty plain. I mean that I rather think our motives are identical."

"Honestly, Marston, I don't understand you," said Mr. Carmel, after another pause.

"Well, it is simply this: that I think Miss Ware a very interesting young lady, and I like being near her—don't you?"

The ecclesiastic flushed crimson; Marston laughed contemptuously.

"I have been away for more than a month," said the priest, a little paler, looking up angrily; "and I leave this to-day for as long a time again."

"Conscious weakness! Weakness of that sentimental kind sometimes runs in families," said the stranger with a sneer. It was plain that the stranger was very angry; the taunt was wicked, and, whatever it meant, stung Mr. Carmel visibly. He trembled, with a momentary quiver, as if a nerve had been pierced.

There was a silence, during which Mr. Carmel's little French clock over the chimney-piece, punctually wound every week by old Rebecca, might be heard sharply tick, tick, ticking.

"I shall not be deterred by your cruel tongue," said he, very quietly, at length, with something like a sob, "from doing my duty."

"Your duty! Of course, it is always duty; jealousy is quite unknown to a man in holy orders. But there is a difference. You can't tell me the least what I'm thinking of; you always suppose the worst of every one. Your duty! And what, pray, is your duty?"

"To warn Miss Ware and her governess," he answered promptly.

"Warn her of what?" said the stranger, sternly.

"Warn her that a villain has got into this house."

The interesting guest sprang to his feet, with his fists clenched. But he did not strike. He hesitated, and then he said:

"Look here; I'll not treat you as I would a man. You wish me to strike you, you Jesuit, and to get myself into hot water. But I shan't make a fool of myself. I tell you what I'll do with you—if you dare to injure me in the opinion of any living creature, by one word of spoken or hinted slander, I'll make it a police-office affair; and I'll bring out the whole story you found it on; and we'll see which suffers most, you or I, when the world hears it. And now, Mr. Carmel, you're warned. And you know I'm a fellow that means what he says."

Mr. Carmel turned with a pale face, and left the room.

I wonder what the stranger thought. I have often pondered over that scene; and, I believe, he really thought that Mr. Carmel would not, on reflection, venture to carry out his threat.

CHAPTER XV.

A WARNING.

E had heard nothing of Mr. Carmel's arrival. He had not passed our windows, but drove up instead by the back avenue; and now he was gone, and there remained no record of his visit but the letter which Laura held in her fingers, while we both examined it on all sides, and turned it over. It was directed, "To Miss Ware and Miss Grey. Malory." And when we opened it we read these words:

"DEAR YOUNG LADIES,—I know a great deal of the gentleman who has been permitted to take up his residence in the house adjoining Malory. It is enough for me to assure you that no acquaintance could be much more objectionable and unsafe, especially for young ladies living alone as you do. You cannot, therefore, exercise too much caution in repelling any advances he may make.— Your true friend, "E. CARMEL."

The shock of reading these few words prevented my speaking for some seconds. I had perfect confidence in Mr. Carmel's warning. I was very much frightened. And the vagueness of his language made it the more alarming. The same thoughts struck us both. What fools we were! How is he to be got out of the house? Whom have we to advise with? What is to be done?

In our first panic we fancied that we had got a burglar or an assassin under our roof. Mr. Carmel's letter, however, on consideration, did not bear out quite so violent a conclusion. We resolved, of course, to act upon that letter; and I blamed myself too late for having permitted the stranger to make, even in so slight a way, my acquaintance.

In great trepidation, I despatched a note to Mrs. Jermyn, to say I could not join her boating party. To the stranger I could send neither note nor message. It did not matter. He would, of course, meet that lady at the jetty, and there learn my resolve. Two o'clock arrived. Old Rebecca came in, and told us that the gentleman in the steward's house had asked her whether Mr. Carmel was gone; and on learning that he had actually driven away, hardly waited till she was out of the room "to burst out a-laughing," and talking to himself, and laughing like mad.

"And I don't think, with his laughing and cursing, he's like a man should be that fears God, and is only a day or two out of the jaws of death!"

This description increased our nervousness. Possibly this person was a lunatic, whose keeper had been drowned in the Conway Castle. There was no solution of the riddle which Mr. Carmel had left us to read, however preposterous, that we did not try; none possible, that was not alarming.

About an hour after, passing through the hall, I saw some one, I thought, standing outside, near the window that commands the steps beside the door. This window has a wire-blind, through which, from outside, it is impossible to see. From within, however, looking towards the light, you can see perfectly. I scarcely thought our now distrusted guest would presume to approach our door so nearly; but there he was. He had mounted the steps, I suppose, with the intention of knocking, but he was, instead, looking stealthily from behind the great elm that grows close beside; his hand was leaning upon its trunk, and his whole attention absorbed in watching some object which, judging from the direction of his gaze, must have been moving upon the avenue. I could not take my eyes off him. He was frowning, with compressed lips and eyes dilated; his attitude betokened caution, and as I looked he smiled darkly.

I recovered my self-possession. I took, directly, Doctor

Mervyn's view of that very peculiar smile. I was suddenly frightened. There was nothing to prevent the formidable stranger from turning the handle of the door and letting himself into the hall. Two or three light steps brought me to the door, and I instantly bolted it. Then drawing back a little into the hall, I looked again through the window, but the intending visitor was gone.

Who had occupied his gaze the moment before? And what had determined the retreat? It flashed upon me suddenly again that he might be one of those persons who are described as "being known to the police," and that Mr. Carmel had possibly sent constables to arrest him.

I waited breathlessly at the window, to see what would come of it. In a minute more, from the direction in which I had been looking for a party of burly policemen, there arrived only my fragile friend, Laura Grey, who had walked down the road to see whether Mr. and Mrs. Jermyn were coming.

Encouraged by this reinforcement, I instantly opened the hall-door, and looked boldly out. The enemy had completely disappeared.

"Did you see him?" I exclaimed.

"See whom?" she asked.

"Come in quickly," I answered. And when I had shut the hall-door, and again bolted it, I continued, "The man in the steward's house. He was on the steps this moment.

"No, I did not see him; but I was not looking towards the hall-door. I was looking up at the trees, counting the broken boughs—there are thirteen trees injured on the right hand, as you come up."

"Well, I vote we keep the door bolted; he shan't come in here," said I. "This is the second siege you and I have stood together in this house. I do wish Mr. Carmel had been a little more communicative, but I scarcely think he would have been so unfriendly as to leave us quite to ourselves if he had thought him a highwayman, and certainly, if he is one, he is a very gentleman-like robber."

"I think he can merely have meant, as he says, to warn us against making his acquaintance," said Miss Grey; "his letter says only that."

"I wish Mr. Carmel would stay about home," I said, "or else that the steward's house were locked up."

I suppose all went right about the boating party, and that Mrs. Jermyn got my note in good time.

No one called at Malory; the dubious stranger did not invade our steps again. We had constant intelligence of his movements from Rebecca Torkill; and there was nothing eccentric or suspicious about them, so far as we could learn.

Another evening passed, and another morning came; no letter by the post, Rebecca hastened to tell us, for our involuntary guest; a certain sign, she conjectured, that we were to have him for another day. Till money arrived he could not, it was plain, resume his journey.

Doctor Mervyn told us, with his customary accuracy and plenitude of information respecting other people's affairs, when he looked in upon us, after his visit to his patient, that he had posted a letter the morning after his arrival, addressed to Lemuel Blount, Esquire, 5, Brunton Street, Regent's Park; and that on reference to the London Directory, in the news-room, it was duly ascertained by the subscribers that "Blount, Lemuel," was simply entered as "Esquire," without any further clue whatsoever to guide an active-minded and inquiring community to a conclusion. So there, for the present, Doctor Mervyn's story ended.

Our panic by this time was very much allayed. The unobtrusive conduct of the unknown, ever since his momentary approach to our side of the house, had greatly contributed to this. I could not submit to a blockade of any duration; so we took heart of grace, and ventured to drive in the little carriage to Cardyllion, where we had some shopping to do.

CHAPTER XVI.

DOUBTS.

HAVE been searching all this morning in vain for a sheet of written note paper, almost grown yellow by time when I last saw it. It contains three stanzas of very pretty poetry. At least I once thought so. I was curious to try, after so many years, what I should think of them now. Possibly they were not even original, though there certainly was no lack in the writer of that sort of cleverness which produces pretty verses.

I must tell you how I came by them. I found that afternoon a note, on the window-stool in our tea-room, addressed "Miss Ethel." Laura Grey did not happen to be in the room at the moment. There might have been some debate on the propriety of opening the note if she had been present. I could have no doubt that it came from our guest, and I opened and read it instantly.

In our few interviews I had discovered, once or twice, a scarcely disguised tenderness in the stranger's tones and looks. A very young girl is always pleased, though ever so secretly, with this sort of incense. I know I was. It is a thing hard to give up; and, after all, what was Mr. Carmel likely to know about this young man?—and if he did not know him, what were the canons of criticism he was likely to apply? And whatever the stranger might be, he talked and looked like a gentleman; he was unfortunate, and for the present dependent, I romantically thought, on our kindness. To have received a copy of verses was very pleasant to my girlish self-importance; and the flattery of the lines themselves was charming.

The first shock of Mr. Carmel's warning had evapo-

rated by this time ; and I was already beginning to explain
away his note. I hid the paper carefully. I loved Laura
Grey ; but I had, in my inmost soul, a secret awe of her ;
I knew how peremptory would be her advice, and I said
not a word about the verses to her. At the first distant
approach of an affair of the heart, how cautious and
reserved we grow, and in most girls how suddenly the
change from kittens to cats sets in ! It was plain he had
no notion of shifting his quarters to the hotel. But a
little before our early tea-hour, Rebecca Torkill came in
and told us what might well account for his not having
yet gone to Cardyllion.

"That poor young man," she said, "he's very bad.
He's lying on his back, with a handkercher full of eau-de-
Cologne on his forehead, and he's sent down to the town
for chloroform, and a blister for the back of his neck.
He called me in, and indeed, though his talk and his
behaviour might well be improved, considering how near
he has just bin to death, yet I could not but pity him.
Says he, ' Mrs. Torkill, for heaven's sake don't shake the
floor, step as light as you can, and close the shutter next
the sun,' which I did ; and says he, ' I'm in a bad way ;
I may die before morning. My doctor in town tells me
these headaches are very dangerous. They come from
the spine.' ' Won't you see Doctor Mervyn, please, sir ?'
say I. ' Not I,' says he. ' I know all about it better
than he '—them were his words—' and if the things that's
coming don't set me to rights, I'm a gone man.' And
indeed he groaned as he might at parting of soul and body
—and here's a nice kettle o' fish, if he should die here,
poor, foolish young man, and we not knowing so much as
where his people lives, nor even his name. 'Tis a
mysterious thing of Providence to do. I can't see how
'twas worth while saving him from drowning, only to
bring him here to die of that headache. But all works
together, we know. Thomas Jones is away down at the
ferry ; a nice thing, among a parcel o' women, a strange
gentleman dying on a sofa, and not a man in the house !
What do you think is best to be done, Miss Grey ?"

"If he grows worse, I think you should send for the
doctor without asking his leave," she answered. "If it

is dangerous, it would not do to have no advice. It is very unlucky."

" Well, it is what I was thinking myself," said the housekeeper; "folks would be talking, as if we let him die without help. I'll keep the boiler full in case he should want a bath. He said his skull was fractured once, where that mark is, near his temple, and that the wound has something to do with it, and, by evil chance, it was just there he got the knock in the wreck of the Conway Castle; the Lord be good to us all!"

So Mrs. Torkill fussed out of the room, leaving us rather uncomfortable; but Laura Grey, at least, was not sorry, although she did not like the cause, that there was no reason to apprehend his venturing out that evening.

Our early tea-things came in. A glowing autumn sunset was declining; the birds were singing their farewell chorus from thick ivy over branch and wall, and Laura and I, each with her own secret, were discussing the chances of the stranger's illness, with exaggerated despondency and alarm. Our talk was interrupted. Through the window, which, the evening being warm, we, secure from intrusion, had left open, we heard a clear manly voice address us as " Miss Ethel and Miss Grey."

Could it be Mr. Carmel come back again? Good Heavens! no; it was the stranger in Mr. Carmel's place, as we had grown to call it. The same window, his hands, it seemed, resting on the very same spot on the windowstone, and his knee, just as Mr. Carmel used to place his, on the stone bench. I had no idea before how stern the stranger's face was; the contrast between the features I had for a moment expected, and those of our guest, revealed the character of his with a force assisted by the misty red beam that glanced on it, with a fierce melancholy, through the trees.

His appearance was as unexpected as if he had been a ghost. It came in the midst of a discussion as to what should be done if, by ill chance, he should die in the steward's house. I can't say how Laura Grey felt; I only know that I stared at his smiling face for some seconds, scarcely knowing whether the apparition was a reality or not.

"I hope you will forgive me; I hope I am not very impertinent; but I have just got up from an astounding headache all right again; and in consequence, in such spirits, that I never thought how audacious I was in venturing this little visit until it was too late."

Miss Grey and I were both too much confounded to say a word. But he rattled on: "I have had a visitor since you were so good as to give me shelter in my shipwrecked state—one quite unexpected. I don't mean my doctor, of course. I had a call to-day much more curious, and wholly unlooked for; an old acquaintance, a fellow named Carmel. I knew him at Oxford, and I certainly never expected to see him again."

"Oh! You know Mr. Carmel?" I said, my curiosity overcoming a kind of reluctance to talk.

"Know him? I rather think I do," he laughed. "Do you know him?"

"Yes," I answered; "that is, not very well; there is, of course, a little formality in our acquaintance—more, I mean, than if he were not a clergyman."

"But do you really know him? I fancied he was boasting when he said so." The gentleman appeared extremely amused.

"Yes; we know him pretty well. But why should it be so unlikely a thing our knowing him?"

"Oh, I did not say that." He still seemed as much amused as a man can quietly be. "But I certainly had not the least idea I should ever see him again, for he owes me a little money. He owes me money, and a grudge besides. There are some men you cannot know anything about without their hating you—that is, without their being afraid of you, which is the same thing. I unluckily heard something about him—quite accidentally, I give you my honour, for I certainly never had the pleasure of knowing him intimately. I don't think he would exactly come to me for a character. I had not an idea that he could be the Mr. Carmel who, they told me, had been permitted by Mr. Ware to reside in his house. I was a good deal surprised when I made the discovery. There can't have been, of course, any inquiry. I should not, I assure you, have spoken to Mr. Carmel had I met him anywhere else; but I could not help telling him how astonished I was at finding him established here. He begged very hard that I would not make a fuss about it, and said that he was going away, and that he would not wait even to take off his hat. So, if that is true, I shan't trouble any-one about him. Mr. Ware would naturally think me very impertinent if I were to interfere."

He now went on to less uncomfortable subjects, and talked very pleasantly. I could see Laura Grey looking at him as opportunity occurred; she was a good deal further in the shade than I and he. I fancied I saw him smile to himself, amused at baffling her curiosity, and he sat back a little further.

"I am quite sorry, Miss Ware," he said, "that I am about to be in funds again. My friends by this time must be weaving my wings—those wings of tissue-paper that come by the post, and take us anywhere. I'm awfully sorry, for I've fallen in love with this place. I shall never forget it." He said these latter words in a tone so low as to reach me only. I was sitting, as I mentioned, very much nearer the window than Laura Grey.

There was in this stranger for me—a country miss, quite inexperienced in the subtle flatteries of voice, manner, looks, which town-bred young ladies accept at their true value—a fascination before which suspicions and alarms melted away. His voice was low and sweet; he was animated, good-humoured, and playful; and his features, though singular, and capable of very grim ex-pression, were handsome.

He talked to me in the same low tone for a few minutes. Happening to look at Laura Grey, I was struck by the anger expressed in her usually serene and gentle face. I fancied that she was vexed at his directing his attentions exclusively to me, and I was rather pleased at my triumph.

"Ethel, dear," she said, "don't you think the air a little cold?"

"Oh, I so very much hope not," he almost whispered to me.

"Cold?" said I. "I think it is so very sultry, on the contrary."

"If you find it too cold, Miss Grey, perhaps you would do wisely, I think, to sit a little further from the window," said Mr. Marston, considerately.

"I am not at all afraid for myself," she answered a little pointedly, "but I am uneasy about Miss Ware. I do think, Ethel, you would do wisely to get a little further from that window."

"But I do assure you I am quite comfortable," I said, in perfect good faith.

I saw Mr. Marston glance for a moment with a malicious smile at Laura Grey. To me the significance of that smile was a little puzzling.

"I see you have got a piano there," he said to me, in his low tones, not meant for her ear. "Miss Grey plays, of course?"

"Yes; very well indeed."

"Well, then, would you mind asking her to play something?"

I had no idea at the time that he wanted simply to find occupation for her, and to fill her ears with her own music, while he talked on with me.

"Laura, will you play that pretty thing of Beethoven's that you tried last night?" I asked.

"Don't ask me, Ethel, dear, to-night; I don't think I could," she answered, I thought a little oddly.

"Perhaps, if Miss Grey knew," he said, smiling, "that she would oblige a shipwrecked stranger extremely, and bind him to do her any service she pleases to impose in return, she might be induced to comply."

"The more you expect from my playing, the less courage I have to play," she said, in reply to his appeal, which was made, I fancied, in a tone of faint irony that seemed to suggest an oblique meaning; and her answer, I also fancied, was spoken as if answering that hidden meaning. It was very quietly done, but I felt the singularity of those tones.

"And why so? Do, I entreat—do play."

"Shouldn't I interrupt your conversation?" she answered.

"I'll not allow you even that excuse," he said; "I'll promise (and won't you, Miss Ware?) to talk whenever we feel inclined. There, now, it's all settled, isn't it? Pray begin."

" No, I am not going to play to-night," she said.

" Who would suppose Miss Grey so resolute ; so little a friend to harmony? Well, I suppose we can do nothing ; we can't prevail ; we can only regret."

I looked curiously at Laura, who had risen, and was approaching the window, close to which she took a chair and sat down.

Mr. Marston was silent. I never saw man look angrier, although he smiled. To his white teeth and vivid eyes his dark skin gave marked effect ; and to me, who knew nothing of the situation, the whole affair was most disagreeably perplexing. I was curious to see whether there would be any sign of recognition ; but I was sitting at the side that commanded a full view of our guest, and the table so near me that Laura could not have introduced her chair without a very pointed disclosure of her purpose. If Mr. Marston was disposed to snarl and snap at Miss Grey, he very quickly subdued that desire. It would have made a scene, and frightened me, and that would never do.

In his most good-humoured manner, therefore, which speedily succeeded this silent paroxysm, he chatted on, now and then almost whispering a sentence or two to me. What a contrast this gay, reckless, and in a disguised way, almost tender talk, presented to the cold, peculiar, but agreeable conversation of the ascetic enthusiast, in whom this dark-faced, animated man of the world had uncomfortably disturbed my faith !

Laura Grey was restless all this time, angry, frightened. I fancied she was jealous and wounded ; and although I was so fond of her, it did not altogether displease me.

The sunlight failed. The reflected glow from the western sky paled into grey, and twilight found our guest still in his place at the window, with his knee on the bench, and his elbows resting on the window-stone, our candles being lighted, chatting, as I thought, quite delightfully, talking sense and nonsense very pleasantly mixed, and hinting a great many very agreeable flatteries.

Laura Grey at length took courage, or panic, which often leads in the same direction, and rising, said quietly, but a little peremptorily : "I am going now, Ethel."

There was, of course, nothing for it but to submit. I confess I was angry. But it would certainly not have been dignified to show my resentment in Mr. Marston's presence. I therefore acquiesced with careless good-humour. The stranger bid us a reluctant good-night, and Laura shut down the window, and drew the little bolt across the window-sash, with, as it seemed to me, a rather inconsistent parade of suspicion. With this ungracious dismissal he went away in high good-humour, notwithstanding.

"Why need we leave the drawing-room so very early ?" said I, in a pet.

"We need not go now, as that man is gone," she said, and quickly closed the window-shutters, and drew the curtains.

Laura, when she had made these arrangements, laid her hand on my shoulder, and looked with great affection and anxiety in my face.

"You are vexed, darling, because I got rid of that person."

"No," said I; "but I'm vexed because you got rid of him rudely."

"I should have prevented his staying at the window for a single minute, if I had been quite sure he is the person I suppose. If he is—oh! how I wish he were a thousand miles away!"

"I don't think you would be quite so hard upon him, if he had divided his conversation a little more equally," I said with the bluntness of vexation.

Laura hardly smiled. There was a pained, disappointed look in her face, but the kindest you can imagine.

"No, Ethel, I did not envy your good fortune. There is no one on earth to whom I should not prefer talking."

"But who is he?" I urged.

"I can't tell you."

"Surely you can say the name of the person you take him for?" I insisted.

"I am not certain; if he be the person he resembles, he took care to place himself so that I could not, or, at least, did not, see him well; there are two or three people

mixed up in a great misfortune, whom I hate to name, or
think of. I thought at one time I recognised him; but
afterwards I grew doubtful. I never saw the person I mean
more than twice in my life; but I know very well what he
is capable of; his name is Marston; but I am not at all
certain that this is he."

"You run away with things," I said. "How do you
know that Mr. Carmel's account may not be a very unfair
one?"

"I don't rely on Mr. Carmel's account of Mr. Marston,
if this is he. I knew a great deal about him. You must
not ask me how that was, or anything more. He is said
to be, and I believe it, a bad, selfish, false man. I am
terrified when I think of your having made his acquaintance. If he continues here, we must go up to town. I
am half distracted. He dare not give us any trouble
there."

"How did he quarrel with Mr. Carmel?" I asked, full
of curiosity.

"I never heard; I did not know that he was even acquainted with him; but I think you may be perfectly
certain that everything he said about Mr. Carmel is untrue.
He knows that Mr. Carmel warned us against making his
acquaintance; and his reason for talking as he does, is
simply to discredit him. I dare say he'll take an opportunity of injuring him also. There is not time to hear
from Mr. Ware. The only course, if he stays here for more
than a day or two, is, as I said, to run up to your papa's
house in town, and stay there till he is gone."

Again my belief in Mr. Marston was shaken; and I re-
viewed my hard thoughts of Mr. Carmel with something
like compunction. The gloom and pallor of Laura's face
haunted me.

CHAPTER XVII.

LEMUEL BLOUNT.

EXT morning, at about half-past ten, as Laura and I sat in our breakfast-room, a hired carriage with two horses, which had evidently been driven at a hard pace, passed our window at a walk. The driver, who was leading his beasts, asked a question of Thomas Jones, who was rolling the gravel on the court-yard before the window; and then he led them round the corner toward the steward's house. The carriage was empty; but in another minute it was followed up by the person whom we might presume to have been its occupant. He turned towards our window as he passed, so that we had a full view of this new visitor.

He was a man who looked past sixty, slow-paced, and very solemn; he was dressed in a clumsy black suit; his face was large, square, and sallow; his cheek and chin were smoothly shorn and blue. His hat was low-crowned, and broad in the brim. He had a cotton umbrella in his big gloved hand, and a coloured pocket-handkerchief sticking out of his pocket. A great bunch of seals hung from his watch-chain under his black waistcoat. He was walking so slowly that we had no difficulty in observing these details; and he stopped before the hall-door, as if doubtful whether he should enter there. A word, however, from Thomas Jones set him right, and he in turn disappeared round the corner.

We did not know what to make of this figure, whom we now conjectured to have come in quest of the shipwrecked stranger.

Thomas Jones ran round before him to the door of the steward's house, which he opened; and the new-comer thanked him with a particularly kind smile. He knocked on chance at the door to the right, and the voice of our unknown guest told him to come in.

"Oh, Mr. Blount!" said the young gentleman, rising, hesitating, and then tendering his hand very respectfully, and looking in the sensible, vulgar face of the old man as if he were by no means sure how that tender might be received. "I hope, sir, I have not quite lost your friendship. I hope I retain some, were it ever so little, of the goodwill you once bore me. I hope, at least, that you will allow me to say that I am glad to see you: I feel it."

The old man bowed his head, holding it a little on one side while the stranger spoke; it was the attitude of listening rather than of respect. When the young gentleman had done speaking, his visitor raised his head again. The young man smiled faintly, and still extended his hand, looking very pale. Mr. Blount did not smile in answer; his countenance was very sombre, one might say sad.

"I never yet, sir, refused the hand of any man living when offered to me in sincerity, especially that of one in whom I felt, I may say, at one time a warm interest, although he may have given me reason to alter the opinion I then entertained of him."

Thus speaking, he gravely took the young man's hand, and shook it in a thoughtful, melancholy way, lowering his head again as he had done before.

"I don't ask how my uncle feels towards me," said the young man, half inquiringly.

"You need not," answered the visitor.

"I am at all events very much obliged to you," said the young man, humbly, "for your friendship, Mr. Blount. There is, I know, but one way of interesting your sympathy, and that is by telling you frankly how deep and true my repentance is; how I execrate my ingratitude; how I deplore my weakness and criminality." He paused, looking earnestly at the old man, who, however, simply bowed his head again, and made no comment.

"I can't justify anything I have done; but in my letter

I ventured to say a few words in extenuation," he continued. "I don't expect to soften my uncle's just resentment, but I am most anxious, Mr. Blount, my best friend on earth, to recover something, were it ever so little, of the ground I have lost in your opinion."

"Time, sir, tries all things," answered the new-comer, gently; "if you mean to lead a new life, you will have opportunity to prove it."

"Was my uncle softened, ever so little, when he heard that the Conway Castle had gone down?" asked the young man, after a short silence.

"I was with him at breakfast when the morning paper brought the intelligence," said Mr. Blount. "I don't recollect that he expressed any regret."

"I dare say; I can quite suppose it; I ought to have known that he was pleased rather."

"No; I don't think he was pleased. I rather think he exhibited indifference," answered Mr. Blount.

With some grim remarks I believe the young man's uncle had received the sudden news of his death.

"Did my uncle see the letter I wrote to you, Mr. Blount?"

"No."

"And why not?"

"You will not think, I hope, that I would for any consideration use a phrase that could wound you unnecessarily when I tell you?"

"Certainly not."

"Your letter mentioned that you had lost your papers and money in the ship. Now, if it should turn out that you had, in short, misstated anything——"

"Told a lie, you mean," interrupted the young man, his face growing white, and his eyes gleaming.

"It would have been discourteous in me to say so, but such was my meaning," he answered, with a very kind look. "It has been one object with me during my life to reconcile courtesy with truth. I am happy in the belief that I have done so, and I believe during a long life I have never once offended against the laws of politeness. Had you deceived him so soon again it would have sunk you finally and for ever. I thought it advisable, there-

fore, to give you an opportunity of reconsidering the statements of your letter before committing you by placing
them before him as fact."

The young man flushed suddenly. It was his misfortune that he could not resent suspicion, however gross,
although he might wince under the insult, all the more
that it was just. Rather sulkily he said :

"I can only repeat, sir, that I have not a shilling, nor
a cheque; I left every paper and every farthing I possessed
in my despatch-box, in my berth. Of course, I can't prove
it; I can only repeat that every guinea I had in the world
has gone to the bottom."

Mr. Blount raised his head. His square face and massive features confronted the younger man, and his hones-
brown eyes were fixed upon him with a grave and undisguised inquiry.

"I don't say that you have any certainty of recovering
a place in your uncle's esteem, but the slightest prevarication in matters of this kind would be simply suicidal.
Now, I ask you, sir, on your honour, did no part of your
money, or of your papers, go by rail either to Bristol or to
London ?"

"Upon my honour, Mr. Blount, not a farthing. I had
only about ten pounds in gold, all the rest was in letters
of credit and cheques ; and, bad as I am, I should scarcely
be fool enough to practise a trick, which, from its nature,
must be almost instantaneously self-exposed. My uncle
could have stopped payment of them; probably he has
done so."

"I see you understand something of business, sir."

"I should have understood a great deal more, Mr.
Blount, and been a much better man, if I had listened to
you long ago. I hope, in future, to be less my own adviser,
and more your pupil."

To this flattering speech the old man listened attentively,
but made no answer.

"Your letter followed me to Chester," said Mr. Blount,
after an interval. "I received it last night. He was in
London when I saw him last ; and my letter, telling him
that you are still living, may not reach him, possibly, for
some days. Thus, you see, you would have the start of

him, if I may so describe it, without rudeness; and you
are aware he has no confidence in you; and, certainly, if
you will permit me to say so, he ought not to have any.
I have a note of the number of the cheque; you can write
a line saying that you have lost it, and requesting that
payment may be stopped; and I will enclose it to Messrs.
Dignum and Budget."

" There's pen and ink here; I'll do it this moment. I
thought you had renounced me also; and I was going to
write again to try you once more, before taking to the high
road," he said, with dismal jocularity.

It wrung the pride of the young man sorely to write the
note. But the bitter pill was swallowed; and he handed
it, but with signs of suppressed anger, to Mr. Blount.

" That will answer perfectly," said the man in black.

" It enables you to stop that cheque by this post, without first seeing my uncle; and it relieves you," said the
young man, with bitter and pitiless irony, " of the folly of
acting in the most trifling matter upon my word of honour.
It is certainly making the most of the situation. I have
made one great slip—a crime, if you like——"

" Quite so, sir," acquiesced Mr. Blount, with melancholy
politeness.

" Under great momentary temptation," continued the
young man, " and without an idea of ultimately injuring
any human being to the amount of a single farthing. I'm
disowned; any one that pleases may safely spit in my face.
I'm quite aware how I stand in this infernal pharisaical
world."

Mr. Blount looked at him gravely, but made him no
answer. The young gentleman did not want to quarrel
with Mr. Blount just then. He could not afford it.

" I don't mean you, of course," he said; " you have
been always only too much my friend. I am speaking of
the world; you know, quite well, if this unlucky thing
takes wind, and my uncle's conduct towards me is the very
thing to set people talking and inquiring, I may as well
take off my hat to you all, drink your healths in a glass of
prussic acid, and try how a trip to some other world agrees
with me."

" You are speaking, of course, sir, in jest," said Mr.

Blount, with some disgust in his grave countenance; "but I may mention that the unfortunate occurrence is known but to your uncle and to me, and to no other person on earth. You bear the name of Marston—you'll excuse me for reminding you, sir—and upon that point he is sensitive and imperious. He considered, sir, that your bearing that name, if I may so say, without being supposed guilty of a rudeness, would slur it; and, therefore, you'll change it, as arranged, on embarking at Southampton. It would be highly inexpedient to annoy your uncle by any inadvertence upon this point. Your contemplating suicide would be— you will pardon the phrase—cowardly and impious. Not, indeed, if I may so say consistently with the rules of politeness," he added, thoughtfully, "that your sudden removal would involve any loss to anybody, except, possibly, some few Jews, and people of that kind."

"Certainly—of course. You need not insist upon that. I feel my degradation, I hope, sufficiently. It is not his fault, at least, if I don't."

"And, from myself, I suggest that he will be incensed, if he learns that you are accepting the hospitality of Mr. Ware's house. I think, sir, that men of the world, especially gentlemen, will regard it, if the phrase be not discourteous, in the light of a shabby act."

"Shabby, sir! what do you mean by shabby?" said Mr. Marston, flaming up.

"I mean, sir—you'll excuse me—paltry; don't you see? —or mean. His feelings would be strongly excited by your partaking of Mr. Ware's hospitality."

"Hospitality! Shelter, you mean; slates, walls—little more than they give a beast in a pound! Why, I don't owe them a crust, or a cup of tea. I get everything from the hotel there, at Cardyllion; and Mr. Ware is a thousand miles away!"

"I speak of it simply as a question of expediency, sir. He will be inflamed against you, if he hears you have, in ever so small a matter, placed yourself under any obligation to Mr. Ware."

"But he need not hear of it; why should you mention it?"

"I cannot practise reserve with a man who treats me

with unlimited confidence," he answered, gently. "Why should you not go to the hotel ?"

"I have no money."

"But you get everything you want there on credit ?"

"Well, yes, that's true ; but it would scarcely do to make that move ; I have been as ill as ever I was in my life since that awful night on the rocks down there. You can have no idea what it was ; and the doctor says I must keep quiet. It isn't worth while moving now ; so soon as I have funds, I'll leave this."

"I will lend you what you require, with much pleasure, sir," proffered Mr. Blout."

"Well, thanks, it is not very much, and it's hard to refuse ; one feels such a fool without a shilling to give to a messenger, or to the servants ; I haven't even a fee for the doctor who has been attending me."

Determined by this pathetic appeal, Mr. Blount took a bank-note of ten pounds from his purse and lent it to Mr. Marston.

"And, I suppose, you'll remove forthwith to the hotel," he said.

"The moment I feel equal to it," he replied. "Why, d—— it, don't you think I'm ready to go, when I'm able ? I—I——Don't mind me, pray. Your looks reprove me. I'm shocked at myself when I use those phrases. I know very well that I have just escaped by a miracle from death. I feel how utterly unfit I was to die ; and, I assure you, I'm not ungrateful. You shall see that my whole future life will be the better for it. I'm not the graceless wretch I have been. One such hour as preceded my scaling that rock out there is a lesson for a life. You have often spoken to me on the subjects that ought to interest us all. I mean when I was a boy. Your words have returned upon me. You derive happiness from the good you do to others. I thought you had cast your bread upon the waters to see it no more ; but you have found it at last. I am very greatful to you."

Did Mr. Marston believe that good people are open, in the manner of their apostleship, to flattery, as baser mortals are in matters of another sort ? It was to be hoped that Mr. Marston felt half what he utttered. His words, however, did produce a favourable and a pleasant impression upon Mr. Blount. His large face beamed for a moment with honest gratification. His eyes looked evil upon him, as if the benevolence of his inmost heart spoke out through them.

"If anything can possibly please him, sir, in connection with you," said Mr. Blount, with all his customary suavity and unconscious bluntness, "it will be to learn that recent events have produced a salutary impression and a total change in you. Not that I suppose he cares very much; but I'm glad to have to represent to him anything favourable in this particular case. I mean to return to London direct, and if your uncle is still there you shall hear in a day or two—at all events very soon; but I wish you were in the hotel."

"Well, I'll go to the hotel, if they can put me up. I'll go at once; address to me to the post-office—Richard Marston, I suppose?"

"Just so, sir, Richard Marston."

Mr. Blount had risen, and stood gravely, prepared to take his leave.

"I have kept you a long time, Mr. Blount; will you take anything?"

Mr. Blount declined refreshments.

"I must leave you now, sir; there is a crisis in every life. What has happened to you is stupendous; the danger and the deliverance. That hour is past. May its remembrance be with you ever—day and night! Do not suppose that it can rest in your mind without positive consequences. It must leave you a great deal better or a great deal worse. Farewell, sir."

So they parted. Mr. Marston seemed to have lost all his spirits and half his energy in that interview. He sat motionless in the chair into which he had thrown himself, and gazed listlessly on the floor in a sulky reverie. At length he said—

"That is a most unpleasant old fellow; I wish he was not so unscrupulously addicted to telling truth."

CHAPTER XVIII.

IDENTIFIED.

T was a gloomy day; I had left Laura Grey in the room we usually occupied, where she was now alone, busy over some of our accounts. I dare say her thoughts now and then wandered into speculations respecting the identity of the visitor who, the night before, evaded her recognition, if indeed he was recognisable by her at all. Her doubts were now resolved. The room door opened, and the tenant of the steward's house entered coolly, and approached the table where she was sitting. Laura Grey did not rise; she did not speak; she sat, pen in hand, staring at him as if she were on the point of fainting. The star-shaped scar on his forehead, fixed there by some old fracture, and his stern and energetic features, were now distinctly before her. He kept his eye fixed upon her, and smiled, dubious of his reception.

"I saw you, Miss Grey, yesterday afternoon, though you did not see me. I avoided your eye then; but it was idle supposing that I could continue even a few days longer in this place without you seeing me. I came last night with my mind made up to reveal myself, but I put it off till we should be to ourselves, as we are now. I saw you half guessed me, but you weren't sure, and I left you in doubt."

He approached till his hands rested upon the table opposite, and said, with a very stern and eager face

"Miss Grey, upon my honour, upon my soul, if I can give you an assurance which can bind a gentleman, I entreat you to believe me. I shan't offer one syllable contrary to what I now feel to be your wishes. I shan't press you, I shan't ask you to hear me upon the one subject you say you object to. You allege that I have done you a wrong. I will spare no pains to redress it. I will do my utmost in any way you please to dictate. I will do all this, I swear by everything a gentleman holds most sacred, upon one very easy condition."

He paused. He was leaning forward, his dark eyes were fixed upon her with a piercing gaze. She did not, or could not, speak. She was answering his gaze with a stare wilder and darker, but her very lips were white.

"I know I have stood in your way; I admit I have injured you, not by accident; it was with the design and wish to injure you, if the endeavour to detach a fellow like that be an injury. You shall forgive me; the most revengeful woman can forgive a man the extravagances of his jealousy. I am here to renounce all, to retrieve everything. I admit the injury; it shall be repaired."

She spoke now for the first time, and said, hardly above her breath:

"It's irreparable. It can't be undone—quite irreparable."

"When I undertake a thing I do it; I'll do this at any sacrifice—yes, at any, of pride or opinion. Suppose I go to the persons in question, and tell them that they have been deceived, and that I deceived them, and now confess the whole thing a tissue of lies?"

"You'll never do that."

"By Heavens, as I stand here, I'll do it! Do you suppose I care for their opinion in comparison with a real object? I'll do it. I'll write and sign it in your presence; you shall have it to lock up in that desk, and do what you please with it, upon one condition."

A smile of incredulity lighted Laura Grey's face faintly, as she shook her head.

"You don't believe me, but you shall. Tell me what will satisfy you—what practicable proof will convince you. I'll set you right with them. You believe in a Providence. Do you think I was saved from that wreck for nothing?"

Laura Grey looked down upon her desk; his fierce eyes were fixed on her with intense eagerness, for he thought he read in her pale face and her attitude signs of compliance. It needed, he fancied, perhaps but a slight impulse to determine her.

"I'll do it all; but, as I told you, on one condition."

There was a silence for a time. He was still watching her intently.

"Let us both be reasonable," he resumed. "I ought, I now know, to have seen long ago, Miss Grey, that there was no use in my talking to you as I did. I have been mad. There's the whole story; and now I renounce it all. I despair; it's over. I'll give you the very best proof of that. I shall devote myself to another, and you shall aid me. Pray, not a word, till you have heard me out; that's the condition. If you accept it, well. If not, so sure as there is life in me, you may regret it."

"There's nothing more you can do I care for now," she broke out with a look of agony. "Oh, Heaven help me!"

"You'll find there is," he continued, with a quiet laugh. "You can talk as long as you please when your turn comes. Just hear me out. I only want you to have the whole case before you. I say you can help me, and you shall. I'm a very good fellow to work with, and a bitter one to work against. Now, one moment. I have made the acquaintance of a young lady whom I wish to marry. Upon my sacred honour, I have no other intention. She is poor; her father is over head and ears in debt; she can never have a guinea more than two thousand pounds. It can't be sordid, you'll allow. There is a Jesuit fellow hanging about this place. He hates me; he has been in here telling lies of me. I expect you to prevent my being prejudiced by that slanderer. You can influence the young lady in my favour, and enable me to improve our acquaintance. I expect you to do so. These are my conditions. She is Miss Ethel Ware."

The shock of a disclosure so entirely unexpected, and the sting possibly of wounded vanity, made her reply more spirited than it would have been. She stood up, and said, quietly and coldly :

"I have neither right nor power in the matter; and if I had, nothing on earth could induce me to exercise them in your favour. You can write, if you please, to Mr. Ware, for leave to pay your addresses to his daughter. But without his leave you shall not visit here, nor join her in her walks; and if you attempt to do either, I will remove Miss Ware, and place her under the care of some one better able than I to protect her."

The young man looked at her with a very pale face.

"I thought you knew me better, Miss Grey," he said, with an angry sneer. "You refuse your chance of reconciliation."

He paused, as if to allow her time to think better of it.

"Very well; I'm glad I've found you out. Don't you think your situation is rather an odd one—a governess in Mr. Ware's country quarters? We all know pretty well what sort of gentleman Mr. Ware is, a gentleman particularly well qualified by good taste and high spirits to make his house agreeable. He was here, I understand, for about a week a little time ago, but his wife does not trouble your solitude much; and now that he is on his travels, he is succeeded by a young friar. I happen to know what sort of person Carmel was, and is. Was ever young lady so fortunate? One only wonders that Mr. Ware, under these circumstances, is not a little alarmed for the Protestantism of his governess. I should scarcely have believed that you had found so easily so desirable a home; but fate has ordained that I should light upon your retreat, and hear with my own ears the good report of the neighbours, and see with my own eyes how very comfortable and how extremely happy you are."

He smiled and bowed ironically, and drew towards the door.

"There was nothing to prevent our being on the friendliest terms—nothing."

He paused, but she made him no answer.

"No reason on earth why we should not. You could have done me a very trifling kindness. I could have served you vitally."

Another pause here,

"I can ascribe your folly to nothing but the most insensate malice. I shall take care of myself. You ought to know me. Whatever befalls, you have to thank but your own infatuated obstinacy for it."

"I have friends still," she cried, in a sudden burst of agony. "Your cowardice, your threats and insults, your persecution of a creature quite defenceless and heartbroken, and with no one near to help her——"

Her voice faltered.

"Find out your friends, if you have got them; tell them what you please; and, if it is worth while, I will contradict your story. I'll fight your friends. I'll pit my oath against yours."

There was no sneer on his features now, no irony in his tones; he was speaking with the bitter vehemence of undisguised fury.

"I shrink from nothing. Things have happened since to make me more reckless, and by so much the more dangerous. If you knew a little more you would scarcely dare to quarrel with me." He dashed his hand as he spoke upon the table.

"I am afraid—I'm frightened; but nothing on earth shall make me do what you ask."

"That's enough—that closes it," said he. There was a little pause. "And remember, the consequences I promise are a great deal nearer than you probably dream of."

With these words, spoken slowly, with studied meaning, he left the room as suddenly as he had appeared. Laura Grey was trembling. Her thoughts were not very clear. She was shocked, and even terrified.

The sea, which had swallowed all the rest, had sent up that one wicked man alive. How many good, kind, and useful lives were lost to earth, she thought, in those dreadful moments, and that one life, barren of all good, profligate and cruel, singled out alone for mercy!

CHAPTER XIX.

PISTOLS FOR TWO.

KNEW nothing of all this. I was not to learn what had passed at that interview till many years later. Laura Grey, on my return, told me nothing. I am sure she was right. There were some things she could not have explained, and the stranger's apparently insane project of marrying penniless me was a secret better in her own keeping than in that of a simple and very self-willed girl.

When I returned there were signs of depression and anxiety in her looks, and her silence and abstraction excited my curiosity. She easily put me off, however. I knew that her spirits sometimes failed her, although she never talked about her troubles; and therefore her dejection was, after all, not very remarkable. We heard nothing more of our guest till next day, when Rebecca Torkill told us that he was again suffering from one of his headaches. The intelligence did not excite all the sympathy she seemed to expect. Shortly after sunset we saw him pass the window of our room, and walk by under the trees.

With an ingrained perversity, the more Laura Grey warned me against this man, the more I became interested in him. She and I were both unusually silent that evening. I think that her thoughts were busy with him; I know that mine were.

"We won't mind opening the window to-night," said Laura.

I

"I was just thinking how pleasant it would be. Why should we not open it?" I answered.

"Because we should have him here again; and he is not the sort of person your mamma would like you to become acquainted with."

I was a little out of humour, but did not persist. I sat in a sullen silence, my eyes looking dreamily through the window. The early twilight had faded into night by the time the stranger re-appeared. I saw him turn the line of his walk near the window; and seeing it shut, pause for a moment. I dare say he was more vexed than I. He made up his mind, however, against a scene. He looked on the ground and over his shoulder, again at the window.

Mr. Marston walked round the corner to the steward's house. The vague shadows and lights of night were abroad by this time. Candles were in his room; he found Rebecca Torkill there, with a small tankard and a tea-cup on a salver, awaiting his return.

"La! sir, to think of you doing such another wild thing, and you, only this minute, at death's door with your head! And how is it now, please, sir?"

"A thousand thanks. My head is as well as my hat. My headache goes as it comes, in a moment. What is this?"

"Some gruel, please, sir, with sugar, white wine, and nutmeg. I thought you might like it."

"Caudle, by Jove!" smiled the gentleman, "isn't it?"

"Well, it is; and it's none the worse o' that."

"All the better," exclaimed Mr. Marston, who chose to be on friendly terms with the old lady. "How can I thank you?"

"It's just the best thing in the world to make you sleep after a headache. You'll take some while it's hot."

"I can't thank you half enough," he said.

"I'll come back, sir, and see you by-and-by," and the good woman toddled out, leaving him alone with his gruel.

"I must not offend her." He poured some out into his cup, tasted it, and laughed quietly. "Sipping caudle! Well, this is rather a change for Richard Marston, by Jove! A change every day. Let us make a carouse of it," he said, and threw it out of the window.

Mr. Marston threw on his loose wrapper, and folded his muffler about his throat, replaced his hat, and with his cane in his fingers, was about to walk down to the town of Cardyllion. A word or two spoken, quite unsuspiciously, by Doctor Mervyn that morning, had touched a sensitive nerve, and awakened a very acute anxiety in Mr. Marston's mind. The result was his intended visit, at the fall of night, to the High-street of the quaint little town.

He was on the point of setting out, when Rebecca Torkill returned with a sliced lemon on a plate.

"Some likes a squeeze of a lemon in it," she observed, "and I thought I might as well leave it here."

"It is quite delicious, really," he replied, as Mrs. Torkill peeped into the open flagon.

"Why," said she, in unfeigned admiration, "I'm blest if he's left a drop! Ah! ah! Well, it was good; and I'll have some more for you before you go to bed. But you shouldn't drink it off, all at a pull, like that. You might make yourself ill that way."

"We men like good liquor so well—so well—we—we —what was I saying? Oh! yes, we like our liquor so well, we never know when we have had enough. It's a bad excuse; but let it pass. I'm going out for a little walk, it always sets me up after one of those headaches. Good evening, Mrs. Torkill."

He was thinking plainly of other matters than her, or her caudle; and, before she had time to reply, he was out of the door.

It was a sweet, soft night; the moon was up. The walk from Malory to the town is lonely and pretty. He took the narrow road that approaches Cardyllion in an inland line, parallel to the road that runs by the shore of the estuary. His own echoing footsteps among the moonlit trees was the only sign of life, except the distant barking of a watch-dog, now and then, that was audible. A melancholy wind was piping high in the air, from over the sea; you might fancy it the aërial lamentations of the drowned.

He was passing the churchyard now, and stopped partly to light a cigar, partly to look at the old church, the effect of which, in the moonlight, was singular. Its gable and towers cast a sharp black shadow across the grass and gravestones, like that of a gigantic hand whose finger pointed towards him. He smiled cynically as the fancy struck him.

"Another grave there, I should not wonder if the news is true. What an ass that fellow is! Another grave, I dare say; and in my present luck, I suppose I shall fill it—fill it! That's ambiguous; yes, the more like an oracle. That shadow does look curiously like a finger pointing at me!"

He smoked for a time, leaning on the pier of the iron wicket that from this side admits to the churchyard, and looking in with thoughts very far from edifying.

"This will be the second disagreeable discovery, without reckoning Carmel, I shall have made since my arrival in this queer corner of the world. Who could have anticipated meeting Laura here?—or what whining fool, Carmel? Who would have fancied that Jennings, of all men, would have turned up in this out-of-the-way nook? By Jove! I'm like Saint Paul, hardly out of the shipwreck when a viper fastens on my hand. Old Sprague made us turn all that into elegiacs. I wonder whether I could make elegiacs now."

He loitered slowly on, by the same old road, into Castle Street, the high-street of the quaint little town of steep roofs and many gables. The hall-door of the "Verney Arms" was open, and the light of the lamp glowed softly on the pavement.

Mr. Marston hated suspense. He would rather make a bad bargain, off-hand, than endure the torture of a long negotiation. He would stride out to meet a catastrophe rather than await its slow, sidelong approaches. This intolerance of uncertainty made him often sudden in action. He had come down to the town simply to reconnoitre. He was beginning, by this time, to meditate something more serious. Under the shadow of the houses opposite, he walked slowly up and down the silent flagway, eyeing the door of the "Verney Arms" askance, as he finished his cigar.

It so happened, that exactly as he had thrown away the stump of it, a smoker, who had just commenced his, came slowly down the steps of the " Verney Arms," and stood upon the deserted flagway, and as he puffed indolently, he looked up the street, and down the street, and up at the sky.

The splendid moon shone full on his face, and Mr. Marston knew him. He was tall and slight, and rather good-looking, with a face of great intelligence, heightened with something of enthusiasm, and stood there smoking, in happy unconsciousness that an unfriendly eye was watching him across the street.

Mr. Marston stood exactly opposite. The smoker, who had emerged from the " Verney Arms," stood before the centre of the steps, and Mr. Marston, on a sudden, as if he was bent on walking straight through him into the hotel, walked at a brisk pace across the street, and halted, within a yard, in front of him.

" I understand," said Marston instantly, in a low, stern tone, " that you said at Black's, when I was away yachting, that you had something to say to me."

The smoker had lowered his cigar, and was evidently surprised, as well he might be ; he looked at him hard for some time, and at length replied as grimly : " Yes, I said so ; yes I do ; I mean to speak to you."

" All right ; no need to raise our voices here though ; I think you had better find some place where we can talk without exciting attention."

" Come this way," said the tall young man, turning suddenly and walking up the street at a leisurely pace. Mr. Marston walked beside him, a yard or two apart. They might be very good friends, for anything that appeared to a passer-by. He turned down a short and narrow by-street, with only room for a house or two, and they found themselves on the little common that is known as the Green of Cardyllion. The sea, at its further side, was breaking in long, tiny waves along the shingle, the wind came over the old castle with a melancholy soughing ; the green was solitary ; and only here and there, from the windows of the early little town, a light gleamed. The moon shone bright on the green, turning the grass to grey, and silvering the ripples on the dark estuary, and whitening the misty outlines of the noble Welsh mountains across the water. A more tranquillising scene could scarcely be imagined.

When they had got to the further end, they stopped, as if by common consent.

"I'm ready to hear you," said Marston.

"Well, I have only to tell you, and I'm glad of this opportunity, that I have ascertained the utter falsehood of your stories, and that you are a coward and a villain."

"Thanks; that will do, Mr. Jennings," answered Marston, growing white with fury, but speaking with cold and quiet precision. "You have clenched this matter by an insult which I should have answered by cutting you across the face with this,"—and he made his cane whistle in the air,—"but that I reserve you for something more effectual, and shall run no risk of turning the matter into a police-office affair. I have neither pistols nor friend here. We must dispense with formalities; we can do all that is necessary for ourselves, I suppose. I'll call to-morrow, early, at the 'Verney Arms.' A word or two will settle everything."

He raised his hat ever so little, implying that that conference, for the present, was over; but before he could turn, Mr. Jennings, who did not choose to learn more than was unavoidable to his honour, said:

"You will find a note at the bar."

"Address it Richard Wynyard, then."

"Your friend?"

"No; myself."

"Oh! a false name?" sneered Mr. Jennings.

"You may use the true one, of course. My tailor is looking for me a little more zealously, I fancy, than you were; and if you publish it in Cardyllion, it may lead to his arresting me, and saving you all further trouble in this, possibly, agitating affair." The young man accompanied these words with a cold laugh.

"Well, Richard Wynyard be it," said Mr. Jennings, with a slight flush.

And with these words the two young men turned their backs on each other. Mr. Jennings walked along beside the shingle, with the sound of the light waves in his ear, and thinking rather hurriedly, as men will, whom so serious a situation has suddenly overtaken. Marston turned, as I said, the other way, and without entering the town again, approached Malory by the narrow road that passes close under the castle walls, and follows the line of the high banks overlooking the estuary.

If there be courage and mental activity, and no conscience, we have a very dangerous devil. A spoiled child, in which self is supreme, who has no softness of heart, and some cleverness and energy, easily degenerates into that sort of Satan. And yet, in a kind of way, Marston was popular. He could spend money freely—it was not his own—and when he was in spirits he was amusing.

When he stared in Jennings' face this evening, the bruise and burning of an old jealousy were in his heart. The pain of that hellish hate is often lightly inflicted; but what is more cruel than vanity? He had abandoned the pursuit in which that jealousy was born, but the hatred remained. And now he had his revenge in hand. It is a high stake, one's life on a match of pistol-shooting. But his brute courage made nothing of it. It was an effort to him to think himself in danger, and he did not make that effort. He was thinking how to turn the situation to account.

CHAPTER XX.

THE WOOD OF PLAS YLWD.

EXT morning, Mr. Marston, we learned, had been down to Cardyllion early. He had returned at about ten o'clock, and he had his luggage packed up, and despatched again to the proprietor of the "Verney Arms." So we might assume that he was gone.

The mountain that had weighed on Laura Grey's spirits was perceptibly lightened. I heard her whisper to herself, "Thank God!" when she heard Rebecca Torkill's report, and the further intelligence that their guest had told her and Thomas Jones that he was going to the town, to return no more to Malory. Laura was now, again, quite like herself. For my part, I was a little glad, and (shall I confess it?) also a little sorry! I had not quite made up my mind respecting this agreeable Mr. Marston, of whom Mr. Carmel and Miss Grey had given each so alarming a character.

About an hour later, I was writing to mamma, and sitting at the window, when, raising my eyes, I saw Laura Grey and Mr. Marston, much to my surprise, walking side by side up the avenue towards the hall-door. They appeared to be in close conversation; Mr. Marston seemed to talk volubly and carelessly, and cut the heads of the weeds with his cane as he sauntered by her side. Laura Grey held her handkerchief to her eyes, except now and then, when she spoke a few words, as it seemed passionately.

When they came to the court-yard, opposite to the hall-door, she broke away from him, hurried across, ran up the steps, and shut the door. He stood where she had left him, looking after her and smiling. I thought he was going to follow; he saw me in the window, and raised his hat, still smiling, and with this farewell salute he turned on his heel and walked slowly away towards the gate. I ran to the hall, and there found Laura Grey. She had been crying, and was agitated.

"Ethel, darling," she said, "let nothing on earth induce you to speak to that man again. I implore of you to give me your solemn promise. If he speaks truth it will not cost you anything, for he says he is going away this moment, not to return."

It certainly looked very like it, for he had actually despatched his two boxes, he had "tipped" the servants handsomely at the steward's house, and having taken a courteous leave of them, and left with Mrs. Torkill a valedictory message of thanks for me, he had got into a "fly" and driven off to the "Verney Arms."

Well, whether for good or ill, he had now unquestionably taken his departure; but not without leaving a sting. The little he had spoken to Miss Grey, at the moment of his flight, had proved, it seemed, a Parthian arrow tipped with poison. She seemed to grow more and more miserable every hour. She had lain down on her bed, and was crying bitterly, and trembling. I began to grow vexed at the cruelty of the man who had deliberately reduced her to that state. I knew not what gave him the power of torturing her. If I was angry, I was also intensely curious. My questions produced no clearer answers than this: "Nothing, dear, that you could possibly understand without first hearing a very long story. I hope the time is coming when I may tell it all to you. But the secret is not mine; it concerns other people; and at present I must keep it."

Mr. Marston had come and gone, then, like a flash of light, leaving my eyes dazzled. The serenity of Malory seemed now too quiet for me; the day was dull. I spent my time sitting in the window, or moping about the place. I must confess that I had, by no means, the horror of this stranger that the warnings of Mr. Carmel and Laura Grey ought, I suppose, to have inspired. On the contrary, his

image came before me perpetually, and everything I looked
at, the dark trees, the window-sill, the garden, the estuary,
and the ribs of rock round which the cruel sea was sporting,
recalled the hero of a terrible romance.

I tried in vain to induce Laura to come with me for a
walk, late in the afternoon. So I set out alone, turning
my back on Cardyllion, in the direction of Penruthyn
Priory. The sun was approaching the western horizon as
I drew near the picturesque old farm-house of Plas Ylwd.

A little to the south of this stretches a fragment of old
forest, covering some nine or ten acres of peaty ground.
It is a decaying wood, and in that melancholy and miserable
plight, I think, very beautiful. I would commend it as a
haunt to artists in search of "studies," who love huge
trees with hollow trunks, some that have "cast" half their
boughs as deer do their antlers; some wreathed and laden
with ivy, others that stretch withered and barkless branches
into the air; ground that is ribbed and unequal, and
cramped with great ringed, snake-like roots, that writhe
and knot themselves into the earth; here and there overspread with little jungles of bramble, and broken and
burrowed by rabbits.

Into this grand and singular bit of forest, now glorified
by the coloured light of evening, I had penetrated some
little way. Arrested in my walk by the mellow song of a
blackbird, I listened in the sort of ecstasy that every one
has, I suppose, experienced under similar circumstances;
and I was in the full enjoyment of this sylvan melody,
when I was startled, and the bird put to flight, by the near
report of fire-arms. Once or twice I had heard boys
shooting at the birds in this wood, but they had always
accompanied their practice with shouting and loud talking.
A dead silence followed this. I had no reason for any
misgivings about so natural an interruption in such a
place, but I did feel an ominous apprehension. I began
to move, and was threading my way through one of these
blackberry thickets, when I heard, close to my side, the
branches of some underwood thrust aside, and Mr.
Marston, looking pale and wicked, walked quickly by. It
was plain he did not see me; I was screened by the stalks
and sprays through which I saw him. He had no weapon

as he passed me; he was drawing on his glove. The
sudden appearance of Mr. Marston whom I believed to be
by this time miles away—at the other side of Cardyllion
—was a shock that rather confirmed my misgivings.

I waited till he was quite gone, and then passed down
the path he had come by. I saw nothing to justify alarm,
so I walked a little in the same direction, looking to the
right and left. In a little opening among the moss-grown
trunks of the trees, I soon saw something that frightened
me. It was a man lying on his back, deadly pale, upon
the ground; his waistcoat was open, and his shirt-front
covered with blood, that seemed to ooze from under his
hand, which was pressed on it; his hat was on the ground,
some way behind. A pistol lay on the grass beside him,
and another not far from his feet.

I was very much frightened, and the sight of blood
made me feel faint. The wounded man saw me, I knew,
for his eyes were fixed on me; his lips moved, and there
was a kind of straining in his throat; he said a word or
two, though I could not at first hear what. With a
horrible reluctance, I came near and leaned a little over
him, and then heard distinctly:

" Pray send help."

I bethought me instantly of the neighbouring farm-
house of Plas Ylwd, and knowing this little forest tract
well, I ran through it nearly direct to the farm-yard, and
quickly succeeded in securing the aid of Farmer Prichard
and all his family, except his wife, who stayed at home to
get a bed ready for the reception of the wounded stranger.
We all trooped back again through the woods, at a trot, I
at their head, quite forgetting my dignity in my excitement. The wounded man appeared fainter. But he
beckoned to us with his hand, without raising his arm,
and with a great effort he said : " The blame is mine—all
my fault—remember, if I die. I compelled this meeting."

I got Prichard to send his son, without a moment's
delay, to Cardyllion, to bring Dr. Mervyn, and as they got
the bleeding man on towards Plas Ylwd, I, in a state of
high excitement, walked swiftly homeward, hoping to
reach Malory before the declining light failed altogether.

CHAPTER XXI.

THE PATIENT AT PLAS YLWD.

GOT home just as the last broad beam of the setting sun was spent, and twilight overspread churchyard and manor-house, sea and land, with its grey mantle. Lights were gleaming from the drawing-room window as I approached; a very welcome light to me, for it told me that Laura Grey had come down, and I was longing to tell her my story. I found her, as I expected, seated quietly at our tea-table, and saw, in her surprised and eager looks, how much she was struck by the excitement which mine exhibited, as, without waiting to take off my hat or coat, I called on her to listen, and stumbled and hurried through the opening of my strange story.

I had hardly mentioned the sudden appearance of Mr. Marston, when Laura Grey rose with her hands clasped:

"Was any one shot ? For God's sake, tell me quickly!"

I described all I had seen. She pressed her hand hard to her heart.

"Oh ! he has killed him—the villain ! His threats are always true—his promises never. Oh ! Ethel, darling, he has been so near me, and I never dreamed it."

"Who ? What is it, Laura ? Don't, darling, be so frightened ; he's not killed—nobody's killed. I daresay it is very trifling, and Doctor Mervyn is with him by this time."

"I am sure he's badly wounded ; he has killed him. He has hated him so long, he would never have left him till he had killed him."

She was growing quite distracted ; I, all the time, doing my utmost to re-assure her.

" What is his name ?" at length I asked.

The question seemed to quiet her. She looked at me, and then down ; and then again at me.

Once or twice she had mentioned a brother whom she loved very much, and who was one of her great anxieties. Was this wounded man he ? If not, was he a lover ? This latter could hardly be ; for she had once, after a long, laughing fencing with my close questions, told me suddenly, quite gravely, " I have no lover, and no admirer, except one whom I despise and dislike as much as I can any one on earth." It was very possible that her brother was in debt, or in some other trouble that made her, for the present, object to disclose anything about him. I thought she was going to tell me a great deal now—but I was disappointed. I was again put off; but I knew she spoke truth, for she was the truest person I ever met, when she said that she longed to tell me all her story, and that the time would soon come when she could. But now, poor thing ! she was, in spite of all I could say, in a state, very nearly, of distraction. She never was coherent, except when, in answer to her constantly repeated questioning, I again and again described the appearance of the wounded man, which each time seemed to satisfy her on the point of identity, but without preventing her from renewing her inquiries with increasing detail.

That evening passed miserably enough for us both. Doctor Mervyn, on his way to his patient, looked in upon us early next morning, intent on learning all he could from me about the circumstances of the discovery of his patient. I had been too well drilled by prudent Rebecca Torkill, to volunteer any information respecting the unexpected appearance of Mr. Marston so suspiciously near the scene of the occurrence. I described, therefore, simply the spectacle presented by the wounded man, on my lighting upon him in the wood, and his removal to the farm-house of Plas Ylwd.

" It's all very fine, saying it was a accident," said the doctor, with a knowing nod and a smile. " Accident, indeed ! If it was, why should he refuse to say who had

a hand in the accident, besides himself? But there's no
need to make a secret of the matter, for unless something
unexpected should occur, he must, in the ordinary course
of things, be well in little more than a week. It's an odd
wound. The ball struck the collar bone and broke it,
glancing upward. If it had penetrated obliquely downward
instead, it might have killed him on the spot."

"Do you know his name?" I inquired.

"No; he's very reserved; fellows in his situation often
are; they don't like figuring in the papers, you understand;
or being bound over to be of good behaviour; or, possibly,
prosecuted. But no trouble will come of this; and he'll
be on his legs again in a very few days."

With this re-assuring news the doctor left us. Miss
Grey was relieved. One thing seemed pretty certain; and
that was that the guilty and victorious duellist would not
venture to appear in our part of the world for some time
to come.

"Will you come with me to-day, to ask how he gets
on?" I said to Laura as soon as the doctor was gone.

"No, I can't do that; but it would be very kind of you:
that is, if you have no objection."

"None in the world; we must get Rebecca to make
broth, or whatever else the doctor may order, and shall I
mention your name to Mrs. Prichard? I mean, do you
wish the patient—shall we call him—to know that you
are here?"

"Oh! no, pray. He is the last person on earth——"

"You are sure?"

"Perfectly. I entreat, dear Ethel, that you run no
risk of my name being mentioned."

"Why, Mr. Marston knows that you are here," I said
persistently.

"Bad as that was, this would be intolerable. I know,
Ethel, I may rely on you."

"Well, I won't say a word—I won't mention your
name, since you so ordain it."

Two or three days passed. As I had been the good
Samaritan, in female garb, who aided the wounded man
in his distress, I was now the visiting Sister of Mercy, the
ministering angel—whatever you are good enough to call

me—who every day saw after his wants, and sent, sometimes soup, and sometimes jelly, to favour the recovery of which the doctor spoke so sanguinely.

I did not feel the romantic interest I ought perhaps to have felt in the object of my benevolence. I had no wish to see his face again. I was haunted by a recollection of him that was ghastly. I am not wanting in courage, physical or moral. But I should have made a bad nurse, and a worse soldier ; at the sight of blood I immediately grow faint, and a sense of indescribable disgust remains.

I sometimes think we women are perverse creatures. For there is an occult interest about the guilty and audacious, if it be elevated by masculine courage and beauty, and surrounded by ever so little of mystery and romance. Shall I confess it ? The image of that wicked Mr. Marston, notwithstanding all Laura's hard epithets, and the startling situation in which I had seen him last, haunted me often, and with something more of fascination than I liked to confess. Let there be energy, cleverness, beauty, and I believe a reckless sort of wickedness will not stand the least in the way of a foolish romance. I think I had energy ; I know I was impetuous. Insipid or timid virtue would have had no chance with me.

I was going to the farm-house one day, I forget how long after the occurrence which had established my interesting relations with Plas Ylwd. My mother had a large cheval-glass ; it had not often reflected her pretty image ; it was the only one in the house, the furniture of which was very much out of date. It had been removed to my room, and before it I now stood, in my hat and jacket, to make a last inspection before I started. What did I see before me ? I have courage to speak my real impressions, for there is no one near to laugh at me. A girl of eighteen, above the middle height, slender, with large, dark, grey eyes and long lashes, not much colour, not pink and white, by any means, but a very clear-tinted and marble-smooth skin ; lips of carmine-scarlet, and teeth very white ; thick, dark brown hair ; and a tendency, when talking or smiling, to dimple in cheek and chin. There was something, too, spirited and energetic in the face that I contemplated with so much satisfaction.

I remained this day a little longer before my glass than usual. Half an hour later, I stood at the heavy stone doorway of Plas Ylwd. It is one of the prettiest farm-houses in the world. Round the farm-yard stand very old hawthorn and lime trees, and the farm-house is a composite building in which a wing of the old Tudor manor-house of Plas Ylwd is incorporated, under a common thatch, which has grown brown and discoloured, and sunk and risen into hillocks and hollows by time. The door is protected by a thatched porch, with worn stone pillars; and here I stood, and learned that "the gentleman upstairs" was very well that afternoon, and sitting up; the doctor thought he would be out for a walk in two or three days. Having learned this, and all the rest that it concerned Rebecca Torkill to hear, I took my leave of good Mrs. Prichard, and crossing the stile from the farm-yard, I entered the picturesque old wood in which the inmate of Plas Ylwd had received his wound. Through this sylvan solitude I intended returning to Malory.

CHAPTER XXII.

THE OUTLAW.

S I followed my path over the unequal flooring of the forest, among the crowded trunks of the trees and the thickets of brambles, I saw, on a sudden, Mr. Marston almost beside me. I was a good deal startled, and stood still. There was something in his air and looks, as he stood with his hat raised, so unspeakably deprecatory, that I felt at once re-assured. Without my permission it was plain he would not dream of accompanying me, or even of talking to me. All Laura's warnings and entreaties sounded at that moment in my ears like a far-off and unmeaning tinkle. He had no apologies to make ; and yet he looked like a penitent. I was embarrassed, but without the slightest fear of him. I spoke ; but I don't recollect what I said.

"I have come here, Miss Ware, as I believe, at some risk ; I should have done the same thing had the danger been a hundred times greater. I tried to persuade myself that I came for no other purpose than to learn how that foolish fellow, who would force a quarrel on me, is getting on. But I came, in truth, on no such errand ; I came here on the almost desperate chance of meeting you, and in the hope, if I were so fortunate, that you would permit me to say a word in my defence. I am unfortunate in having two or three implacable enemies, and fate has perversely collected them here. Miss Grey stands in very confidential relations with you, Miss Ethel ; her prejudices against me are cruel, violent, and in every way monstrous."

K

He was walking beside me as he said this.

"Mr. Marston," I interposed, "I can't hear you say a word against Miss Grey. I have the highest opinion of her; she is my very dearest friend—she is truth itself."

"One word you say I don't dispute, Miss Ware. She means all she says for truth; but she is cruelly prejudiced, and, without suspecting it, does me the most merciless injustice. Whenever she is at liberty to state her whole case against me—at present I haven't so much as heard it—I undertake to satisfy you of its unfairness. There is no human being to whom I would say all this, or before whom I would stoop to defend myself and sue for an acquittal, where I am blameless, but you, Miss Ware."

I felt myself blushing. I think that sign of emotion fired him.

"I could not tell," he said, extending his hand towards Plas Ylwd, "whether that foolish man was dead or living; and this was the last place on earth I should have come to, in common prudence, while that was in doubt; but I was willing to brave that danger for a chance of seeing you once more—I could not live without seeing you."

He was gazing at me, with eyes glowing with admiration. I thought he looked wonderfully handsome. There was dash and recklessness, I thought, enough for an old-world outlaw, in his talk and looks, and, for all I knew, in his reckless doings; and the scene, the shadow, this solemn decaying forest, accorded well, in my romantic fancy, with the wild character I assigned him. There was something flattering in the devotion of this prompt and passionate man.

"Make me no answer," he continued—"no answer, I entreat. It would be mere madness to ask it now; you know nothing of me but, perhaps, the wildest slanders that prejudice ever believed, or hatred forged. From the moment I saw you, in the old garden at Malory, I loved you! Love at first sight! It was no such infatuation. It was the recalling of some happy dream. I had forgotten it in my waking hours; but I recognised, with a pang and rapture, in you, the spirit that had enthralled me. I loved you long before I knew it. I can't escape, Ethel, I adore you!"

I don't know how I felt. I was pretty sure that I ought to have been very angry. And I was half angry with myself for not being angry. I was, however—which answered just as well, a little alarmed; I felt as a child does when about to enter a dark room, and I drew back at the threshold.

"Pray, Mr. Marston, don't speak so to me any longer. It is quite true, I do not know you; you have no right to talk to me in my walks—pray leave me now."

"I shall obey you, Miss Ware; whatever you command, I shall do. My last entreaty is that you will not condemn me unheard; and pray do not mention to my enemies the infatuation that has led me here, with the courage of despair—no, not quite despair, I won't say that. I shall never forget you. Would to Heaven I could! I shall never forget or escape you; who can disenchant me? I shall never forget, or cease to pursue you, Ethel, I swear by Heaven!"

He looked in my face for a moment, raised my hand gently, but quickly, and pressed it to his lips, before I had recovered from my momentary tumult. I did not turn to look after him. I instinctively avoided that, but I heard his footsteps, in rapid retreat, in the direction of the farm-house which I had just left.

It was not until I had got more than half-way on my return to Malory that I began to think clearly on what had just occurred. What had I been dreaming of? I was shocked to think of it. Here was a total stranger admitted to something like the footing of a declared lover! What was I to do? What would papa or mamma say if my folly were to come to their ears? I did not even know where Mr. Marston was to be found. Some one has compared the Iliad to a frieze, which ceases, but does not end; and precisely of the same kind was this awkward epic of the wood of Plas Ylwd. Who could say when the poet might please to continue his work? Who could say how I could now bring the epic to a peremptory termination?

I must confess, however, although I felt the embarrass-

ment of the situation, this lawless man interested me·
Like many whimsical young ladies, I did not quite know
my own mind.

On the step of the stile that crosses the churchyard
wall, near Malory, I sat down, in rather uncomfortable
rumination. I was interrupted by the sound of a step
upon the road, approaching from the direction of Malory.
I looked up, and, greatly to my surprise, saw Mr. Carmel,
quite close to me. I stood up, and walked a few steps to
meet him; we shook hands, he smiling, very glad, I knew,
to meet me.

"You did not expect to see me so soon again, Miss
Ware? And I have ever so much to tell you. I can't
say whether it will please or vex you; but if you and Miss
Grey will give me my old chair at your tea-table, I will
look in for half an hour this evening. I have first to call
at old Parry's, and give him a message that reached me
from your mamma yesterday."

He smiled again, as he continued his walk, leaving me
full of curiosity as to the purport of his news.

CHAPTER XXIII.

A JOURNEY.

BEHOLD us now, about an hour later, at our tea-table. Mr. Carmel, as he had promised, came in and talked, as usual, agreeably; but, if he had any particular news to tell us, he had not yet begun to communicate it.

"You found your old quarters awaiting your return. We have lost our interesting stranger," I said; "I wish you would tell us all you know about him."

Mr. Carmel's head sank; his eyes were fixed, in painful thought, upon the table. "No," he said, looking up sharply, "God knows all, and that's enough. The story could edify no one."

He looked so pained, and even agitated, that I could not think of troubling him more.

"I had grown so attached to this place," said Mr. Carmel, rising and looking from the window, "that I can scarcely make up my mind to say good-bye, and turn my back on it for ever; yet I believe I must in a few days. I don't know. We soldiers, ecclesiastics, I mean, must obey orders, and I scarcely hope that mine will ever call me here again. I have news for you, also, Miss Ethel; I had a letter from your mamma, and a note from Mr. Ware, last night, and there is to be a break-up here, and a movement townward; you are to come out next season, Miss Ethel; your mamma and papa will be in town, for a week or so, in a few days; and, Miss Grey, she hopes you will not leave her on account of the change."

He paused; but she made no answer.

"Oh! darling Laura, you won't leave me?" I exclaimed.

"Certainly not, dear Ethel; and whenever the time for parting comes," she said very kindly, "it will cost me a greater pang than perhaps it will cost you. But though I am neither a soldier nor an ecclesiastic, my movements do not always depend upon myself."

Unrestrained by Mr. Carmel's presence, we kissed each other heartily.

"Here is a note, Miss Grey, enclosed for you," he murmured, and handed it to Laura.

In our eagerness we had got up and stood with Mr. Carmel in the recess of the window. It was twilight, and the table on which the candles burned stood at a considerable distance. To the light Laura Grey took her letter, and as she read it, quite absorbed, Mr. Carmel talked to me in low tones.

As he stood in the dim recess of the window, with trains of withered leaves rustling outside, and the shadow of the sear and half-stript elms upon the court and window, he said, kindly and gently:

"And now, at last, Miss Ethel forsakes her old home, and takes leave of her humble friends, to go into the great world. I don't think she will forget them, and I am sure they won't forget her. We have had a great many pleasant evenings here, and in our conversations in these happy solitudes, the terrors and glories of eternal truth have broken slowly upon your eyes. Beware! If you trifle with Heaven's mercy, the world, or hell, or heaven itself, has no narcotic for the horrors of conscience. In the midst of pleasure and splendour, and the tawdry triumphs of vanity, the words of Saint Paul will startle your ears like thunder. It is impossible for those who were once enlightened, and have tasted of the heavenly gift, and the good word of God, and the powers of the world to come, if they shall fall away, to renew them again unto repentance. The greater the privilege, the greater the liability. The higher the knowledge, the profounder the danger. You have seen the truth afar off; rejoice, therefore, and tremble."

He drew back and joined Miss Grey.

I had been thinking but little, for many weeks, of our many conversations. Incipient convictions had paled in the absence of the sophist or the sage—I knew not which. When he talked on this theme, his voice became cold and stern; his gentleness seemed to me to partake of an awful apathy; he looked like a man who had witnessed a revelation full of horror; my fancy, I am sure, contributed something to the transformation; but it did overawe me. I never was so impressed as by him. The secret was not in his words. It was his peculiar earnestness. He spoke like an eye-witness, and seemed under unutterable fear himself. He had the preacher's master-gift of alarming.

When Mr. Carmel had taken his leave for the night, I told Laura Grey my adventure in the wood of Plas Ylwd. I don't think I told it quite as frankly as I have just described it to you. The story made Miss Grey very grave for a time.

She broke the silence that followed by saying, "I am rather glad, Ethel, that we are leaving this. I think you will be better in town; I know I shall be more comfortable about you. You have no idea, and I earnestly hope you never may have, how much annoyance may arise from an acquaintance with that plausible, wicked man. He won't venture to force his acquaintance upon you in town. Here it is different, of course."

We sat up very late together, chatting this night in my room. I did not quite know how I felt about the impending change. My approaching journey to London was, to me, as great an event as her drive to the ball in her pumpkin-coach was to Cinderella. Of course there was something dazzling and delightful in the prospect. But the excitement and joy were like that of the happy bride who yet weeps because she is looking her last on the old homely life, that will always be dear and dearer as the irrevocable separation goes on. So, though she is sure she is passing into paradise, it is a final farewell to the beloved past. I felt the conflict; I loved Malory better than I could ever love a place again. But youth is the season of enterprise. God has ordained it. We go like the younger son in the parable, selfish, sanguine, adventurous; but the affections revive and turn homeward, and

from a changed heart sometimes breaks on the solitude a
cry, unheard by living ear, of yearning and grief, that
would open the far-off doors, if that were possible, and
return.

Next day arrangements took a definite form. All was
fuss and preparation. I was to go the day following; Mr.
Carmel was to take charge of me on the journey, and place
me safely in the hands of Mrs. Beauchamp, our town
housekeeper. Laura Grey, having wound up and settled
all things at Malory, was to follow to town in less than a
week; and, at about the same time, mamma and papa
were to arrive.

A drive of ten miles or so brought us to the station;
then came a long journey by rail. London was not new
to me; but London with my present anticipations was.
I was in high spirits, and Mr. Carmel made a very agreeable companion, though I fancied he was a little out of
spirits.

I was tired enough that night when I at length took
leave of Mr. Carmel at the door of our house in ——
Street. The street lamps were already lighted. Mrs.
Beauchamp, in a black silk dress, received me with a
great deal of quiet respect, and rustled upstairs before me
to show me my room. Her grave and regulated politeness
contrasted chillily with the hearty, and sometimes even
boisterous welcome of old Rebecca Torkill. Mamma and
papa were to be home, she told me, in a few days—she
could not say exactly the day. I was, after an hour or so,
a great deal lonelier than I had expected to be. I wrote
a long letter to Laura, of whom I had taken leave only
that morning (what a long time it seemed already!), and
told her how much I already wished myself back again in
Malory, and urged her to come sooner than she had
planned her journey.

CHAPTER XXIV.

ARRIVALS.

LAURA had not waited any longer than I for a special justification of a letter. She had nothing to say, and she said it in a letter as long as my own, which reached me at breakfast next morning.

Sitting in a spacious room, looking out into a quiet fashionable street, in a house all of whose decorations and arrangements had an air of cold elegance and newness, the letter, with the friendly Cardyllion postmark on it, seemed to bring with it something of the clear air, and homely comfort, and free life of Malory, and made me yearn all the more for the kind faces, the old house, and beloved scenery I had left behind. It was insufferably dull here, and I soon found myself in that state which is described as not knowing what to do with oneself. For two days no further letter from Laura reached me. On the third, I saw her well-known handwriting on the letter that awaited me on the breakfast-table. As I looked, as people will, at the direction before opening the envelope, I was struck by the postmark "Liverpool," and turning it over and over, I nowhere saw Cardyllion.

I began to grow too uncomfortable to wait longer; I opened the letter with misgivings. At the top of the note there was nothing written but the day of the week. It said—

"MY DEAREST ETHEL,—A sudden and total change in my unhappy circumstances separates me from you. It is impossible that I should go to London now; and it is possible that I may not see you again for a long time, if ever. I write to say farewell; and in doing so to solemnly repeat my warning against permitting the person who obtained a few days' shelter in the steward's house, after the shipwreck, to maintain even the slightest correspondence or acquaintance with you. Pray, dearest Ethel, trust me in this. I implore of you to follow my advice. You may hear from me again. In the meantime, I am sure you will be glad to know that your poor governess is happy—happier than she ever desired, or ever hoped to be. My fond love is always yours, and my thoughts are hourly with you.—Ever your loving

LAURA GREY."

"May God for ever bless you, darling! Good-bye."

I don't think I could easily exaggerate the effect of this letter. I will not weary you with that most tiresome of all relations, an account of another person's grief.

Mamma and papa arrived that evening. If I had lived less at Malory, and more with mamma, I should not, in some points, have appreciated her so highly. When I saw her, for the first time, after a short absence, I was always struck by her beauty and her elegance, and it seemed to me that she was taller than I recollected her. She was looking very well, and so young! I saw papa but for a moment. He went to his room immediately to dress, and then went off to his club. Mamma took me to her room, where we had tea. She said I had grown, and was very much pleased with my looks. Then she told me all her plans about me. I was to have masters, and I was not to come out till April.

She then got me to relate all the circumstances of Nelly's death, and cried a good deal. Then she had in her maid Lexley, and they held a council together over me on the subject of dress. My Malory wardrobe, from which I had brought up to town with me what I considered an unexceptionable selection, was not laughed at, was not even discussed—it was simply treated as non-extant. It gave me a profound sense of the barbarism in which I ad lived.

Laura Grey's letter lay heavy at my heart, but I had

not yet mentioned it to mamma. There was no need, however, to screw my courage to that point. Among the letters brought up to her was one from Laura. When she read it she was angry in her querulous way. She threw herself into a chair in a pet. She had confidence in Laura Grey, and foresaw a good deal of trouble to herself in this desertion. " I am so particularly unfortunate !" she began—" everything that can possibly go wrong ! everything that never happens to any one else ! I could have got her to take you to Monsieur Pontet's, and your drives, and to shop—and—she must be a most un-principled person. She had no right to go away as she has done. It is too bad ! Your papa allows every one of that kind to treat me exactly as they please, and really, when I am at home, my life is one continual misery ! What am I to do now ? I don't believe any one else was ever so entirely at the mercy of her servants. I don't know, my dear, how I can possibly do all that is to be done for you without assistance—and *there* was a person I thought I could depend upon. A total stranger I should not like, and really, for anything I can see at present, I think you must go back again to Malory, and do the best you can. I am not a strong person. I was not made for all this, and I really feel I could just go to my bed, and cry till morning."

My heart had been very full, and I was relieved by this opportunity of crying.

" I wonder at your crying about so good-for-nothing a person," exclaimed mamma, impatiently. " If she had cared the least about you, she could not have left you as she has done. A satisfactory person, certainly, that young lady has turned out !"

Notwithstanding all this, mamma got over her troubles, and engaged a dull and even-tempered lady, named Anna Maria Pounden, whose manners were quiet and unexceptionable, and whose years were about fifty. She was not much of a companion for me, you may suppose. She answered, however, very well for all purposes intended by mamma. She was lady-like and kind, and seemed made for keeping keys, arranging drawers, packing boxes, and taking care of people when they were ill. She spoke

French, besides, fluently, and with a good accent, and mamma insisted that she and I should always talk in that language. All the more persistently for this change, my thoughts were with my beloved friend, Laura Grey.

From Malory, Rebecca Torkill told me, in a rather incoherent letter, the particulars of Laura Grey's departure from Malory. She had gone out for a walk, leaving her things half packed, for she was to go from Malory next day. She did not return ; but a note reached Mrs. Torkill, next morning, telling her simply she could not return ; and that she would write to mamma and to me in London the same day. Mrs. Torkill's note, like mine, had the Liverpool postmark ; and her conjecture was thus expressed : " I don't think, miss, she had no notions to leave that way when she went out. It must have bin something sudding. She went fest, I do sepose to olyhed, and thens to Liverpule in one of them pakkats. Mr. Williams, the town-clerk, and the vicar and his lady, and Doctor Mervyn, is all certing sure it could be no other wise."

Mamma did not often come down to breakfast, during her short stay at this unseasonable time of year in town. On one of those rare occasions, however, something took place that I must describe.

Mamma was in a pretty morning *negligé* as we used to call such careless dresses then, looking as delicately pretty as the old china tea-cups before her. Papa was looking almost as perplexingly young as she, and I made up the little party to the number of the Graces. Mamma must have been forty, and I really don't think she looked more than two-and-thirty. Papa looked about five-and-thirty ; and I think he must have been at least ten years older than he looked. That kind of life that is supposed to wear people out, seemed for them to have had an influence like the elixir vitæ ; and I certainly have seen rustics, in the full enjoyment of mountain breezes, simple fare, and early hours, look many a day older than their years. The old rule, so harped upon, that "early to bed and early to rise" is the secret of perpetual youth, I don't dispute ; but then, if it be early to go to bed at sunset in winter, say four in the evening, and to rise at four in the morning, is it not still earlier to anticipate that hour, and go to bed at

four in the morning, and get up at one in the afternoon ?
At all events, I know that this mode of life seemed to
agree with papa and mamma. I don't think, indeed, that
either suffered much from the cares that poison enjoyment,
and break down strength. Mamma threw all hers un-
examined upon papa ; who threw all his with equal non-
chalance upon Mr. Norman, a kind of factotum, secretary,
comptroller, diplomatist, financier, and every other thing
that comes within the words "making oneself generally
useful."

I never knew exactly what papa had a year to live upon.
Mamma had money also. But they were utterly unfit to
manage their own affairs, and I don't think they ever tried.
Papa had his worries now and then ; but they seldom
seemed to last more than a day, or at most a week or two..
There were a number of what he thought small sums,
varying from two to five thousand pounds, which under old
settlements dropped in opportunely, and extricated him.
These sums ought to have been treated, not as income, but
as capital, as I heard a moneyed man of business say long
ago ; but papa had not the talent of growing rich, or even
of continuing rich, if a good fairy had gifted him with
fortune.

Papa was in a reverie, leaning back in his chair ; mamma
yawned over a letter she was reading ; I was drumming
some dance music with my fingers on my knee under the
table-cloth, when suddenly he said to mamma :

"You don't love your aunt Lorrimer very much ?"

"No, I don't love her—I never said I did, did I ?"

"No, but I mean, you don't like her, you don't care
about her ?"

"No," said mamma, languidly, and looking wonderingly
at him with her large pretty eyes. "I don't very much—
I don't quite know—I have an affection for her."

"You don't love her, and you don't even like her, but
you have an affection for her," laughed papa.

"You are so teasing. I did not say that ; what I mean
is, she has a great many faults and oddities, and I don't
like them—but I have an affection for her. Why should
it seem so odd to you that one should care for one's relations ? I do feel that for her, and there let it rest."

· "Well, but it ought not to rest there—as you do like
her."

"Why, dear—have you heard anything of her ?"

" No ; but there is one thing I should not object to hear
about her just now."

" One thing ?   What do you mean, dear ?"

" That she had died, and left us her money. I know
what a brute I am, and how shocked you are ; but I assure
you we rather want it at this moment. You write to her,
don't you ?"

" N-not very often. Once since we saw her at Naples."

" Well, that certainly is not very often," he laughed.
" But she writes to you. You thought she seemed rather
to like us—I mean you ?"

" Yes."

" She has no one else to care about that I know of. I
don't pretend to care about her—I think her an old fool."

" She isn't that, dear," said mamma, quietly.

" I wish we knew where she is now. Seriously, you
ought to write to her a little oftener, dear ; I wish you
would."

" I'll write to her, certainly, as soon as I am a little
more myself. I could not do it just to-day ; I have not
been very well, you know."

" Oh ! my darling, I did not mean to hurry you. Of
course, not till you feel perfectly well; don't suppose I
could be such a monster. But—I don't want, of course,
to pursue her—but there is a middle course between that
and having to drop her. She really has no one else, poor
old thing ! to care about, or to care about her. Not that
I care about her, but you're her kinswoman, and I don't
see why——"

At this moment the door opened, and there entered, with
the air of an assumed intimacy and a certain welcome, a
person whom I little expected to see there. I saw him
with a shock. It was the man with the fine eyes and great
forehead, the energetic gait and narrow shoulders. The
grim, mean-looking, intelligent, agreeable man of fifty, Mr.
Droqville.

CHAPTER XXV.

THE DOCTOR'S NEWS.

"AH! how do you do, Doctor Droqville?" said mamma, with a very real welcome in looks and accent.

"How d'ye do, Droqville?" said my father, a little dryly, I fancied.

"Have you had your breakfast?" asked mamma.

"Two hours ago."

"We are very late here," said papa.

"I should prefer thinking I am very early, in my primitive quarters," answered Mr. Droqville.

"I had not an idea we should have found you in town, just now."

"In season or out of season, a physician should always be at his post. I'm beginning to learn rather late there's some truth in that old proverb about moss, you know, and rolling stones, and it costs even a bachelor something to keep body and soul together in this mercenary, tailoring, cutlet-eating world." At this moment he saw me, and made me a bow. "Miss Ware?" he said, a little inquiringly to mamma. "Yes, I knew perfectly it was the young lady I had seen at Malory. Some faces are not easily forgotten," he added, gallantly, with a glance at me. "I threatened to run away with her, but she was firm as fate," he smiled and went on; "and I paid a visit to our friend Carmel, you know."

"And how did you think he was?" she asked; and I listened with interest for the answer.

"He's consumptive. He's at this side of the Styx, it is true; but his foot is in the water, and Charon's obolus is

always between his finger and thumb. He'll die young.
He may live five years, it is true; but he is not likely to
live two. And if he happens to take cold and begins to
cough, he might not last four months."

"My wife has been complaining," said papa; "I wish
you could do something for her. You still believe in
Doctor Droqville? I think she half believes you have taken
a degree in divinity as well as in medicine; if so, a miracle,
now and then, would be quite in your way."

"But I assure you, Doctor Droqville, I never said any
such thing. It was you who thought," she said to my
father, "that Doctor Droqville was in orders."

Droqville laughed.

"But, Doctor Droqville, I think," said mamma, "you
would have made a very good priest."

"There are good priests, madame, of various types;
Madame de Genlis, for instance, commends an abbé of her
acquaintance; he was a most respectable man, she says,
and never ridiculed revealed religion but with moderation."

Papa laughed, but I could see that he did not like
Doctor Droqville. There was something dry, and a little
suspicious in his manner, so slight that you could hardly
define it, but which contrasted strikingly with the decision
and *insouciance* of Doctor Droqville's talk.

"But, you know, you never do that, even with moderation; and you can argue so closely when you please."

"There, madame, you do me too much honour. I am
the worst logician in the world. I wrote a part of an essay
on Christian chivalry, and did pretty well, till I began to
reason; the essay ended, and I was swallowed up in this
argument—pray listen to it. To sacrifice your life for the
lady you adore is a high degree of heroism; but to sacrifice
your soul for her is the highest degree of heroism. But
the highest degree of heroism is but another name for
Christianity; and, therefore, to act thus can't sacrifice
your soul, and if it doesn't you don't practise a heroism,
and therefore no Christianity, and, therefore, you do sacrifice your soul. But if you do sacrifice your soul, it is the
highest heroism—therefore Christianity; and, therefore,
you don't sacrifice your soul, and so, *da capo*, it goes on
for ever—and I can't extricate myself. When I mean to

make a boat, I make a net; and this argument that I invented to carry me some little way on my voyage to truth, not only won't hold water, but has caught me by the foot, entangles, and drowns me. I never went on with my essay."

In this cynical trifling there was a contemptuous jocularity quite apparent to me, although mamma took it all in good faith, and said:

"It is very puzzling, but it can't be true; and I should think it almost a duty to find out where it is wrong."

Papa laughed, and said:

"My dear, don't you see that Doctor Droqville is mystifying us?"

I was rather glad, for I did not like it. I was vexed for mamma. Doctor Droqville's talk seemed to me an insolence.

"It is quite true, I am no logician; I had better continue as I am. I make a tolerable physician; if I became a preacher, with my defective ratiocination, I should inevitably lose myself and my audience in a labyrinth. You make but a very short stay in town, I suppose?" he broke off suddenly. "It isn't tempting, so many houses sealed—a city of the dead. One does not like, madame, as your Doctor Johnson said to Mrs. Thrale, to come down to vacuity."

"Well, it is only a visit of two or three days. My daughter Ethel is coming out next spring, and she came up to meet us here. I wish her to have a few weeks with masters, and there are more things to be thought of than you would suppose. Do you think there is anything a country miss would do well to read up that we might have forgotten?"

"Read? read? Oh! yes, two things."

"What are they?"

"If she has a sound knowledge of the heathen mythology, and a smattering of the Bible, she'll do very well."

"But she won't talk about the Bible," laughed papa; "people who like it, read it to themselves."

"Very true," said Doctor Droqville, "you never mention it; but, quite unconsciously, you are perpetually

L

alluding to it. Nothing strikes a stranger more, if he understands your language as I do. You had a note from Lady Lorrimer?"

" No," said mamma.

The word " note," I think, struck papa as implying that she was nearer than letter-writing distance, and he glanced quickly at Doctor Droqville.

" And where is Lady Lorrimer now?" asked papa.

" That is what I came to tell you. She is at Mivart's. I told her you were in town, and I fancied you would have had a note from her; but I thought I might as well look in and tell you."

" She's quite well, I hope?" said mamma.

" Now did you ever, Mrs. Ware, in all your life, see her quite well? I never did. She would lose all pleasure in life, if she thought she wasn't leaving it. She arrived last night, and summoned me to her at ten this morning. I felt her pulse. It was horribly regular. She had slept well, and breakfasted well, but that was all. In short, I found her suffering under her usual chronic attack of good health, and, as the case was not to be trifled with, I ordered her instantly some medicine which could not possibly produce any effect whatever; and in that critical state I left her, with a promise to look in again in the afternoon to ascertain that the more robust symptoms were not gaining ground, and in the interval I came to see you and tell you all about it."

" I suppose, then, I should find her in her bed?" said mamma.

" No; I rather think she has postponed dying till after dinner—she ordered a very good one—and means to expire in her sitting-room, where you'll find her. And you have not been very well?"

" Remember the story he has just told you of your aunt Lorrimer, and take care he doesn't tell her the same story of you," said papa, laughing.

" I wish I could," said Doctor Droqville; " few things would please me better. That pain in the nerves of the head is a very real torment."

So he and mamma talked over her head-aches in an undertone for some minutes; and while this was going on there came in a note for mamma. The servant was was waiting for an answer in the hall.

"Shall I read it?" said papa, holding it up by the corner. "It is Lady Lorrimer's, I'm sure."

"Do, dear," said mamma, and she continued her confidences in Doctor Droqville's ear.

Papa smiled a little satirically as he read it. He threw it across the table, saying:

"You can read it, Ethel; it concerns you rather."

I was very curious. The hand was youthful and pretty, considering Lady Lorrimer's years. It was a whimpering, apathetic, selfish little note. She was miserable, she said, and had quite made up her mind that she could not exist in London smoke. She had sent for the doctor.

She continued: "I shall make an effort to see you, if you can look in about three, for a few minutes. Have you any of your children with you? If they are very quiet I should like to see them. It would amuse me. It is an age since I saw your little people, and I really forget their ages, and even their names. Say if I am to expect you at three. I have told the servant to wait."

People who live in the country fancy themselves of more importance than they really are. I was mortified, and almost shocked at the cool sentences about "the little people," etc.

"Well, you promise to be very quiet, won't you? You won't pull the cat's tail, or light paper in the fire, or roar for plum-cake?" said papa.

"I don't think she wants to see us. I don't think she cares the least about us. Perhaps mamma won't go," I said, resentfully, hoping that she would not pay that homage to the insolent old woman.

Doctor Droqville stood up, having written a prescription.

"Well, I'm off; and I think this will do you a world of good. Can I do any commission for you about town; I shall be in every possible direction in the next three hours?"

No, there was nothing; and this man, whom I somehow liked less than ever, although he rather amused me, vanished, and we saw his cab drive by the window.

"Well, here's her note. You'll go to see her, I suppose?" said papa.

"Certainly; I have a great affection for my aunt. She was very kind to me when there was no one else to care about me."

Mamma spoke with more animation than I believed her capable of—I thought I even saw tears in her eyes. It struck me that she did not like papa's tone in speaking about her. The same thing probably struck him.

"You are quite right, darling, as you always are in a matter of feeling, and you'll take Ethel, won't you?"

"Yes, I should like her to come."

"And you know, if she should ask you, don't tell her I'm a bit better off than I really am. I have had some awful losses lately. I don't like bothering you about business, and it was no fault or negligence of mine; but I really—it is of very great importance she should not do anything less that she intended for you, or anything whimsical or unjust. I give you my honour there isn't a guinea to spare now, it would be a positive cruelty."

Mamma looked at him, but she was by this time so accustomed to alarms of that kind that they did not make a very deep impression upon her.

"I don't think she's likely to talk about such matters, dear," said mamma; "but if she should make any inquiries, I shall certainly tell her the truth."

I remembered Lady Lorrimer long ago at Malory. It was a figure seen in the haze of infancy, and remembered through the distance of many years. I recollect coming down the stairs, the nursery-maid holding me by the hand, and seeing a carriage and servants in the court before the door. I remember, as part of the same dream, sitting in the lap of a strange lady in the drawing-room, who left a vague impression of having been richly dressed, who talked to me in a sweet, gentle voice, and gave me toys, and whom I always knew to have been Lady Lorrimer. How much of this I actually saw, and how much was picked up with the vivid power of reproducing pictures from description that belongs to children, I cannot say; but I always heard of Aunt Lorrimer afterwards with interest, and now at length I was about to see her. Her note had disappointed me, still I was curious.

CHAPTER XXVI.

LADY LORRIMER.

MY curiosity was soon gratified. After luncheon we drove to Mivart's, and there in her sitting-room I saw Lady Lorrimer. I was agreeably surprised. Her figure was still beautiful. She was, I believe, past sixty then; but, like all our family whom I have ever seen, she looked a great deal younger than her years. I thought her very handsome, very like my idea of Mary Queen of Scots in her later years; and her good looks palpably owed nothing to "making up." Her smile was very winning, and her eyes still soft and brilliant. Through so many years, her voice as she greeted us returned with a strange and very sweet recognition upon my ear.

She put her arms about mamma's neck, and kissed her tenderly. In like manner she kissed me. She made me sit beside her on a sofa, and held my hands in hers. Mamma sat opposite in a chair.

Lady Lorrimer might be very selfish—lonely people often are; but she certainly was very affectionate. There were tears in her fine eyes as she looked at me. It was not such a stare as a dealer might bestow on a picture, to which, as a child, I had sometimes been subjected by old friends in search of a likeness. By-and-by she talked of me.

"The flight of my years is so silent," she said, with a sad smile to mamma, "that I forgot, as I wrote to you, how few are left me, and that Ethel is no longer a child. I think her quite lovely; she is like what I remember you, but it is only a likeness—not the same; she does not sacrifice her originality. I'm not afraid, dear, to say all that before you," she said, turning on me for a moment her engaging smile. "I think, Ethel, in this world, where people without a particle of merit are always pushing themselves to the front, young people who have beauty should know it. But, my dear," she said, looking on me again, "good looks don't last very long. Your mamma, there, keeps hers wonderfully; but look at me. I was once a pretty girl, as you are now; and see what I am!

> 'Le même cours des planètes
> Régle nos jours et nos nuits;
> On me vit ce que vous êtes,
> Vous serez ce que je suis.'

So I qualify my agreeable truths with a little uncomfortable morality. She'll be coming out immediately?"

Mamma told her, hereupon, all her plans about me.

"And so sure as you take her out, her papa will be giving her away; and, remember, I'm to give her her diamonds whenever she marries. You are to write to me whenever anything is settled, or likely to come about. They always know at my house here, when I am on my travels, where a letter will find me. No, you're not to thank me," she interrupted us. "I saw Lady Rimington's, and I intend that your daughter's shall be a great deal better than hers."

Our old Malory housekeeper, Rebecca Torkill, had a saying, "Nothing so grateful as pride." I think I really liked my aunt Lorrimer better for her praises of my good looks than for her munificent intentions about my bridal brilliants. But for either I could only show my pleasure by my looks. I started up to thank her for her promised diamonds. But, as I told you, she would not hear a word, and drew me down gently with a smile again beside her.

Then she talked, and mamma talked. For such a recluse, Lady Lorrimer was a wonderful gossip, and devoured all mamma's news, and told her old stories of all the old people who figured in such oral history. I must do her justice. There seemed to me to be no malice whatever in her stories. The comic was what she enjoyed most. Her lively pictures amused even me, who knew nothing of the originals ; and the longer I sat with her, the more confidence did I feel in her good-nature.

A good deal of this conversation was all but whispered, and she had despatched me with her maid to look at some china she had brought home for her cabinets in London, at the other end of the room. When I returned their heads were still very near, and they were talking low with the same animation. I sat down again beside Lady Lorrimer. I had spun out my inspection of the china as long as I could. Lady Lorrimer patted my head gently, as I sat down again, without, I fancy, remembering at the moment that I had been away. She was answering, I think, a remark of mamma's, and upon a subject which had lain rather heavily at my heart since Monsieur Droqville's visit to our breakfast-table that morning.

"I don't know," she said ; "Monsieur Droqville is a clever physician, but it seems to me he has always made too much of Mr. Carmel's illness, or delicacy, or whatever it is. I do not think Mr. Carmel is in any real danger—I don't think there is anything seriously wrong with him—more, in fact, than with any other thin young man, and now and then he has a cough. Three years ago, when I first made his acquaintance—and what a charming creature he is !—Monsieur Droqville told me he could not live more than two years ; and this morning, when I asked how Mr. Carmel was, he allowed him three years still to live ; so if he goes on killing him at that easy rate, he may live as long as Old Parr. And now that I think of it, did you hear a rumour about Sir Harry ?"

"There are so many Sir Harrys," said mamma. "Do you mean Sir Harry Rokestone ?"

"Of course I mean Sir Harry Rokestone," she answered ; "have you heard anything of him ?"

"Nothing, but the old story," said mamma.

"And what is that ?" asked Lady Lorrimer.

"Only that he hates us with all his heart and soul, and never loses an opportunity of doing us all the mischief he can. He has twice prevented my husband getting into the House—and cost him a great deal more money than he could afford ; and he has had opportunities, from those

old money dealings that you know of between the two
families, of embarrassing my poor husband most cruelly.
If you knew what enormous law expenses we have been
put to, and all the injuries he has done us, you would say
that you never heard of anything so implacable, so malig-
nant, and——"

" So natural," said Lady Lorrimer. "I don't mean to
fight Sir Harry Rokestone's battle for him. I dare say
he has been stern and vindictive; he was a proud, fierce
man; and, my dear Mabel, you treated him very ill; so
did Francis Ware. If he treats you as you have treated
him, nothing can be much worse. I always liked him
better than your husband; he was better, and is better.
I use the privilege of an old kinswoman; and I say
nothing could have been more foolish than your treatment
of him, except your choice of a husband. I think Francis
Ware is one of those men who never ought to have married. He is a clever man; but in some respects, and
these of very great importance, he has always acted like
a fool. Harry Rokestone was worth twenty of him, and
would have made a much better husband than ever he did.
I always thought he was the handsomer man; he had
twice the real ability of Francis Ware; he had all the
masculine attributes of mind. I say nothing about his
immensely superior wealth; that you chose to regard as
a point quite unworthy of consideration. The only thing
not in his favour was that he was some years older."

"Twenty years nearly," said mamma.

" Well, my dear, a man with his peculiar kind of good
looks, and his commanding character, wears better than
a younger man. You recollect the answer of the old
French mareschal to the young *petit-maître* who asked
him his age. '*Je ne vous le dirai pas precisement; mais
soyez sur qu'un âne est plus âgé à vingt ans qu'un homme ne
l'est à soixante.*' I don't say that the term would have
fairly described Francis Ware. I know very well he was
brilliant; but those talents, if there are no more solid
gifts to support them, grow less and less suitable as men
get into years, until they become frivolous. However, I
am sure that Harry Rokestone does hate you both; and
he's just the man to make his hatred felt. The time has

passed for forgiveness. When the fire of romance has expired, the metal that might have taken another shape cools down and hardens in the mould. He will never forgive or change, I am afraid; and you must both lay your account with his persevering animosity. But, you say, you haven't heard any story about him lately ?"

" No, nothing."

" Well, old Mrs. Jennings, of Golden Friars, sometimes writes to me, and she says he is going to marry that rich spinster, Miss Goulding of Wrybiggins. She only says she hears so; and I thought you might know."

"I should not wonder—it is not at all an unlikely thing. I don't see that they could do better; there's nothing to prevent it, so far as I can see."

But although mamma thus applauded the arrangement, I could see that in her inmost heart she did not like it. There is something of desertion in these late marriages of long-cast-off lovers, who have worshipped our shadows in secret, through lonely years; and I could see dimly a sad little mortification in mamma's pretty face.

As we drove home I mused over Lady Lorrimer. The only disagreeable recollection that disturbed my pleasant retrospect was that part of her conversation that referred to papa. She said she " used the privilege of an old kinswoman." I should have said abused it rather. But mamma did not seem to resent it—I suppose they were on terms to discuss him; and they either forgot me, or thought I had no business to be in the way. In every other respect, I was very much pleased with my visit, as I well might be. She was much more clever than I expected, more animated, more fascinating. I was haunted with the thought how lovely she must have been when she was young !

" Don't a great many older women than Lady Lorrimer go out a great deal ?" I asked.

" Yes," answered mamma, " but they have young people to take out very often."

" But papa mentioned some this morning, who are everywhere, and never chaperon any one."

" I suppose they enjoy it, as they can't live without it. Pull up that window, dear."

"I wonder very much she doesn't go out; she's so handsome, really beautiful, considering her years, I think; and so very agreeable."

"I suppose she doesn't care," she answered, a little drily.

"But she complained of being lonely," I resumed, "and I thought she sighed when she spoke of my coming out, as if she would like a look at the gay world again."

"My dear, you bore me; I suppose Lady Lorrimer will do, with respect to that, as she does about everything else —precisely what pleases her best."

These words mamma spoke in a way that very plainly expressed: "Now you have heard, once for all, everything I mean to say on this subject; and you will be good enough to talk and think of something quite different."

CHAPTER XXVII.

WHAT CAN SHE MEAN?

E had promised to go and see Lady Lorrimer again next day at the same hour. My head was still full of her. Mamma did not come down to breakfast; so I interrupted papa at his newspaper to sound him, very much as I had sounded her.

"Why doesn't she stay at home, and go out?" he repeated, smiling faintly as he did so. "I suppose she understands her own business; I can't say—but you mustn't say anything of that kind before her. She has done some foolish things, and got herself talked about; and you'll hear it all, I daresay, time enough. She's not a bit worse than other people, but a much greater fool; so don't ask people those questions, it would vex your mamma, and do nobody any good, do you see?"

Shortly after this, Miss Pounden came down to tell me that we were not going to see Lady Lorrimer that day. I was horribly disappointed, and ran up to the drawing-room, where mamma then was, to learn the cause of our visit being put off.

"Here, dear, is my aunt's note," she said, handing it to me, and scarcely interrupting her consultation with her maid about the millinery they were discussing. It was open, and I read these words:

"My DEAR MABEL,—I must say good-bye a little earlier than I had intended. My plans are upset. I find my native air insupportable, and fly northward for my life! I am thinking at present of Buxton for a few days; the weather is so genial here, that my doctor tells me I may find it still endurable in that cold region. It grieves me not to see your dear faces before I go. Do not let your pretty daughter forget me. I may, it is just possible, return through London—so we may meet soon again. I shall have left Mivart's and begun my journey before this note reaches you. God bless you, my dear Mabel!—Your affectionate   AUNT."

So she was actually gone! What a dull day it would be! Well, there was no good in railing at fate. But was I ever to see that charming lady more?

In my drive that day with Miss Pounden, thinking it was just possible that Lady Lorrimer, whimsical as she was said to be, might have once more changed her mind, I called at Mivart's to inquire. She was no longer there. She had left with bag and baggage, and all her servants, that morning at nine o'clock. I had called with very little hope of finding that her journey had been delayed, and I drove away with even that small hope extinguished. She was my Mary, Queen of Scots. She had done something too rash and generous for the epicurean, sarcastic, and specious society of London. From the little that papa had said, I conjectured that Lady Lorrimer's secession from society was not quite voluntary; but she interested me all the more. In my dull life the loss of my new acquaintance so soon was a real blow. Mamma was not much of a companion to me. She liked to talk of people she knew, and to people who knew them. Except what concerned my dress and accomplishments, we had as yet no topics in common.

Dear Laura Grey, how I missed you now! The resentment I had felt at first was long since quite lost in my real sorrow, and there remained nothing but affectionate regrets.

I take up the thread of my personal narrative where I dropped it on the day of my ineffectual visit at Lady Lorrimer's hotel. In the afternoon Doctor Droqville came to see mamma. He had been to see Lady Lorrimer that morning, just before she set out on her journey.

"She was going direct to Buxton, as she hinted to you," said Doctor Droqville, "and I advised her to make a week's stay there. When she leaves it, she says she is going on to Westmoreland, and to stay for a fortnight or three weeks at Golden Friars. She's fanciful; there was gout in her family, and she is full of gouty whims and horrors. She is as well as a woman of her years need be, if she would only believe it."

"Have you heard lately from Mr. Carmel?" asked mamma.

I listened with a great deal of interest for the answer.

"Yes, I heard this morning," he replied. "He's in Wales."

"Not at Malory?" said mamma.

"No, not at Malory; a good way from Malory."

I should have liked to ask how long he had been in Wales, for I had been secretly offended at his apparent neglect of me; but I could not muster courage for the question.

Next morning I took it into my head that I should like a walk; and with mamma's leave, Miss Pounden and I set out, of course keeping among the quiet streets in the neighbourhood. While, as we walked, I was in high chat with Miss Pounden, who was chiefly a listener, and sometimes, I must admit, a rather absent one, I raised my eyes and could scarcely believe their report. Not ten yards away, walking up the flagged way towards us, were two figures. One was Lady Lorrimer I was certain. She was dressed in a very full velvet cloak, and had a small book in her hand. At her left, at a distance of more than a yard, walked a woman in a peculiar costume. This woman looked surly, and stumped beside her with a limp, as if one leg were shorter than the other. They approached at a measured pace, looking straight before them, and in total silence.

My eyes were fixed on Lady Lorrimer with a smile, which I every moment expected would be answered by one of recognition from her. But no such thing. She must have seen me; but nearer and nearer they came. They never deviated from their line of march. Lady Lorrimer continued to look straight before her. It was the sternest possible "cut," insomuch that I felt actually incredulous, and began to question my first identification. Her velvet actually brushed my dress as I stood next the railings. She passed me with her head high, and the same stony look.

" Shall we go on, dear ?" asked Miss Pounden, who did not understand why we had come to a standstill.

I moved on in silence ; but the street being a very quiet one, I turned about for a last look. I saw them ascend the steps of a house, and at the same moment the door opened, and Mr. Carmel came out, with his hat in his hand, and followed the two ladies in. The door was then shut. We resumed our walk homeward. We had a good many streets to go through, and I did not know my way. I was confounded, and walked on in utter silence, looking down in confused rumination on the flags under my feet.

Till we got home I did not say a word; and then I sat down in my room, and meditated on that odd occurrence, as well as my perturbation would let me. It was a strange mixture of surprise, doubt, and intense mortification. It was very stupid of me not to have ascertained at the time the name of the street which was the scene of this incident. Miss Pounden had never seen either Lady Lorrimer or Mr. Carmel; and the occurrence had not made the least impression upon her. She could not therefore help me, ever so little, next day, to recover the name of the street in which I had stood still for a few seconds, looking at she knew not what. There was just a film of doubt, derived from the inexplicable behaviour of the supposed Lady Lorrimer. When I told mamma, she at first insisted it was quite impossible. But, as I persisted, and went into detail, she said it was very odd. She was thoughtful for a little time, and sighed. Then she made me repeat all I had told her, and seemed very uncomfortable, but did not comment upon it. At length she said:

" You must promise me. Ethel, not to say a word about it to your papa. It would only lead to vexation. I have good reasons for thinking so. Speak of it to no one. Let the matter rest. I don't think I shall ever understand some people. But let us talk about it no more."

And with this charge the subject dropped.

CHAPTER XXVIII.

A SEMI-QUARREL.

MAMMA did not remain long in town. Bleak as the weather now was, she and papa went to Brighton for a fortnight. They then went, for a few days, to Malory; and from that, north-ward, to Golden Friars. I dare say papa would have liked to find Lady Loorrimer there. I don't know that he did.

I, meanwhile, was left in the care of Miss Pounden, who made a very staid and careful chaperon. I danced every day, and pounded a piano, and sang a little, and spoke French incessantly to Miss Pounden. My spirits were sustained by the consciousness that I was very soon to come out. I was not entirely abandoned to Miss Pounden's agreeable society. Mr. Carmel re-appeared. Three times a week he came in and read, and spoke Italian with me for an hour, Miss Pounden sitting by—at least, she was supposed to be sitting there on guard—but she really was as often out of the room as in it. One day I said to him:

"You know Lady Lorrimer, my aunt?"

"Yes," he answered, carelessly.

"Did you know she was my aunt?"

"Your great-aunt, yes."

"I wonder, then, why you never mentioned her to me," said I.

"There is nothing to wonder at," he replied, with a smile. "Respecting her, I have no curiosity, and nothing to tell."

"Oh! But you must know something about her—ever

so little—and I really know nothing. Why does she lead
so melancholy a life ?"

" She has sickened of gaiety, I have been told."

" There's something more than that," I insisted.

" She's not young, you know, and society is a laborious
calling."

" There's some reason; none of you will tell me," I
said. " I used to tell every one everything, until I found
that no one told me anything; now I say, ' Ethel, seal
your lips, and open your ears; don't you be the only fool
in this listening, sly, suspicious world.' But, if you'll tell
nothing else, at least you'll tell me this. What were you
all about when you opened the door of a house, in some
street not far from this, to Lady Lorrimer, and an odd-
looking woman who was walking beside her, on the day
after she had written to mamma to say she had actually
left London. What was the meaning of that deception ?"

" I don't know whether Lady Lorrimer out-stayed the
time of her intended departure or not," he answered;
" she would write what she pleased, and to whom she
pleased, without telling me. And now I must tell you, if
Lady Lorrimer had confided a harmless secret to me, I
should not betray it by answering either ' yes' or ' no' to
any questions. Therefore, should you question me upon
any such subject, you must not be offended if I am
silent."

I was vexed.

" One thing you must tell me," I persisted. " I have
been puzzling myself over her very odd looks that day;
and also over the odd manner and disagreeable countenance of the woman who was walking at her side. Is
Lady Lorrimer, at times, a little out of her mind ?"

" Who suggested that question ?" he asked, fixing his
eyes suddenly on me.

" Who suggested it ?" I repeated. " No one. People,
I suppose, can ask their own questions."

I was surprised and annoyed, and I suppose looked so.
I continued: " That woman looked like a keeper, I fancied, and Lady Lorrimer—I don't know what it was—but
there was something so unaccountable about her."

" I don't know a great deal of Lady Lorrimer, but I am

grateful to her for, at least, one great kindness, that of
having introduced me to your family," he said; "and I
can certainly testify that there is no clearer mind anywhere. No suspicion of that kind can approach her; she
is said to be one of the cleverest, shrewdest intellects, and
the most cultivated, you can imagine. But people say
she is an *esprit fort*, and believes in nothing. It does not
prevent her doing a kind office for a person such as I.
She has more charity than many persons who make loud
professions of faith."

I had felt a little angry at this short dialogue. He was
practising reserve, and he looked at one time a little stern,
and unlike himself.

"But I want to ask you a question—only one more," I
said, for I wished to clear up my doubts.

"Certainly," he said, more like himself.

"About my meeting Lady Lorrimer that day, and
seeing you, as I told you." I paused, and he simply sat
listening. "My question," I continued, "is this—I may
as well tell you; the whole thing appeared to me so unaccountable that I have been ever since doubting the
reality of what I saw; and I want you simply to tell me
whether it did happen as I have described?"

At this renewed attack, Mr. Carmel's countenance un-
derwent no change, even the slightest, that could lead me
to an inference; he said, with a smile:

"It might, perhaps, be the easiest thing in the world
for me to answer distinctly, 'no;' but I remember that
Dean Swift, when asked a certain question, said that Lord
Somers had once told him never to give a negative
answer, although truth would warrant it, to a question of
that kind; because, if he made that his habit, when he
could give a denial, whenever he declined to do so, would
amount to an admission. I think that a wise rule, and
all such questions I omit to answer."

"That is an evasion," I replied, in high indignation.

"Forgive me, it is no evasion—it is simply silence."

"You know it is cowardly, and indirect, and—characteristic," I persisted, in growing wrath.

He was provokingly serene.

"Well, let me give you another reason for silence re-

specting Lady Lorrimer. Your mamma has specially
requested me to keep silence on the subject; and in your
case, Miss Ethel, her daughter, can I consider that request
otherwise than as a command?"

"Not comprehending casuistry, I don't quite see how
your promise to papa, to observe silence respecting the
differences of the two Churches, is less binding than your
promise to mamma of silence respecting Lady Lorrimer."

"Will you allow me to answer that sarcasm?" he
asked, flushing a little.

"How I hate hypocrisy and prevarication!" I repeated,
rising even above my old level of scorn.

"I have been perfectly direct," he said, "upon that
subject; for the reason I have mentioned, I can't and
won't speak."

"Then for the present, I think, we shall talk upon no
other," I said, getting up, going out of the room, and
treating him at the door to a haughty little bow.

So we parted for that day.

I understood Mr. Carmel, however; I knew that he had
acted as he always did when he refused to do what other
people wished, from a reason that was not to be overcome;
and I don't recollect that I ever renewed my attack. We
were on our old terms in a day or two. Between the
stanzas of Tasso, often for ten minutes unobserved, he
talked upon the old themes—eternity, faith, the Church,
the saints, the Blessed Virgin. He supplied me with
books; but this borrowing and lending was secret as the
stolen correspondence of lovers.

I have thought over that strange period of my life: the
little books that wrought such wonders, the spell of whose
power is broken now; the tone of mind induced by them,
by my solitude, my agitations, the haunting affections of
the dead; and all these influences re-acting again upon
the cold and supernatural character of Mr. Carmel's talk.
My exterior life had been going on, the rural monotony of
Malory, its walks, its boating, its little drives; and now
the dawning ambitions of a more vulgar scene, the town
life, the excitement of a new world were opening. But
among these realities, ever recurring, and dominating all,
there seemed to be ever present a stupendous vision!

So it seemed to me my life was divided between frivolous realities and a gigantic trance. Into this I receded every now and then, alone and unwatched. The immense perspective of a towering cathedral aisle seemed to rise before me, shafts and ribbed stone, lost in smoke of incense floating high in air; mitres and gorgeous robes, and golden furniture of the altar, and chains of censers and jewelled shrines, glimmering far off in the tapers' starlight, and the inspired painting of the stupendous Sacrifice reared above the altar in dim reality. I fancied I could hear human voices, plaintive and sublime as the aërial choirs heard high over dying saints and martyrs by faithful ears; and the mellow thunder of the organ rolling through unseen arches above. Sometimes, less dimly, I could see the bowed heads of myriads of worshippers, "a great multitude, which no man could number, of all nations, and kindreds, and peoples, and tongues." It was, to my visionary senses, the symbol of the Church. Always the self-same stupendous building, the same sounds and sights, the same high-priest and satellite bishops; but seen in varying lights—now in solemn beams, striking down and crossing the shadow in mighty bars of yellow, crimson, green, and purple through the stained windows, and now in the dull red gleam of the tapers.

Was I more under the influence of religion in this state? I don't believe I was. My imagination was exalted, my anxiety was a little excited, and the subject generally made me more uncomfortable than it did before. Some of the forces were in action which might have pushed me, under other circumstances, into a decided course. One thing, which logically had certainly no bearing upon the question, did affect me, I now know, powerfully. There was a change in Mr. Carmel's manner which wounded me, and piqued my pride. I used to think he took an interest in Ethel Ware. He seemed now to feel none, except in the discharge of his own missionary duties, and I fancied that, if it had not been for his anxiety to acquit himself of a task imposed by others, and exacted by his conscience, I should have seen no more of Mr. Carmel.

I was a great deal too proud to let him perceive my re-sentiment—I was just as usual—I trifled and laughed, read my Italian, and made blunders, and asked questions; and, in those intervals of which I have spoken, I listened to what he had to say, took the books he offered, and thanked him with a smile, but with no great fervour. The temperature of our town drawing-room was perceptibly cooler than that of Malory, and the distance between our two chairs had appreciably increased. Nevertheless, we were apparently, at least, very good friends.

But terms like these are sometimes difficult to maintain. I was vexed at his seeming to acquiesce so easily in my change of manner, which, imperceptible to any one else, I somehow knew could not be hidden from him. I had brought down, and laid on the drawing-room table at which we sat, the only book which I then had belonging to Mr. Carmel. It was rather a dark day. Something in the weather made me a little more cross than usual. Miss Pounden was, according to her wont, flitting to and fro, and not minding in the least what we read or said. I laid down my Tasso, and laughed. Mr. Carmel looked at me a little puzzled.

"That, I think, is the most absurd stanza we have read. I ought, I suppose, to say the most sublime. But it is as impossible to read it without laughing as to read the rest without yawning."

I said this with more scorn than I really felt, but it certainly was one of those passages in which good Homer nods. A hero's head is cut off, I forget his name—a kinsman, I daresay, of Saint Denis; and he is so engrossed with the battle that he forgets his loss, and goes on fighting for some time.

"I hope it is not very wrong, and very stupid, but I am so tired of the *Gerusalemme Liberata.*"

He looked at me for a moment or two. I think he did not comprehend the spirit in which I said all this, but perhaps he suspected something of it—he looked a little pained.

"But, I hope, you are not tired of Italian? There are other authors."

"Yes, so there are. I should like Ariosto, I daresay. I like fairy-tales, and that is the reason, I think, I like read-

ing the lives of the saints, and the other books you have
been so kind as to lend me."

I said this quite innocently, but there was a great deal
of long-husbanded cruelty in it. He dropped his fine
eyes to the table, and leaned for a short time on his hand.

"Well, even so, it is something gained to have read
them," meditated Mr. Carmel, and looking up at me, he
added, "and we never know by what childish instincts
and simple paths we may be led to the sublimest elevations."

There was so much gentleness in his tone and looks
that my heart smote me. My momentary compunction,
however, did not prevent my going on, now that I had got
fairly afloat.

"I have brought down the book you were so kind as to
lend me last week. I am sure it is very eloquent, but
there's so much I cannot understand."

"Can I explain anything?" he began, taking up the
book at the same time.

"I did not mean that—no. I was going to return it,
with my very best thanks," I said. "I have been reading
a great deal that is too high for me—books meant for
wiser people and deeper minds than mine."

"The mysteries of faith remain, for all varieties of
mind, mysteries still," he answered sadly. "No human
vision can pierce the veil. I do not flatter you, but I
have met with no brighter intelligence than yours. In
death the scales will fall from our eyes. Until then, yea
must be yea, and nay, nay, and let us be patient."

"I don't know, Mr. Carmel, that I ought to read these
books without papa's consent. I have imperceptibly glided
into this kind of reading. 'I will tell you about Sweden-
borg,' you said; 'we must not talk of Rome or Luther—
we can't agree, and they are forbidden subjects,' do you
remember? And then you told me what an enemy Swe-
denborg was of the Catholic Church—you remember that?
And then you read me what he said about vastation, as
he calls it; and you lent me the book to read; and when
you took it back, you explained to me that his account of
vastation differs in no respect from purgatory; and in the
same way, when I read the legends of the saints, you told

me a great deal more of your doctrine; and in the same
way, also, you discussed those beautiful old hymns, so
that in a little while, although, as you said, Rome and
Luther were forbidden subjects, or rather names, I found
myself immersed in a controversy, which I did not understand, with a zealous and able priest. You have been
artful, Mr. Carmel!"

"Have I been artful in trying to save you?" he answered
gently.

"You would not, I think, practise the same arts with
other people—you treat me like a fool," I said. "You
would not treat that Welsh lady so, whom you visit—I
mean—I really forget her name, but you remember all
about her."

He rose unconsciously, and looked for a minute from
the window.

"A good priest," he said, returning, "is no respecter of
persons. Blessed should I be if I could beguile a be-
nighted traveller into safety! Blessed and happy were
my lot if I could die in the endeavour thus to save one
human soul bent on self-destruction!"

His answer vexed me. The theological level on which
he placed all human souls did not please me. After all
our friendly evenings at Malory, I did not quite understand his being, as he seemed to boast, no "respecter of
persons."

"I am sure that it is quite right," I said, carelessly,
"and very prudent, too, because, if you were to lose your
life in converting me, or a Hottentot chief, or any one else,
you would, you think, go straight to heaven; so, after all,
the wish is not altogether too heroic for this selfish world."

He smiled; but there was doubt, I thought, in the eyes
which he turned for a moment upon me.

"Our motives are so mixed," he said, "and death,
besides, is to some men less than happier people think;
my life has been austere and afflicted; and what remains
of it will, I know, be darker. I see sometimes where all
is drifting. I never was so happy, and I never shall be,
as I have been for a time at Malory. I shall see that
place perhaps no more. Happy the people whose annals
are dull!" he smiled. "How few believe that well-worn

saying in their own case! Yet, Miss Ethel, when you left Malory, you left quiet behind you, perhaps for ever!"

He was silent; I said nothing. The spirit of what he had said echoed, though he knew it not, the forebodings of my own heart. The late evening sun was touching with its slanting beams the houses opposite, and the cold grimy brick in which the dingy taste of our domestic architecture some forty years before delighted; and as I gazed listlessly from my chair, through the window, on the dismal formality of the street, I saw in the same sunlight nothing of those bricks and windows: I saw Malory and the church-tower, the trees, the glimmering blue of the estuary, the misty mountains, all fading in the dreamy quietude of the declining light, and I sighed.

"Well, then," he said, closing the book, "we close Tasso here. If you care to try Ariosto, I shall be only too happy. Shall we commence to-morrow? And as for our other books, those I mean that you were good enough to read——"

"I'm not afraid of them," I said: "we shan't break our old Malory custom yet; and I ought to be very grateful to you, Mr. Carmel."

His countenance brightened, but the unconscious reproach of his wounded look still haunted me. And after he was gone, with a confusion of feelings which I could not have easily analysed, I laid my hands over my eyes, and cried for some time bitterly.

CHAPTER XXIX.

MY BOUQUET.

 REMEMBER so vividly the night of my first ball. The excitement of the toilet; mamma's and the maid's consultations and debates; the tremulous anticipations; the "pleasing terror;" the delightful, anxious flutter, and my final look in the tall glass. I hardly knew myself. I gazed at myself with the irrepressible smile of elation. I never had looked so well. There are degrees of that delightful excitement that calls such tints to girlish cheeks, and such fire. to the eyes, as visit them no more in our wiser after-life, The enchantment wanes, and the flowers and brilliants fade and we soon cease to see them. I went down to the drawing-room to wait for mamma. The candles were lighted, and whom should I find there but Mr. Carmel?

"I asked your mamma's leave to come and see you dressed for your first ball," he said. "How very pretty it all is!"

He surveyed me, smiling with a melancholy pride, it seemed to me, in my good looks and brilliant dress.

"No longer, and never more, the Miss Ethel of my quiet Malory recollections. Going out at last! If any one can survive the ordeal and come forth scathless, you, I think, will. But to me it seems that this is a farewell, and that my pupil dies to-night, and a new Miss Ethel returns. You cannot help it; all the world cannot prevent it, if so it is to be. As an old friend, I knew I might bring you these."

" Oh, Mr. Carmel, what beautiful flowers!" I ex-claimed.

It was certainly an exquisite bouquet ; one of those beautiful and costly offerings that perish in an hour, and seems to me like the pearl thrown into the cup of wine.

"I am so grateful. It was so kind of you. It is too splendid a great deal. It is quite impossible that there can be anything like it in the room."

I was really lost in wonder and admiration, and I suppose looked delighted. I was pleased that the flowers should have come from Mr. Carmel's hand.

"If you think that the flowers are worthy of you, you think more highly than I do of them," he answered, with a smile that was at once sad and pleased. "I am such an old friend, you know ; a month at quiet Malory counts for a year anywhere else. And as you say of the flowers, I may say more justly of my pupil, there will be no one like her there. It is the compensation of being such as I, that we may speak frankly, like good old women, and no one be offended. And, oh, Miss Ethel, may God grant they be not placed like flowers upon a sacrifice or on the dead. Do not forget your better thoughts. You are entering scenes of illusion, where there is little charity, and almost no sincerity, where cruel feelings are instilled, the love of flattery and dominion awakened, and all the evil and enchantments of the world beset you. En-courage those good thoughts ; watch and pray, or a pain-less and even pleasant death sets in, and no one can arrest it."

How my poor father would have laughed at such an exhortation at the threshold of a ball-room ! No doubt it had its comic side, but not for me, and that was all Mr. Carmel cared for.

This was a ball at an official residence, and besides the usual muster, Cabinet and other Ministers would be there, and above all, that judicious rewarder of public virtue, and instructor of the conscience of the hustings, the patronage secretary of the Treasury. Papa had at last discovered a constituency which he thought promised success, he had made it a point, of course, to go to places where he had opportunities for a talk with that important

personage. Papa was very sanguine, and now, as usual,
whenever he had a project of that kind on hand, was in
high spirits.

He came into the drawing-room. He always seemed to
me as if he did not quite know whether he liked or disliked
Mr. Carmel. Whenever I saw them together, he appeared
to me, like Mrs. Malaprop, to begin with a little aversion,
and gradually to become more and more genial. He
greeted Mr. Carmel a little coldly, and brightened as he
looked on me; he was evidently pleased with me, and
talked me over with myself very good-humouredly. I took
care to show him my flowers. He could not help admiring
them.

"These are the best flowers I have seen anywhere.
How did you contrive to get them? Really, Mr. Carmel,
you are a great deal too kind. I hope Ethel thanked you.
Ethel, you ought really to tell Mr. Carmel how very much
obliged you are."

"Oh! she has thanked me a great deal too much; she
has made me quite ashamed," said he.

And so we talked on, waiting for mamma, and I remember papa said he wondered how Mr. Carmel, who had
lived in London and at Oxford, and at other places, where
in one kind of life or another one really does live, contrived
to exist month after month at Malory, and he drew an
amusing and cruel picture of its barbarism and the naked-
ness of the town of Cardyllion. Mr. Carmel took up the
cudgels for both, and I threw in a word wherever I had one
to say. I remember this laughing debate, because it led to
this little bit of dialogue.

"I fortunately never bought many things there—two
brushes, I remember; all their hairs fell out, and they were
bald before the combs they sent for to London arrived. If
I had been dependent on the town of Cardyllion, I should
have been reduced to a state of utter simplicity."

"Oh, but I assure you, papa, they have a great many
very nice things at Jones's shop in Castle Street," I re-
monstrated.

"Certainly not for one's dressing room. There are
tubs at the regattas, and sponges at their dinners, I daresay," papa began, in a punning vein.

"But you'll admit that London supplies no such cosmetics as Malory," said Mr. Carmel, with a kind glance at me.

"Well, you have me there, I admit," laughed papa, looking very pleasantly at me, who, no doubt, was at that moment the centre of many wild hopes of his.

Mamma came down now; there was no time to lose. My heart bounded, half with fear. Mr. Carmel came downstairs with us, and saw us into the carriage. He stood at the door-steps smiling, his short cloak wrapped about him, his hat in his hand. Now the horses made their clattering scramble forward; the carriage was in motion. Mr. Carmel's figure, in the attitude of his last look, receded; he was gone; it was like a farewell to Malory, and we were rolling on swiftly towards the ball-room, and a new life for me.

I am not going to describe this particular ball, nor my sensations on entering this new world, so artificial and astonishing. What an arduous life, with its stupendous excitement, fatigues, and publicity! There were in the new world on which I was entering, of course, personal affections and friendships, as among all other societies of human beings. But the canons on which it governs itself are, it seemed to me, inimical to both. The heart gives little, and requires little there. It assumes nothing deeper than relations of acquaintance; and there is no time to bestow on any other. It is the recognised business of every one to enjoy, and if people have pains or misfortunes they had best keep them to themselves, and smile. No one has a right to be ailing or unfortunate, much less to talk as if he were so, in that happy valley. Such people are "tainted wethers of the flock," and are bound to abolish themselves forthwith. No doubt kind things are done, and charitable, by people who live in it. But they are no more intended to see the light of that life than Mr. Snake's good-natured actions were. This dazzling microcosm, therefore, must not be expected to do that which it never undertook. Its exertions in pursuit of pleasure are enormous; its exhaustion prodigious; the necessary restorative cycle must not be interrupted by private agonies, small or great. If that were permitted, who could recruit for his daily task? I am relating, after an interval of very many years, the impressions of a person who, then very young, was a denizen of "the world" only for a short time; but the application of these principles of selfishness seemed to me sometimes ghastly.

One thing that struck me very much in a little time was that society, as it is termed, was so limited in numbers. You might go everywhere, it seemed to me, and see, as nearly as possible, the same people night after night. The same cards always, merely shuffled. This, considering the size and wealth of England and of London, did seem to me unaccountable.

My first season, like that of every girl who is admired and danced with a great deal, was glorified by illusions, chief among which was that the men who danced with me as they could every night did honestly adore me. We learn afterwards how much and how little those triumphs mean; that new faces are liked simply because they are new; and that girls are danced with because they are the fashion and dance well. I am not boasting—I was admired; and papa was in high good-humour and spirits. There is sunshine even in that region; like winter suns, bright but cold, Such as it is, let the birds of that enchanted forest enjoy it while it lasts; flutter their wings and sing in its sheen, for it may not be for long.

CHAPTER XXX.

THE KNIGHT OF THE BLACK CASTLE.

Y readings with Mr. Carmel totally ceased; in fact, there was no time for any but that one worship which now absorbed me altogether. Every now and then, however, he was in London, and mamma, in the drawing-room, used at times to converse with him, in so low a tone, so earnestly and so long, that I used to half suspect her of making a shrift, and receiving a whispered absolution. Mamma, indeed, stood as it were with just one foot upon the very topmost point of our "high church," ready to spread her wings, and to float to the still more exalted level of the cross on the dome of St. Peter's. But she always hesitated when the moment for making the aërial ascent arrived, and was still trembling in her old attitude on her old pedestal.

I don't think mamma's theological vagaries troubled papa. Upon all such matters he talked like a good-natured Sadducee; and if religion could have been carried on without priests, I don't think he would have objected to any of its many forms.

Mamma had Mr. Carmel to luncheon often, during his stay in town. Whenever he could find an opportunity, he talked with me. He struggled hard to maintain his hold upon me. Mamma seemed pleased that he should; yet I don't think that she had made up her mind even upon my case. I daresay, had I then declared myself a "Catholic," she would have been in hysterics. Her own religious state, just then, I could not perfectly understand. I don't think she did. She was very uncomfortable about once a fort-

night. Her tremors returned when a cold or any other
accident had given her a dull day.

When the season was over, I went with papa and mamma
to some country houses, and while they completed their
circuit of visits Miss Pounden and I were despatched to
Malory. The new world which had dazzled me for a time
had not changed me. I had acquired a second self; but
my old self was still living. It had not touched my heart,
nor changed my simple tastes. I enjoyed the quiet of
Malory, and its rural ways, and should have been as happy
there as ever, if I could only have recovered the beloved
companions whom I missed.

My loneliness was very agreeably relieved one day, as I
was walking home from Penruthyn Priory, by meeting Mr.
Carmel. He joined me, and we sauntered towards home
in very friendly talk. He was to make a little stay at the
steward's house. We agreed to read *I Promessi Sposi*
together. Malory was recovering its old looks. I asked
him all the news that he was likely to know and I cared
to hear.

"Where was Lady Lorrimer?" I inquired.

Travelling, he told me, on the Continent, he could not
say where. "We must not talk of her," he said, with a
shrug and a laugh. "I think, Miss Ware, we were never
so near quarrelling upon any subject as upon Lady Lorrimer,
and I then resolved never again to approach that irritating
topic."

So with common consent we talked of other things,
among which I asked him:

"Do you remember Mr. Marston?"

"You mean the shipwrecked man who was quartered
for some days at the steward's house?" he asked. "Yes
—I remember him very well." He seemed to grow rather
pale as he looked at me, and added, "Why do you ask?"

"Because," I answered, "you told me that he was in
good society, and I have not seen him anywhere—not
once."

"He was in society; but he's not in London, nor in
England now, I believe. I once knew him pretty well,
and I know only too much of him. I know him for a
villain; and had he been still in England I should have

warned you again, Miss Ethel, and warned your mamma, also, against permitting him to claim your acquaintance. But I don't think he will be seen again in this part of the world—not, at all events, until after the death of a person who is likely to live a long time."

"But what has he done?" I asked.

"I can't tell you—I can't tell you how cruelly he has wounded me," he answered. "I have told you in substance all I know, when I say he is a villain."

"I do believe, Mr. Carmel, your mission on earth is to mortify my curiosity. You won't tell me anything of any one I'm the least curious to hear about."

"He is a person I hate to talk of, or even to think of. He is a villain—he is incorrigible—and, happen what may, a villain, I think, he will be to the end."

I was obliged to be satisfied with this, for I had learned that it was a mere waste of time trying to extract from Mr. Carmel any secret which he chose to keep.

Here, then, in the old scenes, our quiet life began for awhile once more. I did not see more of Mr. Carmel now than formerly, and there continued the slightly altered tone, in talk and manner, which had secretly so sorely vexed me in town, and which at times I almost ascribed to my fancy.

Mr. Carmel's stay at Malory was desultory, too, as before; he was often absent for two or three days together. During one of these short absences, there occurred a very trifling incident, which, however, I must mention.

The castle of Cardyllion is a vast ruin, a military fortress of the feudal times, built on a great scale, and with prodigious strength. Its ponderous walls and towers are covered thick with ivy. It is so vast that the few visitors who are to be found there when the summer is over, hardly disquiet its wide solitudes and its silence. For a time I induced Miss Pounden to come down there nearly every afternoon, and we used to bring our novels, and she, sometimes her work; and we sat in the old castle, feeling, in the quiet autumn, as if we had it all to ourselves. The inner court is nearly two hundred feet square, and, ascending a circular stair in the angle next the great gate, you find yourself at the end of a very dark stone-floored corridor, running the entire length of the building. This long passage is lighted at intervals by narrow loopholes placed at the left; and in the wall to the right, after having passed several doors, you come, about mid-way, to one admitting to the chapel. It is a small stone-floored chamber, with a lofty groined roof, very gracefully proportioned; a tall stone-shafted window admits a scanty light from the east, over the site of the dismantled altar; deep shadow prevails everywhere else in this pretty chapel, which is so dark in most parts that, in order to read or work, one must get directly under the streak of light that enters through the window, necessarily so narrow as not to compromise the jealous rules of mediæval fortification. A small arch, at each side of the door, opens a view of this chamber from two small rooms, or galleries, reached by steps from this corridor.

We had placed our camp-stools nearly under this window, and were both reading; when I raised my eyes they encountered those of a very remarkable-looking old man, whom I instantly recognised, with a start. It was the man whom we used, long ago, to call the Knight of the Black Castle. His well-formed, bronzed face and features were little changed, except for those lines that time deepens or produces. His dark, fierce eyes were not dimmed by the years that had passed, but his long black hair, which was uncovered, as tall men in those low passages were obliged to remove their hats, was streaked now with grey. This stern old man was gazing fixedly on me, from the arch beside the door, to my left, as I looked at him, and he did not remove his eyes as mine met his. Sullen, gloomy, stern was the face that remained inflexibly fixed in the deep shadow which enhanced its pallor. I turned with an effort to my companion, and said:

"Suppose we come out, and take a turn in the grounds."

To which, as indeed to everything I proposed, Miss Pounden assented.

I walked for a minute or two about the chapel before I stole a glance backward at the place where I had seen the apparition. He was gone. The arch, and the void space behind, were all that remained; there was nothing but deep shadow where that face had loomed. I asked Miss Pounden if she had seen the old man looking in ; she had not.

Well, we left the chapel, and retraced our steps through the long corridor, I watching through the successive loop-holes for the figure of the old man pacing the grass beneath; but I did not see him. Down the stairs we came, I peeping into every narrow doorway we passed, and so out upon the grassy level of the inner court. I looked in all directions there, but nowhere could I see him. Under the arched gateway, where the portcullis used to clang, we passed into the outer court, and there I peeped about, also in vain.

I dare say Miss Pounden, if she could wonder at anything, wondered what I could be in pursuit of; but that most convenient of women never troubled me with a question.

Through the outer gate, in turn, we passed, and to Richard Pritchard's lodge, at the side of the gate admitting visitors from Castle Street to the castle grounds. Tall Richard Pritchard, with his thin stoop, his wide-awake hat, brown face, lantern jaws, and perpetual smirk, listened to my questions, and answered that he had let in such a gentleman, about ten minutes before, as I described. This gentleman had given his horse to hold to a donkey-boy outside the gate, and Richard Pritchard went on to say, with his usual volubility, and his curious interpolation of phrases of politeness, without the slightest regard to their connection with the context, but simply to heighten the amiability and polish of his discourse :

"And he asked a deal, miss, about the family down at Malory, I beg your pardon ; and when he heard you were there, miss, he asked if you ever came down to the town —yes, indeed. So when I told him you were in the castle now—very well, I thank you, miss—he asked whereabout in the castle you were likely to be—yes, indeed, miss, very true—and he gave me a shilling—he did, indeed—and I showed him the way to the chapel—I beg your pardon, miss—where you very often go—very true indeed, miss ; and so I left him at the top of the stairs. Ah, ha! yes, indeed, miss ; and he came back

N

just two or three minutes, and took his horse and rode
down towards the water gate—very well, I thank you,
miss.

This was the substance of Richard Pritchard's information. So, then, he had ridden down Castle Street and
out of the town. It was odd his caring to have that look
at me. What could he mean by it? His was a countenance ominous of nothing good. After so long an
interval, it was not pleasant to see it again, especially
associated with inquiries about Malory and its owners,
and the sinister attraction which had drawn him to the
chapel to gaze upon me, and, as I plainly perceived, by
no means with eyes of liking. The years that had immediately followed his last visit, I knew had proved years
of great loss and peril to papa. May heaven avert the
omen! I silently prayed. I knew that old Rebecca
Torkill could not help to identify him, for I had been
curious on the point before. She could not bring to her
recollection the particular scene that had so fixed itself
upon my memory; for, as she said, in those evil years
there was hardly a day that did not bring down some
bawling creditor from London to Malory in search
of papa.

CHAPTER XXXI.

RUSTICATION.

MALORY was not visited that year by either papa or mamma. I had been so accustomed to a lonely life there that my sojourn in that serene and beautiful spot never seemed solitary. Besides, town life would open again for me in the early spring. Had it not been for that near and exciting prospect, without Laura Grey, I might possibly have felt my solitude more; but the sure return to the whirl and music of the world made my rural weeks precious. They were to end earlier even than our return to town. I was written for, to Roydon, where mamma and papa then were making a short visit, and was deposited safely in that splendid but rather dull house by Miss Pounden, who sped forthwith to London, where I suppose she enjoyed her liberty in her own quiet way.

I enjoyed very much our flitting from country-house to country-house, and the more familiar society of that kind of life. As these peregrinations and progresses, however, had no essential bearing upon my history, I shall mention them only to say this. At Roydon I met a person whom I very little expected to see there. The same person afterwards turned up at a very much pleasanter house—I mean Lady Mardykes's house at Carsbrook, where a really delightful party were assembled. Who do you think this person was? No titled person—not known to the readers of newspapers, except as a name mentioned now and then as forming a unit in a party at some distinguished house; no brilliant name in the lists of talent; a man apparently not worth propitiating on any score: and yet everywhere, and knowing everybody! Who, I say, do you suppose he was? Simply Doctor Droqville! In London I had seen him very often. He used to drop in at balls or garden-parties for an hour or two, and vanish. There was a certain decision, animation, and audacity in his talk, which seemed, although I did not like it, to please better judges very well. No one appeared to know much more about him than I did. Some people, I suppose, like mamma, did know quite enough; but by far the greater part took him for granted, and seeing that other people had him at their houses, did likewise.

Very agreeably the interval passed; and in due time we found ourselves once more in London.

My second season wanted something of the brilliant delirium of the first; and yet, I think I enjoyed it more. Papa was not in such spirits by any means. I dare say, as my second season drew near its close, he was disappointed that I was not already a peeress. But papa had other grounds for anxiety; and very anxious he began to look. It was quite settled now that at the next election he was to stand for the borough of Shillingsworth, with the support of the Government. Every one said he would do very well in the House; but that we ought to have begun earlier. Papa was full of it; but somehow not quite so sanguine and cheery as he used to be about his projects. I had seen ministers looking so haggard and overworked, and really suffering at times, that I began to think that politics were as fatiguing a pursuit almost as pleasure. The iron seemed to have entered into poor papa's soul already.

Although our breakfast hour was late, mamma was hardly ever down to it, and I not always. But one day when we did happen to be all three at breakfast together, he put down his newspaper with a rustle on his knee, and said to mamma, "I have been intending to ask you this long time, and I haven't had an opportunity—or at least it has gone out of my head when I might have asked; have you been writing lately to Lady Lorrimer?"

"Yes, I—at least, I heard from her, a little more than

a week ago—a very kind letter—she wrote from Naples—
she has been there for the winter."

"And quite well?"

"Complaining a little, as usual; but I suppose she is
really quite well."

"I wish she did not hate me quite so much as she
does," said papa. "I'd write to her myself—I dare say
you haven't answered her letter?"

"Well, really, you know, just now it is not easy to find
time," mamma began.

"Oh! hang it, time! Why, you forget you have really
nothing to do," answered papa, more tartly than I had
ever heard him speak to mamma before. "You don't
answer her letters, I think; at least not for months after
you get them! I don't wish you to flatter her—I wish
that as little as you do—but I think you might be civil—
where's the good of irritating her?"

"I never said I saw any," answered mamma, a little
high.

"No; but I see the mischief of it," he continued; "it's
utter folly—and it's not right, besides. You'll just lose
her, that'll be the end of it—she is the only one of your
relations who really cares anything about you—and she
intends making Ethel a present—diamonds—it is just, I
do believe, that she wishes to show what she intends
further. You are the person she would naturally like to
succeed her in anything she has to leave; and you take
such a time about answering her letters, you seem to wish
to vex her. You'll succeed at last—and, I can tell you,
you can't afford to throw away friendship just now. I
shall want every friend, I mean every real friend, I can
count upon. More than you think depends on this affair.
If I'm returned for Shillingsworth, I'm quite certain I
shall get something very soon—and if I once get it,
depend upon it, I shall get on. Some people would say
I'm a fool for my pains, but it is money very well spent—
it is the only money, I really think, I ever laid out wisely
in my life, and it is a very serious matter our succeeding
in this. Did not your aunt Lorrimer say that she thought
she would be at Golden Friars again this year?"

"Yes, I think so; why?" said mamma, listlessly.

"Because she must have some influence over that beast Rokestone—I often wonder what devil has got hold of my affairs, or how Rokestone happens to meet me at so many points—and if she would talk to him a little, she might prevent his doing me a very serious mischief. She is sure to see him when she goes down there."

"He's not there often, you know; I can always find a time to go to Golden Friars without a chance of seeing him. I shall never see him again, I hope." I thought mamma sighed a little, as she said this. "But I'll write and ask Lady Lorrimer to say whatever you wish to him, when her visit to Golden Friars is quite decided on."

So the conversation ended, and upon that theme was not resumed, at least within my hearing, during the remainder of our stay in town.

My journal, which I kept pretty punctually during that season, lies open on the table before me. I have been aiding my memory with it. It has, however, helped me to nothing that bears upon my story. It is a register, for the most part, of routine. Now we lunched with Lady This—now we went to the Duchess of So-and-so's garden-party—every night either a ball, or a musical party, or the opera. Sometimes I was asked out to dinner, sometimes we went to the play. Ink and leaves are discoloured by time. The score years and more that have passed, have transformed this record of frivolity into a solemn and melancholy Mentor. So many of the names that figure there have since been carved on tombstones! Among those that live still, and hold their heads up, there is change everywhere—some for better, some for worse; and yet riven, shattered, scattered, as this muster-roll is, with perfect continuity and solidity, that smiling Sadduceeic world without a home, the community that lives out of doors, and accepts, as it seems to me, satire and pleasure in lieu of the affections, lives and works on upon its old principles and aliment; diamonds do not fail, nor liveries, nor high-bred horses, nor pretty faces, nor witty men, nor chaperons, nor fools, nor rascals.

I must tell you, however, what does not distinctly appear in this diary. Among the many so-called admirers who asked for dances in the ball-room, were two who appeared to like me with a deeper feeling than the others. One was handsome Colonel Saint-George Dacre, with an estate of thirty thousand a year, as my friends told mamma, who duly conveyed the fact to me. But young ladies, newly come out and very much danced with, are fastidious, and I was hard to please. My heart was not pre-occupied, but even in my lonely life I had seen men who interested me more. I liked my present life and freedom too well, and shrank from the idea of being married. The other was Sir Henry Park, also rich, but older. Papa, I think, looked even higher for me, and fancied that I might possibly marry so as to make political connection for him. He did not, therefore, argue the question with me; but overrating me more than I did myself, thought he was quite safe in leaving me free to do as I pleased.

These gentlemen, therefore, were, with the most polite tenderness for their feelings, dismissed—one at Brighton, in August; the other, a little later, at Carsbrook, where he chose to speak. I have mentioned these little affairs in the order in which they occurred, as I might have to allude to them in the pages that follow.

Every one has, once or twice, in his or her life, I suppose, commenced a diary which was to have been prosecuted as diligently and perseveringly as that of Samuel Pepys. I did, I know, oftener than I could now tell you; I have just mentioned one of mine, and from this fragmentary note-book I give you the following extracts, which happen to help my narrative at this particular point.

"At length, thank Heaven! news of darling Laura Grey. I can hardly believe that I am to see her so soon. I wonder whether I shall be able, a year hence, to recall the delight of this expected moment. It is true, there is a great deal to qualify my happiness, for her language is ominous. Still it will be delightful to meet her, and hear her adventures, and have one of our good long talks together, such as made Malory so happy.

"I was in mamma's rooom about half-an-hour ago; she was fidgeting about in her dressing-gown and slippers, and had just sat down before her dressing-table, when Wentworth (her maid) came in with letters by the early post. Mamma has as few secrets, I think, as most people, and her correspondence is generally very uninteresting. Whenever I care to read them, she allows me to amuse myself with her letters when she has opened and read them herself. I was in no mood to do so to-day; but I fancied I saw a slight but distinct change in her careless looks as she peeped into one. She read it a second time, and handed it to me. It is, indeed, from Laura Grey! It says that she is in great affliction, and that she will call at our town house 'to-morrow,' that is to-day, 'Thursday,' at one o'clock, to try whether mamma would consent to see her.

"'I think that very cool. I don't object to seeing her, however,' said mamma; 'but she shall know what I think of her.'

"I don't like the idea of such an opening as mamma would make. I must try to see Laura before she meets her. She must have wonders to tell me; it cannot have been a trifling thing that made her use me, apparently, so unkindly.

"Thursday—half-past one. No sign of Laura yet.

"Thursday—six o'clock. She has not appeared! What am I to think?

"Her letter is written, as it seems to me, in the hurry of agitation. I can't understand what all this means.

"Thursday night—eleven o'clock. Before going to bed. Laura has not appeared. No note. Mamma more vexed than I have often seen her. I fancy she had a hope of getting her back again, as I know I had.

"Friday. I waked in the dark, early this morning, thinking of Laura, and fancying every horrible thing that could have befallen her since her note of yesterday morning was written.

"Went to mamma, who had her breakfast in her bed, and told her how miserable I was about Laura Grey. She said, 'There is nothing the matter with Miss Grey, except that she does not know how to behave herself." I don't agree with mamma, and I am sure that she does not really think any such thing of Laura Grey. I am still very uneasy about her; there is no address to her note.

"I have just been again with mamma, to try whether she can recollect anything by which we could find her out.

She says she can remember no circumstance by which we can trace her. Mamma says she had been trying to find a governess at some of the places where lists of ladies seeking such employment are kept, but without finding one who exactly answered ; papa had then seen an advertisement in the *Times*, which seemed to promise satisfactorily, and Miss Grey answered mamma's note, and referred to a lady, who immediately called on her ; mamma could only recollect that she knew this lady's name, that she had heard of her before, and that she spoke with the greatest affection of Miss Grey, and shed tears while she lamented her determination to seek employment as a governess, instead of living at home with her. The lady had come in a carriage, with servants, and had all the appearance of being rich, and spoke of Laura as her cousin. But neither her name nor address could mamma recollect, and there remained no clue by which to trace her. It was some comfort to think that the lady who claimed her as a kinswoman, and spoke of her with so much affection, was wealthy, and anxious to take her to her own home ; but circumstances are always mutable, and life transitory—how can we tell where that lady is now?"

"I have still one hope—Laura may have written one o'clock 'Thursday,' and meant Friday. It is only a chance—still I cling to it.

" Friday—three o'clock. Laura has not appeared. What are we to think? I can't get it out of my head that something very bad has happened. My poor Laura !

" Saturday night—a quarter to eleven. Going to bed. Another day, and no tidings of Laura. I have quite given up the hope of seeing her."

She did not come next day. On the subject on which mamma felt so sharply, she had not an opportunity of giving her a piece of her mind then, or the next day.

So the season being over, behold us again in the country !

After our visit to Carsbrook, mamma and papa were going to Haitly Abbey. For some reason, possibly the very simple one that I had been forgotten in the invitation, I was not to accompany them ; I was despatched in charge of old Lady Hester Wigmore, who was going that way, to Chester, where Miss Pounden took me up; and with her, "to my great content," as old Samuel Pepys says, I went to Malory, which I always re-visited with an unutterable affection, as my only true home.

Nothing happened during my stay at Malory, which was unexpectedly interrupted by a note from mamma appointing to meet me at Chester. Papa had been obliged to go to town to consult with some friends, and he was then to go down to Shillingsworth to speak at a public dinner. She and I were going northward. She would tell me all when we met. I need not bring any of my finery with me.

With this scanty information, and some curiosity as to our destination in the North, I arrived at Chester, and there met mamma, from whom I soon learned that our excursion was to lead us into wild and beautiful scenery quite new to me.

CHAPTER XXXII.

AT THE GEORGE AND DRAGON.

E had to wait for a long time at some station, I forget its name. The sun set, and night overtook us before we reached the end of our journey by rail. We had then to drive about twelve miles. The road, for many miles, lay through a desolate black moss. I could not have believed there was anything so savage in England. A thin mist was stretched like a veil over the more distant level of the dark expanse, on which, here and there, a wide pool gleamed faintly under the moonlight. To the right there rose a grand mass of mountain. We were soon driving through a sort of gorge, and found ourselves fenced in by the steep sides of gigantic mountains, as we followed a road that wound and ascended among them. I shall never forget the beautiful effect of the scene suddenly presented, and for the first time, as the road reached its highest elevation, and I saw, with the dark receding sides of the mountain we had been penetrating for a proscenium, my first view of Golden Friars. Oh! how beautiful!

Surrounded by an amphitheatre of Alpine fells, the broad mere of Golden Friars glimmered cold under the moonlight, and the quaint little town of steep gables, built of light grey stone, rose from its grasy margin surrounded by elms, single or in clumps, that looked almost black in contrast with the gleaming lake and the white masonry of the town. It looked like enchanted ground. A silvery hoar-frost seemed to cover the whole scene, giving it a filmy and half-visionary character that enhanced its beauty. I was exclaiming in wonder and delight as every minute some new beauty unfolded itself to view. Mamma was silent, as she looked from the window; I saw that she cried gently, thinking herself unobserved. A beautiful scene, where childish days were passed, awakes so many sweet and bitter fancies! The yearnings for the irrevocable, the heartache of the memory, opened the fountains of her tears; and I was careful not to interrupt her lonely thoughts. I left her to the enjoyment of that melancholy luxury, and gazed on in strange delight.

Here, then, was the dwelling-place of that redoubted enemy of our house whom fate seemed to have ordained as our persecutor. Here lived the old enchanter whose malign spells were woven about us, in busy London and quiet Malory, or the distant scenes of France and Italy. Even this thought added interest to the romantic scene.

We had now descended to the level of the shore of the lake, along whose margin our road swept in a gentle curve. The fells from this level rose stupendous, all around, striking their silvery peaks into the misty moonlight, and looking so aërial that one might fancy a stone thrown would pass through their sides as if they were vapour. Now we passed under the shadow of the first clump of mighty elms; and now the white fronts and chimneys of the village houses rose in the foreground. There was no sign of life but the barking of the watch-dogs, and the cackling of the vigilant geese, and the light that glanced from the hall of the "George and Dragon," the substantial old inn that, looking across the road, faces the lake and distant fells. At the door of this ancient and comfortable inn drew up our chaise and four horses, no mere ostentation, but a simple necessity, where carriage and luggage were pulled, towards the close of so long a stage, over the steeps where the road pushes its way high among the fells.

So our journey was over; and we stood in the hall. Before we went up to our rooms mamma inquired whether Lady Lorrimer had arrived. Yes, her ladyship had been there since the day before yesterday. Mamma seemed nervous and uncomfortable. She sent down her maid to find out whether Sir Harry Rokestone was in the country;

and when the servant returned and told her that he was
not expected to arrive at Dorracleugh before a fortnight,
she sighed, and I heard her say faintly, " Thank God!"

I confess it was rather a disappointment than a relief
to me. I rather wished to see this truculent old wizard.
After a sound sleep, which we both needed, I got up and
had a little peep at that beautiful place, in the early sunlight, before breakfast. Lady Lorrimer's maid came with
inquiries from her mistress, for mamma and me. Her
ladyship was not very well, and could not see us till about
twelve. She was so vexed at having to put us off, and
hoped we were not tired ; and also that we would take our
dinner with her. To this mamma agreed.

I was curious to see Lady Lorrimer once more. My
ideas had grown obscure, and my theory of that kinswoman
had been disagreeably disturbed, ever since the evening on
which she, or her double, had passed by me so resolutely
in the street.

Having heard that she was quite ready to see us, we
paid our visit. I wondered how she would receive me,
and my suspense amounted almost to excitement as I
reached the door. A moment more, and I could not believe
that Lady Lorrimer and the woman who so resembled her
were the same. Nothing could be more affectionate than
Lady Lorrimer. She received us with a very real welcome, and so much pleasure in her looks, tones, and words.
She was not, indeed, looking well, but her spirits seemed
cheerful. She embraced mamma, and kissed her very
fondly ; then she kissed me over and over again. I was
utterly puzzled, and more than doubted the identity of this
warm-hearted, affectionate woman with the person who
had chosen to cut me with such offensive and sinister
persistence.

" See how this pretty creature looks at me !" she said
to mamma, laughing, as she detected my conscious
scrutiny.

I blushed and looked down ; I did not know what to
say.

" I'm very much obliged to you, dear, for looking at
me, so few people do now-a-days ; and I was just going
to steal a good look at you, when I found I was anticipated.

I have just been saying to your mamma that I have ordered
a boat, and we must all have a sail together on the lake
after dinner ; what do you say ?"

Of course I was delighted ; I thought the place perfectly
charming.

" I lived the earlier part of my life here," she resumed,
"and so did your mamma, you know—when she was a
little girl, and until she came to be nineteen or twenty—I
forget which you were, dear, when you were married?"
she said, turning to mamma.

" Twenty-two," said mamma, smiling.

" Twenty-two ? Really ! Well, we lived at Mardykes.
I'll point out the place on the water when we take our
sail ; you can't see it from these windows."

" And where does Sir Harry Rokestone live ?" I asked.

" You can't see that either from these windows. It is
further than Mardykes, at the same side. But we shall
see it from the boat."

Then she and mamma began to talk, and I went to the
window and looked out.

Lady Lorrimer, with all her airs of conventual seclusion,
hungered and thirsted after gossip ; and whenever they
met, she learned all the stories from mamma, and gave
her, in return, old scandal and ridiculous anecdotes about
the predecessors of the people with whose sayings, doings,
and mishaps mamma amused her.

Two o'clock dinners, instead of luncheons, were the rule
in this part of the world. And people turned tea into a
very substantial supper, and were all in bed and asleep
before the hour arrived at which the London ladies and
gentlemen are beginning to dress for a ball.

You are now to suppose us, on a sunny evening, on
board the boat that had been moored for some time at
the jetty opposite the door of the " George and Dragon."
We were standing up the lake, and away from the Golden
Friars shore, towards a distant wood, which they told me
was the forest of Clusted.

" Look at that forest, Ethel," said Lady Lorrimer. " It
is the haunted forest of Clusted—the last resort of the
fairies in England. It was there, they say, that Sir Bale
Mardykes, long ago, made a compact with the Evil One,"

Through the openings of its magnificent trees, as we nearer, from time to time, the ivied ruins of an old manor-house were visible. In this beautiful and, in spite of the monotony of the gigantic fells that surround the lake, ever-varying scenery, my companions gradually grew silent for a time; even I felt the dreamy influence of the scene, and liked the listless silence, in which nothing was heard but the rush of the waters, and the flap of the sail now and then. I was living in a world of fancy: they in a sadder one of memory.

In a little while, in gentle tones, they were exchanging old remembrances; a few words now and then sufficed; the affecting associations of scenes of early life revisited were crowding up everywhere. As happens to some people when death is near, a change, that seemed to be quite beautiful, came over mamma's mind in the air and lights of this beautiful place! How I wished that she could remain always as she was now!

With the old recollections seemed to return the simple rural spirit of the early life. What is the town life, of which I had tasted, compared with this? How much simpler, tenderer, sublimer, this is! How immensely nearer heaven! The breeze was light, and the signs of the sky assured the boatmen that we need fear none of those gusts and squalls that sometimes burst so furiously down through the cloughs and hollows of the surrounding mountains. I, with the nautical knowledge acquired at Malory, took the tiller, under direction of the boatmen. We had a good deal of tacking to get near enough to the shore at Clusted to command a good view of that fine piece of forest. We then sailed northward, along the margin of the " mere," as they call the lake; and, when we had gone in that direction for a mile or more, turned the boat's head across the water, and ran before the breeze towards the Mardykes side. There is a small island near the other side, with a streak of grey rock and bushes nearly surrounding what looked like a ruined chapel or hermitage, and Lady Lorrimer told me to pass this as nearly as I could.

The glow of evening was by this time in the western sky. The sun was hidden behind the fells that form a noble barrier between Golden Friars and the distant moss of Dardale, where stands Haworth Hall. In deepest purple shadow the mountains here closely overhang the lake. Under these, along the margin, Lady Lorrimer told me to steer.

We were gliding slowly along, so that there was ample leisure to note every tree and rock upon the shore as we passed. As we drifted, rather than sailed, along the shore, there suddenly opened from the margin a narrow valley, reaching about a quarter of a mile. It was a sudden dip in the mountains that here rise nearly from the edge of the lake. Steep-sided and wild was this hollow, and backed by a mountain that, to me, looking up from the level of the lake, appeared stupendous.

The valley lay flat in one unbroken field of short grass. A broad-fronted, feudal tower, with a few more modern buildings about it, stood far back, fronting the river. A rude stone pier afforded shelter to a couple of boats, and a double line of immense lime-trees receded from that point about half-way up to the tower. Whether it was altogether due to the peculiar conformation of the scene, or that it owed its character in large measure to its being enveloped in the deep purple shadow cast by the surrounding mountain, and the strange effect of the glow reflected downward from the evening clouds, which touched the summits of the trees, and the edges of the old tower, like the light of a distant conflagration, I cannot say; but never did I see a spot with so awful a character of solitude and melancholy.

In the gloom we could see a man standing alone on the extremity of the stone pier, looking over the lake. This figure was the only living thing we could discover there.

"Well, dear, now you see it. That's Dorracleugh—that's Harry Rokestone's place," said Lady Lorrimer. "What a spot! Fit only for a bear or an anchorite. Do you know," she added, turning to mamma, "he is there a great deal more than he used to be, they tell me. I know if I were to live in that place for six months I should never come out of it a sane woman. To do him justice, he does not stay very long here when he does come, and for years he never came at all. He has other places, far away from this; and if a certain event had happened about two-and-twenty years ago," she added, for my behalf, "he intended building quite a regal house a little higher up, on a site that is really enchanting, but your mamma would not allow him; and so, and so——" Lady Lorrimer had turned her glasses during her sentence upon the figure which stood motionless on the end of the pier; and she said, forgetting what she had been telling me, "I really think—I'm nearly certain—that man standing there is Harry Rokestone!"

Mamma started. I looked with all my eyes; little more than a hundred yards interposed, but the shadow was so intense, and the effect of the faint reflected light so odd and puzzling, that I could be certain of nothing, but that the man stood very erect, and was tall and power-fully built. Lady Lorrimer was too much absorbed in her inspection to offer me her glasses, which I was long-ing to borrow, but for which I could not well ask, and so we sailed slowly by, and the hill that flanked the valley gradually glided between us and the pier, and the figure disappeared from view. Lady Lorrimer, lowering her glasses, said:

"I can't say positively, but I'm very nearly certain it was he."

Mamma said nothing, but was looking pale, and during the rest of our sail seemed absent and uncomfortable, if not unhappy.

CHAPTER XXXIII.

NOTICE TO QUIT.

WE drank tea with Lady Lorrimer. Mamma continued very silent, and I think she had been crying in her room.

"They can't tell me here whether Harry has arrived or not," said Lady Lorrimer. "He might have returned by the Dardale Road, and if so, he would not have passed through Golden Friars, so it is doubtful. But I'm pretty sure that was he."

"I wish I were sure of that," said mamma.

"Well, I don't know," said Lady Lorrimer, "what to advise. I was just going to say it might be a wise thing if you were to make up your mind to see him, and to beard the lion in his den."

"No," said mamma; "if you mean to meet him and speak to him, I could not do that. I shall never see him again—nothing but pain could come of it; and he would not see me, and he ought not to see me; and he ought not to forgive me—never!"

"Well, dear, I can't deny it, you did use him very ill. And he is, and always was, a fierce and implacable enemy," answered Lady Lorrimer. "I fancied, perhaps, if he did see you, the old chord might be touched again, and yield something of its old tone on an ear saddened by time. But I daresay you are right. It was a Quixotic inspiration, and might have led to disaster; more probably, indeed, than to victory."

"I am quite sure of that—in fact, I know it," said mamma.

And there followed a silence.

"I sometimes think, Mabel—I was thinking so all this evening," said Lady Lorrimer, "it might have been happier for us if we had never left this lonely place. We might have been happier if we had been born under harder conditions; the power of doing what pleases us best leads us so often into sorrow."

Another silence followed. Mamma was looking over her shoulder, sadly, through the window at the familiar view of lake and mountain, indolently listening.

"I regret it, and I don't regret it," continued Lady Lorrimer. "If I could go back again into my early self—I wish I could—but the artificial life so perverts and enervates one, I hardly know, honestly, what I wish. I only know there is regret enough to make me discontented, and I think I should have been a great deal happier if I had been compelled to stay at Golden Friars, and had never passed beyond the mountains that surround us here. I have not so long as you to live, Mabel, and I'm glad of it. I am not quite so much of a Sadducee as you used to think me, and I hope there may be a happier world for us all. And, now that I have ended my homminy, as they call such long speeches in this country, will you, dear Ethel, give me a cup of tea?"

Lady Lorrimer and I talked. I was curious about some of the places and ruins I had seen, and asked questions, which it seemed to delight her to answer. It is a region abounding in stories strange and marvellous, family traditions, and legends of every kind.

"I think," said mamma, *à propos des bottes,* "if he has returned they are sure to know in the town before ten to-night. Would you mind asking again by-and-by?"

"You mean about Harry Rokestone?"

"Yes."

"I will. I'll make out all about him. We saw his castle to-day," she continued, turning to me. "Our not knowing whether he was there or not made it a very interesting contemplation. You remember the short speech Sheridan wrote to introduce Kelly's song at Drury Lane

—'There stands my Matilda's cottage! She must be in it, or else out of it?'"

Again mamma dropped out, and the conversation was maintained by Lady Lorrimer and myself. In a little while mamma took her leave, complaining of a headache; and our kinswoman begged that I would remain for an hour or so, to keep her company. When mamma had bid her good night, and was gone, the door being shut, Lady Lorrimer laughed, and said:

"Now, tell me truly, don't you think if your papa had been with us to-day in the boat, and seen the change that took place in your mamma's looks and spirits from the moment she saw Dorracleugh, and the tall man who stood on the rock, down to the hour of her headache and early good night, he would have been a little jealous?"

I did not quite know whether she was joking or serious, and I fancy there was some puzzle in my face as I answered:

"But it can't be that she liked Sir Harry Rokestone; she is awfully afraid of him—that is the reason, I'm sure, she was so put out. She never liked him."

"Don't be too sure of that, little woman," she answered, gaily.

"Do you really think mamma liked him? Why, she was in love with papa."

"No, it was nothing so deep," said Lady Lorrimer; "she did not love your papa. It was a violent whim, and if she had been left just five weeks to think, she would have returned to Rokestone."

"But there can be no sentiment remaining still," I remarked. "Sir Harry Rokestone is an old man!"

"Yes, he is an old man; he is—let me see—he's fifty six. And she did choose to marry your papa. But I'm sure she thinks she made a great mistake. I am very sure she thinks that, with all his faults, Rokestone was the more loveable man, the better man, the truer. He would have taken good care of her. I don't know of any one point in which he was your papa's inferior, and there are fifty in which he was immeasurably his superior. He was a handsomer man, if that is worth anything. I think I never saw so handsome a man, in his peculiar style. You think me a very odd old woman to tell you my opinion of your father so frankly; but I am speaking as your mamma's friend and kinswoman, and I say your papa has not used her well. He is good-humoured, and has good spirits, and he has some good-nature, quite subordinated to his selfishness. And those qualities, so far as I know, complete the muster-roll of his virtues. But he has made her, in no respect, a good husband. In some a very bad one. And he employs half-a-dozen attorneys, to whom he commits his business at random; and he is too indolent to look after anything. Of course he's robbed, and everything at sixes and sevens; and he has got your mamma to take legal steps to make away with her money for his own purposes; and the foolish child, the merest simpleton in money matters, does everything he bids her; and I really believe she has left herself without a guinea. I don't like him—no one could who likes *her*. Poor, dear Mabel, she wants energy; I never knew a woman with so little will. She never showed any but once, and that was when she did a foolish thing, and married your father."

"And did Sir Harry Rokestone like mamma very much?" I asked.

"He was madly in love with her," and when she married your papa, he wanted to shoot him. I think he was, without any metaphor, very nearly out of his mind. He has been a sort of anchorite ever since. His money is of no use to him. He is a bitter and eccentric old man."

"And he can injure papa now?"

"So I'm told. Your papa thinks so; and he seldom takes the trouble to be alarmed about danger three or four months distant."

Then, to my disappointment and, also, my relief, that subject dropped. It had interested and pained me; and sometimes I felt that it was scarcely right that I should hear all she was saying, without taking up the cudgels for papa. Now, with great animation, she told me her recollections of her girlish days here at Golden Friars, when the old gentry were such bores and humorists as are no longer to be met with anywhere. And as she made me

laugh at these recitals, her maid, whom she had sent down
to "the bar" to make an inquiry, returned, and told her
something in an undertone. As soon as she was gone,
Lady Lorrimer said :

"Yes, it is quite true. Tell your mamma that Harry
Rokestone is at Dorracleugh."

She became thoughtful. Perhaps she was rehearsing
mentally the mediatory conference she had undertaken.

We had not much more conversation that night; and
we soon parted with a very affectionate good-night. My
room adjoined mamma's, and finding that she was not yet
asleep, I went in and gave her Lady Lorrimer's message.
Mamma changed colour, and raised herself suddenly on
her elbow, looking in my face.

"Very well, dear," said she, a little flurried. "We
must leave this to-morrow morning."

CHAPTER XXXIV.

SIR HARRY'S ANSWER.

ABOUT eleven o'clock next morning our chaise was at the door of the "George and Dragon." We had been waiting with our bonnets on to say good-bye to Lady Lorrimer. I have seen two or three places in my life to which my affections were drawn at first sight, and this was one of them. I was standing at the window, looking my last at this beautiful scene. Mamma was restless and impatient. I knew she was uneasy lest some accident should bring Sir Harry Rokestone to the door before we had set out upon our journey.

At length Lady Lorrimer's foreign maid came to tell us that milady wished to see us now. Accordingly we followed the maid, who softly announced us.

The room was darkened; only one gleam, through a little opening in the far shutter, touched the curtains of her bed, showing the old-fashioned chintz pattern, like a transparency, through the faded lining. She was no longer the gay Lady Lorrimer of the evening before. She was sitting up among her pillows, nearly in the dark, and the most melancholy, whimpering voice you can imagine came through the gloom from among the curtains.

"Is my sweet Ethel there, also?" she asked when she had kissed mamma. "Oh, that's right; I should not have been happy if I had not bid you good-bye. Give me your hand, darling. And so you are going, Mabel? I'm sorry you go so soon, but perhaps you are right—I think you are. It would not do, perhaps, to meet. I'll do what I can, and write to tell you how I succeed."

Mamma thanked and kissed her again.

"I'm not so well as people think, dear, nor as I wish to think myself. We may not meet for a long time, and I wish to tell you, Mabel—I wish to tell you both—that I won't leave you dependent on that reckless creature, Francis Ware. I want you two to be safe. I have none but you left me to love on earth." Here poor Lady Lorrimer began to cry. "Whenever I write to you, you must come to me; don't let anything prevent you. I am so weak. I want to leave you both very well, and I intend to put it out of my power to change it—who's that at the door? Just open it, Ethel, dear child, and see if any one is there—my maid, I mean—you can say you dropped your handkerchief—hush!"

There was no one in the lobby.

"Shut it quietly, dear; I'll do what I say—don't thank me—don't say a word about it to any one, and if you mention it to Francis Ware, charge him to tell no one else. There, dears, both, don't stay longer. God bless you! Go, go; God bless you!"

And with these words, having kissed us both very fondly, she dismissed us.

Mamma ran down, and out to the carriage very quickly, and sat back as far as she could at the far side. I followed, and all being ready, in a minute more we were driving swiftly from the "George and Dragon," and soon town, lake, forest, and distant fells were hidden from view by the precipitous sides of the savage gorge, through which the road winds its upward way.

Our drive into Golden Friars had been a silent one, and so was our drive from it, though from different causes. I was thinking over our odd interview with poor Lady Lorrimer. In what a low, nervous state she seemed, and how affectionately she spoke! I had no inquisitive tendencies, and I was just at the age when people take the future for granted. No sordid speculations therefore, I can honestly say, were busy with my brain.

We were to have stayed at least ten days at Golden Friars, and here we were flying from it before two days were spent. All our plans were upset by the blight of Sir Harry Rokestone's arrival at least a fortnight before the

date of his usual visit, just as Napoleon's Russian calcula-
tions were spoilt by the famous early winter of 1812.
I was vexed in my way. I should not have been sorry to hear
that he had been well ducked in the lake. Mamma was vexed
in her own way, also, when, about an hour after, she
escaped from the thoughts that agitated her at first, and
descended to her ordinary level. A gap of more than a
week was made in her series of visits. What was to be
done with it ?

"Where are you going, mamma ?" I asked, innocently
enough.

"Nowhere—everywhere. To Chester," she answered,
presently.

"And where then ?" I asked.

"Why do you ask questions that I can't answer ? Why
should you like to make me more miserable than I am ?
Everything is thrown into confusion. I'm sure I don't
know the least. I have no plans. I literally don't know
where we are to lay our heads to-night. There's no one
to take care of us. As usual, whenever I want assistance,
there's none to be had, and my maid is so utterly helpless,
and your papa in town. I only know that I'm not strong
enough for this kind of thing ; you can write to your papa
when we come to Chester. We shan't see him for Heaven
knows how long—he may have left London by this time ;
and he'll write to Golden Friars—and now that I think of
it—oh ! how am I to live through all this !—I forgot to
tell the people there where to send our letters. Oh ! dear,
oh ! dear, it is such a muddle ! And I could not have told
them, literally, for I don't know where we are going. We
had better just stay at Chester till he comes, whenever
that may be ; and I really could just lie down and cry."

I was glad we were to ourselves, for mamma's looks and
tones were so utterly despairing that in a railway carriage
we should have made quite an excitement. In such matters
mamma was very easy to persuade by any one who would
take the trouble of thinking on himself, and she consented
to come to Malory instead ; and there, accordingly, we
arrived next day, much to the surprise of Rebecca Torkill,
who received us with a very glad welcome, solemnized a
little by a housekeeper's responsibilities.

Mamma enjoyed her simple life here wonderfully—more,
a great deal, than I had ventured to hope. She seemed
to me naturally made for a rural life, though fate had
consigned her to a town one. She reminded me of the
German prince mentioned in Tom Moore's journal, who
had a great taste for navigation, but whose principality
unfortunately was inland.

Papa did not arrive until the day before that fixed for
his and mamma's visit to Dromelton. He was in high
spirits, everything was doing well; his canvass was pro-
spering, and now Lady Lorrimer's conversation at parting,
as reported by mamma, lighted up the uncertain future
with a steady glory, and set his sanguine spirit in a blaze.
Attorneys, foreclosures, bills of exchange hovering threaten-
ingly in the air, and biding their brief time to pounce upon
him, all lost their horrors, for a little, in the exhilarating
news.

Mamma had been expecting a letter from Lady Lorrimer
—one, at length, arrived this morning. Papa had walked
round by the mill-road to visit old Captain Etheridge.
Mamma and I were in the drawing-room as she read it.
It was a long one. She looked gloomy, and said, when
she had come to the end :

"I was right—it was not worth trying. I'm afraid
this will vex your papa. You may read it. You heard
Aunt Lorrimer talk about it. Yes, I was right. She
was a great deal too sanguine."

I read as follows :—

"MY DEAREST MABEL,—I have a disagreeable letter to
write. You desired me to relate with rigour every savage
thing he said—I mean Harry Rokestone, of course—and
I must keep my promise, although I think you will hate
me for it. I had almost given him up, and thinking that
for some reason he was resolved to forget his usual visit
to me, and I being equally determined to make him see
me, was this morning thinking of writing him a little
cousinly note, to say that I was going to see him in his
melancholy castle. But to-day, at about one, there came
on one of those fine thunder-storms among the fells that
you used to admire so much. It grew awfully dark—

portentous omen!—and some enormous drops of rain, as
big as bullets, came smacking down upon the window-
stone. Perhaps these drove him in; for in he came,
announced by the waiter, exactly as a very much nearer
clap of thunder startled all the echoes of Golden Friars
into a hundred reverberations; a finer heralding, and
much more characteristic of the scene and man than that
flourish of trumpets to which kings always enter in
Shakespeare. In he came, my dear Mabel, looking so
king-like, and as tall as the Catstean on Dardale Moss,
and gloomy as the sky. He is as like Allan Macaulay, in
the 'Legend of Montrose,' as ever. A huge dog, one of
that grand sort you remember long ago at Dorracleugh,
came striding in beside him. He used to smile long ago.
But it is many years, you know, since fortune killed that
smile; and he took my poor thin fingers in his colossal
hand, with what Clarendon calls a 'glooming' countenance. We talked for some time as well as the thunder
and the clatter of the rain, mixed with hail, would let us.

"By the time its violence was a little abated, I, being
as you know, not a bad diplomatist, managed, without
startling him, to bring him face to face with the subject
on which I wished to move him. I may as well tell you
at once, my dear Mabel, I might just as well (to return
to my old simile) have tried to move the Catstean. When
I described the danger in which the proceedings would
involve you, as well as your husband, he suddenly smiled;
it was his first smile, so far as I remember, for many a
day. It was not pleasant sunlight—it was more like the
glare of the lightning.

"'We have not very far to travel in life's journey,' I
said, 'you and I. We have had our enemies and our
quarrels, and fought our battles stoutly enough. It is
time we should forget and forgive.'

"'I have forgotten a great deal,' he answered. 'I'll
forgive nothing.'

"'You can't mean you have forgotten pretty Mabel?' I
exclaimed.

"'Let me bury my dead out of my sight,' was all he
said. He did not say it kindly. It was spoken sulkily
and peremptorily.

" 'Well, Harry,' I said, returning upon his former speech, I can't suppose you really intend to forgive nothing.'

"It is a hypocritical world,' he answered. 'If it were anything else, every one would confess what every one knows, that no one ever forgave any one anything since man was created.'

" 'Am I, then, to assume that you will prosecute this matter, to their ruin, through revenge ?' I asked, rather harshly.

" 'Certainly not,' said he. 'That feud is dead and rotten. It is twenty years and more since I saw them. I'm tired of their names. The man I sometimes remember—I'd like to see him flung over the crags of Darness Heugh—but the girl I never think of—she's clean forgot. To me they are total strangers. I'm a trustee in this matter; why should I swerve from my duty, and incur, perhaps, a danger for those whom I know not ?'

" 'You are not obliged to do this—you know you are not,' I urged. 'You have the power, that's all, and you choose to exercise it.'

" 'Amen, so be it; and now we've said enough,' he replied.

" 'No,' I answered, warmly, for it was impossible to be diplomatic with a man like this. 'I must say a word more. I ask you only to treat them as you describe them, that is as strangers. You would not put yourself out of your way to crush a stranger. There was a time when you were kind.'

" 'And foolish,' said he.

" 'Kind,' I repeated; 'you were a kind man.'

" 'The volume of life is full of knowledge,' he answered, ' and I have turned over some pages since then.'

" 'A higher knowledge leads us to charity,' I pleaded.

" 'The highest to justice,' he said, with a scoff. 'I'm no theologian, but I know that fellow deserves the very worst. He refused to meet me, when a crack or two of a pistol might have blown away our feud, since so you call it—feud with such a mafflin !' Every now and then, when he is excited, out pops one of these strange words. They came very often in this conversation, but I don't remember them. 'The mafflin ! the coward!'

"I give you his words; his truculent looks I can't give you. It is plain he has not forgiven him, and never will. Your husband, we all know, did perfectly right in declining that wild challenge. All his friends so advised him. I was very near saying a foolish thing about you, but I saw it in time, and turned my sentence differently; and when I had done, he said:

"'I am going now—the shower is over.' He took my hand, and said 'Good-bye.' But he held it still, and looking me in the face with his gloomy eyes, he added: 'See, I like you well; but if you will talk of those people, or so much as mention their names again, we meet as friends no more.'

"'Think better of it, do, Harry,' I called after him, but he was already clanking over the lobby in his cyclopean shoes. Whether he heard me or not, he walked down the stairs, with his big brute at his heels, without once looking over his shoulder.

"And now, dear Mabel, I have told you everything. You are, of course, to take for granted those Northumbrian words and idioms which drop from him, as I reminded you, as he grows warm in discussion. This is a 'report' rather than a letter, and I have sat up very late to finish it, and I send it to the post-office before I go to bed. Good night, and Heaven bless you, and I hope this gloomy letter may not vex you as much as its purport does me; disappoint you, judging from what you said to me when we talked the matter over, I scarcely think it can."

There is a Latin proverb, almost the only four words of Latin I possess, which says, *Omne ignotum pro magnifico*, for which, and for its translation, I am obliged to Mr. Carmel: "The unknown is taken for the sublime." I did not at the time at all understand the nature of the danger that threatened, and its vagueness magnified it. Papa came in. He read the letter, and the deeper he got in it the paler his face grew, and the more it darkened. He drew a great breath as he laid it down.

"Well, it's not worse than you expected?" said mamma at last. "I hope not. I've had so much to weary, and worry, and break me down; you have no idea what the journey to the Golden Friars was to me. I have not been at all myself. I've been trying to do too much. Ethel there will tell you all I said to my aunt ; and really things go so wrong and so unluckily, no matter what one does, that I almost think I'll go to my bed and cry."

"Yes, dear," said papa, thinking, a little bewildered. " It's—it's—it is—it's very perverse. The old scoundrel! I suppose this is something else."

He took up a letter that had followed him by the same post, and nervously broke the seal. I was watching his face intently as he read. It brightened.

"Here—here's a bit of good luck at last! Where's Mabel ? Oh, yes! it's from Cloudesly. There are some leases just expired at Ellenston, and we shall get at least two thousand pounds, he thinks, for renewing. That makes it all right for the present. I wish it had been fifteen hundred more ; but it's a great deal better than nothing. We'll tide it over, you'll find." And papa kissed her with effusion.

"And you can give three hundred pounds to Le Panier and Tarlton ; they have been sending so often lately," said mamma, recovering from her despondency.

CHAPTER XXXV.

LADY MARDYKES'S BALL.

THE autumn deepened, and leaves were brown, and summer's leafy honours spead drifting over the short grass and the forest roots. Winter came, and snow was on the ground, and presently spring began to show its buds, and blades, and earliest flowers; and the London season was again upon us.

Lady Lorrimer had gone, soon after our visit to Golden Friars, to Naples for the winter. She was to pass the summer in Switzerland, and the autumn somewhere in the north of Italy, and again she was to winter in her old quarters at Naples. We had little chance, therefore, of seeing her again in England for more than a year. Her letters were written in varying spirits, sometimes cheery, sometimes *de profundis*. Sometimes she seemed to think that she was just going to break up and sink; and then her next letter would unfold plans looking far into the future, and talking of her next visit to England. There was an uneasy and even violent fluctuation in these accounts, which did not exactly suggest the idea of a merely fanciful invalid. She spoke at times, also, of intense and exhausting pain. And she mentioned that in Paris she had been in the surgeons' hands, and that there was still uncertainty as to what good they might have done her. This may have been at the root of her hysterical vacillations. But, in addition to this, there was something very odd in Lady Lorrimer's correspondence.

She had told mamma to write to her once a fortnight, and promised to answer punctually; but nothing could be more irregular. At one time, so long an interval as two whole months passed without bringing a line from her. Then, again, she would complain of mamma's want of punctuality. She seemed to have forgotten things that mamma had told her; and sometimes she alluded to things as if she had told them to mamma, which she had never mentioned before. Either the post-office was playing tricks with her letters, or poor Lady Lorrimer was losing her head.

I think, if we had been in a quiet place like Malory, we should have been more uneasy about Lady Lorrimer than, in the whirl of London, we had time to be. There was one odd passage in one of her letters; it was as follows: " Send your letters, not by the post, I move about so much; but, when you have an opportunity, send them by a friend. I wish I were happier. I don't do always as I like. If we were for a time together—but all I do is so uncertain !"

Papa heard more than her letters told of her state of health. A friend of his, who happened to be in Paris at the time, told papa that one of the medical celebrities whom she had consulted there had spoken to him in the most desponding terms of poor Lady Lorrimer's chances of recovery, I do not know whether it was referable to that account of her state of health or simply to the approach of the time when he was to make his *début* in the House; but the fact is that papa gave a great many dinner-parties this season; and mamma took her drives in a new carriage, with a new and very pretty pair of horses; and a great deal of new plate came home; and it was plain that he was making a fresh start in a style suited to his new position, which he assumed to be certain and near. He was playing rather deep upon this throw. It must be allowed, however, that nothing could look more promising.

Sir Luke Pyneweck, a young man, with an estate and an overpowering influence in the town of Shillingsworth, had sat for three years for that borough, not in the House, but in his carriage, or a Bath-chair, in various watering-

places at home and abroad—being, in fact, a miserable invalid. This influential young politician had written a confidential letter, with only two or three slips in spelling and grammar, to his friend the Patronage Secretary, telling him to look out for a man to represent Shillingsworth till he had recovered his health, which was not returning quite so quickly as he expected, and promising his strenuous support to the nominee of the minister. Papa's confidence, therefore, was very reasonably justified, and the matter was looked upon by those sages of the lobbies who count the shadowy noses of unborn Houses of Commons as settled. It was known that the dissolution would take place early in the autumn.

Presently there came a letter to the "whip," from his friend Sir Luke Pyneweck, announcing that he was so much better that he had made up his mind to try once more before retiring.

This was a stunning blow to papa. Sir Luke could do without the government better than the government could do without him. And do or say what they might, no one could carry the borough against him. The Patronage Secretary really liked my father; and, I believe, would have wished him, for many reasons, in the House. But what was to be done? Sir Luke was neither to be managed nor bullied; he was cunning and obstinate. He did not want anything for himself, and did not want anything for any other person. With a patriot of that type who could do anything?

It was a pity the "whip" did not know this before every safe constituency was engaged. A pity papa did not know it before he put an organ into Shillingsworth church, and subscribed six hundred pounds towards the building of the meeting-house. I never saw papa so cast down and excited as he was by this disappointment. Looking very ill, however, he contrived to rally his spirits when he was among his friends, and seemed resolved, one way or other, to conquer fortune.

Balls, dinners, concerts, garden-parties, nevertheless, devoured our time, and our drives, and shopping, and visits went on, as if nothing had happened, and nothing was impending.

P

Two notable engagements for the next week, because
they were connected, in the event, with my strange story,
I mention now. On Tuesday there was Lady Mardykes's
ball, on that day week papa had a political party to dinner,
among whom were some very considerable names indeed.
Lady Mardykes's balls were always, as you know, among the
most brilliant of the season. While dancing one of those
quadrilles that give us breathing time between the round
dances, I saw a face that riveted my attention, and excited
my curiosity. A slight old gentleman, in evening costume,
with one of those obsolete under-waistcoats, which seemed
to me such a pretty fashion (his was of blue satin), was
the person I mean. A forbidding-looking man was this,
with a thin face, as brown as a nut, hawk's eyes and beak,
thin lips, and a certain character of dignified ill-temper,
and even insolence, which, however, did not prevent its
being a very gentleman-like face. I instantly recognised
him as the old man, in the chocolate-coloured coat, who
had talked so sharply, as it seemed to me and poor Nelly,
with Laura Grey on the Milk-walk, in the shadow of the
steep bank and the overhanging trees.

"Who is that old gentleman standing near the door at
the end of the room, with that blue satin about his neck?
Now he's speaking to Lady Westerbroke."

"Oh! that's Lord Rillingdon," answered my friend.

"He does not go to many places? I have seen him, I
think, but once before," I said.

"No, I fancy he does not care about this sort of
thing."

"Doesn't he speak very well? I think I've heard——"

"Yes, he speaks only in Indian debates. He's very well
up on India—he was there, you know."

"Don't you think he looks very cross?" I said.

"They say he is very cross," said my informant, laughing: and here the dance was resumed, and I heard no
more of him.

Old Lord Rillingdon had his eyes about him. He
seemed, as much as possible, to avoid talking to people,
and I thought was looking very busily for somebody. As
I now and then saw this old man, who, from time to time,
changed his point of observation, my thoughts were busy

with Laura Grey, and the pain of my uncertainty returned—pain mingled with remorse. My enjoyment of
this scene contrasted with her possible lot, upbraided me,
and for a time I wished myself at home.

A little later I thought I saw a face that had not been
seen in London for more than a year. I was not quite
sure, but I thought I saw Monsieur Droqville. In rooms
so crowded, one sometimes has so momentary a peep of a
distant face that recognition is uncertain. Very soon I
saw him again, and this time I had no doubt whatever.
He seemed as usual, chatty, and full of energy; but I
soon saw, or at least fancied, that he did not choose to
see mamma or me. It is just possible I may have been
doing him wrong. I did not see him, it is true, so much
as once glance towards us; but Doctor or Monsieur Droqville was a man who saw everything, as Rebecca Torkill
would say, with half an eye—always noting everything
that passed; full of curiosity, suspicion, and conclusion,
and with an eye quick and piercing as a falcon's.

This man, I thought, had seen, and was avoiding us,
without wishing to appear to do so. It so happened,
however, that some time later, in the tea-room, mamma
was placed beside him. I was near enough to hear.
Mamma recognised him with a smile and a little bow.
He replied with just surprise enough in his looks and
tones to imply that he had not known, up to that moment,
that she was there.

"You are surprised to see me here?" he said; "I can
scarcely believe it myself. I've been away thirteen
months—a wanderer all over Europe; and I shall be off
again in a few days. By-the-bye, you hear from Lady
Lorrimer sometimes: I saw her at Naples, in January.
She was looking flourishing then, but complaining a good
deal. She has not been so well since—but I'll look in
upon you to-morrow or the next day. I shall be sure to
see her again, immediately. Your friends, the Wiclyffs,
were at Baden this summer, so were the D'Acres. Lord
Charles is to marry that French lady; it turns out she's
rather an heiress; it is very nearly arranged, and they
seemed all very well pleased. Have you seen my friend
Carmel lately?"

"About three weeks ago; he was going to North Wales," she said.

"He is another of those interesting people who are always dying, and never die," said Monsieur Droqville.

I felt a growing disgust for this unfeeling man. He talked a little longer, and then turned to me and said:

"There's one advantage, Miss Ware, in being an old fellow—one can tell a young lady, in such charming and brilliant looks as yours to-night, what he thinks, just as he might give his opinion upon a picture. But I won't venture mine; I'll content myself with making a petition. I only ask that, when you are a very great lady, you'll remember a threadbare doctor, who would be very glad of an humble post about the court, and who is tired of wandering over the world in search of happiness, and finding a fee only once in fifty miles."

I do not know what was in this man's mind at that moment. If he was a Jesuit, he certainly owed very little to those arts and graces of which rumour allows so large a share to the order. But brusque and almost offensive as I thought him, there was something about him that seemed to command acceptance, and carry him everywhere he chose to go. He went away, and I saw him afterwards talking now to one great lady, and now to another. Lord Rillingdon, who looked like the envious witch whom Madame D'Aulnois introduces sometimes at the feasts of her happy kings and queens, throwing a malign gloom on all about them, had vanished.

That night, however, was to recall, as unexpectedly, another face, a more startling reminder of Malory and Laura Grey.

CHAPTER XXXVI.

NEWS OF LADY LORRIMER.

LD Lord Verney, of all persons in the world, took a fancy to take me down to the tea-room. I think he believed, as other wiser people did, that papa, who was certainly clever, and a very shrewd club-house politician, might come to be somebody in the House, in time.

As usual, he was telling an interminable story, without point or beginning or end, about himself, and all mixed up with the minister, and the opposition leader, and an amendment, and some dismal bill, that I instantly lost my way in. As we entered the tea-room, a large room opening from the landing, he nodded, without interrupting his story, to a gentleman who was going downstairs. My eye followed this recognition, and I saw a tall, rather good-looking young man. I saw him only for a moment. I was so startled that I involuntarily almost stopped Lord Verney as we passed; but I recovered myself instantly. It was tantalising. He always talks as if he were making a speech; one can't, without rudeness, edge in a word; he is so pompous, I dare not interrupt him. He did that office for himself, however, by taking an ice; and I seized the transitory silence, and instantly asked him the name of the gentleman to whom he had bowed; I thought he said, "Mr. Jennings," and as a clever artist of that odd name had lately painted a portrait of Lord Verney, I was satisfied that I had heard him aright.

This was to be a night of odd recognitions. I was engaged to Lord John Roxford, who came up, and saying, "I think this is our dance, Miss Ware?" took me away,

to my great relief, from Lord Verney. Well, we danced
and talked a little ; and I learned nothing that I remember, except that he was to return to Paris the next day.
Before he took me to mamma, however, he said :

"A very dear friend has asked me, as the greatest
favour I can do him, to introduce him to you, Miss Ware ;
you will allow me ?"

He repeated, I thought—for he was looking for him,
and his face at that moment was turned a little away, and
the noise considerable—the same name that Lord Verney
had mentioned. As Rebecca Torkill used to say, "my
heart jumped into my mouth," as I consented. A moment
more, and I found myself actually acquainted with the
very man ! How strange it seemed ! Was that smiling
young man of fashion the same I had seen stretched on
the rugged peat and roots at Plas Ylwd, with white face
and leaden lips, and shirt soaked in blood ? He was, with
his white-gloved hand on the pier-table beside me, inquiring what dance I could give him. I was engaged for this ;
but I could not risk the chance of forfeiting my talk with
my new acquaintance. I gave it to him, and having the
next at my disposal, transferred it to the injured man
whom I had ousted.

The squabble, the innocent surprise, the regrets, the
other hypocrisies, and finally the compromise over, away
we went to take our places in the quadrille. I was glad it
was not a round dance. I wanted to hear him talk a
little. How strange it seemed to me, standing beside him
in this artifical atmosphere of wax-light and music ! Each
affecting the air of an acquaintance made then and there ;
each perfectly recognising the other, as we stood side by
side talking of the new primo tenore, the play, the Aztecs,
and I know not what besides !

This young man's manner was different from what I
had been accustomed to in ball-rooms. There was
none of the trifling, and no sign of the admiration
which the conversation and looks of others seemed to
imply. His tone, perfectly gentleman-like, was merely
friendly, and he seemed to take an interest in me, much
as I fancied an unknown relation might. We talked of
things of no particular interest, until he happened to

ask something of my occasional wanderings in the country.
It was my opportunity, and I seized it like a general.

" I like the country," I said. " I enjoy it thoroughly ;
I've lived nearly all my life in the country, in a place I
am so fond of, called Malory. I think all about there so
beautiful ! It is close to Cardyllion—have you ever seen
Cardyllion ?"

" Yes, I've been to Cardyllion once—only once, I think.
I did not see a great deal of it. But you, now, see a great
deal more of the country—you have been to the lakes ?"

" Oh ! yes ; but I want to ask how you liked Cardyllion.
How long is it since you were there ?"

"About two years, or a little more, perhaps," he
answered.

" Oh ! that's just about the time the Conway Castle
was wrecked—how awful that was ! I had a companion
then, my dearest friend—Laura Grey was her name ; she
left us so suddenly, when I was away from Malory, and I
have never seen her since. I have been longing so to
meet any one who could tell me anything about her. You
don't happen to know any one, do you, who knows a young
lady of that name ? I make it a rule to ask every one I
can ; and I'm sure I shall make her out at last."

"Nothing like perseverance," said he. " I shall be
most happy to be enlisted ; and if I should light upon a
lady of that name, I may tell her that Miss Ware is very
well, and happy ?"

"No, not happy—at least, not quite happy, until she writes
to tell me where she is, or comes to see me ; and tell her I
could not have believed she would have been so unkind."

Conversations are as suddenly cut short in ball-rooms
as they are in a beleaguered city, where the head of one of
the interlocutors is carried off by a round-shot. Our
dialogue ended with the sudden arrival of the ill-used man,
whom I could no longer postpone, and who carried me off,
very much vexed, as you may suppose, and scarcely giving
my companion time to make a bow.

Never was "fast dance" so slow as this ! At length it
was over, and wherever I went my eyes wandered hither
and thither in search of the tall young man with whom I
had danced. The man who had figured in a scene which

had so often returned to my imagination was now gone;
I saw him neither in the dancing-rooms nor in any others.
By this time there was a constant double current to and
from the supper-room, up and down the stairs. As I went
down, immediately before me was Monsieur Droqville.
He did not follow the stream, but passed into the hall.

Monsieur Droqville put on his loose black wrapper, and
wound a shawl about his throat, and glanced, from habit,
with his shrewd, hard eyes at the servants as he passed
through them in the hall. He jumped into a cab, told
the driver where to stop, lighted a cigar, and smoked.
He got out at the corner of a fashionable but rather
dingy street not very far away. Then he dismissed his
vehicle, walked up the pavement smoking, passed into a
still quieter street, also fashionable, that opens from it at
an obtuse angle. Here he walked slowly, and, as it were,
softly. The faint echo of his own steps was the only
sound that met him as he entered it. He crossed, threw
his head back, and shrewdly scanned the upper windows,
blowing out a thin stream of tobacco-smoke as he looked.
"Not flown yet, *animula, vagula blandula?* Still on
the perch," he said, as he crossed the street again.
His cigar was just out, and he threw it away as he
reached the steps. He did not need to knock or ring; he
admitted himself with a latch-key. A bedroom candlestick in the hall had a candle still burning in it. He took
it and walked quietly up. The boards of the stairs and
lobbies were bare, and a little dust lay on the wall and
bannister, indicating the neglected state of a house abandoned by its tenants for a journey or a very long stay in
the country. He opened the back drawing-room door and
put his head in. A pair of candles lighted the room. A
thin elderly lady, in an odd costume, was the only person
there. She wore a white, quilted headcloth, a black robe,
and her beads and cross were at her side. She was reading, with spectacles on, a small book which she held open
in both hands, as he peeped in. With a slight start she
rose. There was a little crucifix on the table, and a
coloured print of the Madonna hung on the wall, on the
nail from which a Watteau had been temporarily removed.

"Has your patient been anointed yet?" said Monsieur Droqville, in his short nasal tones.

"Not yet, reverend father," she answered. They were both speaking French.

"Has she been since nearly *in articulo?*"

"At about eleven o'clock, reverend father, her soul seemed at her very lips."

"In this complaint so it will often be. Is Sister Cecilia upstairs?"

"Yes, reverend father."

"Father Edwyn here?"

"Yes, reverend father."

He withdrew his head, closed the door, and walked upstairs. He tapped gently at the door of the front bedroom.

A French nun, in a habit precisely similar to that of the lady downstairs, stood noiselessly at the door. She was comparatively young, wore no spectacles, and had a kind and rather sad countenance. He whispered a word to her, heard her answer softly, and then he entered the room with a soundless step—it was thickly carpeted, and furnished luxuriously—and stood at the side of a huge four-post bed, with stately curtains of silk, within which a miserable shrunken old woman, with a face brown as clay, sunk and flaccid, and staring feebly with wide glassy eyes, with her back coiled into a curve, and laden with shawls, was set up, among pillows, breathing, or rather gasping, with difficulty.

Here she was, bent, we may say, in the grip of two murderers, heart complaint and cancer. The irresistible chemistry of death had set in; the return of "earth to earth" was going on. Who could have recognised, in this breathing effigy of death, poor Lady Lorrimer? But disease now and then makes short work of such transformations.

The good nurse here, like the other downstairs, had her little picture against the wall, and had been curtseying and crossing herself before it, in honest prayer for the dying old lady, to whom Monsieur Droqville whispered something, and then leaned his ear close to her lips. He felt her pulse, and said, "Madame has some time still to meditate and pray."

Again his ear was to her lips. "Doubt it not, madame. Every consolation."

She whispered something more; it lasted longer, and was more earnest this time. Her head was nodding on her shoulders, and her eyes were turned up to his dark energetic face, imploringly.

"You can't do that, madame—it is not yours—you have given it to God."

The woman turned her eyes on him with a piteous look.

"No, madame," he said, sharply; "it is too late to withhold a part. This, madame, is temptation—a weakness of earth; the promises are to her that overcometh."

Her only answer was an hysterical whimper and imperfect sobbing.

"Be calm," he resumed. "It is meritorious. Discharge your mind of it, and the memory of your sacrifice will be sweeter, and its promise more glorious the nearer you draw to your darkest hour on earth."

She had another word to say; her fingers were creeping on the coverlet to his hand.

"No, madame, there won't be any struggle—you will faint, that is all, and waken, we trust among the blest. I'm sorry I can't stay just now. But Father Edwyn is here, and Dr. Garnet."

Again she turned her wavering head towards him, and lifted her eyes, as if to speak.

"No, no, you must not exert yourself—husband your strength—you'll want it, madame."

It was plain, however, she would have one last word more, and a little sourly he stooped his ear again.

"Pardon me, madame, I never said or supposed that after you signed it you were still at liberty to deal with any part; if you have courage to take it back, it is another matter. I won't send you before the Judge Eternal with a sacrilege in your right hand."

He spoke quietly, but very sternly, raising his finger upward, with his eyes fixed upon her, while his dark face looked pale.

She answered only with the same helpless whimper. He beckoned to the nun.

"Let me see that book."

He looked through its pages.

"Read aloud to madame the four first elevations; agony is near."

As he passed from the room, he beckoned the lady in the religious habit again, and whispered in her ear in the lobby:

"Lock this door, and admit none but those you know."

He went down this time to the front drawing-room, and entered it suddenly. Mr. Carmel was seated there, with candles beside him, reading. Down went his book instantly, and he rose.

"Our good friend upstairs won't last beyond three or four hours—possibly five," began Monsieur Droqville. "Garnet will be here in a few minutes; keep the doors bolted! people might come in and disturb the old lady. You need not mind now. I locked the hall-door as I came in. Why don't you make more way with Miss Ware? Her mother is no obstacle—favourable rather. Her father is a mere pagan, and never at home; and the girl likes you."

Mr. Carmel stared.

"Yes, you are blind; but I have my eyes. Why don't you read your Montaigne? '*Les agaceries des femmes sont des declarations d'amour.*' You interest her, and yet you profit nothing by your advantage. There she is, romantic, passionate, Quixotic, and makes, without knowing it, a hero of you. You are not what I thought you."

Mr. Carmel's colour flushed to his very temples; he looked pained and agitated; his eyes were lowered before his superior.

"Why need you look like a fool? Understand me," continued Monsieur Droqville, in his grim, harsh nasals. "The weaknesses of human nature are Heaven's opportunities. The godly man knows how to use them with purity. She is not conscious of the position she gives you; but you should understand its powers. You can illuminate, elevate, save her."

He paused for a moment; Mr. Carmel stood before him with his eyes lowered.

"What account am I to give of you?" he resumed. "Remember, you have no business to be afraid. You

must use all influences to save a soul, and serve the
Church. A good soldier fights with every weapon he has
—sword, pistol, bayonet, fist—in the cause of his king.
What shall I say of you? A loyal soldier, but wanting
head, wanting action, wanting presence of mind. A
theorist, a scholar, a deliberator. But not a man for the
field; no *coup d'œil*, no promptitude, no perception of a
great law, where it is opposed by a small quibble, no power
of deciding between a trifle and an enormity, between seeing your king robbed or breaking the thief's fingers. Why,
can't you see that the power that commands is also the
power that absolves? I thought you had tact—I thought
you had insinuation. Have I been mistaken? If so, we
must cut out other work for you. Have you anything
to say?"

He paused only for a second, and in that second Mr.
Carmel raised his head to speak; but with a slight downward motion of his hand, and a frown, Droqville silenced
him, and proceeded:

"True, I told you not to precipitate matters. But you
need not let the fire go out, because I told you not to set
the chimney in a blaze. There is Mrs. Ware; her most
useful position is where she is, *in equilibrio*. She can
serve no one by declaring herself a Catholic; the *éclat* of
such a thing would spoil the other mission, that must be
conducted with judgment and patience. The old man I
told you of is a Puritan, and must see or suspect nothing.
While he lives there can be no avowal. But up to that
point all must now proceed. Ha! there goes a carriage
—that's the third I have heard—Lady Mardykes's party
breaking up. The Wares don't return this way. I'll see
you again to-morrow. To-night you accomplish your
duty here. The old woman upstairs will scarcely last till
dawn."

He nodded and left the room as suddenly as he had
entered it.

CHAPTER XXXVII.

A LAST LOOK.

T about eleven o'clock next morning, mamma came to my bedside, having thrown her dressing-gown on, and holding a note in her hand. I was awakened by her calling me by my name; and the extraordinary exertion of getting out of her bed at such an hour, the morning after a ball, even if there had not been consternation in her looks, would have satisfied me that something unusual had happened. I sat up staring at her.

"Oh, dear Ethel, here's a note from Doctor Droqville; I'm so shocked—poor, dear Aunt Lorrimer is dead." And mamma burst into tears, and, sobbing, told me to read the note, which, so soon as I had a little collected myself, I did. It said :

"DEAR MRS. WARE,—I could not, of course, last night tell you the sad news about Lady Lorrimer. She arrived, it seems, on Tuesday last, to die in England. On leaving Lady Mardykes's last night, I went to her house to make inquiries; she was good enough to wish to see me. I found her in a most alarming state, and quite conscious of her danger. She was sinking rapidly. I was, therefore, by no means surprised, on calling about half an hour ago, to learn that she was no more. I lose no time in communicating the sad intelligence. It will be consolatory to you to learn that the nurses, who were present during her last moments, tell me that she died without any pain or struggle. I shall call to morrow, as near twelve as I can, to learn whether there is anything in which you think my poor services can be made available.—I remain, dear Mrs. Ware, Ever yours sincerely,

P. DROQVILLE."

I was very sorry. I even shed some tears, a thing oftener written about than done.

Mamma cried for a long time. She had now no near kinswoman left. When we are "pretty well on," and the thinned ranks of one generation only stand between us and death, the disappearance of the old over the verge is a serious matter. Between mamma and Lady Lorrimer, too, there were early recollections and sympathies in common, and the chasm was not so wide.

But for the young, and I was then young, the old seem at best a sort of benevolent ghosts, whose presence, more or less, chills and awes, and whose home is not properly with the younger generation. Their memories are busy with a phantom world that passed away before we were born. They are puckered masks and glassy eyes, peeping from behind the door of the sepulchre that stands ajar, closing little by little to shut them in for ever. I am now but little past forty, yet I feel this isolation stealing upon me. I acquiesce in the law of nature, though it seems a cynical one. I know I am no longer of the young; I grow shy of them; there is a real separation between us.

The world is for the young—it belongs to them, and time makes us ugly, and despised, and solitary, and prepares for our unregretted removal, for nature has ordained that death shall trouble the pleasure and economy of the vigorous, high-spirited world as little as may be.

Mamma was more grieved, a great deal, than I at all expected. I am writing now in solitude, and from my interior convictions, under a sort of obligation to tell, not only nothing but the truth, but the whole truth also; and I confess that mamma was selfish, and, in a degree, exacting. The education of her whole married life had tended to form those habits; but she was also affectionate, and her grief was vehement, and did not subside, as I thought it would, after its first outburst. The only practical result of her grief was a determination to visit the house, and see the remains of the poor lady.

I never could understand the comfort that some people seem to derive from contemplating such a spectacle! To me the sight is simply shocking. Mamma made it a point, however, that I should accompany her. She could not make up her mind to go that day. The next day Doctor Droqville called. Mamma saw him. After they had talked for a little, mamma declared her intention of seeing poor Lady Lorrimer as she lay in her bed.

"Allow me to advise you, as a physician, to do no such thing," said Droqville. "You'll inflict a great deal of pain on yourself, and do nobody any good."

"But unless I see her once more I shall be miserable," pleaded mamma.

"You have not nerve for such scenes," he replied; "you'd not be yourself again for a month after."

I joined my entreaties to Doctor Droqville's representations, and I thought we had finally prevailed over mamma's facile will.

He gave us a brief account of Lady Lorrimer's illness and last moments, and then talked on other subjects; finally he said, "You told me you wished me to return a bracelet that does not answer, to St. Aumand, when I pass again through Paris. I find I shall be there in a few days—can you let me have it now?"

Mamma's maid was out, so she went to get it herself, and, while she was away, Doctor Droqville said to me, with rather a stern look:

"Don't you allow her to go; your mamma has a form of the same affection of the heart. We can't tell her that; but quiet nerves are essential to her. She touches the spring of the mischief, and puts it in action at any moment by agitating herself."

"I think she has given up that intention," I answered; "but for Heaven's sake, Doctor Droqville, tell me, is mamma in any danger?"

"No, if she will only keep quiet. She may live for many years to come; but every woman, of course, who has a weakness of the kind, may kill herself easily and quickly; but—I hear her—don't allow her to go."

Mamma returned, and Doctor Droqville soon took his departure, leaving me very miserable, and very much alarmed. She now talked only of postponing her last look at poor Lady Lorrimer until to-morrow. Her vacillations were truly those of weakness, but they were sometimes violent; and when her emotions overcame her indolence, she was not easily managed.

The dark countenance of Doctor Droqville, as he urged his prohibition, excited vague suspicions. It was by no means benevolent—it was grim, and even angry. It struck me instinctively that he might have some motive, other than the kind one which he professed, in wishing to scare away mamma from the house of death.

Doctor Droqville was, I believe, a very clever physician; but his visits to England, being desultory, he could not, of course, take the position of any but an occasional adviser. He had acquired an influence over mamma, and I think if he had been a resident in London, she would have consulted no other. As matters were, however, Sir Jacob Lake was her "physician in ordinary." To him I wrote the moment I had an opportunity, stating what had occurred, enclosing his fee, and begging of him to look in about two next day, on any pretext he could think of, to determine the question.

Next day came, and with two o'clock, just as we were sitting down to lunch, Sir Jacob arrived. I ran up instantly to the drawing-room, leaving mamma to follow, for sages of his kind have not many minutes to throw away. He relieved my mind a little about mamma, but not quite, and before he had spoken half-a-dozen sentences she came in. He made an excuse of poor Lady Lorrimer's death, and had brought with him two or three letters of hers, describing her case, which he thought might be valuable should any discussion arise respecting the nature of her disease.

The conversation thus directed, I was enabled to put the question on which Doctor Droqville had been so peremptory. Sir Jacob said there was nothing to prevent mamma's going, and that she was a great deal more likely to be agitated by a dogged opposition to a thing she had so set her heart on.

Now that mamma found herself quite at liberty to go, I think she grew a little frightened. She was looking ill; she had eaten nearly nothing for the last two days, seen nobody but Doctor Droqville and the doctor who had just now called, and her head was full of her mourning and

mine. Her grief was very real. Through Lady Lorrimer's
eyes she had been accustomed to look back into her own
early life. They had both seen the same scenes and people
that she remembered, and now there was no one left with
whom she could talk over old times. Mamma was irresolute till late in the afternoon, and then at last she made
up her mind.

We drove through half-a-dozen streets. I did not know
in what street my poor aunt Lorrimer's house was. We
suddenly pulled up, and the footman came to the door to
say that there was a chain across the street at each end.
We had nothing for it but to get out and to walk past the
paviors who had taken possession of it. The sun was, I
suppose, at this time about setting. The sunlight fell
faintly on the red brick chimneys above, but all beneath
was dark and cold. In its present state it was a melancholy and silent street. It was, I instantly saw, the very
same street in which Lady Lorrimer had chosen to pass
me by.

"Is that the house, the one with the tan before it?" I
asked.

It was. I was now clear upon the point. Into that
house I had seen her go. The woman in the odd costume
who had walked beside her, Mr. Carmel's thin figure and
melancholy ascetic face, and the silence in which they
moved, were all remembered, and recalled the sense of
curious mystery with which I had observed the parting,
more than two years ago, and mingled an unpleasant ingredient in the gloom that deepened about me as I now
approached the door.

It was all to be cleared up soon. The door was instantly
opened by a man in black placed in the hall. A man also
in black, thin, very perpendicular, with a long neck, sallow
face, and black eyes, very stern, passed us by in silence
with a glance. He turned about before he reached the hall
door, and in a low tone, a little grimly, inquired our business. I told him, and also who we were.

We were standing at the foot of the stairs. On hearing
our names he took off his hat, and, more courteously,
requested us to wait for a moment where we were, till he
should procure a person to conduct us to the room. This

Q

man was dressed something in the style of our own High-Church divines, except that his black coat was longer, I think. He had hardly left us when there was a ring at the bell, and a poor woman, holding a little girl by the hand, came in, whispered to the man in the hall, and then, passing us by, went up the stairs in silence and disappeared. They were met by a second clergyman coming down, rather corpulent, with a tallowy countenance and spectacles, who looked at us suspiciously, and went out just as a party of three came into the hall, and passed us by like the former.

Almost immediately the clergyman we had first met returned, and conducted us up the stairs as far as the first landing, where we were met by a lady in a strange brown habit, with a rosary, and a hood over her head, whom I instantly knew to be a nun. We followed her up the stairs. There was a strange air of mystery and of publicity in the proceedings; the house seemed pretty well open to all comers; no one who whispered a few words satisfactorily to the porter in the hall failed to obtain immediate access to the upper floor of the house. Everything was carried on in whispers, and there was a perpetual tramping of feet slowly going up and down stairs.

It was much more silent as we reached the level of the drawing-rooms. The nun opened the back drawing-room, and without more ceremony than a quiet movement of her hand, signed to us to go in. I think mamma's heart half failed her; I almost hoped she would change her mind, for she hesitated, and sighed two or three times heavily, with her hand pressed to her heart, and looked very faint.

The light that escaped through the half-opened door was not that of day, but the light of candles. Mamma took my arm, and in silence hurried me into the room.

Now I will tell you what I saw. The room was hung with black, which probably enhanced the effect of its size, for it appeared very large. The windows were concealed by the hangings of black cloth, which were continued without interruption round all the walls of the room. A great many large wax candles were burning in it, and the black background, reflecting no light, gave to all the objects standing in the room an odd sharpness and relief.

At the far end of the apartment stood a sort of platform,

about as wide as a narrow bed, covered with a deep velvet
cushion, with a drapery of the same material descending
to the floor. On this lay the body of Lady Lorrimer,
habited in the robes and hood of the order, I think, of the
Carmelites; her hands were placed together on her breast,
and her rosary was twined through her fingers. The hood
was drawn quite up about the head and cheeks of the
corpse. Her dress, the cushion on which she lay, the
pillow creased by the pressure of her cold head, were strewn
with flowers. I had resolved not to look at it—such sights
haunt me afterwards; but an irresistible curiosity overcame me. It was just one momentary glance, but the
picture has remained on my inner sight ever since, as if I
had gazed for an hour.

There was at the foot of this catafalque an altar, on
which was placed a large crucifix; huge candlesticks with
tall tapers stood on the floor beside it. Many of the
strangers who came in kneeled before the crucifix and
prayed, no doubt for the departed spirit. Many smaller
crucifixes were hung upon the walls, and before these also
others of the visitors from time to time said a prayer.
Two nuns stood one at each side of the body, like effigies
of contemplation and prayer, telling their beads. It seemed
to me that there was a profusion of wax-lights. The
transition from the grey evening light, darker in the house,
into this illumination of tapers, had a strange influence
upon my imagination. The reality of the devotion, and
the more awful reality of death, quite overpowered the
theatrical character of the effect.

I saw the folly of mamma's irrepressible desire to come
here. I thought she was going to faint; I dare say she
would have done so, she looked so very ill, but that tears
relieved her. They were tears in which grief had but a
subordinate share; they were nervous tears, the thunder-
shower of the hysteria which had been brewing ever since
she had entered the room. I don't know whether she was
sorry that she had come. I am sure she would have been
better if she had never wished it.

CHAPTER XXXVIII.

STORM.

A FEW days later, mamma and I were talking in the drawing-room, when the door opened, and papa came in, his umbrella in his hand, and his hat on his head, looking as white as death. He stood for a time without speaking. We were both staring in his face, as dumb as he.

"Droqville's a villain!" he said, suddenly. "They have got that miserable old fool's money—every guinea. I told you how it would be, and now it has all happened!"

"What has happened?" asked mamma, still gazing at him, with a look of terror. I was myself freezing with horror. I never saw despair so near the verge of madness in a human face before as in papa's.

"What? We're ruined! If there's fifty pounds in the bank it's all, and only that between us and nothing."

"My God!" exclaimed mamma, whiter than ever, and almost in a whisper.

"Your God! What are you talking about? It is you that have done it all—filling the house with priests and Jesuits. I knew how it would be, you fool!"

Papa was speaking with the sternness of actual fury.

"I'm not to blame—it is not my doing. Frank, for Heaven's sake, don't speak so—you'll drive me mad! I don't know what they have done—I don't understand it!" cried mamma, and burst into a helpless flood of tears.

"You may as well stop that crying—you can do it in the streets by-and-by. Understand it? By Heaven, you'll understand it well enough before long. I hope you may, as you deserve it!"

With those dreadful looks, and a voice hoarse with

passion, poor papa strode out of the room, and we heard him shut the hall-door after him with a crash.

We were left with the vaguest ideas of the nature of our misfortune; his agitation was so great as to assure me that an alarming calamity had really befallen us. Mamma cried on. She was frightened by his evident alarm, and outraged by his violence, so shocking in one usually so gay, gentle, and serene. She went up to her room to cry there, and to declare herself the most miserable of women. Her maid gave her sal-volatile, and I, seeing no good or comfort in my presence, ran down to the drawing-room. I had hardly got into the room, when whom should I see arriving at the door in a cab, with some papers in his hand, but Mr. Forrester, papa's principal attorney. I knew papa was out, and I was so afraid of his attorney's going away without giving us any light on the subject of our alarms that I ran downstairs, and told the servant to show him into the dining-room, and on no account to let him go away. I went into the room myself, and there awaited him. In came Mr. Forrester, and looked surprised at finding me only.

"Oh! Mr. Forrester," I said, going quickly to him, and looking up in his eyes, "what is this about Lady Lorrimer, and—are we quite ruined?"

"Ruined?" he repeated. "Oh, dear, not at all," and he threw a cautionary glance towards the door, and lowered his voice a little. "Why should you be ruined? It's only a disappointment. It has been very artfully done, and I was only this moment at the Temple talking the will over with one of the best men at the Bar, to whom I'm to send a brief, though I can't see, myself, any good that is likely to come of it. Everything has been done, you see, under the best possible advice, and all the statutes steered clear of. Her estates were all turned into money—that is, the reversions sold—two years ago. The whole thing is very nearly a quarter of a million, all in money, and the will declares no trust—a simple bequest. I haven't the slightest hope of any case on the ground of undue influence. I daresay she was, in the meaning of the law, a perfectly free agent; and if she was not, depend upon it we shall never find it out."

"But does it do us any particular injury?" I inquired, not understanding one sentence in three that he spoke.

"Why, no injury, except a disappointment. In the natural course of things, all this, or the bulk of it, might very likely have come to you here. But only that. It now goes elsewhere: and I fear there is not the least chance of disturbing it."

"Then we are not ruined?" I repeated.

He looked at me, as if he were not quite sure of my meaning, and with a smile, answered:

"You are not a bit worse off than you were a year ago. She might have left you money, but she could take nothing from you. You have property at Cardyllion, I think, a place called Malory, and more at Golden Friars, and other things besides. But your country solicitors would know all about those things."

And thus having in some measure reassured me, he took his leave, saying he would go to papa's clubs to look for him.

I ran up to mamma, more cheerful than when I had left her. She, also, was cheered by my report, and being comforted on the immediate subject of her alarm, she began to think that his excitement was due to some fresh disappointment in his electioneering projects, and her resentment at his ill-temper increased.

This was the evening of papa's political dinner-party. A gentleman's party strictly it was to be, and he did not choose to allow poor Aunt Lorrimer's death to prevent it. Perhaps he was sorry now that he had not postponed it; but it was too late to think of that. We were very near the close of the session. The evenings were perceptibly shortening. I remember every particular connected with that evening and night, with a sharp precision.

Papa came in at dusk. He ran upstairs, and before dressing he came into mamma's bedroom, where I was sitting at her bedside. He looked tired and ill, but was comparatively tranquil now.

"Never mind, May," he said; "it will all come right, I daresay. I wish this dinner was not to be till to-morrow. They are talking of putting me up for Dawling. One way or other, we must not despair yet. I'll come up

and see you when they go away. We are a small party
—only nine, you know—and I don't think there are two
among them who won't be of very real use to me. If I
get in, I don't despair. I have been very low before, two
or three times, and we've got up again. I don't see why
we shouldn't now, as we did before."

Judging by his looks, you would have said that papa
had just got out of a sick-bed, pale, ill, haggard. He
looked at his watch ; it was later than he thought, and he
went away. We heard him ring for his man, and presently
the double knocks began at the hall-door, and his party
were arriving. Mamma was not very well, and whenever
she was, or fancied herself ill, papa slept in another bed-
room, adjoining hers, with a dressing-room off it. Ours was
a large house, handsomer than would naturally have fallen
to our lot ; it had belonged to my grandfather, Lord
Chellwood, and when he built the new house in Blank
Street settled this upon his younger son.

Mamma and I had some dinner in her room, and some
tea there also. She had got over her first alarm. Papa's
second visit had been re-assuring, and she took it very
nearly for granted that, after some harassing delays, and
possibly a good deal of worry, the danger, whatever it
was, would subside, as similar dangers had subsided
before, and things would run again in their accustomed
channel.

It was a very animated party ; we could hear the muffled
sound of their talking and laughing from the drawing-room,
where they were now taking their tea and coffee, and
talking, as it seemed, nearly all together. At length, however, the feast was ended, the guests departed, and papa,
according to promise, came upstairs, and, with hardly a
knock at the door, came in. Had he been drinking more
than usual ? I don't know. He was in high spirits. He
was excited, and looked flushed, and talked incessantly,
and laughed ever so much at what seemed to me very
indifferent jokes.

I tried to edge in a question or two about the election
matters, but he did not seem to mind, or even to hear what
I said, but rattled and laughed on in the same breathless
spirits.

"I'm going to bed now," he said, suddenly. "I've ever so much to do to-morrow, and I'm tired. I shall be glad when this thing is all ended."

Mamma called after him, "But you did not bid us good-night." The candle, however, vanished through the second bed-room into the dressing-room, and we heard him shut the door.

"He did not hear," said mamma; "his head is so full of his election. He seems very well. I suppose everything will be right, after all."

So mamma and I talked on for a little; but it was high time that she should settle to rest. I kissed her, and away I went to my own room. There my maid, as she brushed my hair, told me all the rumours of the servants' hall and the housekeeper's room about papa's electioneering prospects. All promised great things, and, absurd as these visions were, there was something cheering in listening to them. It was past twelve by the time my maid left

Very shortly after I heard a step come to my door, and papa asked, "Can I come in, dear, to say a word?"

"Oh! yes; certainly, papa," I answered, a little curious.

"I won't sit down," he said, looking round the room vaguely. He laid his candle on my table; he had a small box in his hand, in which mamma had told me he kept little lozenges of opium, his use of which had lately given her a great deal of secret uneasiness. "I have found it all out. It was that villain Droqville who did it all. He has brought us very low—broken my heart, my poor child!' He heaved a great sigh. "If that woman had never lived, if we had never heard of her, I should not have been so improvident. But that's all over. You must read your Bible, Ethel; it is a good book; there's something in it—something in it. That governess, Miss Grey, was a good woman. I say you are young; you are not spoiled yet. You must read a little bit every night, or I'll come and scold you. Do you mind? You look very well, Ethel. You must not let your spirits down—your courage. I wish it was morning. All in good time. Get to sleep, darling. Good night—good-bye." He kissed me on the cheek and departed.

I was soon fast asleep. I think the occurrences of the earlier part of the day had made me nervous. I awoke with a start, and a vague consciousness of having been in the midst of an unpleasant dream. I thought I heard mamma call me. I jumped out of bed, threw my dressing-gown about me, and, with bare feet, walked along the lobby, now quite dark, towards mamma's door. When I got almost to it I suddenly recollected that I could not have heard mamma's voice in my room from hers. In total darkness, solitude, and silence, I experienced the sort of chill which accompanies the discovery of such an illusion. I was just turning about, to make a hasty retreat to my own room, when I did hear mamma's voice. I heard her call papa's name, and then there was a silence. I changed my mind. I went on, and tapped at her door. Rather nervously she asked, "Who's there?" and on hearing me answer, told me to come in. There was only the night-light she usually had burning in her room. She was sitting up in her bed, and told me she had been startled by seeing papa looking in at the door (she nodded toward the one that opened to his bedroom). The night-light was placed on a little table close beside it.

"And oh! my dear Ethel, he looked so horribly ill I was frightened; I hardly knew him, and I called to him, but he only said, 'That's enough,' and drew back, and shut the door. He looked so ill, that I should have followed him in, but I found the door locked, and I heard him shut the door of his dressing-room. Do you think he is ill?"

"Oh! no, mamma; if he had been ill he'd have told you so; I'm sure it was the miserable light in this room—everything looks so strange in it." And so with a few words more we bid good-night once again; and, having seen her reclining with her head on her pillow, I made my way back again to my own room.

I felt very uncomfortable; the few words mamma had said presented an image that somehow was mysterious and ill-omened. I held my door open, and listened with my head stretched into the dark. Papa's dressing-room door was nearly opposite. I was re-assured by hearing his step on the floor; then I heard something move; I closed my door once more, and got into bed.

The laws of acoustics are, I believe, well ascertained; and, of course, they never vary. But their action, I confess, has often puzzled me.

In the house where I now write, there are two rooms separated only by a narrow passage, in one of which, under a surgical operation, three dreadful shrieks were uttered, not one of which was, even faintly, heard in the other room, where two near and loving relations awaited the result in the silence and agony of suspense. In the same way, but not so strikingly, because the interposing space is considerably greater, no sound was ever heard in mamma's room, from papa's dressing-room, when the doors were shut. But from my door, when the rest of the house was silent, you could very distinctly hear a heavy step, or any other noise, in that room.

My visit to mamma's room had, as nurses say, "put my sleep astray," and I lay awake until I began to despair of going to sleep again till morning. From my meditations in the dead silence, I was suddenly startled by a sound like the clapping of the dressing-room door with one violent clang. I jumped up again; I thought I should hear papa's step running down the stairs, and all my wild misgivings returned. I put my head out of the door, and listened. I heard no step—nothing stirring. Once more in my dressing-gown I stole out; his candle was still burning, for I saw a ray of light slanting towards the lobby floor from the keyhole of his room, with the motes quivering in it. It pointed like a wand to something white that lay upon the ground. I remembered that this was the open leaf of the old Bible—too much neglected book, alas! in our house—that had fallen from its little shelf on the lobby, and which I had been specially moved to replace as I passed it an hour or two before, seeing, in my superstitious mood, omens in all things. Hurried on, however, by mamma's voice calling me, I had not carried out my intention.

"Dislodged from your place, you may be," I now thought, as I stooped to take the book in my hand; "but never to be trampled on!"

I was interrupted by a voice, a groan, I thought from inside the dressing-room.

I was not quite certain; staring breathlessly at the door, I listened; no sound followed. I stepped to the door and knocked. No answer came. With my lips close to the door, and my hand upon the handle, I called, "Papa, papa, papa!" I was frightened; I pushed open the door, and hesitated. I called again, "Papa—answer, answer! Are you there, papa?" I was calling upon silence. With a little effort I stepped in.

The candle was burning on the table; there was a film of blue smoke hovering in the air—a faint smell of burning. I saw papa lying on the floor; he appeared to have dropped from the arm-chair, and to have fallen over on his back; a pistol lay by his half-open hand; the side of his face looked black and torn, as if a thunderbolt had scorched him, and a stream of blood seemed throbbing from his ear.

The smell of powder, the smoke, the pistol on the ground, told what had happened. Freezing with terror, I screamed the words, "Papa, papa! O God! speak! He's killed!" I was on my knees beside him; he was not quite dead. His eyes were fixed in the earnest stare of the last look, and there was a faint movement of the mouth, as if he were trying to speak. It was only for a few seconds. Then all motion ceased—his jaw fell—he was dead.

I staggered back against the wall, uttering a frightful scream.

Under excitement so tremendous as mine, people, I think, are more than half spiritualized. We seem to find ourselves translated from place to place by thought rather than effort.

It seemed to me only a second after I had left that frightful room, that I stood beside Miss Pounden's bed upstairs. She slept with not only her shutters, but the window open. It was so perfectly silent, the street as well as the house, that through the wall from the nursery next door I could faintly hear a little baby crying. The moonlight shone dazzlingly on the white curtains of Miss Pounden's bed. I shook her by the shoulder, and called her. She started up, and I rememember the odd effect of her wide open eyes, lighted by the white reflection, and staring from the shadow at me with a horror that she caught from my looks.

"Merciful Heaven! Miss Ware—my dear child—why are you here?—what is it?"

"Come with me; we must get help. Papa is dreadfully hurt in the dressing-room. Mamma knows nothing of it; don't say a word as you pass her door."

Together we went down, steadily drawing towards the awful room, from which we saw, at the end of the dark passage, the faint flush of the candle fall on the carpet.

When I told Miss Pounden what had happened, nothing would induce her to come with me beyond the lobby. I had to go into the room alone; I had to look in to be sure that he was actually dead. Oh! it was appalling, incredible. I, Ethel Ware, looking at my handsome, gay, good-natured father, killed by his own hands, the smoke of the fatal shot not yet quite cleared away! Why was there no pitying angel near to call me but a minute earlier? My tap at the door would have arrested his hand, and the moment of temptation would have passed harmlessly by. All too late—for time and eternity all is irretrievable now. One glance was sufficient. I could not breathe; I could not, for some dreadful moments, withdraw my eyes. With a faint cry, I stepped backward. I was trembling violently as I asked Miss Pounden to send any one of the servants for Sir Jacob Lake, and to tell whoever was going not to leave his house without him.

I waited in the drawing-room while she went down, and I heard her call to the servants over the stairs. The message was soon arranged, and the messenger gone. I had not cried all this time; I continued walking quickly about the drawing-room, with my hands clenched together, talking wildly to myself and to God. When Miss Pounden returned, I implored of her not to leave me.

"Come up to my room; we'll wait there till Sir Jacob Lake comes. Mamma must not know it, except as he advises. If she learned it too suddenly, she would lose her mind."

CHAPTER XXXIX.

FAREWELL, MISS WARE.

I DO not mean to describe the terrible scenes that followed. When death comes attended with a scandal like this, every recollection connected with it is torture. The gross and ghastly publicity, the merciless prying into details, and over all the gloom of the maddest and most mysterious of crimes! You look in vain in the shadow for the consoling image. of hope and repose ; a medium is spread around that discolours and horrifies, and the Tempter seems to haunt the house.

Then the outrage of a public tribunal canvassing the agitations and depressions of "the deceased" in the house which within a few days was his own, handling the fatal pistol, discussing the wounds, the silent records of a mental agony that happy men cannot even imagine, and that will for life darken the secret reveries of those who loved the dead !

But as one of our proverbs, old as the days of Glaston-bury, says :

" Be the day never so long,
At length cometh the even song."

Mamma is now in her crape and widow's cap ; I in my deep mourning also, laden with crape. A great many people have called to inquire, and have left cards. A few notes, which could not be withheld, of embarrassed condolence, have come from the more intimate, who thought themselves obliged to make that sacrifice and exertion. Two or three were very kind indeed. Sore does one feel at the desertions that attend a great and sudden change of fortune. But I do not, on fairly thinking it over, believe that there is more selfishness or less good-nature in the world in which we were living than in that wider world which lies at a lower social level. We are too ready to take the intimacies of pleasure or mere convenience as meaning a great deal more than they ever fairly can mean. They are not contracted to involve the liabilities of friendship. If they did, they would be inconveniently few. You must not expect people to sacrifice themselves for you merely because they think you good company or have similar tastes. When you begin the *facilis deccensus*, people won't walk with you very far on the way. The most you can expect is a graceful, and sometimes a compassionate, farewell.

It was about a fortnight after poor papa's death that some law-papers came, which, understanding as little about such matters as most young ladies do, I sent, with mamma's approval, to Mr. Forrester, who, I mentioned, had been poor papa's man of business in town.

Next day he called. I was with mamma in her room at the time, and the servant came up with a little pencilled note. It said, "The papers are important, and the matter must be looked after immediately, to prevent unpleasantness." Mamma and I were both startled. "Business," which we had never heard of before, now met us sternly face to face, and demanded instant attention. The servant said that Mr. Forrester was waiting in the drawing-room, to know whether mamma wished to see him. She asked me to go down instead, which accordingly I did.

As I entered, he was standing looking from the window with a thoughtful and rather disgusted countenance, as if he had something disagreeable to tell. He came forward and spoke very kindly, and then told me that the papers were notices to the effect that unless certain mortgages were paid off upon a certain early day, which was named, the house and furniture would be sold. He saw how startled I was. He looked very kindly, and as if he pitied me.

"Has your mamma any relation, who understands business, to advise with under her present circumstances?" he asked.

"Chellwood, I think, ought," I began.

"I know. But this will be very troublesome; and they say Lord Chellwood is not a man of business. He'll never undertake it, I'm sure. We can try, if you like; but I think it is merely losing time and a sheet of paper, and he's abroad, I know, at Vichy; for I wrote to him to try to induce him to take an assignment of this very mortgage, and he would not, or said he could not, which means the same thing. I don't think he'll put himself out of his way for anybody. Can you think of no one else ?"

"We have very few kinsmen," I answered; "they are too remote, and we know too little about them, to have any chance of their taking any trouble for us."

"But there was a family named Rokestone connected with you at Golden Friars ?"

"There is only Sir Harry Rokestone, and he is not friendly. We have reason to know he is very much the reverse," I answered.

"I hope, Miss Ware, you won't think me impertinent, but it is right you should ascertain, without further loss of time, how you stand. There are expenses going on. And all I positively know is that poor Mr. Ware's affairs are left in a very entangled state. Does your mamma know what balance there is in the bank ?"

"How much money in the bank?" I repeated. "Papa said there was fifty pounds."

"Fifty pounds! Oh, there must be more than that," he replied, and looked down, with a frown, upon the floor, and, with his hands in his pockets, meditated for a minute or two.

"I don't like acting alone, if it can be helped," he began again; "but if Mrs. Ware, your mamma, wishes it, I'll write to the different professional men, Mr. Jarlcot at Golden Friars, and Mr. Williams at Cardyllion, and the two solicitors in the south of England, and I'll ascertain for her, as nearly as we can, what is left, and how everything stands, and we must learn at the bank what balance stands to your credit. But I think your mamma should know that she can't possibly afford to live in the way she has been accustomed to, and it would only be prudent and right that she should give all the servants, except two or three whom she can't do without, notice of discharge. Is there a will?"

"I don't know. I think not—mamma thinks not," I said.

"I don't believe there is," he added. "It's not likely, and the law makes as good a will for him as he could have made for himself." He thought for a minute, and then went on. "I felt a great reluctance, Miss Ware, to talk upon these unpleasant subjects: but it would not have been either kind or honest to be silent. You and your mamma will meet your change of circumstances with good sense and good feeling, I am sure. A very great change, I fear, it will be. You are not to consider me as a professional man, tell your mama. I am acting as a friend. I wish to do all I can to prevent expense, and to put you in possession of the facts as quickly and clearly as I can, and then you will know exactly the case you have to deal with."

He took his leave, with the same air of care, thought, and suppressed fuss which belongs to the overworked man of business.

When these people make a present of their time, they are giving us something more than gold. I was not half grateful enough to him then. Thought and years have enabled me to estimate his goodnature.

I was standing at the window of a back drawing-room, a rather dark room, pondering on the kind but alarming words, at which, as at the sound of a bell, the curtain seemed to rise for a new act in my life. These worldly terrors were mingling a new poison in my grief. The vulgar troubles, which are the hardest to bear, were near us. At this inopportune moment I heard the servant announce some one, and, looking over my shoulder quickly, I saw Mr. Carmel come in. I felt myself grow pale. I saw his eye wander for a moment in search, I fancied, of mamma. I did not speak or move. The mirror reflected my figure back upon myself as I turned towards him. What did he see? Not quite the same Ethel Ware he had been accustomed to. My mourning-dress made me look taller, thinner, and paler than before. I could not have expected to see him; I looked, I suppose, as I felt, excited, proud, pained, resentful.

He came near; his dark eyes looked at me inquiringly.
He extended his hand, hesitated, and said:

"I am afraid I did wrong. I ought not to have asked
to see you."

"We have not seen any one—mamma or I—except one
old friend, who came a little time ago."

My own voice sounded cold and strange in my ear; I
felt angry and contemptuous. Had I not reason? I did
not give him my hand, or appear to perceive that he had
advanced his. I could see, though I did not look direct
at him, that he seemed pained.

"I thought, perhaps, that I had some claim, also, as an
old friend," he began, and paused.

"Oh! I quite forgot that," I repeated, in the same
tones; "an old friend, to be sure." I felt that I smiled
bitterly.

"You look at me as if you hated me, Miss Ware," he
said—"why should you? What have I done?"

"Why do you ask me? Ask yoursel. Look into your
conscience. I think, Mr. Carmel, you are the last person
who should have come here."

"I won't affect to misunderstand you; you think I in-
fluenced Lady Lorrimer," he said.

"The whole thing is coarse and odious," I said. "I
hate to speak or think of it; but, shocking as it is, I must.
Lady Lorrimer had no near relations but mamma; and
she intended—she told her so in my hearing—leaving
money to her by her will. It is, I think, natural and
right that people should leave their money to those they
love—their own kindred—and not to strangers. I would
not complain if Lady Lorrimer had acted of her own
thought and will in the matter. But it was far otherwise;
a lady, nervous and broken in health, was terrified, as
death approached, by people, of whom you were one, and
thus constrained to give all she possessed into the hands
of strangers, to forward theological intrigues, of which
she could understand nothing. I say it was unnatural,
cruel, and rapacious. That kind lady, if she had done as
she wished, would have saved us from all our misery."

"Will you believe me, Miss Ware?" he said, in the
lowest possible tones, grasping the back of the chair, on

R

which his hand rested, very hard, "I never knew, heard, or suspected that Lady Lorrimer had asked or received any advice respecting that will, which I see has been publicly criticised in some of the papers. I never so much as heard that she had made a will. I entreat, Miss Ware, that you will believe me."

"In matters where your Church is concerned, Mr. Carmel, I have heard that prevarication is a merit. With respect to all that concerns poor Lady Lorrimer, I shall never willingly hear another word from you, nor ever speak to you again."

I turned to the window, and looked out for a minute or two, with my fingers on the window-sash. Then I turned again rather suddenly. He was standing on the same spot, in the same attitude, his hands clasped together, his head lowered, his eyes fixed in a reverie on the ground, and I thought I saw the trace of tears on his cheek.

My moving recalled him, and he instantly looked up and said:

"Let me say a word—whatever sacrifice my holy calling may impose, I accept with gratitude to Heaven. We are not pressed into this service—we are volunteers. The bride at the altar never took vow more freely. We have sworn to obey, to suffer, to fight, to die. Forewarned, and with our eyes opened, we have cast all behind us: the vanities, hopes, and affections of mortality—according to the word of God, hating father, mother, sister, brother; we take up the heavy cross, and follow in the blood-stained footsteps of our Master, pressing forward; with blind obedience and desperate stoicism, we smile at hunger, thirst, heat and cold, sickness, perils, bonds, and death. Such soldiers, you are right in thinking, will dare everything but treason. If I had been commanded to withhold information from my dearest friend, to practise any secresy, or to exert for a given object any influence, I should have done so. All human friendship is subject with me to these inexorable conditions. Is there any prevarication there? But with respect to Lady Lorrimer's will, I suggested nothing, heard nothing, thought nothing."

All this seemed to me very cool. I was angry. I smiled again, and said:

" You must think all that very childish, Mr. Carmel.
You tell me you are ready to mislead me upon any subject,
and you expect me to believe you upon this."

" Of course that strikes you," he said, " and I have no
answer but this : I have no possible motive in deceiving
you—all that is past, inexorable, fixed as death itself !"

" I neither know nor care with what purpose you speak.
It is clear to me, Mr. Carmel, that with your principles,
as I suppose I must call them, you could be no one's
friend, and no one but a fool could be yours. It seems to
me you are isolated from all human sympathies ; toward
such a person I could feel nothing but antipathy and fear ;
you don't stand before me like a fellow-creature, but like
a spirit—and not a good one."

" These principles, Miss Ware, of which you speak so
severely, Protestants, the most religious, practise with as
little scruple as we, in their warfare, in their litigation, in
their diplomacy, in their ordinary business, wherever, in
fact, hostile action is suspected. If a Laodicean community were as earnest about winning souls as they are about
winning battles, or lawsuits, or money, or elections, we
should hear very little of such weak exceptions against
the inevitable strategy of zeal and faith."

I made him no answer; perhaps I could not do so at
the moment. I was excited; his serene temper made me
more so.

" I have described my obligations, Miss Ware," he said.
" Your lowest view of them can now charge me with no
treachery to you. It is true I cannot be a friend in the
sense in which the world reads friendship. My first alle-
giance is to Heaven ; and in the greatest, as in the minutest
things, all my obedience is due to that organ of its will
which Heaven has placed above me. If all men thought
more justly, such relations would not require to be disclosed or defended ; they would simply be taken for granted
—reason deduces them from the facts of our faith ; we
are the creatures of one God, who has appointed one
Church to be the interpreter of his will upon earth."

" Every traitor is a sophist, sir ; I have neither skill
nor temper for such discussions," I answered, proving my
latter position sufficiently. " I had no idea that you could

have thought of visiting here, and I hoped I should have been spared the pain of seeing you again. Nor should I like to continue this conversation, because I might be tempted to say even more pointedly what I think than I care to do. Good-bye, Mr. Carmel, good-bye, sir," I repeated, with a quiet emphasis meant to check, as I thought, his evident intention to speak again.

He so understood it. He paused for a moment, undecided, and then said:

"Am I to understand that you command me to come no more?"

"Certainly," I answered, coldly and angrily.

His hand was on the door, and he asked very gently, but I thought with some little agitation:

"And that you now end our acquaintance?"

"Certainly," I repeated, in the same tone.

"Heaven has sent my share of sorrow," he said; "but no soldier of Christ goes to his grave without many scars. I deserve my wounds and submit. It must be long before we meet again under any circumstances; never, perhaps, in this life."

He looked at me. He was very pale, and his large eyes were full of kindness. He held out his hand to me silently, but I did not take it. He sighed deeply, and placed it again on the handle of the door, and said, very low:

"Farewell, Miss Ware—Ethel—my pupil, and may God for ever bless you!" So the door opened, and he went.

I heard the hall door shut. That sullen sound smote my heart like a signal telling me that my last friend was gone.

Few people who have taken an irrevocable step on impulse, even though they have done rightly, think very clearly immediately after. My own act for a while confounded me. I don't think that Mr. Carmel was formed by nature for deception. I think, in my inmost soul, I believed his denial, and was sure that he had neither act nor part in the management of Lady Lorrimer's will. I know I felt a sort of compunction, and I experienced that melancholy doubt as to having been quite in the right, which sometimes follows an angry scene. In this state I returned to mamma to tell her all that had passed.

CHAPTER XL.

A RAINY DAY.

AMMA knew nothing distinctly about the state of our affairs, but she knew something generally of the provision made at her marriage, and she thought we should have about a thousand a year to live upon.

I could hardly recognise the possibility of this, with Mr. Forrester's forbodings. But if that, or even something like it, were secured to us, we could go down to Malory, and live there very comfortably. Mamma's habits of thinking, and the supine routine of her useless life, had sustained a shock, and her mind seemed now to rest with pleasure on the comparative solitude and quiet of a country life.

All our servants, except one or two, were under notice to go. I had also got leave from mamma to get our plate, horses, carriages, and other superfluous things valued, and fifty other trifling measures taken to expedite the winding-up of our old life, and our entrance upon our new one, the moment Mr. Forrester should tell us that our income was ascertained, and available.

I was longing to be gone, so also was mamma. She seemed very easy about our provision for the future, and I, alternating between an overweening confidence and an irrepressible anxiety, awaited the promised disclosures of Mr. Forrester, which were to end our suspense.

Nearly a fortnight passed before he came again. A note reached us the day before, saying that he would call at four, unless we should write in the meantime to put him off. He did come, and I shall never forget the interview that followed. Mamma and I were sitting in the front drawing-room, expecting him. My heart was trembling. I know of no state so intolerable as suspense upon a vital issue. It is the state in which people in money troubles are, without intermission. How it is lived through for years, as often as it is, and without the loss of reason, is in my eyes the greatest physical and psychological wonder of this sorrowful world.

A gloomier day could hardly have heralded the critical exposition that was to disclose our future lot. A dark sky, clouds dark as coal-smoke, and a steady down-pour of rain, large-dropped and violent, that keeps up a loud and gusty drumming on the panes, down which the wet is rushing in rivers. Now and then the noise rises to a point that makes conversation difficult. Every minute at this streaming window I was looking into the street, where cabs and umbrellas, few and far between, were scarcely discoverable through the rivulets that coursed over the glass.

At length I saw a cab, like a waving mass of black mist, halt at the door, and a double knock followed. My breath almost left me. In a minute or two the servant, opening the door, said, " Mr. Forrester," and that gentleman stepped into the gloomy room, with a despatch-box in his hand, looking ominously grave and pale. He took mamma's hand, and looked, I thought, with a kind of doubtful inquiry in her face, as if measuring her strength to bear some unpleasant news. I almost forgot to shake hands with him, I was so horribly eager to hear him speak.

Mamma was much more confident than I, and said, as soon as he had placed his box beside him, and sat down :

" I'm so obliged to you, Mr. Forrester ; you have been so extremely kind to us. My daughter told me that you intended making inquiries, and letting us know all you heard ; I hope you think it satisfactory ?"

He looked down, and shook his head in silence. Mamma flushed very much, and stood up, staring at him, and then grew deadly pale.

"It is not—it can't be less—I hope it's not—than nine hundred a year. If it is not that, what is to become of us?"

Mamma's voice sounded hard and stern, though she spoke very low. I, too, was staring at the messenger of fate with all my eyes, and my heart was thumping hard.

"Very far from satisfactory. I wish it were anything at all like the sum you have named," said Mr. Forrester, very dejectedly, but gathering courage for his statement as he proceeded. "I'll tell you, Mrs. Ware, the result of my correspondence, and I am really pained and grieved that I should have such a statement to make. I find that you opened your marriage settlement, except the provision for your daughter, which, I regret to say, is little more than a thousand pounds, and she takes nothing during your life, and then we can't put it down at more than forty pounds a year."

"But—but I want to know," broke in poor mamma, with eyes that glared, and her very lips white, "what there is—how much we have got to live on?"

"I hope from my heart there may be something, Mrs. Ware, but I should not be treating you fairly if I did not tell you frankly that it seems to me a case in which relations ought to come forward."

I felt so stunned that I could not speak.

"You mean, ask their assistance?" said mamma. "My good God! I can't—we can't—I could not do that!"

"Mamma," said I, with white lips, "had not we better hear all that Mr. Forrester has to tell us?"

"Allow me," continued mamma, excitedly; "there must be something, Ethel—don't talk folly. We can live at Malory, and, however small our pittance, we must make it do. But I won't consent to beg." Mamma's colour came again as she said this, with a look of haughty resentment at Mr. Forrester. That poor gentleman seemed distressed, and shifted his position a little uneasily.

"Malory," he began, "would be a very suitable place, if an income were arranged. But Malory will be in Sir Harry Rokestone's possession in two or three days, and without his leave you could not get there; and I'm afraid I dare not encourage you to entertain any hopes of a favourable, or even a courteous, hearing in that quarter. Since I had the pleasure of seeing Miss Ware here, about ten days or a fortnight since, I saw Mr. Jarlcot, of Golden Friars; a very intelligent man he evidently is, and does Sir Harry Rokestone's business in that part of the world, and seemed very friendly; but he says that in that quarter"—Mr. Forrester paused, and shook his head gloomily, looking on the carpet—" we have nothing good to look for. He bears your family, it appears an implacable animosity, and does not scruple to express it in very violent language indeed."

"I did not know that Sir Harry Rokestone had any claim upon Malory," said mamma; "I don't know by what right he can prevent our going into my house."

" I'm afraid there can be no doubt as to his right as a trustee; but it was not obligatory on him to enforce it. Some charges ought to have been paid off four years ago; it is a very peculiar deed, and, instead of that, interest has been allowed to accumulate. I took the liberty of writing to Sir Harry Rokestone a very strong letter, the day after my last interview with Miss Ware; but he has taken not the slightest notice of it, and that is very nearly a fortnight ago, and Jarlcot seems to think that, if he lets me off with silence, I'm getting off very easily. They all seem afraid of him down there."

I fancied that Mr. Forrester had been talking partly to postpone a moment of pain. If there was a shock coming, he wanted resolution to precipitate the crisis, and looked again with a perplexed and uneasy countenance on the carpet. He glanced at mamma, once or twice, quickly, as if he had nearly made up his mind to break the short silence that had followed. While he was hesitating, however, I was relieved by mamma's speaking, and very much to the point.

" And how much do you think, Mr. Forrester, we shall have to live upon?"

"That," said he, looking stedfastly on the table, with a very gloomy countenance, "is the point on which, I fear, I have nothing satisfactory—or even hopeful," he added, raising his head, and looking a little stern, and even frightened, "to say. You must only look the misfortune in the face; and a great misfortune it is, accustomed as you have been to everything that makes life happy and easy. It is, as I said before, a case in which relations who are wealthy, and well able to do it, should come forward."

"But do say what it is," said mamma, trembling violently. "I shan't be frightened, only say distinctly. Is it only four hundred?—or only three hundred a year?" She paused, looking imploringly at him.

"I should be doing very wrong if I told you there was anything—anything like that—anything whatever certain, in fact, however small. There's nothing certain, and it would be very wrong to mislead you. I don't think the assets and property will be sufficient to pay the debts."

"Great Heaven! Sir—oh! oh!—is there nothing left?"

He shook his head despondingly. The murder was out now; there was no need of any more questioning—no case could be simpler. We were not worth a shilling!

If in my vain and godless days the doctor at my bedside had suddenly told me that I must die before midnight, I could not have been more bewildered. Without knowing what I did, I turned and walked to the window, on which the rain was thundering, and rolling down in rivers. I heard nothing—my ears were stunned.

CHAPTER XLI.

THE FLITTING.

E were ruined! What must the discovery have been to poor mamma? She saw all the monstrous past—the delirium was dissipated. An abyss was between her and her former life. In the moment of social death, all that she was leaving had become almost grotesque, incredibly ghastly. Here in a moment was something worse than poverty, worse even than death.

During papa's life the possibility of those vague vexations known as "difficulties" and "embarrassments," might have occurred to me, but that I should ever have found myself in the plight in which I now stood had never entered my imagination.

Suppose, on a fine evening, a ship, with a crash like a cannon, tears open her planks on a hidden rock, and the water gushes and whirls above the knees, the waists, the throats of the polite people round the tea-table in the state-cabin, without so much as time interposed to say God bless us! between the warning and the catastrophe, and you have our case!

Young ladies, you live in a vague and pleasant dream. Gaslight in your hall and lobbies, wax lights, fires, decorous servants, flowers, spirited horses, millinery, soups and wines, are products of nature, and come of themselves. There is, nevertheless, such a thing as poverty, as there is such a thing as death. We hold them both as doctrines, and, of course, devoutly believe in them, but when either lays its cold hand on your shoulder, and you look it in the face, you are as much appalled as if you had never heard its name before.

Carelessness, indolence, a pleasurable supineness, without any other grievous fault or enormous mistake, had, little by little, prepared all for the catastrophe. Mamma was very ill that night. In the morning Mr. Forrester came again. Mamma could not see him; but I had a long interview with him. He was very kind. I will tell you, in a few words, the upshot of our conference.

In the first place, the rather startling fact was disclosed that we had, in the world, but nine pounds, eight shillings, which mamma happened still to have in her purse, out of her last money for dress. Nine pounds, eight shillings! That was all that interposed between us and the wide republic of beggary. Then Mr. Forrester told me that mamma must positively leave the house in which we were then residing, to avoid being made, as he said, "administratrix in her own wrong," and put to great annoyance, and seeing any little fund that relations might place at her disposal wasted in expenses and possible litigation.

So it was settled we were to leave the house, but where were we to go? That was provided for. Near High Holborn, in a little street entered between two narrow piers, stood an odd and ancient house, as old as the times of James the First, which was about to be taken down to make way for a model lodging-house. The roof was sound, and the drainage good, that was all he could say for it; and he could get us leave to occupy it, free of rent, until its demolition should be commenced. He had, in fact, already arranged that for mamma.

Poor papa had owed him a considerable sum for law costs. He meant, he said, to remit the greater part of it, and whatever the estate might give him, on account of them, he would hand over to mamma. He feared the sum would be a small one. He thought it would hardly amount to a hundred pounds, but in the meantime she could have fifty pounds on account of it.

She might also remove a very little furniture, but no more than would just suffice, in the scantiest way, for our bed-rooms and one sitting-room, and such things as a servant might take for the kitchen. He would make himself responsible to the creditors for these.

I need not go further into particulars. Of course there

were many details to be adjusted, and the conduct of all
these arrangements devolved upon me. Mr. Forrester
undertook all the dealings with the servants whom it was
necessary to dismiss and pay forthwith.

The house was now very deserted. There was no life
in it but that feverish fuss like the preparations that
condemned people make for their executions. The arrangements for our sorrowful flight went on like the
dismal worry of a sick dream. In our changed state we
preferred country servants, and I wrote for good old
Rebecca Torkill and one of her rustic maids at Malory,
who arrived, and entered on their duties the day before
our departure. How outlandish these good creatures
appeared when transplanted from the primitive life and
surroundings of Malory to the artificial scenes of London!
But how comfortable and kindly was their clumsiness
compared with the cynical politeness and growing contempt of the cosmopolitan servants of London!

Well, at last we were settled in our strange habitation.
It was by no means so uncomfortable as you might have
supposed. We found ourselves in a sitting-room of
handsome dimensions, panelled with oak up to its
ceiling, which, however, from the size of the room,
appeared rather low. It was richly moulded, after the
style of James the First's reign, but the coarse smear of
newly-applied whitewash covered its traceries.

Our scanty furniture was collected at the upper end of
the apartment, which was covered with a piece of carpet,
and shut off from the lower part of the room by a folding
screen. Some kind friend had placed flowers in a glass
on the table, and three pretty plants in full blow upon
the window-stones. Some books from a circulating
library were on the table, and some volumes also of
engravings. These little signs of care and refinement
took off something of the gaunt and desolate character
which would have, otherwise, made this habitation
terrifying.

A rich man, with such a house in the country, might
have made it curiously beautiful; but where it was,
tenanted by paupers, and condemned to early demolition,
who was to trouble his head about it?

Mamma had been better in the morning, but was now suffering, again, from a violent palpitation, and was sitting up in her bed; it was her own bed, which had been removed for her use. Rebecca Torkill, who had been for some hours managing everything to receive her, was now in her room. I was in our "drawing-room," I suppose I am to call it, quite alone. My elbows rested on the table, my hands were over my eyes, and I was crying vehemently. These were tears neither of cowardice nor of sorrow. They were tears of rage. I was one of those impracticable and defiant spirits who, standing more in need than any other of the chastisements of Heaven, resent its discipline as an outrage, and upbraid its justice with impious fury. I dried my eyes fiercely. I looked round our strange room with a bitter smile. Black oak floor, black oak panelling up to the ceiling; as evening darkened how melancholy this grew!

I looked out of the window. The ruddy sky of evening was fading into grey. A grass-grown brick wall, as old as the house perhaps, and springing from the two piers, enclosed the space once occupied by the street in which it had stood. Nothing now remained of the other houses but high piles of rubbish, broken bricks, and plaster, through which, now and then, a black spar or plank of worn wood was visible in this dismal enclosure; beyond these hillocks of ruin, and the jagged and worn brick wall, were visible the roofs with slates no bigger than oyster-shells, and the clumsy old chimneys of poverty-stricken dwellings, existing on sufferance, and sure to fall before long beneath the pick and crowbar; beyond these melancholy objects spread the expiring glow of sunset with a veil of smoke before it.

As I looked back upon this sombre room, and then out upon the still more gloomy and ruinous prospect, with a feeling of disgust and fear, and the intolerable consciousness that we were here under the coercion of actual poverty, you may fancy what my ruminations were. I don't know whether, in my family, there was a vein of that hereditary melancholy called suicidal. I know I felt, just then, its horrible promptings. Like the invitations of the Erl-king in Goethe's ballad, it "whispered low in mine ear." There is nothing so startling as the first real allurement to this tremendous step. There remains a sense of an actual communication at which mind and soul tremble. I felt it once afterwards.

Its insidiousness and power are felt on starting from the dream, and finding oneself, as I did, alone, with silence and darkness and frightful thoughts. I think that, but for mamma, it would have been irresistible. The sudden exertion of my will, and in spite of my impious mood, I am sure, an inward cry to God for help, scared away the brood that had gathered about me with their soft monotonous seduction. Have you ever experienced the same thing? The temptation breaks from you like a murmur changed to a laugh, and leaves you horrified. I hated life; my energies were dead already. Why should I drag on, with broken heart, in solitude and degradation?

Some pitying angel kept me in remembrance of mamma, sick, helpless, so long and entirely in the habit of leaning upon others for counsel and for action. When sickness follows poverty, fate has little left to inflict. One good thing in our present habitation was the fact of its being as completely out of sight as the inmost cavern of the catacombs. That was consolatory. I felt, at first, as if I never should wish to see the light again. But every expression of life is strong in the young; energy, health, spirits, hope.

The dread of this great downfall began to subside, and I could see a little before me; my head grew clearer, and was already full of plans for earning my bread. That, I dare say, would have been easy enough, if I could have made up my mind to leave mamma, or if she could have consented to part with me. But there were many things I could do at home. Mamma was sometimes better, but her spirits never rallied. She cried almost incessantly; I think she was heart-broken. If she could have given me some of her gentleness, and if I could inspired her with some of my courage, we should have done better.

The day after our arrival, as I looked out of the window listlessly, I saw a van drive between the piers. Two men were on the driver's seat. They stopped before they had got very far. It was difficult navigation among the

promontories and islands of rubbish. The driver turned
a disgusted look up towards our windows, and made some
remark to his companion. They got down and led the
horses with circumspection, and with many turns and
windings up to the door, and then began to speak to our
servant ; but, at this interesting moment, I was summoned
by Rebecca Torkill to mamma's room, where I forgot all
about the van.

But, on returning a few minutes later, I found a piano
in our drawing-room. Our rustic maid had not heard or
even asked from whom it came ; and when a tuner arrived
an hour later, I found that nothing could prevail on him
to disclose the name of the person or place from which it
had come. It had not any indication but the maker's
name and that was no guide.

Two or three days after our flight to this melancholy
place, Mr. Forrester called. I saw him in our strange
sitting -room. It was pleasant to see a friendly face. He
had not many minutes to give me. He listened to my
plans, and rather approved of them ; told me that he had
some clients who might be useful, and that he would make
it a point to do what he could with them. Then I thanked
him very much for the flowers, and the books, and the
piano. But it was not he who had sent them. I began
to be rather unpleasantly puzzled about the quarter from
which these favours came. Our melancholy habitation
must be known to more persons than we supposed. I was
thinking uncomfortably on this problem when he went on
to say :

"As Mrs. Ware is not well enough to see me, I should
like to read to you a draft of the letter I was thinking of
sending to-day to Lord Chellwood's house. He's to be
home, I understand, for a day or two before the end of this
week ; and I want to hit him on the wing, if I can."

He then read the letter for me.

" Pray leave out what you say of me," I said.

" Why, Miss Ware ?"

"Because, if I can't live by my own labour, I will die,"
I answered. " I think it is his duty to do something for
mamma, who is ill, and the widow of his brother, and who
has lost her provision by poor papa's misfortunes; but I

mean to work; and I hope to earn quite enough to support
me; and if I can't, as I said, I don't wish to live. I will
accept nothing from him."

"And why not from him, Miss Ware? You know he's
your uncle. Whom could you more naturally look to in
such an emergency?"

"He's not my uncle; papa was his half-brother only, by
a later marriage. He never liked papa—nor us."

"Never mind—he'll do something. I've had some
experience; and I tell you, he can't avoid contributing
in a case like this; it comes too near him," said Mr.
Forrester.

"I have seen him—I have heard him talk; I know the
kind of person he is. I have heard poor papa say, ' I wish
some one would relieve Norman's mind: he seems to fancy
we have a design on his pocket, or his will. He is always
keeping us at arm's-length. I don't think my wife is ever
likely to have to ask him for anything.' I have heard poor
papa say, I think, those very words. Bread from his hand
would choke me, and I can't eat it."

"Well, Miss Ware, if you object to that passage, I shall
strike it out, of course. I wrote a second time to Sir
Harry Rokestone, and have not yet had a line in reply,
and I don't think it likely I ever shall. I'll try him once
more; and if that doesn't bring an answer, I think we may
let him alone for some time to come."

And now Mr. Forrester took his leave and was gone.
The forlorn old house was silent again.

CHAPTER XLII.

A FORLORN HOPE.

ANOTHER week passed; mamma was better—not much better in spirits, but very much apparently in health. She was now a good deal more tranquil, though in great affliction. Poor mamma! No book interested her now but the Bible; the great, wise, gentle friend so seldom listened to when all goes well—always called in to console, when others fail.

Mr. Forrester had got me some work to do—work much more interesting than I had proposed for myself. It was to make a translation of a French work for a publisher. For a few days it was simply experimental, but it was found that I did it well and quickly enough; and I calculated that if I could only obtain constant employment of this kind, I might earn about seventy pounds a year. Here was a resource—something between us and actual want—something between me and the terrible condition of dependence. My ambition was humble enough now.

For about two days this discovery of my power, under favourable circumstances, to make sixty or seventy pounds a year, actually cheered me; but this healthier effect was of short duration. The miseries of our situation were too obvious and formidable to be long kept out of view. Gloom and distraction soon returned—the same rebellious violence inflamed by the fresh alarm of mamma's returning illness.

She was very ill again the night but one after the good news about my translation—breathless, palpitating. I began to grow frightened and desponding about her. I had fancied before that her symptoms were mere indications of her state of mind; but now, when her mind

s

seemed more tranquil, and her nerves quiet, their return
was ominous. I was urging her to see Sir Jacob Lake,
when Mr. Forrester called, and I went to our drawing-
room to see him. He had got a note, cold and petulant,
from my uncle, Lord Chellwood, that morning. This
letter said that " no person who knew of the number and
magnitude of the charges affecting his property could be
so unreasonable as to suppose that he could, even if he
had the power, which was not quite so clear, think of
charging an annuity upon it, however small, for the
benefit of any one." That " he deeply commiserated the
distressing circumstances in which poor Frank's widow
found herself; but surely he, Lord Chellwood, was not to
blame for it. He had never lost an opportunity of pressing upon his brother the obligation he conceived every
married man to be under, to make provision for his wife;
and had been at the trouble to show him, by some very
pertinent figures, how impracticable it was for him to add
to the burdens that weighed on the estates, and how
totally he, Lord Chellwood, was without the power of
mitigating to any extent the consequences of his rashness,
if he should leave his wife without a suitable provision."
So it went on ; and ended by saying that " he might possibly be able, next spring, to make—it could be but a
small one—a present to the poor lady, who had certainly
much to answer for in the imprudent career in which she
had contributed to engage her husband, and during which
she had wilfully sacrificed her settlement to the pleasures
and vanities of an expensive and unsuitable life." The
letter went on in this strain, and hinted that the present
he spoke of could not exceed a hundred and fifty pounds,
and could not possibly be repeated.

" This looks very black, you see," said the good-
natured solicitor. " But I hope it may not be quite so
bad as he says. If he could be got to do a little more, a
small annuity might be purchased."

I did not like my uncle. It is very hard to get over
first impressions, and the repulsion of an entirely uncon-
genial countenance. There was nothing manly in his
face—it was narrow, selfish, conceited. He was pale as
wax. He had manners at once dry and languid; and

whether it was in his eye or not, I can't say, but there was something in his look, though he smiled as much as was called for, and never said a disagreeable thing, that conveyed very clearly to me, although neither papa nor mamma seemed to perceive it, that he positively disliked us, each and every one, not even excepting poor, gay, good-natured papa. We all knew he was stingy; he had one hobby, and that was the nursing and rehabilitation of the estates which had come to him, with the title, in a very crippled state.

With these feelings, and the pride which is strongest in youth, I fancied that I should have died rather than have submitted to the humiliation of accepting, much less asking, money from his hand.

I must carry you three weeks further on. It was dark; I can't tell you now what o'clock it was; I am sure it was not much earlier than nine. I had my cloak and bonnet on; Rebecca Torkill was at my side, and her thin · hand was upon my arm.

"And where are you going, my darling, at this time of night?" she said, looking frightened into my face.

"To see Lord Chellwood; to see papa's unnatural brother; to tell him that mamma must die unless he helps her."

"But, my child, this is no time—you would not go out through them wicked streets at this hour—you shan't go!" she said sturdily, taking a firm hold of my arm.

I snatched it from her grasp angrily, and walked quickly away. I looked over my shoulder, as I reached the two piers, and saw the figure of old Rebecca looking black in the doorway, with a background of misty light from the candle at the foot of the stairs. I think she was wavering between the risk of leaving the house and mamma only half protected, and the urgent necessity of pursuing and bringing me back. I was out of her reach, however, before she could make up her mind.

I was walking as quickly as I could through the streets that led towards Regent Street. I had studied them on the map.

These out-of-the-way streets were quiet now, but not deserted; now and then I passed the blaze of a gin-palace. It was a strange fear and excitement to me to be walking through these poor by-streets by gas-light. No fugitive

threading the streets of a town in the throes of revolution
had a keener sense of danger, or moved with eye and
sinew more ready every moment to start from a walk into
a run. I suppose they allow poor people, such as I might
well be taken for, walking quickly upon their business, to
pass undisturbed. I was not molested.

At length I was in Regent Street. I felt safe now; the
broad pavement, the stream of traffic, the long line of
gas-lamps, and the still open shops, enabled me, without
fear, a little to slacken my pace. I required this relief.
I had been ill for two days, and was worse. I felt chilly
and aguish; I was suffering from one of those stupendous headaches which possibly give the sufferer some idea
of the action of that iron "cap of silence" with which,
during the reign of good King Bomba, so many Neapolitan
citizens were made acquainted. I can afford to speak
lightly of it now; but I was very ill. I ought to have
been in my bed. Nothing but my tremor about mamma
would have given me nerve and strength for this excursion.

She had that day had a sudden return of the breathlessness
and palpitation from which she had suffered so much, and I
had succeeded in getting Sir Jacob Lake to come to see her.

It was a hurried visit, as his visits always were. He
saw her, gave some general directions, wrote a prescription, spoke cheerfully to her, and his manner seemed to
say he apprehended nothing. I came with him to the
stairs, which we went down together, and in the drawing-
room I heard the astounding words that told me mamma
could not live many months, and might be carried off at
any moment in one of those attacks. He told me to get
her to the country, her native air, if that could be
managed, immediately. That might prolong her life a
little. It was only a chance, and at best a reprieve. But
without it he could not answer for a week. He told me
that I must be careful not to let mamma know that he
thought her in danger. She was in a critical state, and
any agitation might be fatal. He took his leave, and I
was alone with his dreadful words in my ears.

Now, how was I to carry out his directions? The
journey to Golden Friars, as he planned it, would cost us
at least twenty pounds, and he ordered claret, then a very

expensive wine, for mamma. He did not know that he
was carrying away our last guinea in his pocket. I had
but half a sovereign and a few shillings in my purse.
Mr. Forrester was out of town; and even if he were
within reach, it was scarcely likely that he would lend or
bestow anything like the sum required. The work was
not sufficiently advanced to justify a hope that he would
give me, a stranger, a sum of money on account of a
task which I might never complete. Poverty had come
in its direst shape. In the distraction of that dreadful
helplessness my pride broke down. This was the reason
of my wild excursion.

As I now walked at a more moderate pace, I felt the
effect of my unnatural exertion more painfully—every
pulse was a throb of torture. It was an effort to keep
my mind clear, and to banish perpetually rising con-
fusions, the incipient exhalations of fever. What drowsi-
ness is to the system in health, this tendency to drop into ·
delirium is to the sick.

I found myself, at length, almost exhausted, at my noble
kinsman's door. I knocked; I asked to see him. The footman did not recognise me. He simply said, looking across
the street over my head, with a careless disdain:

"I say, what's the row, miss?"

Certainly such a visitor as I, and at such an hour, had
no very recognisable claim to a ceremonious reception.

"Charles," I said, "don't you know me?—Miss Ware."

The man started a little, looked hard at me, drew
himself up formally, as he made his salutation, receding
a step, with the hall-door open in his hand.

"Is his lordship at home?" I asked.

"No, miss, he dined out to-day."

"But I must see him, Charles. If he knew it was I
he could not refuse. Tell him mamma is dangerously ill,
and I have no one to help me."

"He is out, miss; and he sleeps out of town—at
Colonel Anson's to-night."

I uttered an exclamation of despair.

"And when is he to return?"

"He will not be in town again for a fortnight, miss;
he's going to Harleigh Castle."

I stood on the steps for a minute, stunned by the disappointment, staring helplessly into the man's face.

"Please, shall I call a cab, miss?"

"No—no," I said dreamily. I turned and went away
quickly. It troubled me little what the servants might
say or think of my strange visit."

This blow was distracting. The doctor had distinctly
said that mamma's immediate removal to country air
was a necessity.

As people will under excitement, I was walking at
the swiftest pace I could. I was pacing under the evergreens of the neighbouring square, back and forward,
again and again; I saw young ladies get from a house
opposite into a carriage, and drive away, as I once used
to do. I hated them—I hated every one who was as
fortunate as I once was. I hated the houses on the
other side with their well-lighted halls. I hated even
the great prosperous shop-keeping class, with their over-
grown persons and purses. Why did not fortune take
other people, the purse-proud, the scheming, the vicious,
the arrogant, the avaricious, instead of us—drag them
from their places, and batter and trundle them in the
gutter? Here was I, for no fault—none, none!—reduced
to a worse plight than a beggar's. The beggar has been
brought up to his calling, and can make something of it;
while I could not set about it, had not even that form of
pluck which people call meanness, and was quite past the
age at which the art is to be learned.

All this time I was growing more and more ill. The
breathless walking and the angry agitation were precipi-
tating the fever that was already upon me. I had an
increasing horror of the dismal abode which was now my
home. Distraction like mine demands rapid locomotion
as its proper and only anodyne. Despair and quietude
quickly subside into madness.

Some public clock not far off struck the hour; I did
not count it; but it reminded me suddenly of the risk of
exciting alarm at home by delaying my return. So with an
effort, and as it were an awakening, I began to direct my
steps homewards. But before I reached that melancholy
goal, an astounding adventure was fated to befall me.

CHAPTER XLIII

COLD STEEL.

I AM quite certain now that the impious sophistries to which some proud minds in affliction abandon themselves, are the direful suggestions of intelligences immensely superior in power to themselves. When they call to us in the air we listen; when they knock at the door we go down and open to them; we take them in to sup with us, we make them our guests, they become sojourners in the house, and are about our paths, and about our beds, and spying out all our ways; their thoughts become our thoughts, their wickedness our wickedness, their purposes our purposes, till, without perceiving it, we are their slaves. And then when a fit opportunity presents itself, they make, in Doctor Johnson's phrase, "a snatch of us." Something like this was near happening to me. You shall hear.

I grew, on a sudden, faint and cold; a horror of returning home stole over me. I could not go home, and yet I had no other choice but death. I had scarcely thought of death, when a longing seized me. Death grew so beautiful in my eyes! The false smile, the mysterious welcome, the sweep of deep waters, the vague allurement of a profound endless welcome, drew me on and on.

Two men chatting passed me by as one said to the other, "The tide's full in at Waterloo Bridge now; the moon must look quite lovely there." It was spoken in harmony with my thoughts. I had read in my happier

days in the papers how poor girls had ended their misery
by climbing over the balustrade of Waterloo Bridge, over
the black abyss, dotted with the reflected lamps, and step-
ping off it into the dark air into death. I was going now
to that bridge—people would direct me—by the time I
reached it the thoroughfare would be still and deserted
enough. I can't say I had determined upon this—I can't
say I ever thought about it—it was only that the scene
and the event had taken possession of me, with the longing of a child for its home.

The streets were quieter now; but some shops were still
open. Among these was a jeweller's. The shutters were up,
and only the door open. I stepped in, I don't in the least
know why. The fever, I suppose, had touched my brain.
There were only three men in the shop—one behind the
counter, a smiling, ceremonious man, whom I believe to have
been the owner—the two others were customers. One was a
young man, sitting on a chair with his elbow on the counter,
examining and turning over some jewellery that glittered
in a little heap on the counter. The other, older and
dressed in black, was leaning over the counter, with his
back to me, and discussing, in low, careless tones, the
merits of a dagger, which, from their talk, not distinctly
heard, I conjectured the young man had been recommend-
ing as a specific against garotters. I was in no condition
to comprehend or care for the debate. The elder man, as
he talked, sometimes laid the little weapon down upon
the counter, and sometimes took it up, fitting it in his hand.

The intense light of the gas striking on my eyes made
them ache acutely. I don't know why, or how, I entered
the shop; I only know that I found myself standing within the door in a blaze of gaslight.

The jeweller, looking at me sharply across the counter,
said :

"Well, ma'am ?"

I answered :

"Can you give me change for a sovereign ?"

I must have been losing my head; for though I spoke
in perfect good faith, I had not a shilling about me. It
was not forgetfulness, but distinctly an illusion; for
I not only had the picture of the imaginary sovereign

distinctly before me, but thought I had it actually in my hand.

The jeweller was talking in subdued and urbane accents to his customer, and pointing out, no doubt, the special beauties and workmanship of his *bijouterie*.

"Sorry I can't oblige you; you must try elsewhere," he said, again directing a hard glance at me. I think he was satisfied that I was not a thief; and he continued his talk with the young man who was making his selection, and who was probably a little hard to please. I turned to leave the shop, and the jeweller went into the next room, possibly in search of something more likely to please his fastidious client at the counter.

I had not yet seen the face of either of the visitors to the shop, but I was conscious that the younger of the two had once or twice looked over his shoulder at me. He now said, taking his purse from his pocket—it was but as a parenthesis in his talk with his companion:

"I beg pardon; perhaps I can manage that change for you."

I drew nearer. What occurred next appeared to me like an incident in a dream, in which our motives are often so obscure that our own acts take us by surprise. Whether it was a mad moment or a lucid moment I don't know; for in extreme misery, if our courage does not fail us, our thoughts are always wicked.

I stood there, a slight figure, in crape, cloaked, veiled —in pain, giddy, confused. I cannot tell you what interest the common-place spectacle before me had for me, nor why I stayed there, gazing towards the three gas lamps that seemed each girt with a dazzling halo that made my eyes ache. What sounds and sights smote my sick senses with a jarring recognition? The hard, nasal tones of the elderly man in black, who leaned over the counter, and the pallid, scornful face, with its fine, rest- less eyes and sinister energy, were those of Monsieur Droqville!

He was talking to his companion, and did not trouble himself to look at me. He little dreamed what an image of death stood at his elbow!

They were not talking any longer about the pretty

dagger that lay on the counter, by his open fingers.
Monsieur Droqville was now indulging his cynical vein
upon another theme. He was finishing a satirical sum-
ming up of poor papa's character. I saw the sneer, the
shrug; I heard in his hard, bitter talk the name made
sacred to me by unutterable calamity; I listened to the
outrage from the lips of the man who had done all. Oh,
beloved, ruined father! Can I ever forget the pale smile
of despair, the cold, piteous voice with which, on that
frightful night, he said, "Droqville has done it all—he
has broken my heart." And here was the very Droqville,
with the scoff, the contempt, the triumph in his pitiless
face; and poor papa in his bloody shroud, and mamma
dying! What cared I what became of me? An icy chill
seemed to stream from my brain through me, to my feet,
to my finger tips; as a shadow moves, I had leaned over,
and the hand that holds this pen had struck the dagger
into Droqville's breast.

In a moment his face darkened, with a horrified,
vacant look. His mouth opened, as if to speak or call
out, but no sound came; his deep-set eyes, fixed on
me, were darkening; he was sinking backward, with
a groping motion of his hand, as if to ward off another
blow.

Was it real? For a second I stared, freezing with
horror; and then, with a gasp, darted through the shop-
door.

An accident, as I afterwards learned, had lamed Droqville's companion, and thus favoured my escape. Before
many seconds, however, pursuit was on my track. I soon
heard its cry and clatter. The street was empty when I
ran out. My echoing steps were the only sound there for
some seconds. I fled with the speed of the wind. I
turned to the left down a narrow street, and from that to
the right into a kind of stable lane. I heard shouting
and footsteps in pursuit. I ran for some time, but the
shouting of sounds and pursuit continued. My strength
failed me; I stopped short behind a kind of buttress,
beside a coach-house gate; I was hardly a second there.
An almost suicidal folly prompted me. I know not why,
but I stepped out again from my place of concealment,

intending to give myself up to my pursuers. I walked slowly back a few steps towards them. One was now close to me. A man without a hat, crying, "Stop, stop, police!" ran furiously past me. It clearly never entered his mind that I, walking slowly towards him, could possibly be the fugitive.

So this moment, as I expected of perdition, passed innocuously by.

By what instinct, chance, or miracle I made the rest of my way home, I know not. When I reached the doorstone, Rebecca Torkill was standing there watching for me in irrepressible panic.

When she was sure it was I, she ran out, crying, "Oh! God be thanked, miss, it's you, my child!" She caught me in her arms, and kissed me with honest vehemence. I did not return her caress—I was worn out; it all seemed like a frightful dream. Her voice sounded ever so far away. I saw her, as raving people see objects mixed with unrealities. I did not say a word as she conveyed me upstairs with her stalwart arm round my waist.

I heard her say, "Your mamma's better; she's quite easy now." I could not say, "Thank God!" I was conscious that I showed no trace of pleasure, nor even of comprehension, in my looks.

She was looking anxiously in my face as she talked to me, and led me into the drawing-room. I did not utter a word, nor look to the right or left. With a moan I sat down on the sofa. I was shivering uncontrollably.

Another phantom was now before me, talking with Rebecca. It was Mr. Carmel; his large, strange eyes—how dark and haggard they looked—fixed on my face with a gaze almost of agony! Something fell from my hand on the table as my fingers relaxed. I had forgotten that I held anything in them. I saw them both look at it, and then on one another with a glance of alarm, and even horror. It was the dagger, stained with blood, that had dropped upon that homely table.

I was unable to follow their talk. I saw him take it up quickly, and look from it to me, and to Rebecca again, with a horrible uncertainty. It was, indeed, a rather sinister waif to find in the hand of a person evidently so

ill as I was, especially with a mark of blood also upon
that trembling hand. He looked at it again very carefully; then he put it into Rebecca's hand, and said something very earnestly.

They talked on for a time. I neither understood nor
cared what they said; nor cared, indeed, at all what became of me.

"You're not hurt, darling?" she whispered, with her
earnest old eyes very near mine.

"I? No. Oh, no!" I answered.

"Not with that knife?"

"No," I repeated.

I was rapidly growing worse.

A little time passed thus, and then I saw Mr. Carmel
pray with his hands clasped for a few moments, and I
heard him distinctly say to Rebecca, "She's very ill. I'll
go for the doctor;" and he added some words to her. He
looked ghastly pale: as he gazed in my face, his eyes
seemed to burn into my brain. Then another figure was
added to the group; our maid glided in, and stood beside
Rebecca Torkill, and as it seemed to me, murmured
vaguely. I could not understand what she or they said.
She looked as frightened as the rest. I had perception
enough left to feel that they all thought me dying. So
the thought filled my darkened mind that I was indeed
passing into the state of the dead. The black curtain
that had been suspended over me for so long at last descended, and I remember no more for many days and
nights.

The secret was, for the present, mine only. I lay, as
the old writers say, "at God's mercy," the sword's point
at my throat, in the privation, darkness, and utter helplessness of fever. Safe enough it was with me. My brain
could recall nothing; my lips were sealed. But though
I was speechless, another person was quickly in possession
of the secret.

Some weeks, as I have said, are simply struck out of
my existence. When gradually the cold, grey light
of returning life stole in upon me, I almost hoped it
might be fallacious. I hated to come back to the frightful routine of existence. I was so very weak that even

after the fever left me I might easily have died at any moment.

I was promoted at length to the easy-chair, in which, in dressing-gown and slippers, people recover from dangerous illness. There, in the listlessness of exhaustion, I used to sit for hours, without reading, without speaking, without even thinking. Gradually, by little, my spirit revived, and, as life returned, the black cares and fears essential to existence glided in, and gathered round with awful faces.

One day old Rebecca, who, no doubt, had long been anxious, asked :

" How did you come by that knife, Miss Ethel, that you fetched home in your hand the night you took ill ?"

" A knife ? Did I ?" I spoke, quietly suppressing my horror. " What was it like ?"

I was almost unconscious until then that I had really taken away the dagger in my hand. This speech of Rebecca's nearly killed me. They were the first words I had heard connecting me distinctly with that ghastly scene.

She described it, and repeated her question.

" Where is it ?" I asked.

" Mr. Carmel took it away with him," she replied, " the same night."

" Mr. Carmel ?" I repeated, remembering with a new terror his connexion with Monsieur Droqville. " You had no business to allow him to see it, much less—good Heaven !—to take it."

I stood up in my terror, but I was too weak, and stumbled back into the chair.

I would answer no question of hers. She saw that she was agitating me, and desisted.

The whole scene in the jeweller's shop remained emblazoned in vivid tints and lights on my memory. But there was something more, and that perhaps the most terrible ingredient in it.

I had recognised another face besides Droqville's. It started between me and the wounded man as I recoiled from my own blow. One hand was extended towards me, to prevent my repeating the stroke—the other held up the wounded man.

Sometimes I doubted whether the whole of that frightful episode was not an illusion. Sometimes it seemed only that the pale face, so much younger and handsomer than Monsieur Droqville's—the fiery eyes, the frown, the scarred forehead, the suspended smile that had for only that dreadful moment started into light before me so close to my face, were those of a spectre.

The young man who had been turning over the jewels at the counter, and who had offered to give me change for my imaginary sovereign, was the very man I had seen shipwrecked at Malory; the man who had in the wood near Plas Ylwd fought that secret duel; and who had afterwards made, with so reckless an audacity, those mad declarations of love to me; the man who, for a time, had so haunted my imagination, and respecting whom I had received warnings so dark and formidable.

Nothing could be more vivid than this picture, nothing more uncertain than its reality. I did not see recognition in the face; all was so instantaneous. Well, I cared not. I was dying. What was the world to me? I had assigned myself to death; and I was willing to accept that fate rather than re-ascend to my frightful life.

My poor mother, who knew nothing of my strange adventure, had experienced one of those deceitful rallies which sometimes seem to promise a long reprieve, in that form of heart-complaint under which she suffered. She only knew that I had had brain-fever. How near to death I had been she never knew. She was spared, too, the horror of my dreadful adventure. I was now recovering rapidly and surely; but I was so utterly weak and heart-broken that I fancied I must die, and thought that they were either deceived themselves, or trying kindly, but in vain, to deceive me. I was at length convinced by finding myself able, as I have said, to sit up. Mamma was often with me, cheered by my recovery. I dare say she had been more alarmed than Rebecca supposed.

I learned from mamma that the money that had main-

tained us through my illness had come from Mr. Carmel.
Little as it was, it must have cost him exertion to get it;
for men in his position cannot, I believe, own money of
their own. It was very kind. I said nothing, but I was
grateful; his immovable fidelity touched me deeply. I
wondered whether Mr. Carmel had often made inquiries
during my illness, or had shown an interest in my recovery. But I dared not ask.

CHAPTER XLIV.

AN OMINOUS VISIT.

 HAVE sometimes felt that, even without a revelation, we might have discovered that the human race was born to immortality. Death is an intrusion here. Children can't believe in it. When they see it first, it strikes them with curiosity and wonder. It is a long time before they comprehend its real character, or believe that it is common to all; to the end of our days we are hardly quite sincere when we talk of our own deaths.

Seeing mamma better, I thought no more of her danger than if the angel of death had never been within our doors, and I had never seen the passing shadow of that spectre in her room.

As my strength returned, I grew more and more gloomy and excited. I was haunted by never-slumbering, and very reasonable, fore-castings of danger. In the first place, I was quite in the dark as to whether Monsieur Droqville was dangerously or mortally hurt, and I had no way of learning anything of him. Rebecca, it is true, used to take in, for her special edification, a Sunday paper, in which all the horrors of the week were displayed, and she used to con it over regularly, day after day, till the next number made its appearance. If Monsieur Droqville's name, with which she was familiar, had occurred in this odious register, she had at least had a fair chance of seeing it, and if she had seen it, she would be pretty sure to have mentioned it. Secretly, however,

I was in miserable fear. Mr. Carmel had not returned since my recovery had ceased to be doubtful, and he was in possession of the weapon that had fallen from my hand.

In his retention of this damning piece of evidence, and his withdrawing himself so carefully from my presence, coupled with my knowledge of the principles that bound him to treat all private considerations, feelings, and friendships as non-existent, when they stood ever so little in the way of his all-pervading and supreme duty to his order—there was a sinister augury. I lived in secret terror ; no wonder I was not recovering quickly.

One day, when we had sat a long time silent, I asked Rebecca how I was dressed the night I had gone to Lord Chellwood's. I was immensely relieved when she told me, among other things, that I had worn a thick black veil. This was all I wanted to be assured of; for I could not implicitly rely upon my recollection through the haze and mirage of fever. It was some comfort to think that neither Monsieur Droqville nor Mr. Marston could have recognised my features.

In this state of suspense I continued for two or three weeks. At the end of that time a little adventure happened. I was sitting in an arm-chair, in our drawing-room, with pillows about me, one afternoon, and had fallen into a doze. Mamma was in the room, and, when I had last seen her, was reading her Bible, which she now did sometimes for hours together—sometimes with tears, always with the trembling interest of one who has lost everything else.

I had fallen asleep. I was waked by tones that terrified me. I thought that I was still dreaming, or that I had lost my reason. I heard the nasal and energetic tones of Monsieur Droqville, talking with his accustomed rapidity in the room—not to mamma, for, as I afterwards found, she had left the room while I was asleep, but to Rebecca.

Happily for me, a screen stood between me and the door, and I suppose he did not know that I was in the room. At every movement of his foot on the floor, at every harsh emphasis in his talk, my heart bounded. I was afraid to move, almost to breathe, lest I should draw his attention to me.

T

My illness had quite unnerved me. I was afraid that, restless and inquisitive as I knew him to be, he would peep round the screen, and see and talk to me. I did not know the object of his visit; but in terror I surmised it, and I lay among my pillows, motionless, and with my eyes closed, while I heard him examine Rebecca, sharply, as to the date of my illness, and the nature of it.

"When was Miss Ware last out, before her illness?" he asked at length.

"I could not tell you that exactly, sir," answered Rebecca, evasively. "She left the house but seldom, just before she was took ill; for her mamma being very bad, she was but little out of doors then."

He made a pretence of learning the facts of my case simply as a physician, and he offered in that capacity to see me at the moment. He asked the question in an off-hand way. "I can see her, I dare say? I'm a doctor, you know. Where is Miss Ware?"

The moment of silence that intervened before her answer seemed to me to last five minutes. She answered, however, quite firmly:

"No, sir; I thank you. She's attended by a doctor, quite reg'lar, and she's asleep now."

Rebecca had heard me speak with horror of Monsieur Droqville, and did not forget my antipathy.

He hesitated. I heard his fingers drumming, as he mused, upon the other side of the screen.

"Well," he said, dwelling on the word meditatively, "it doesn't matter much. I don't mind; only it might have been as well. However, you can tell Mrs. Ware a note to my old quarters will find me, and I shall be very happy."

And so saying, I heard him walk, at first slowly, from the room, and then run briskly down the stairs. Then the old hall-door shut smartly after him.

The fear that this man inspired, and not without reason, in my mind, was indescribable. I can't be mistaken in my recollection upon that point, for, as soon as he was gone, I fainted.

When I recovered, my fears returned. No one who has not experienced that solitary horror, knows what it is to keep an undivulged secret, full of danger, every hour in-

spiring some new terror, with no one to consult, and no
courage but your own to draw upon. Even mamma's
dejected spirits took fire at what she termed the audacity
of Monsieur Droqville's visit. My anger, greater than
hers, was silenced by fear. Mamma was roused; she ran
volubly—though interrupted by many sobs and gushes of
tears—over the catalogue of her wrongs and miseries, all
of which she laid to Monsieur Droqville's charge.

The storm blew over, however, in an hour or so. But
later in the evening mamma was suffering under a return
of her illness, brought on by her agitation. It was not
violent; still there was suffering; and, to me, gloomier
proof that her malady was established, and the grave in a
nearer perspective. This turned my alarms into a new
channel.

She was very patient and gentle. As I sat by her bedside, looking at her sad face, what unutterable tenderness,
what sorrow trembled at my heart! At about six o'clock
she had fallen asleep, and with this quietude my thoughts
began to wander, and other fears returned. It was for no
good, I was sure, that Monsieur Droqville had tracked us
to our dismal abode. Whatever he might do in this affair
of my crime, or mania, passion would not guide it, nor
merely social considerations; it would be directed by a
policy the principles of which I could not anticipate. I
had no clue to guide me; I was in utter darkness, and
surrounded by all the fancies that imagination conjures
from the abyss.

I was not destined to wait very long in uncertainty.

CHAPTER XLV.

CONFIDENTIAL.

THE sun was setting, when, on tip-toe, scarcely letting my dress rustle, so afraid I was of disturbing mamma's sleep, I stole from her room, intending to give some directions to Rebecca Torkill. As I went down the dusky stairs I passed our Malory maid, who said something, pointing to the drawing-room. I saw her lips move, but, as will happen when one is pre-occupied, I took in nothing of what she said, but, with a mechanical acquiescence, followed the direction of her hand, and entered the sitting-room.

Our house stood upon high ground, and the nearest houses between our front windows and the west were low, so that the last beams of sunset, red with smoke and mist, passed over their roofs, and shone dimly on the oak panels opposite. The windows were narrow, and the room rather dark. I saw some one standing at the window-frame in the shade. I was startled, and hesitated, close to the door. The figure turned quickly, the sun glancing on his features. It was Mr. Carmel. He came towards me quickly; and he said, as I fancied, very coldly,

"Can you spare me two or three minutes alone, Miss Ware? I have but little to say," he added, as I did not answer. "But it is important, and I will make my words as few as possible."

We were standing close to the door. I assented. He closed it gently, and we walked slowly, side by side, to the window where he had been standing. He turned. The faint sun, like a distant fire, lighted his face. What singular dark eyes he had, so large, so enthusiastic! and had ever human eye such a character of suffering? I knew very well what he was going to speak of. The face, sad, sombre, ascetic, with which I was so familiar, I now, for the first time, understood.

The shadow of the confessional was on it. It was the face of one before whom human nature, in moments of terrible sincerity, had laid bare its direful secrets, and submitted itself to a melancholy anatomisation. To some minds, sympathetic, proud, sensitive the office of the confessor must be full of self-abasement, pain, and horror. We who know our own secrets, and no one else's, know nothing of the astonishment, and melancholy, and disgust that must strike some minds on contemplating the revelations of others, and discovering, for certain, that the standard of human nature is not above such and such a level.

"I have brought you this," he said, scarcely above his breath, holding the knife so that it lay across the hollow of his hand. His haggard eyes were fixed on me, and he said, "I know the whole story of it. Unless you forbid me, I will drop it into the river to-night; it is the evidence of an act for which you are, I thank God, no more accountable than a somnambulist for what she does in her dream. Over Monsieur Droqville I have neither authority nor influence; on the contrary, he can command me. But of this much I am sure—so long as your friends do not attack Lady Lorrimer's will—and I believe they have no idea of taking any such step—you need fear no trouble whatever from him."

I made him no reply, but I think he saw something in my face that made him add, with more emphasis:

"You may be sure of that."

I was immensely and instantly relieved, for I knew that there was not the slightest intention of hazarding any litigation on the subject of the will.

"But," he resumed, in the same cold tones, and with the same anxiety in his dark eyes, "there is a person from whom you may possibly experience annoyance. There are circumstances of which, as yet, you know nothing, that may, not unnaturally, bring you once more into contact with Mr. Marston. If that should happen, you must be on your guard. I understand that he said something that implies his suspicions. It may have been no more than conjecture. It may be that it was impossible he could have recognised you with certainty. If, I repeat, an untoward destiny should bring you together under the same roof, be wise, stand aloof from him, admit nothing; defeat his suspicions and his cunning by impenetrable caution. He has an interest in seeking to disgrace you, and where he has an object to gain he has neither conscience nor mercy. I wish I could inspire you with the horror of that mean and formidable character which so many have acquired by a bitter experience. I can but repeat my warning, and implore of you to act upon it, if the time should come. This thing I retain for the present"—he glanced at the weapon in his hand—" and dispose of it to-night, as I said."

There was no emotion in his manner; no sign of any special interest in me; but his voice and looks were unspeakably earnest, and inspired me with a certain awe.

I had not forgiven Mr. Carmel yet, or rather my pride would not retract; and my parting with him at our former house was fresh in my recollection. So it was, I might suppose, in his; for his manner was cold, and even severe.

" Our old acquaintance ended, Miss Ware, by your command, and, on reflection, with my own willing submission. When last we parted, I thought it unlikely that we should ever meet again, and this interview is not voluntary— necessity compelled it. I have simply done my duty, and, I earnestly hope, not in vain. It must be something very unlooked for, indeed, that shall ever constrain me to trouble you again."

He showed no sign of wishing to bid me a kindlier farewell. The actual, as well as metaphorical, distance between us had widened; he was by this time at the door; he opened it, and took his leave, very coldly. It was very unlike his former parting. I had only said:

" I am very grateful, Mr. Carmel, for your care of me— miserable me!"

He made no answer; he simply repeated his farewell, as gently and coldly as before, and left the room, and I saw him walk away from our door in the fast-fading light.

Heavier and heavier was my heart, as I saw him move quickly away. I had yearned, during our cold interview, to put out my hand to him, and ask him, in simple phrase, to make it up with me. I burned to tell him that I had judged him too hardly, and was sorry ; but my pride forbade it. His pride too, I thought, had held him aloof, and so I had lost my friend. My eyes filled with tears, that rolled heavily over my cheeks.

I sat at one of our windows, looking, over the distant roofs, towards the discoloured and disappearing tints of evening and the melancholy sky, which even through the smoke of London has its poetry and tenderness, until the light faded, and the moon began to shine through the twilight. Then I went upstairs, and found mamma still sleeping. As I stood by the bed looking at her, Rebecca Torkill at my side whispered :

" She's looking very pale, poor thing, don't you think, miss ? Too pale, a deal."

I did think so ; but she was sleeping tranquilly. Every change in her looks was now a subject of anxiety, but her hour had not quite come yet. She looked so very pale that I began to fear she had fainted ; but she awoke just then, and said she would sit up for a little time. Her colour did not return ; she seemed faint, but thought she should be more herself by-and-by.

She came down to the drawing-room, and soon did seem better, and chatted more than she had done, I think, since our awful misfortune had befallen us, and appeared more like her former self ; I mean, that simpler and tender self that I had seen far away from artificial London, among the beautiful solitudes of her birthplace.

While we were talking here, Rebecca Torkill, coming in now and then, and lending a word, after the manner of privileged old rustic servants, to keep the conversation going, the business of this story was being transacted in other places.

Something of Mr. Carmel's adventures that night I afterwards learned. He had two or three calls to make before he went to his temporary home. A friend had lent him, during his absence abroad, his rooms in the Temple. Arrived there, he let himself in by a latch-key. It was

night, the shutters unclosed, the moon shining outside,
and its misty beams, slanting in at the dusky windows,
touched objects here and there in the dark room with a
cold distinctness.

To a man already dejected, what is more dispiriting
than a return to empty and unlighted rooms? Mr. Carmel
moved like a shadow through this solitude, and in his
melancholy listlessness, stood for a time at the window.

Here and there a light, from a window in the black line
of buildings opposite, showed that human thought and
eyes were busy; but if these points of light and life made
the prospect less dismal, they added by contrast to the
gloom that pervaded his own chambers.

As he stood, some dimly-seen movement caught his eye,
and, looking over his shoulder, he saw the door through
which he himself had come in slowly open, and a man put
in his head, and then enter silently, and shut the door.
This figure, faintly seen in the imperfect light, resembled
but one man of all his acquaintance, and he the last man
in the world, as he thought, who would have courted a
meeting. Carmel stood for a moment startled and chilled
by his presence.

"I say, Carmel, don't you know me?" said a very
peculiar voice. "I saw you come in, and intended to
knock; but you left your door open."

By this time he had reached the window, and stood
beside Mr. Carmel, with the moonlight revealing his
features sharply enough. That pale light fell upon the
remarkable face of Mr. Marston.

"I'm not a ghost, though I've been pretty near it two
or three times. I see what you're thinking—death may
have taken better men? I might have been very well
spared? and having escaped it, I should have laid the
lesson to heart? Well, so I have. I was very nearly
killed at the great battle of Fuentas. I fought for the
Queen of Spain, and be hanged to her! She owes me
fifteen pounds ten and elevenpence, British currency, to
this day. It only shows my luck. In that general action
there were only four living beings hit so as to draw blood
—myself, a venerable orange-woman, a priest's mule, and
our surgeon-in-chief, whose thumb and razor were broken

off by a spent ball, as he was shaving a grenadier, under an umbrella, while the battle was raging. You see the Spaniard is a discreet warrior, and we very seldom got near enough to hurt each other. I was hit by some blundering beast. He must have shut his eyes, like Gil Blas, for there was not a man in either army who could ever hit anything he aimed at. No matter, he very nearly killed me; half an inch higher, and I must have made up my mind to see you, dear Carmel, no more, and to shut my eyes on this sweet, jesuitical world. It was the first ugly wound of the campaign, and the enemy lived for a long time on the reputation of it. But the truth is, I have suffered a great deal in sickness, wounds, and fifty other ways. I have been as miserable a devil as any righteous man could wish me to be; and I am changed; upon my honour, I'm as different a man from what I was as you are from me. But I can't half see you; do light your candles, I entreat."

"Not while you are here," said Carmel.

"Why, what are you afraid of?" said Marston. "You haven't, I hope, got a little French milliner behind your screen, like Joseph Surface, who, I think, would have made a very pretty Jesuit. Why should you object to light?"

"Your ribaldry is out of place here," said Carmel, who knew very well that Marston had not come to talk nonsense, and recount his adventures in Spain; and that his business, whatever it may be, was likely to be odious. "What right have you to enter my room? What right to speak to me anywhere?"

"Come, Carmel, don't be unreasonable; you know very well I can be of use to you."

"You can be of none," answered Carmel, a little startled; "and if you could, I would not have you. Leave my room, sir."

"You can exorcise some evil spirits, but not me, till I've said my say," answered Marston, with a smile that looked grim and cynical in the moonlight. "I say I can be of use to you."

"It's enough; I won't have it; go," said Carmel, with a sterner emphasis.

Marston smiled again, and looked at him.

"Well, I can be of use," he said, "and I don't want particularly to be of use to you; but you can do me a kindness, and it is better to do it quietly than upon compulsion. Will you be of use to me? I'll show you how?"

"God forbid!" said Carmel, quickly. "It is nothing good, I'm sure."

Marston looked at him with an evil eye; it was a sneer of intense anger.

After some seconds he said, his eyes still fixed askance on Mr. Carmel:

"Forgive us our trespasses, as we forgive, et cætera—eh? I suppose you sometimes pray your paternoster? A pretty time you have kept up that old grudge against me—haven't you—about Ginevra?"

He kept his eyes on Carmel, as if he enjoyed the spectacle of the torture he applied, and liked to see the wince and quiver that accompanied its first thrill.

At the word, Edwyn Carmel's eyes started up from the floor, to which they had been lowered, with a flash to the face of his visitor. His forehead flushed; he remained speechless for some seconds. Marston did not smile; his features were fixed, but there was a secret, cruel smile in his eyes as he watched these evidences of agitation.

"Well, I should not have said the name; I should not have alluded to it; I did wrong," he said, after some seconds; "but I was going, before you riled me, to say how really I blame myself, now, for all that deplorable business. I do, upon my soul! What more can a fellow say, when reparation is impossible, than that he is sorry? Is not repentance all that a man like me can offer? I saw you were thinking of it; you vexed me; I was angry, and I could not help saying what I did. Now do let that miserable subject drop; and hear me, on quite another, without excitement. It is not asking a great deal."

Carmel placed his hand to his head, as if he had not heard what he said, and then groaned.

"Why don't you leave me?" he said, piteously, turning again towards Marston; "don't you see that nothing but pain and reproach can result from your staying here?"

"Let me first say a word," said Marston; "you can assist me in a very harmless and perfectly unobjectionable matter. Every fellow who wants to turn over a new leaf marries. The lady is poor—there is that proof, at least, that it is not sordid; you know her, you can influence her——."

"Perhaps I do know her; perhaps I know who she is— I may as well say, at once, I do. I have no influence; and if I had, I would not use it for you. I think I know your reasons, also; I think I can see them."

"Well, suppose there are reasons, it's not the worse for that," said Marston, growing again angry. "I thought I would just come and try whether you chose to be on friendly terms. I'm willing; but if you won't, I can't help you. I'll make use of you all the same. You had better think again. I'm pleasanter as a friend than an enemy."

"I don't fear you as an enemy, and I do fear you as a friend. I will aid you in nothing; I have long made up my mind," answered Carmel, savagely.

"I think, through Monsieur Droqville, I'll manage that. Oh, yes, you will give me a lift."

"Why should Monsieur Droqville control my conduct?" asked Mr. Carmel sharply.

"It was he who made you a Catholic; and I suspect he has a fast hold on your conscience and obedience. If he chooses to promote the matter, I rather think you must."

"You may think as you please," said Carmel.

"That's a great deal from your Church," sneered Marston; and, changing his tone again, he said: "Look here, Carmel, once more; where's the good in our quarrelling? I won't press that other point, if you don't like; but you must do this, the most trifling thing in the world—you must tell me where Mrs. Ware lives. No one knows since old Ware made a fool of himself, poor devil! But I think you'll allow that, with my feelings, I may, at least, speak to the young lady's mother? Do tell me where they are. You know, of course?"

"If I did know, I should not tell you; so it does not matter," answered Carmel.

Marston looked very angry, and a little silence followed.

"I suppose you have now said everything," resumed Carmel; "and again I desire that you will leave me."

"I mean to do so," said Marston, putting on his hat with a kind of emphasis, "though it's hard to leave such romantic, light, and brilliant company. You might have had peace, and you prefer war. I think there are things you have at heart that I could forward, if all went right with me." He paused, but Carmel made no sign. "Well, you take your own way now, not mine; and, by-and-by, I think you'll have reason to regret it."

Marston left the room, with no other farewell. The clap with which he shut the door, as he went, had hardly ceased to ring round the walls, when Carmel saw him emerge in the court below, and walk away with a careless air, humming a tune in the moonlight.

Why is it that there are men upon earth whose secret thoughts are always such as to justify fear; and nearly all whose plans, if not through malice, from some other secret obliquity, involve evil to others? We have most of us known something of some such man; a man whom we are disposed to watch in silence; who, smile as he may, brings with him a sense of insecurity, and whose departure is a real relief. Such a man seems to me a stranger on earth; his confidences to be with unseen companions; his mental enjoyments not human; and his mission here cruel and mysterious. I look back with wonder and with thankfulness. Fearful is the strait of any one who, in the presence of such an influence, under such a fascination, loses the sense of danger.

CHAPTER XLVI.

AFTER OFFICE HOURS.

EXT day our doctor called. He was very kind. He had made mamma many visits, and attended me through my tedious fever, and would never take a fee after the first one. I daresay that other great London physicians, whom the world reputes worldly, often do similar charities by stealth. My own experience is that affliction like ours does not lower the sufferer's estimate of human nature. It is a great discriminator of character, and sifts men like wheat. Those among our friends who are all chaff it blows away altogether; those who have noble attributes, it leaves all noble. There is no more petulance, no more hurry or carelessness; we meet, in after-contact with them, be it much or little, only the finer attributes, gentleness, tenderness, respect, patience.

I do not remember one of those who had known us in better days, among the very few who now knew where to find us, who did not show us even more kindness than they could have had opportunity of showing if we had been in our former position. Who could be kinder than Mr. Forrester? Who more thoughtful than Mr. Carmel, to whom at length we had traced the flowers, and the books, and the piano, that were such a resource to me; and who had, during my illness, come every day to see mamma?

In his necessarily brief visits, Sir Jacob Lake was energetic and cheery; there was in his manner that which inspired confidence; but I fancied this day, as he was taking his leave of mamma, that I observed something like a shadow on his face, a transitory melancholy, that alarmed me. I accompanied him downstairs, and he stopped for a moment in the lobby outside the drawing-room.

"Has there been anything done since about that place—Malory, I think you call it?" he asked.

"No," I answered; "there is not the least chance. Sir Harry Rokestone is going to sell it, Mr. Jarlcot says; just through hatred of us, he thinks. He's an old enemy of ours; he says he hates our very name; and he won't write; he hasn't answered a single letter of Mr. Forrester's."

"I was only going to say that it wouldn't do; she could not bear so long a journey just now. I think she had better make no effort; she must not leave this at present."

"I'm afraid you think her very ill," I said, feeling myself grow pale.

"She is ill; and she will never be much better; but she may be spared to you for a long time yet. This kind of thing, however, is always uncertain; and it may end earlier than we think—I don't say it is likely, only possible. You must send for me whenever you want me; and I'll look in now and then, and see that all goes on satisfactorily."

I began to thank him earnestly, but he stopped me very good-naturedly. He could spare me little more than a minute; I walked with him to the hall-door, and although he said but little, and that little very cautiously, he left me convinced that I might lose my darling mother any day or hour. He had implied this very vaguely, but I was sure of it. People who have suffered great blows like mine, regard the future as an adversary, and believe its threatenings.

In flurry and terror I returned to the drawing-room, and shut the door; then, with the instinct that prevails, I went to mamma's room and sat down beside her.

I suppose every one has felt as I have felt. How magically the society of the patient, if not actually suffering, reassures us! The mere contiguity, the voice, the interest she takes in the common topics of our daily life, the cheerful and easy tone, even the little peevishness about the details of the sick-room, soon throw death again into perspective, and the instinct of life prevails against all facts and logic.

The form of heart-complaint from which my mother suffered had in it nothing revolting. I think I never remember her so pretty. The tint of her lips, and the colour of her cheeks, always lovely, were now more delicately brilliant than ever; and the lustre of her eyes, thus enhanced, was quite beautiful. The white tints a little paler, and her face and figure slightly thinner, but not unbecomingly, brought back a picture so girlish that I wondered while I looked; and when I went away the pretty face haunted me as the saddest and gentlest I had ever seen.

So many people have said that the approach of death induces a change of character, that I almost accept it for a general law of nature. I saw it, I know, in mamma. Not exactly an actual change, perhaps, but, rather, a subsidence of whatever was less lovely in her nature, and a proportionate predominance of all its sweetness and gentleness. There came also a serenity very different from the state of mind in which she had been from papa's death up to the time of my illness. I do not know whether she was conscious of her imminent danger. If she suspected it, she certainly did not speak of it to me or to Rebecca Torkill. But death is a subject on which some people, I believe, practise as many reserves as others do in love.

Next day mamma was much better, and sat in our drawing-room, and I read and talked to her, and amused her with my music. She sat in slippers and dressing-gown in an easy-chair, and we talked over a hundred plans which seemed to interest her. The effort to cheer mamma did me good, and I think we were both happier that day than we had been since ruin had so tragically overtaken us.

While we were thus employed at home, events connected with us and our history were not standing still in other places.

Mr. Forrester's business was very large; he had the assistance of two partners; but all three were hard worked. The offices of the firm occupied two houses in one of the streets which run down from the Strand to the river, at no great distance from Temple Bar. I saw these offices but once in my life; I suppose there was little to distinguish them and their arrangements from those of other well-frequented chambers; but I remember being struck with their air of business and regularity, and by the complicated topography of two houses fused into one.

Mr. Forrester, in his private office, had locked up his

desk. He was thinking of taking his leave of business for
the day. It was now past four, and he had looked into
the office where the collective firm did their business, and
where his colleagues were giving audience to a deputation
about a complicated winding-up. This momentary delay
cost him more time than he intended, for a clerk came in
and whispered in his ear:

" A gentleman wants to see you, sir."

" Why, hang it! I've left the office," said Mr. Forrester,
tartly—" don't you see ? Here's my hat in my hand ! Go
and look for me in my office, and you'll see I'm not there."

Very deferentially, notwithstanding this explosion, the
messenger added :

" I thought, sir, before sending him away, you might
like to see him ; he seemed to think he was doing us a
favour in looking in, and he has been hearing from you,
and would not take the trouble to write ; and he won't
call again."

" What's his name ?" asked Mr. Forrester, vacillating
a little.

" Sir Harry Rokestone," he said.

" Sir Harry Rokestone ? Oh ! Well, I suppose I must
see him. Yes, I'll see him ; bring him up to my private
room."

Mr. Forrester had hardly got back, laid aside his hat
and umbrella, and placed himself in his chair of state
behind his desk, when his aide-de-camp returned and
introduced " Sir Harry Rokestone ?"

Mr. Forrester rose, and received him with a bow. He
saw a tall man, with something grand and simple in his
gait and erect bearing, with a brown handsome face, and
a lofty forehead, noble and stern as if it had caught something of the gloomy character of the mountain scenery
among which his home was. He was dressed in the rustic
and careless garb of an old-fashioned country gentleman,
with gaiters up to his knees, as if he were going to stride
out upon the heather with his gun on his shoulder and his
dogs at his heel.

Mr. Forrester placed a chair for this gentleman, who,
with hardly a nod, and without a word, sat down. The
door closed, and they were alone.

CHAPTER XLVII.

SIR HARRY SPEAKS.

"YOU'RE Mr. Forrester?" said Sir Harry, in a deep, clear voice, quite in character with his appearance, and with a stern eye fixed on the solicitor.

That gentleman made a slight inclination of assent.

"I got all your letters, sir—every one," said the rustic baronet.

Mr. Forrester bowed.

"I did not answer one of them."

Mr. Forrester bowed again.

"Did it strike you, as a man of business, sir, that it was rather an odd omission your not mentioning where the ladies representing the late Mr. Ware's interests—if he had any remaining, which I don't believe—are residing?"

"I had actually written——" answered Mr. Forrester, turning the key in his desk, and slipping his hand under the cover, and making a momentary search. He had hesitated on the question of sending the letter or not; but, having considered whether there could be any possible risk in letting him know, and having come to the conclusion that there was none, he now handed this letter, a little obsolete as it was, to Sir Harry Rokestone.

"What's this?" said Sir Harry, breaking the seal and looking at the contents of the note, and thrusting it, thinking as it seemed all the time of something different, into his coat-pocket.

"The present address of Mrs. and Miss Ware, which I understood you just now to express a wish for," answered Mr. Forrester.

"Express a wish, sir, for their address!" exclaimed Sir Harry, with a scoff. "Dall me if I did, though! What the deaul, man, should I want o' their *address*, as ye call it? They may live where they like for me. And so Ware's dead—died a worse death than the hangman's; and died not worth a plack, as I always knew he would. And what made you write all those foolish letters to me? Why did you go on plaguing me, when you saw I never gave you an answer to one of them? You that should be a man of head, how could ye be such a mafflin?" His northern accent became broader as he became more excited.

The audacity and singularity of this old man disconcerted Mr. Forrester. He did not afterwards understand why he had not turned him out of his room.

"I think, Sir Harry, you will find my reasons for writing very distinctly stated in my letters, if you are good enough to look into them."

"Ay, so I did; and I don't understand them, nor you neither."

It was not clear whether he intended that the reasons or the attorney were beyond his comprehension. Mr. Forrester selected the first interpretation, and, I daresay, rightly, as being the least offensive.

"Pardon me, Sir Harry Rokestone," said he, with a little dry dignity; "I have not leisure to throw away upon writing nonsense; I am one of those men who are weak enough to believe that there are rights besides those defined by statute or common law, and duties, consequently, you'll excuse me for saying, even more obligatory—Christian duties, which, in this particular case, plainly devolve upon you."

"Christian flam! Humbug! and you an attorney!"

"I'm not accustomed, sir, to be talked to in that way," said Mr. Forrester, who felt that his visitor was becoming insupportable.

"Of course you're not; living in this town you never hear a word of honest truth," said Sir Harry; "but I'm not so much in the dark ; I understand you pretty well, now ; and I think you a precious impudent fellow."

Both gentlemen had risen by this time, and Mr. Forrester, with a flush in his cheeks, replied, raising his head as he stooped over his desk while turning the key in the lock :

"And I beg to say, sir, that I, also, have formed my own very distinct opinion of you !"

Mr. Forrester flushed more decidedly, for he felt, a little too late, that he had perhaps made a rather rash speech, considering that his visitor seemed to have so little control over his temper, and also that he was gigantic.

The herculean baronet, however, who could have lifted him up by the collar, and flung him out of the window, only smiled sardonically, and said :

"Then we part, you and I, wiser men than we met. You write me no more letters, and I'll pay you no more visits."

With another cynical grin, he turned on his heel, and walked slowly down the stairs, leaving Mr. Forrester more ruffled than he had been for many a day.

CHAPTER XLVIII.

THE OLD LOVE.

THE hour had now arrived at which our room looked really becoming. It had been a particularly fine autumn; and I have mentioned the effect of a warm sunset streaming through the deep windows upon the oak panelling. This light had begun to fade, and its melancholy serenity had made us silent. I had heard the sound of wheels near our door, but that was nothing unusual, for carts often passed close by, carrying away the rubbish that had accumulated in the old houses now taken down.

Annie Owen, our Malory maid, peeped in at the door—came in, looking frightened and important, and closed it before she spoke. She was turning something about in her fingers.

"What is it, Anne?" I asked.

"Please, miss, there's an old gentleman downstairs; and he wants to know, ma'am," she continued, now addressing mamma, "whether you'll be pleased to see him."

Mamma raised herself, and looked at the girl with anxious, startled eyes.

"What is that you have got in your hand?" I asked.

"Oh! I beg your pardon, ma'am; he told me to give you this, please." And she handed a card to mamma. She looked at it and grew very pale. She stood up with a flurried air.

"Are you sure?" she said.

"Please, ma'am?" inquired the girl in perplexity.

"No matter. Ethel, dear, it is he. Yes, I'll see him," she said to the girl, in an agitated way; "show him up. Ethel, it's Harry Rokestone—don't go; he is so stern—I know how he'll speak to me—but I ought not to refuse to see him."

I was angry at my mother's precipitation. If it had

rested with me, what an answer the savage old man should have had! I was silent. By this time the girl was again at the hall-door. The first moment of indignation over, I was thunderstruck. I could not believe that anything so portentous was on the eve of happening.

The moments of suspense were not many. My eyes were fixed on the door as if an executioner were about to enter by it. It opened, and I saw—need I tell you?—the very same tall, handsome old man I had seen in the chapel of Cardyllion Castle.

"Oh! Mabel," he said, and stopped. It was the most melancholy, broken voice I had ever heard. "My darling!"

My mother stood with her hand stretched vaguely towards him, trembling.

"Oh! Mabel, it is you, and we've met at last!"

He took her hand in one of his, and laid the other suddenly across his eyes and sobbed. There was silence. for a good while, and then he spoke again.

"My pretty Mabel! I lost ye; I tried to hate ye, Mabel; but all would not do, for I love ye still. I was mad and broken-hearted—I tried to hate ye, but I couldn't; I'd a' given my life for you all the time, and you shall have Malory—it's your own—I've bought it—ye'll not be too proud to take a gift from the old man, my only darling! The spring and summer are over, it's winter now wi' the old fellow, and he'll soon lie under the grass o' the kirk-garth, and what does it all matter then? And you, bonny Mabel, there's wonderful little change wi' you!"

He was silent again, and tears coursed one another down his rugged cheeks.

"I saw you sometimes a long way off, when you didn't think I was looking, and the sight o' ye wrung my heart, that I didn't hold up my head for a week after. A lonely man I've been for your sake, Mabel; and down to Gouden Friars, and among the fells, and through the lonnins of old Clusted Forest, and sailin' on the mere, where we two often were, thinkin' I saw ye in the shaddas, and your voice in my ear as far away as the call o' the wind—dreams, dreams—and now I've met ye."

He was holding mamma's hand in his, and she was crying bitterly.

"I knew nothing of all this till to-day—I got all Forrester's letters together. I was on the Continent—and you've been complaining, Mabel; but you're looking so young and bonny! It was care, care was the matter, care and trouble; but that's all over, and you shall never know anxiety more—you'll be well again—you shall live at Malory, if you like it, or Gouden Friars—Mardykes is to let. I've a right to help you, Mabel, and you have none to refuse my help, for I'm the only living kinsman you have. I don't count that blackguard lord for anything. You shall never know care again. For twenty years and more an angry man and dow I've been, caring for no one, love or likin,' when I had lost yours. But now it is past and over, and the days are sped."

A few melancholy and broken words more, and he was gone, promising to return next day at twelve, having seen Mr. Forrester in the meantime at his house in Piccadilly, and had a talk with him.

He was gone. He had not spoken a word to me—had not even appeared conscious that I was present. I daresay he was not. It was a little mortifying. To me he appeared a mixture, such as I never saw before, of brutality and tenderness. The scene had moved me.

Mamma was now talking excitedly. It had been an agitating meeting, and, till he had disclosed his real feelings, full of uncertainty. To prevent her from exerting herself too much, I took my turn in the conversation, and, looking from the window, still in the direction in which his cab had disappeared, I descanted with immense delight on the likelihood of his forthwith arranging that Malory should become our residence.

As I spoke, I turned about to listen for the answer I expected from mamma. I was shocked to see her look so very ill. I was by her side in a moment. She said a few words scarcely audible, and ceased speaking before she had ended her sentence. Her lips moved, and she made an eager gesture with her hand; but her voice failed. She made an effort, I thought, to rise, but her strength forsook her, and she fainted.

CHAPTER XLIX.

ALONE IN THE WORLD.

SIR HARRY did not find Mr. Forrester at home; the solicitor was at a consultation in the Temple. Thither drove the baronet, who was impetuous in most things, and intolerant of delay where an object lay near his heart. Up to the counsel's chambers in the Temple mounted Sir Harry Rokestone. He hammered his double knock at the door as peremptorily as he would have done at his own hall-door.

Mr. Forrester afforded him just half a minute; and they parted good friends, having made an appointment for the purpose of talking over poor mamma's affairs, and considering what was best to be done.

Sir Harry strode with the careless step of a mountaineer, along the front of the buildings, till he reached the entrance to which, in answer to a sudden inquiry, Mr. Forrester had directed him. Up the stairs he marched, and stopped at the door of the chambers occupied by Mr. Carmel. There he knocked again as stoutly as before. The door was opened by Edwyn Carmel himself.

"Is Mr. Carmel here?" inquired the old man.

"I am Mr. Carmel," answered he.

"And I am Sir Harry Rokestone," said the baronet. "I found a letter from you this morning; it had been lying at my house unopened for some time," said the baronet.

Mr. Carmel invited him to come in. There were candles

lighted, for it was by this time nearly dark; he placed a
chair for his visitor: they were alone.

Sir Harry Rokestone seated himself, and began:

"There was no need, sir, of apology for your letter;
intervention on behalf of two helpless and suffering ladies
was honourable to you; but I had also heard some particulars from their own professional man of business;
that, however, you could not have known. I have called
to tell you that I quite understand the case. So much for
your letter. But, sir, I have been informed that you are
a Jesuit."

"I am a Catholic priest, sir."

"Well, sir, I won't press the point; but the ruin of
that family has been brought about, so far as I can learn,
by gentlemen of that order. They got about that poor
foolish creature, Lady Lorrimer; and, by cajoleries and
terror, they got hold of every sixpence of her fortune,
which, according to all that's right and kind in nature,
should have gone to her nearest kindred."

Sir Harry's eyes were fixed on him, as if he expected
an answer.

"Lady Lorrimer did, I suppose, what pleased her best
in her will," said the young man, coldly; "Mrs. Ware
had expectations, I believe, which have been, you say,
disappointed."

"And do you mean to tell me that you don't know that
fact for certain?" said the old gentleman, growing hot.

"I'm not certain of anything of which I have no proof,
Sir Harry," answered Mr. Carmel. "If I were a Jesuit,
and your statement were a just one, still I should know
no more about the facts than I do now; for it would not
be competent for me to inquire into the proceedings of my
superiors in the order. It is enough for me to say that I
know nothing of any such influence exerted by any human
being upon Lady Lorrimer; and I need scarcely add that
I have never, by word or act, endeavoured ever so slightly
to influence Lady Lorrimer's dealings with her property!
Your ear, sir, has been abused by slander."

"By Jea! Here's modesty!" said Sir Harry, explod-
ing in a gruff laugh of scorn, and standing up. "What
a pack o' gaumless gannets you must take us for! Look-

ye, now, young sir. I have my own opinion about all that.
And tell your superiors, as you call them, they'll never
get a plack of old Harry Rokestone's money, while hand
and seal can bind, and law's law ; and if I catch a priest
in my house, ye may swear he'll get out of it quicker than
he came in. I'd thank you more for your letter, sir, if I
was a little more sure of the motive ; and now I've said
my say, and I wish ye good evening."

With a fierce smile, the old man looked at him steadily
for a few seconds, and then turning abruptly, left the room
and shut the door, with a firm clap, after him.

That was, to me, an anxious night. Mamma continued
ill; I had written rather a wild note for our doctor ; but
he did not come for many hours. He did not say much ;
he wrote a prescription, and gave some directions; he was
serious and reserved, which, in a physician, means alarm.
In answer to my flurried inquiries, as I went downstairs
by his side, he said :

"I told you, you recollect, that it is a capricious kind
of thing ; I hope she may be better when I look in in the
morning ; the nature of it is that it may end at any time,
with very little warning ; but with caution she may live
a year, or possibly two years. I've known cases, as dis-
couraging as hers, where life has been prolonged for three
years."

Next morning came, and I thought mamma much better.
I told her all that was cheery in the doctor's opinion, and
amused her with plans for our future. But the hour was
drawing near when doctors' opinions, and friends' hopes
and flatteries, and the kindly illusions of plans looking
pleasantly into an indefinite future, were to be swallowed
in the tremendous event.

About half an hour before our kind doctor's call,
mamma's faintness returned. I now began, and not an
hour too soon, to despair. The medicine he had ordered
the day before, to support her in those paroxysms, had
lost its power. Mamma had been for a time in the drawing-room, but having had a long fainting-fit there, I persuaded her, so soon as she was a little recovered, to return
to her bed.

I find it difficult, I may say, indeed, impossible, to

reduce the occurrences of this day to order. The picture is not, indeed, so chaotic as my recollection of the times and events that attended my darling Nelly's death. The shock, in that case, had affected my mind. But I do not believe that any one retains a perfectly arranged recollection of the flurried and startling scenes that wind up our hopes in the dread catastrophe. I never met a person yet who could have told the story of such a day with perfect accuracy and order.

I don't know what o'clock it was when the doctor came. There is something of the character of sternness in the brief questions, the low tone, and the silent inspection that mark his last visit to the sick-room. What is more terrible than the avowed helplessness that follows, and his evident acquiescence in the inevitable?

"Don't go. Oh, don't go yet; wait till I come back, only a few minutes; there might be a change, and something might be done."

I entreated; I was going up to mamma's room; I had come down with him to the drawing-room.

"Well, my dear, I'll wait." He looked at his watch. "I'll remain with you for ten minutes."

I suppose I looked very miserable, for I saw a great compassion in his face. He was very good-natured, and he added, placing his hand upon my arm, and looking gently in my face, "But, my poor child, you must not flatter yourself with hopes, for I have none—there are none."

But what so headstrong and so persistent as hope? Terrible must be that place where it never comes.

I had scarcely left the drawing-room, when Sir Harry Rokestone, of the kindly change in whom I had spoken to our good doctor, knocked at the hall-door. Our rustic maid, Anne Owen, who was crying, let him in, and told him the sudden news; he laid his hand against the door-post and grew pale. He did not say a word for as long as you might count twenty, then he asked:

"Is the doctor here?"

The girl led the way to the drawing-room.

"Bad news, doctor?" said the tall old man, in an agitated voice, as he entered, with his eyes fixed on Sir

Jacob Lake. "My name is Rokestone—Sir Harry Rokestone. Tell me, is it so bad as the servant says? You have not given her up?"

The doctor shook his head; he advanced slowly a step or two to meet Sir Harry, and said, in a low tone:

"Mrs. Ware is dying—sinking very fast."

Sir Harry walked to the mantelpiece, laid his hand on it, and stood there without moving. After a little he turned again, and came to Sir Jacob Lake.

"You London doctors—you're so hurried," he said, a little wildly, "from place to place. I think—I think—look, doctor; save her! save her, man!"—he caught the doctor's wrist in his hand—"and I'll make your fortune. Ye need never do an hour's work more. Man was never so rewarded, not for a queen."

The doctor looked very much offended; but, coarse as the speech was, it was delivered with a pathetic and simple vehemence that disarmed him.

"You mistake me, sir," he said. "I take a very deep interest in this case. I have known Mrs. Ware from the time when she came to live in London. I hope I do my duty in every case, but in this I have been particularly anxious, and I do assure you, if——— What's that?"

It was, as Shakespeare says, "a cry of women," the sudden shrilly clamour of female voices heard through distant doors.

The doctor opened the door, and stood at the foot of the stairs.

"Ay, that's it," he said, shaking his head a little. "It's all over."

CHAPTER L.

A PROTECTOR.

WAS in mamma's room; I was holding up her head; old Rebecca and Anne Owen were at the bedside. My terrified eyes saw the doctor drawing near softly in the darkened room. I asked him some wild questions, and he answered gently, "No, dear; no, no."

The doctor took his stand at the bedside, and, with his hands behind his back, looked down at her face sadly. Then he leaned over. He laid his hand gently on mamma's, put his fingers to her wrist, felt, also, for the beating of her heart, looked again at her face, and rose from his stooping posture with a little shake of the head and a sigh, looked in the still face once more for a few seconds, and turning to me, said tenderly:

"You had better come away, dear; there's nothing more to be done. You must not distress yourself."

That last look of the physician at his patient, when he stands up, and becomes on a sudden no more than any other spectator, his office over, his command ended, is terrifying.

For two or three minutes I scarcely knew who was going or coming. The doctor, who had just gone down-stairs, returned with an earnest request from Sir Harry Rokestone that in an hour or so he might be permitted to come back and take a last look of mamma. He did come back, but his heart failed him. He could not bear to see her now. He went into the drawing-room, and, a few minutes later, Rebecca Torkill came into my room, where, by this time, I was crying alone, and said:

" Ye mustn't take on so, my darling; rouse yourself a bit. That old man, Sir Harry Rokestone, is down in the drawing-room in a bit of a taking, and he says he must see you before he goes."

" I can't see him, Rebecca," I said.

" But what am I to say to him ?" said she.

" Simply that. Do tell him I can't go down to see anybody."

" But ain't it as well to go and have it over, miss ?— for see you he will, I am sure of that; and I can't manage him."

" Does he seem angry ?" I said, " or only in grief? I daresay he is angry. Yesterday, when he was here, he never spoke one word to me—he took no notice of me whatever."

At another time an interview with Sir Harry Rokestone might have inspired many more nervous misgivings ; as it was, I had only this : I knew that he had hated papa, and . I, as my father's child, might well " stand within his danger," as the old phrase was. And the eccentric and violent old man, I thought, might, in the moment and agony of having lost for ever the object of an affection which my father had crossed, have sent for me, his child, simply to tell me that with my father's blood I had inherited his curse.

" I can't say, miss, indeed. He was talking to himself, and stamping with his thick shoes on the floor a bit as he walked. But ain't it best to have done with him at once, if he ain't friendly, and not keep him here, coming and going ?—for see you he will, sooner or later."

" I don't very much care. Perhaps you are right. Yes, I will go down and see him," I said. " Go you down, Rebecca, and tell him that I am coming."

I had been lying on my bed, and required to adjust my hair, and dress a little.

As I came downstairs a few minutes later, I passed poor mamma's door ; the key turned in it. Was I walking in a dream? Mamma dead, and Sir Harry Rokestone waiting in the drawing-room to see me ! I leaned against the wall, feeling faint for a minute.

As I approached the drawing-room door, which was

open, I heard Rebecca's voice talking to him; and then the old man said, in a broken voice:

"Where's the child? Bring her here. I will see the bairn."

I was the "bairn" summoned to his presence. This broad north-country dialect, the language, I suppose, of his early childhood, always returned to him in moments when his feelings were excited. I entered the room, and he strode towards me.

"Ha! the lassie," he cried, gently. There was a little tremor in his deep voice; a pause followed, and he added, vehemently, "By the God above us, I'll never forsake you!"

He held me to his heart for some seconds without speaking.

"Gimma your hand. I love you for her sake," he said, and took my hand firmly and kindly in his, and he looked earnestly in my face for awhile in silence. "You're like her; but, oh! lassie, you'll never be the same. There'll never be another such as Mabel."

Tears, which he did not dry or conceal, trickled down his rugged cheeks.

He had been talking with Rebecca Torkill, and had made her tell him everything she could think of about mamma.

"Sit ye down here, lass," he said to me, having recovered his self-possession. "You are to come home wi' me, to Gouden Friars, or wherever else you like best. You shall have music and flowers, and books and dresses, and you shall have your maid to wait on you, like other young ladies, and you shall bring Rebecca with you. I'll do my best to be kind and helpful; and you'll be a blessing to a very lonely old man; and as I love you now for Mabel's sake, I'll come to love you after for your own."

I did not think his stern old face could look so gentle and sorrowful, and the voice, generally so loud and commanding, speak so tenderly. The light of that look was full of compassion and melancholy, and indicated a finer nature than I had given the uncouth old man credit for. He seemed pleased by what I said; he was doing, he felt, something for mamma in taking care of the child she had left so helpless.

Days were to pass before he could speak to me in a more business-like way upon his plans for my future life, and those were days of agitation and affliction, from which, even in memory, I turn away.

I am going to pass over some little time. An interval of six weeks finds me in a lofty wainscoted room, with two stone-shafted windows, large and tall, in proportion, admitting scarcely light enough however, to make it cheerful. These windows are placed at the end of an oblong apartment, and the view they command is melancholy and imposing. I was looking through the sudden hollow of a mountain gorge, with a level of pasture between its craggy sides, upon a broad lake, nearly three hundred yards away, a barrier of mountains rising bold and purple from its distant margin. A file of gigantic trees stretches from about midway down to the edge of the lake, and partakes of the sombre character of the scene. On the steeps at either side, in groups or singly, stand some dwarf oak and birch-trees, scattered and wild, very picturesque, but I think enhancing the melancholy of the view.

For me this spot, repulsive as it would have been to most young people, had a charm ; not, indeed, that of a " happy valley," but the charm of seclusion, which to a wounded soul is above price. Those who have suffered a great reverse will understand my horror of meeting the people whom I had once known, my recoil from recognition, and how welcome are the shadows and silence of the cloister compared with the anguish of a comparative publicity.

Experience had early dissipated the illusions of youth, and taught me to listen to the whisperings of hope with cold suspicion. I had no trust in the future—my ghastly mischances had filled me with disgust and terror. My knowledge haunted me ; I could not have learned it from the experience of another, though my instructor had come to me from the dead. I was here, then, under no constraint, not the slightest. It was of my own free choice that I came, and remained here. Sir Harry Rokestone would have taken me anywhere I pleased.

Other people spoke of him differently ; I can speak only

of my own experience. Nothing could be more considerate and less selfish than his treatment of me, nothing more tender and parental. Kind as he was, however, I always felt a sort of awe in his presence. It was not, indeed, quite the awe that is founded on respect—he was old—in most relations stern—and his uneducated moral nature, impetuous and fierce, seemed capable of tragic things. It was not a playful nature, with which the sympathies and spirits of a young person could at all coalesce.

Thormen Fell, at the north of the lake, that out-topped the rest, and shielded us from the wintry wind, rearing its solemn head in solitude, snowy, rocky, high in air, the first of the fells visible, the first to greet me, far off in the sunshine, with its dim welcome as I returned to Golden Friars. It was friendly, it was kindly, but stood aloof and high, and was always associated in my mind with danger, isolation, and mystery. And I think my liking for Sir Harry Rokestone partook of my affection for Thormen Fell.

So, as you have no doubt surmised, I was harboured in the old baronet's feudal castle of Dorracleugh. A stern, wild, melancholy residence, but one that suited wonderfully my present mood.

He was at home; another old gentleman, whose odd society I liked very well, was also at that time an inmate of the house. I will tell you more about him in my next chapter.

CHAPTER LI.

A WARNING.

THE old gentleman I speak of, I had seen once before—it was at Malory. He was that very Mr. Lemuel Blount whom I and Laura Grey had watched with so much interest as he crossed the court-yard before our windows, followed by a chaise.

As Sir Harry and I, at the end of our northward journey from London, arrived before the door of his ancient house of Dorracleugh, Mr. Blount appeared at the threshold in the light, and ran down, before the servant could reach it, to the door of our chaise. There was something kindly and pleasant in the voice of this old man, who was so earnest about our comforts. I afterwards found that he was both wise and simple, a sound adviser, and as merry often as a good-natured boy. He contrasted, in this latter respect, very agreeably for me, with Sir Harry Rokestone, whom solitary life, and a habit of brooding over the irreparable, had made both gloomy and silent.

Mr. Blount was easily amused, and was something of an innocent gossip. He used to go down to the town of Golden Friars every day, and gather all the news, and bring home his budget, and entertain me with it, giving all the information I required with respect to the *dramatis personæ*. He liked boating as well as I did, and although the storms of the equinox prevailed, and the surrounding mountains, with their gorges, made the winds squally and uncertain, and sailing upon the lake in certain states of the weather dangerous, he and I used to venture out I daresay oftener than was strictly prudent. Sir Harry used to attack him for these mad adventures, and once or twice

grew as tempestuous almost as the weather. Although I
was afraid of Sir Harry, I could not help laughing at Mr.
Blount's frightened and penitent countenance, and his stolen
glances at Sir Harry, so like what I fancied those of a fat
schoolboy might be when called up for judgment before
his master.

Sir Harry knew all the signs of the weather, and it
ended by his putting us under condition never to go out
without his leave, and old Mr. Blount's pleadings and
quarrelsome resentment under his prohibition were almost
as laughable as his alarms.

In a little time neighbours began to call upon me, and I
was obliged, of course, to return these visits; but neighbours do not abound in these wild regions, and my quiet,
which I had grown to love, was wonderfully little disturbed.

One morning at breakfast, among the letters laid beside
Sir Harry was one, on opening which his face darkened
suddenly, and an angry light glowed in his deep-set eyes.
He rapped his knuckles on the table, he stood up and
muttered, sat down again in a little while, and once more
looked into the letter. He read it through this time; and
then turning to Lemuel Blount, who had been staring at
him in silence, as it seemed to me knowing very well what
the subject of the letter must be:

"Look at that," said the Baronet, whisking the letter
across the table to Mr. Blount. "I don't understand him
—I never did."

Mr. Blount took the letter to the window and read it
thoughtfully.

"Come along," said the Baronet, rising, and beckoning
him with his finger, "I'll give him an answer."

Sir Harry, with these words, strode out of the room,
followed by Mr. Blount; and I was left alone to my vain
conjectures. It was a serene and sunny day; the air, as
in late autumn it always is, though the sun has not lost
its power, was a little sharp. Some hours later, I and
my old comrade, Mr. Blount, had taken to the water.
A boatman sat in the bow. I held the tiller, abandoned
to me by my companion, in right of my admitted
superiority in steering, an art which I had learned on the

estuary at Cardyllion. Mr. Blount was not so talkative as usual. I said to him at last:

"Do you know, Mr. Blount, I once saw you, before I met you here."

"Did you?" said he. "But I did not see you. Where was that?"

"At Malory, near Cardyllion, after the wreck of the Conway Castle, when Mr. Marston was there."

"Yes, so he was," said the old gentleman; "but I did not know that any of Mr. Ware's family were at home at the time. You may have seen me, but I did not see you —or, if I did, you made no impression upon me."

This was one of my good friend's unconscious compliments which often made me smile.

"And what became of that Mr. Marston?" I asked. "He had a wonderful escape!"

"So he had—he went abroad."

"And is he still abroad?"

"About six weeks ago he left England again; he was here only for a flying visit of two or three months. It would be wise, I think, if he never returned. I think he has definitely settled now, far away from this country, and I don't think we are likely to see his face again. You're not keeping her near enough to the wind."

I was curious to learn more about this Mr. Marston, of whom Mr. Carmel and Laura Grey—each judging him, no doubt, from totally different facts, and from points of view so dissimilar—had expressed such singularly ill opinions.

"You know Mr. Marston pretty well, do you?" I asked.

"Yes, very well; I have been trying to do him a service," answered Mr. Blount. "See, see, there—see— those can't be wild ducks? Blessed are the peace-makers. I wish I could, and I think I may. Now, I think you may put her about, eh?"

I did as he advised.

"I have heard people speak ill of that Mr. Marston," I said; "do you know any reason why he should not be liked?"

"Why, yes—that is by people who sit in judgment

upon their neighbours—he has been an ill friend to
himself. I know but one bad blot he has made, and that,
I happen to be aware, hurt no one on earth but himself;
but there is no use in talking about him, it vexes
me."

"Only one thing more—where is he now?"

"In America. Put this over your feet, please—the air
is cold—allow me to arrange it. Ay, the Atlantic is wide
enough—let him rest—out of sight, out of mind, for the
present at least, and so best."

Our talk now turned upon other subjects, and returned
no more to Mr. Marston during our sail.

In this house, as in most other old country-houses,
there is a room that is called the library. It had been
assigned to Mr. Blount as his special apartment. He had
made me free of it—either to sit there and read, whenever
I should take a fancy to do so, or to take away any of the
books to the drawing-room. My life was as quiet and
humdrum as life could be; but never was mortal in the
enjoyment of more absolute liberty. Except in the matter
of drowning myself and Mr. Blount in the mere, I could
do in all respects exactly as I pleased. Dear old Rebecca
Torkill was established as a retainer of the house, to my
great comfort—she talked me to sleep every night, and
drank a cup of tea every afternoon in my room. The
quietude and seclusion of my life recalled my early days,
and the peaceful routine of Malory. Of course, a time
might come when I should like all this changed a little
—for the present, it was the only life I thought endurable.

About a week after my conversation with Mr. Blount
during our sail, Sir Harry Rokestone was called away for
a short time by business; and I had not been for many
days in the enjoyment of my *tête-à-tête* with Mr. Blount,
when there occurred an incident which troubled me extremely, and was followed by a state of vague suspense
and alarm, such as I never expected to have known in that
quiet region.

One morning as I sat at breakfast with Mr. Blount for
my *vis-à-vis*, and no one by but the servant who had just
handed us our letters, I found before me an envelope
addressed with a singularity that struck me as a little

ominous. The direction was traced, not in the ordinary handwriting, but in Roman characters, in imitation of printing; and the penmanship was thin and feeble, but quite accurate enough to show that it was not the work of a child.

I was already cudgelling my brains to discover whether I could remember among my friends any waggish person who might play me a trick of this kind; but I could recollect no one; especially at a time when my mourning would have made jesting of that kind so inopportune. Odder still, it bore the Malory post-mark, and unaccountable as this was, its contents were still more so. They were penned in the same Roman character, and to the following effect:

" Miss Ware,—Within the next ten days, a person will probably visit Golden Friars, who intends you a mischief. So soon as you see, you will recognize your enemy. Yours,—A Friend."

My first step would have been to consult Mr. Blount upon this letter; but I could tell him nothing of my apprehensions from Monsieur Droqville, in whom my fears at once recognised the " enemy " pointed at by the letter. It might possibly, indeed, be some one else, but by no means, I thought so probable as the other. Who was my "friend," who subscribed this warning? If it was not Mr. Carmel, who else could he be ? And yet, why should not Mr. Carmel write to me as frankly as he had spoken and written before? If it came from him, the warning could not point to Monsieur Droqville. There was more than enough to perplex and alarm one in this enigmatical note.

CHAPTER LII.

 WAS afraid to consult even Rebecca Torkill; she was a little given to talking, and my alarms might have become, in a day or two, the property of Sir Harry's housekeeper. There is no use in telling you all the solutions which my fears invented for this riddle.

In my anxiety I wrote to the Rector's wife at Cardyllion, telling her that I had got an anonymous note, bearing the Malory post-mark, affecting so much mystery that I was totally unable to interpret it. I begged of her therefore to take every opportunity of making out, if possible, who was the author, and to tell me whether there was any acquaintance of mine at present there, who might have written such a note by way of a practical joke to mystify me; and I entreated of her to let me know her conjectures. Then I went into the little world of Cardyllion and inquired about all sorts of people, great and small, and finally I asked if Mr. Carmel had been lately there.

In addition to this, I wrote to the post-master, describing the appearance of the letter I had got, and asked whether he could help me to a description of the person who had posted it? Every time a new theory struck me, I read my "friend's" note over again.

At length I began to think that it was most probably the thoughtless production of some real but harmless friend, who intended herself paying me a visit here, on visiting the Golden Friars. A female visitor was very likely, as the note was framed so as to indicate nothing of the sex of the "enemy;" and two or three young lady friends, not very reasonable, had been attacking me in their letters for not answering more punctually.

My mind was perpetually working upon this problem. I was very uncomfortable, and at times frightened, and even agitated. I don't, even now, wonder at the degree to which I suffered.

A note of a dream in one of my fragmentary diaries at that time will show you how nervous I was. It is set down in much greater detail than you or I can afford it here. I will just tell you its "heads," as old sermons say. I thought I had arrived here, at Dorracleugh, after a long journey. Mr. Blount and a servant came in carrying one of my large black travelling boxes, and tugged it along the ground. The servant then went out, and Mr. Blount, who I fancied was very pale, looked at me fixedly, and placing his finger to his lip in token of silence, softly went out, also, and shut the door, leaving me rather awe-struck. My box, I thought, on turning my eyes upon it again, from my gaze at Mr. Blount, seemed much longer, and its shape altered ; but such transformations do not trouble us in our dreams, and I began fumbling with the key, which did not easily fit the lock. At length I opened it, and instead of my dresses I saw a long piece of rumpled linen, and perceived that the box was a coffin. With the persistent acquiescence in monstrosities by which dreams are characterized, I experienced the slightest possible bewilderment at this, and drew down the linen covering, and discovered the shrouded face of Mr. Marston. I was absolutely horrified, and more so when the dead man sat up, with his eyes open, in the coffin, and looked at me with an expression so atrocious that I awoke with a scream, and a heart bounding with terror, and lay awake for more than an hour. This dream was the vague embodiment of one of my conjectures, and pointed at one of the persons whom, against all probability, I had canvassed as the "enemy" of my warning.

Solitude and a secret fear go a long way towards making us superstitious. I became more and more nervous as the suspense extended from day to day. I was afraid to go into Golden Friars, lest I should meet my enemy. I made an excuse, and stayed at home from church on

Sunday for the same reason. I was afraid even of passing a boat upon the lake. I don't know whether Mr. Blount observed my increased depression; we played our hit of backgammon, nevertheless, as usual, in the evening, and took, when the weather was not boisterous, our little sail on the lake.

I heard from the Rector's wife. She was not able, any more than the Cardyllion postmaster, to throw the least light upon my letter. Mr. Carmel had not been in that part of the world for a long time. I was haunted, nevertheless, by the image of Mr. Marston, whom my dream had fixed in my imagination.

These letters had reached me as usual as we sat at breakfast. Mine absorbed me, and by demolishing all theories, had directed me upon new problems. I sat looking into my tea-cup, as if I could divine from it. I raised my eyes at length and said:

"When did you say—I forget—you last heard from Mr. Marston?"

He looked up. I perceived that he had been just as much engrossed by his letter as I had been with mine. He laid it down, and asked me to repeat my question. I did. Mr. Blount smiled.

"Well, that is very odd. I have just heard from him," said he, raising the letter he had been reading by the corner. "It came by the mail that reached London yesterday evening."

"And where is he?" I asked.

"He's at New York now; but he says he is going in a few days to set out for Canada, or the backwoods—he has not yet made up his mind which. I think, myself, he will choose the back-settlements; he has a passion for adventure."

At these words of Mr. Blount, my theories respecting Mr. Marston fell to the ground, and my fears again gathered about the meaner figure of Monsieur Droqville; and as soon as breakfast was ended, I sat down in the window, and studied my anonymous letter carefully once more.

Business called Mr. Blount that evening to Golden Friars; and after dinner I went into the library, and sat looking out at the noble landscape. A red autumnal sunset illuminated the summits of the steep side of the glen, at my left, leaving all the rest of the cleugh in deep, purple-grey shadow. It opens, as I told you, on the lake, which stretched before me in soft shadow, except where its slow moving ripple caught the light with a fiery glimmer; and far away the noble fells, their peaks and ribs touched with the same misty glow, stood out like majestic shadows, and closed the view sublimely.

I sat here, I can't say reading, although I had an old book open upon my knees. I was too anxious, and my head too busy, to read. Twilight came, and then gradually a dazzling, icy moonlight transformed the landscape. I leaned back in my low chair, my head and shoulders half hidden among the curtains, looking out on the beautiful effect.

This moonlight had prevailed for, I dare say, ten or fifteen minutes, when something occurred to rouse me from my listless reverie. Some object moved upon the window-stone, and caught my eye. It was a human hand suddenly placed there; its fellow instantly followed; an elbow, a hat, a head, a knee; and a man kneeled in the moonlight upon the window-stone, which was there some eight or ten feet from the ground.

Was I awake or in a dream? Gracious Heaven! There were the scarred forehead and the stern face of Mr. Marston with knit brows, and his hand shading his eyes, as he stared close to the glass into the room.

I was in the shadow, and cowered back deeper into the folds of the curtain. He plainly did not see me. He was looking into the further end of the room. I was afraid to cry out; it would have betrayed me. I remained motionless, in the hope that, when he was satisfied that there was no one in the room, he would withdraw from his place of observation, and go elsewhere.

I was watching him with the fascinated terror of a bird, in its ivied nook, when a kite hovers at night within a span of it.

He now seized the window-sash—how I prayed that it had been secured—and with a push or two the window ascended, and he stepped in upon the floor. The cold night air entered with him; he stood for a minute looking into the room, and then very softly he closed the window. He seemed to have made up his mind to establish himself here, for he lazily pushed Mr. Blount's easy-chair into the recess at the window, and sat down very nearly opposite to me. If I had been less shocked and frightened, I might have seen the absurdity of my situation.

He leaned back in Mr. Blount's chair, like a tired man, and extended his heels on the carpet; his hand clutched the arm of the chair. His face was in the bright white light of the moon, his chin was sunk on his chest. His features looked haggard and wicked. Two or three times I thought he saw me, for his eyes were fixed on me for more than a minute; but my perfect stillness, the deep shadow that enveloped me, and the brilliant moonlight in his eyes, protected me.

Suddenly I heard a step—it was Mr. Blount; the door opened, and the step was arrested; to my infinite relief a voice, it was Mr. Blount's, called a little sternly:

" Who's that ?"

" The prodigal, the outcast," answered Mr. Marston's deep voice, bitterly. "I have been, and am, too miserable not to make one more trial, and to seek to be reconciled. You, sir, are very kind—you are a staunch friend; but you have never yet done all you could do for me. Why have you not faith ? Your influence is unlimited."

" My good gracious !" exclaimed Mr. Blount, not moving an inch from where he stood. "Why, it is only this morning I received your letter from New York. What is all this ? I don't understand."

" I came by the same mail that brought my letter. Second thoughts are the best. I changed my mind," said the young man, standing up. "Why should I live the sort of life he seems to have planned for me, if he intends anything better at any time ? And if he don't, what do I owe him ? It is vindictive and unnatural. I'm worn out; my patience has broken down."

" I could not have believed my eyes," said Mr. Blount. "I did not—dear, dear me ! I don't know what to make of it; he'll be very much displeased. Mr. Marston, sir, you seem bent on ruining yourself with him, quite."

"I don't know—what chance have I out there? Out of sight out of mind, you used to say. He'd have forgotten me, you'd have forgotten me; I should not have had a friend soon, who knew or cared whether I was alive or dead. Speak to him; tell him he may as well listen to me. I'm perfectly desperate," and he struck his open hand on the back of the chair, and clenched the sentence with a bitter oath.

"I am not to blame for it," said Mr. Blount.

"I know that; I know it very well, Mr. Blount. You are too good a friend of our family. I know it, and I feel it—I do, indeed; but look here, where's the good of driving a fellow to desperation? I tell you I'll do something that will bring it to a crisis; I can't stand the hell I live in. And let him prosecute me if he likes; it is very easy for me to put a pistol to my head—it's only half a second and it's over—and I'll leave a letter telling the world how he has used me, and then see how he'll like the mess he has made of it."

"Now, pardon me, sir," said Mr. Blount, ceremoniously, "that's all stuff; I mean he won't believe you. When I have an unacceptable truth to communicate, I make it a rule to do so in the most courteous manner; and, happily, I have, hitherto, found the laws of truth and of politeness always reconcilable; he has told me, my dear sir, fifty times, that you are a great deal too selfish ever to hurt yourself. There is no use, then, in trying, if I may be permitted the phrase, to bully him. If you seek, with the smallest chance of success, to make an impression upon Sir Harry Rokestone, you must approach him in a spirit totally unlike that. I'll tell you what you must do. Write me a penitent letter, asking my intercession, and if you can make, with perfect sincerity, fair promises for the future, and carefully avoid the smallest evidence of the spirit you chose to display in your last—and it is very strange if you have learned nothing—I'll try again what I can do."

The young man advanced, and took Mr. Blount's hand and wrung it fervently.

I don't think Mr. Blount returned the demonstration with equal warmth. He was rather passive on the occasion.

" Is he—here ?" asked Mr. Marson.

"No, and you must not remain an hour in this house, nor at Golden Friars, nor shall you go to London, but to some perfectly quiet place ; write to me, from thence, a letter such as I have described, and I will lay it before him, with such representations of my own as perhaps may weigh with him, and we shall soon know what will come of it. Have the servants seen you ?"

" No one."

" So much the better."

" I scaled your window about ten minutes ago. I thought you would soon turn up, and I was right. I know you will forgive me."

" Well, no matter, you had better get away as you came ; how was that ?"

" By boat, sir ; I took it at the Three Oaks."

" It is all the better you were not in the town ; I should not like him to know you are in England, until I have got your letter to show him ; I hope, sir, you will write in it no more than you sincerely feel. I cannot enter into any but an honest case. Where did your boat wait ?"

" At the jetty here ?"

"Very good ; as you came by the window, you may as well go by it, and I will meet you a little way down the path ; I may have something more to say."

" Thank you, sir, from my heart," said Marston.

" No, no, don't mind, I want you to get away again; there, get away as quickly as you can." He had opened the window for him. " Ah, you have climbed that many a time when you were a boy; you should know every stone by heart."

" I'll do exactly as you tell me, sir, in all things," said the young man, and dropped lightly from the window-stone to the ground, and I saw his shadowy figure glide swiftly down the grass, towards the great lime-trees that stand in a receding row between the house and the water. Mr. Blount lowered the window quietly, and looked for a moment after him.

" Some men are born to double sorrow—sorrow for others—sorrow for themselves. I don't quite know what to make of him."

The old man sighed heavily, and left the room. I felt very like a spy, and very much ashamed of myself for having overheard a conversation certainly not intended for my ears. I can honestly say it was not curiosity that held me there ; that I was beyond measure distressed at my accidental treachery ; and that, had there been a door near enough to enable me to escape unseen I should not have overheard a sentence of what had passed. But I had not courage to discover myself ; and wanting nerve at the beginning to declare myself, I had, of course, less and less as the conference proceeded, and my situation became more equivocal.

The departure of Mr. Blount, whom I now saw descending the steps in pursuit of his visitor, relieved me, and I got away from the room, haunted by the face that had so lately appeared to me in my ominous dream, and by the voice whose tones excited a strange tremor, and revived stranger recollections.

In the drawing-room, before a quarter of an hour, I was joined by Mr. Blount. Our *tête a tête* was an unusually silent one, and, after tea, we played a rather spiritless hit or two at backgammon.

I was glad when the time came to get to my room, to the genial and garrulous society of Rebecca Torkill ; and after my candle was put out, I lay long enough awake, trying to put together the as yet imperfect fragments of a story and a situation which were to form the ground-work of the drama in which I instinctively felt that I was involved.

CHAPTER LIII.

ONE MORE CHANCE.

SIR HARRY came home, and met me more affectionately and kindly than ever. I soon perceived that there was something of more than usual gravity under discussion between him and Mr. Blount. I knew, of course, very well what was the question they were debating. I was very uncomfortable while this matter was being discussed; Mr. Blount seemed nervous and uneasy; and it was plain that the decision was not only suspended but uncertain. I don't suppose there was a more perturbed little family in all England at that moment, over whom, at the same time, there hung apparently no cloud of disaster.

At last I could perceive that something was settled; for the discussions between Mr. Blount and Sir Harry seemed to have lost the character of debate and remonstrance, and to have become more like a gloomy confidence and consultation between them. I can only speak of what I may call the external appearance of these conversations, for I was not permitted to hear one word of their substance.

In a little while Sir Harry went away again. This time his journey, I afterwards learned, was to one of the quietest little towns in North Wales, where his chaise drew up at the Bull Inn. The tall northern baronet got out of the chaise, and strode to the bar of that rural hostelry.

"Is there a gentleman named Marston staying here?" he asked of the plump elderly lady who sat within the bow-window of the bar.

"Yes, sir, Mr. Marston, Number Seven, up one pair o stairs."

"Upstairs now?" asked Sir Harry.

"He'll be gone out to take his walk, sir, by this time," answered the lady.

"Can I talk to you for a few minutes, anywhere, madam, in private?" asked Sir Harry.

The old lady looked at him, a little surprised.

"Yes, sir," she said. "Is it anything very particular, please?"

"Yes, ma'am, very particular," answered the baronet.

She called to her handmaid, and installed her quickly in her seat, and so led the baronet to an occupied room on the ground-floor. Sir Harry closed the door, and told her who he was. The landlady recognised his baronetage with a little courtesy.

"I'm a relation of Mr. Marston's, and I've come down here to make an inquiry; I want to know whether he has been leading an orderly, quiet life since he came to your house."

"No one more so, please, sir; a very nice regular gentleman, and goes to church every Sunday he's been here, and that is true. We have no complaint to make of him, please, sir; and he has paid his bill twice since he came here."

The woman looked honest, with frank, round eyes.

"Thank you, ma'am," said Sir Harry; "that will do."

An hour later it was twilight, and Mr. Marston, on entering his sitting-room after his walk, saw the baronet, who got up from his chair before the fire as he came in.

The young man instantly took off his hat, and stood near the door, the very image of humility. Sir Harry did not advance, or offer him his hand; he gave him a nod. Nothing could be colder than this reception.

"So, Richard, you have returned to England, as you have done most other things, without consulting me," said the cold, deep voice of Sir Harry.

"I've acted rashly sir, I fear. I acted on an impulse. I could not resist it. It was only twelve hours before the ship left New York when the thought struck me. I ought to have waited. I ought to have thought it over. It seemed to me my only chance, and I'm afraid it has but sunk me lower in your esteem."

"It is clear you should have asked my leave first, all things considered," said Sir Harry, in the same tone.

The young man bowed his head.

"I see that very clearly now, sir; but I have been so miserable under your displeasure, and I do not always see things as my calmer reason would view them. I thought of nothing but my chance of obtaining your forgiveness, and, at so great a distance, I despaired."

"So it was to please me you set my authority at naught? By Jea! that's logic."

Sir Harry spoke this with a scornful and angry smile.

"I am the only near kinsman you have left, sir, of your blood and name."

"My name, sir!" challenged Sir Harry, fiercely.

"My second name is Rokestone—called after you," pleaded Mr. Marston.

"By my sang, young man, if you and I had borne the same name, I'd have got the. Queen's letter, and changed mine to Smith."

To this the young gentleman made no reply. His uncle broke the silence that followed.

"We'll talk at present, if you please, as little as need be ; there's nothing pleasant to say between us. But I'll give you a chance ; I'll see if you are a changed man, as your letter says. I'll try what work is in you, or what good. You said you'd like farming. Well, we'll see what sort of farmer you'll make. You'll do well to remember 'tis but a trial. In two or three days Mr. Blount will give you particulars by letter. Good evening. Don't come down; stay here. I'll go alone. Say no more ; I'll have no thanks or professions. Your conduct, steadiness, integrity, shall guide me. That's all. Farewell."

Mr. Marston, during this colloquy, had gradually advanced a little, and now stood near the window. Sir Harry accompanied his farewell with a short nod, and stalked down the stairs. Mr. Marston knew he meant what he said, and therefore did not attempt to accompany him downstairs. And so, with a fresh pair of horses, Sir Harry immediately started on his homeward journey.

I, who knew at the time nothing of what I afterwards
learned, was still in a suspense which nobody suspected.
It was ended one evening by Sir Harry Rokestone, who
said :

"To-morrow my nephew, Richard Marston, will be
here to stay, I have not yet determined for how long. He
is a dull young man. You'll not like him; he has not a
word to throw at a dog."

So, whatever his description was worth, his announce-
ment was conclusive, and Richard Marston was to become
an inmate of Dorracleugh next day. I find my diary
says, under date of the next day :

"I have been looking forward, with a trepidation I can
hardly account for, to the arrival which Sir Harry
announced yesterday. The event of the day occurred at
three o'clock. I was thinking of going out for a walk,
and had my hat and jacket on, and was standing in the
hall. I wished to postpone, as long as I could, the
meeting with Mr. Marston, which I dreaded. At that
critical moment his double knock at the hall-door, and
the distant peal of our rather deep-mouthed bell, startled
me. I guessed it was he, and turned to run up to my
room, but met Sir Harry, who said, laying his hand
gently on my shoulder :

"'Wait, dear—this is my nephew. I saw him from
the window. I want to introduce him.'

"Of course I had to submit. The door was opened.
There he was, the veritable Mr. Marston, of Malory, the
hero of the Conway Castle, of the duel, and likewise of so
many evil stories—the man who had once talked so
romantically and so madly to me. I felt myself growing
pale, and then blushing. Sir Harry received him coldly
enough, and introduced me, simply mentioning my name
and his ; and then I ran down the steps, with two of the
dogs as my companions, while the servants were getting
in Mr. Marston's luggage.

"I met him again at dinner. He is very little changed,
except that he is much more sun-burnt. He has got a
look, too, of command and melancholy. I am sure he
has suffered, and suffering, they say, makes people better.
He talked very little during dinner, and rather justified

Y

Sir Harry's description. Sir Harry talked about the farm he intends for him—they are to look at it to-morrow together. Mr. Blount seems to have got a load off his mind.

"The farm is not so far away as I had imagined—it is only at the other side of the lake, about five hundred acres at Clusted, which came to Sir Harry, Mr. Blount says, through the Mardykes family. I wonder whether there is a house upon it—if so, he will probably live at the other side of the lake, and his arrival will have made very little difference to us. So much the better, perhaps.

"I saw him and Sir Harry, at about eight o'clock this morning, set out together in the big boat, with two men, to cross the lake.

"Farming is, I believe, a very absorbing pursuit. He won't feel his solitude much; and Mr. Blount says he will have to go to fairs and markets. It is altogether a grazing farm."

The reader will perceive that I am still quoting my diary.

"To-day, old Miss Goulding, of Wrybiggins, the old lady whom the gossips of Golden Friars once assigned to Sir Harry as a wife, called with a niece who is with her on a visit, so I suppose they had heard of Mr. Marston's arrival, and came to see what kind of person he is. I'm rather glad they were disappointed. I ordered luncheon for them, and I saw them look toward the door every time it opened, expecting, I am sure, to see Mr. Marston. I maliciously postponed telling them, until the very last moment, that he was at the other side of the mere, as they call the lake, although I suffered for my cruelty, for they dawdled on here almost interminably.

"Sir Harry and Mr. Marston did not return till tea-time, when it was quite dark; they had dined at a farmhouse at the other side. Sir Harry seems, I think a little more friendly with him. They talked, it is true, of nothing but farming and live stock; and Mr. Blount joined. I took, therefore, in solitude, to my piano, and, when I was tired of that, to my novel.

"A very dull evening—the dullest, I think, I've passed since we came to Dorracleugh. I daresay Mr. Marston

will make a very good farmer. I hope very much there
may be a suitable residence found for him at the other
side of the lake."

Next my diary contains the following entry:

" Mr. Marston off again at eight o'clock to his farm.
Mr. Blount and I took a sail to-day, with Sir Harry's
leave, in the small boat. He tells me that there is no necessity for Mr. Marston's going every day to the farm—that
Sir Harry has promised him a third of whatever the farm,
under his management, makes. He seems very anxious
to please Sir Harry. I can't conceive what can have
made me so nervous about the arrival of this very humdrum squire, whose sole object appears to be the pro-
sperity of his colony of cows and sheep.

" Sunday.—Of course to-day he has taken a holiday,
but he has not given us the benefit of it. He chose to
walk all day, instead of going to church with us to Golden
Friars. It is not far from Haworth. So he prefers a
march of four and twenty miles to the fatigue of our
society !"

On the Tuesday following I find, by the same record,
Sir Harry went to visit his estate of Tarlton, about forty
miles from Golden Friars, to remain away for three or
four days. That day I find also Mr. Marston was, as
usual, at his farm at Clusted, and did not come home till
about nine o'clock.

I went to my room immediately after his arrival, so that
he had an uninterrupted *tête-à-tête* with Mr. Blount.

Next day he went away at his usual early hour, and
returned not so late. I made an excuse of having some
letters to write, and left the two gentlemen to themselves
a good deal earlier than the night before.

" Mr. Marston certainly is very little in my way; I
have not spoken twenty words to him since his arrival. I
begin to think him extremely impertinent."

The foregoing is a very brief note of the day, considering how diffuse and particular I often was when we were
more alone. I make up for it on the following day. The
text runs thus:

" Mr. Marston has come off his high horse, and broken
silence at last. It was blowing furiously in the morning,

Y 2

and I suppose, however melancholy he may be, he has no intention of drowning himself. At all events, there has been no crossing the mere this morning.

" He has appeared, for the first time since his arrival, at breakfast. Sir Harry's absence seems to have removed a great constraint. He talked very agreeably, and seemed totally to have forgotten the subject of farming; he told us a great deal of his semi-military life in Spain, which was very amusing. I know he made me laugh heartily. Old Mr. Blount laughed also. Our breakfast was a very pleasant meal. Mr. Blount was himself in Spain for more than a year when he was young, and got up and gave us a representation of his host, an eccentric fan-maker, walking with his toes pointed and his chest thrown out, and speaking sonorous Spanish with pompous gesture. I had no idea he had so much fun in him. The good-natured old man seemed quite elated at our applause and very real laughter.

" Mr. Marston suddenly looked across the lake, and recollected his farm.

" ' How suddenly that storm went down !' he said. ' I can't say I'm glad of it, for I suppose I must make my usual trip, and visit my four-footed friends over the way.'

" ' No,' said Mr. Blount; ' let them shift for themselves to-day; I'll take it on myself. There's no necessity for you going every day as you do.'

" ' But how will it be received by the authorities? Will my uncle think it an omission ? I should not like him to suppose that, under any temptation, I had forgotten my understanding with him.'

" He glanced at me. Whether he thought me the temptation, or only wished to include me in the question, I don't know.

" ' Oh ! no,' said Mr. Blount; ' stay at home for this once—I'll explain it all; and we can go out and have a sail, if the day continues as fine as it promises.'

" Mr. Marston hesitated ; he looked at me as if for an opinion, but I said nothing.

" ' Well,' he said, ' I can't resist. I'll take your advice, Mr. Blount, and make this a holiday.'

" I think Mr. Marston very much improved in some

respects. His manners and conversation are not less
spirited, but gentler; and he is so very agreeable! I
think he has led an unhappy life, and no doubt was often
very much in the wrong. But I have remarked that we
condemn people not in proportion to their moral guilt,
but in proportion to the inconvenience their faults inflict
on us. I wonder very much what those stories were which
caused Mr. Carmel and Laura Grey to speak of him so
bitterly and sternly? They were both so good that things
which other people would have thought lightly enough of,
would seem to them enormous. I dare say it is all about
debt, or very likely play; and people who have possibly
lost money by his extravagance have been exaggerating
matters, and telling stories their own way. He seems
very much sobered now, at all events. One can't help
pitying him.

"He went down to the jetty before luncheon. I found
afterwards that it was to get cloaks and rugs arranged
for me.

"He lunched with us, and we were all very talkative.
He certainly will prevent our all falling asleep in this
drowsy place. We had such a pleasant sail. I gave him
the tiller; but his duties as helmsman did not prevent his
talking. We could hear one another very well, in spite of
the breeze, which was rather more than Sir Harry would
have quite approved of.

"Mr. Marston had many opportunities to-day of talking to me without any risk of being overheard. He did
not, however, say a single word in his old vein. I am
very glad of this; it would be provoking to lose his conversation, which is amusing, and, I confess, a great resource in this solitude.

"He is always on the watch to find if I want anything,
and gets or does it instantly. I wish his farm was at this
side of the lake. I dare say when Sir Harry comes back we
shall see as little as ever of him. It will end by his being
drowned in that dangerous lake. It seems odd that Sir
Harry, who is so tender of my life and Mr. Blount's,
should have apparently no feeling whatever about his.
But it is their affair. I'm not likely to be consulted; so I
need not trouble my head about it.

"I write in my room, the day now over, and dear old Rebecca Torkill is fussing about from table to wardrobe, and from wardrobe to drawers, pottering, and fidgeting, and whispering to herself. She has just told me that Mrs. Shackleton, the housekeeper here at Dorracleugh, talked to her a good deal this evening about Mr. Marston. She gives a very good account of him. When he went to school, and to Oxford, she saw him only at intervals, but he was a manly, good-natured boy she said, ' and never, that she knew, any harm in him, only a bit wild, like other young men at such places.' I write, as nearly as I can, Rebecca's words.

"The subject of the quarrel with Sir Harry Rokestone, Mrs. Shackleton says, was simply that Mr. Marston positively refused to marry some one whom his uncle had selected for a niece-in-law. That is exactly the kind of disobedience that old people are sometimes most severe upon. She told Rebecca to be very careful not to say a word of it to the other servants, as it was a great secret.

"After all there may be two sides to this case, as to others, and Mr. Marston's chief mutiny may have been of that kind which writers of romance and tragedy elevate into heroism.

"He certainly is very much improved."

Here my diary for that day left Mr. Marston, and turned to half-a-dozen trifles, treated, I must admit, with much comparative brevity.

CHAPTER LIV.

DANGEROUS GROUND.

OLD Mr. Blount was a religious man. Sir Harry, whose ideas upon such subjects I never could exactly divine, went to church every Sunday; but he scoffed at bishops, and neither loved nor trusted clergymen. He had, however, family prayers every morning, at which Mr. Blount officiated, with evident happiness and peace in the light of his simple countenance.

No radiance of this happy light was reflected on the face of Sir Harry Rokestone, who sat by the mantelpiece, in one of the old oak arm chairs, a colossal image of solitude, stern and melancholy, and never, it seemed to me, so much alone as at those moments which seem to draw other mortals nearer. I fancied that some associations connected with such simple gatherings long ago, perhaps, recalled mamma to his thoughts. He seemed to sit in a stern and melancholy reverie, and he would often come over to me, when the prayer was ended, and, looking at me with great affection, ask gently:

"Well, my little lass, do they try to make you happy here? Is there anything you think of that you'd like me to get down from Lunnon? You must think. I'd like to be doing little things for you; think, and tell me this evening." And at such times he would turn on me a look of full-hearted affection, and smoothe my hair caressingly with his old hand.

Sometimes he would say: "You like this place, you

tell me; but the winters here, I'm thinking, will be too hard for you."

"But I like a good, cold, frosty winter," I would answer him. "There is nothing I think so pleasant."

"Ay, but maybe ye'll be getting a cough or something."

"No, I assure you I'm one of the few persons on earth who never take cold," I urged, for I really wished to spend the winter at Golden Friars.

"Well, pretty lass, ye shall do as you like best, but you mustn't fall sick; if you do, what's to become o' the auld man?"

You must allow me here to help myself with my diary once more. I am about to quote from what I find there, dated the following Sunday:

"We went to Golden Friars to church as usual; and Mr. Marston, instead of performing his devotions twelve miles away, came with us.

"After the service was ended, Sir Harry, who had a call to make, took leave of us. The day was so fine that we were tempted to walk home instead of driving.

"We chose the path by the lake, and sent the carriage on to Dorracleugh.

"Mr. Blount chooses to talk over the sermon, and I am sure thinks it profane to mention secular subjects on Sunday. I think this a mistake; and I confess I was not sorry when good Mr. Blount stopped and told us he was going into Shenstone's cottage. I felt that a respite of five minutes from the echoes of the good vicar's sermon would be pleasant. But when he went on to say that he was going in to read some of the Bible and talk a little with the consumptive little boy, placing me under Mr. Marston's escort for the rest of the walk, which was about a mile, I experienced a new alarm. I had no wish that Mr. Marston should return to his old heroics.

I did not well know what to say or do, Mr. Blount's good-bye came so suddenly. My making a difficulty about walking home with Mr. Marston would to him, who knew nothing of what had passed at Malory, have appeared an unaccountable affectation of prudery. I asked Mr. Blount whether he intended staying any time. He answered,

'Half an hour at least; and if the poor boy wishes it, I shall stay an hour,' he added.

"Mr. Marston, who, I am sure, perfectly understood me, did not say a word. I had only to make the best of an uncomfortable situation, and, very nervous, I nodded and smiled my farewell to Mr. Blount, and set out on my homeward march with Mr. Marston.

"I need not have been in such a panic—it was very soon perfectly plain that Mr. Marston did not intend treating me to any heroics.

"'I don't know any one in the world I have a much higher opinion of than Mr. Blount,' he said; 'but I do think it a great mercy to get away from him a little on Sundays: I can't talk to him in his own way, and I turn simply into a Trappist—I become, I mean, perfectly dumb.'

"I agreed, but said that I had such a regard for Mr. Blount that I could not bring myself to vex him.

"'That is my rule also,' he said, 'only I carry it a little further, ever since I received my education,' he smiled, darkly; 'that is, since I begun to suffer, about three years ago, I have learned to practise it with all my friends. You would not believe what constraint I often place upon myself to avoid saying that which is in my heart and next my lips, but which I fear—I fear with too good reason—might not be liked by others. There was a time, I daresay, when Hamlet blurted out everything that came into his mind, before he learned in the school of sorrow to say, " But break my heart, for I must hold my tongue." '

"He looked very expressively, and I thought I knew perfectly what he meant, and that if by any blunder I happened to say a foolish thing, I might find myself, before I knew where I was, in the midst of a conversation as wild as that of the wood of Plas Ylwd.

"In reply to this I said, not very adroitly:

"And what a beautiful play *Hamlet* is! I have been trying to copy Retsch's outline, but I have made such a failure. The faces are so fine and forcible, and the expression of the hands is so wonderful, and my hands are so tame and clumsy; I can do nothing but the ghost, and that is because he is the only absurd figure in the series."

" 'Yes,' he acquiesced, ' like a thing in an *opera boufe.*'

" I could perceive very plainly that my rather-precipitate
and incoherent excursion into Retsch's outlines, into which
he had followed me with the best grace he could, had
wounded him. It was equally plain, however, that he
was in good faith practising the rule he had just now
mentioned, and was by no means the insolent and over-
bearing suitor he had shown himself in that scene, now
removed alike by time and distance, in which I had before
seen him.

" No one could be more submissive than he to my distinct decision that there was to be no more such wild talk.

" For the rest of our walk he talked upon totally indifferent subjects. Certainly, of the two, I had been the
most put out by his momentary ascent to a more tragic
level. I wonder now whether I did not possibly suspect
a great deal more than was intended. If so, what a fool
I must have appeared ! Is there anything so ridiculous
as a demonstration of resistance where no attack is meditated ? I began to feel so confused and ashamed that I
hardly took the trouble to follow what he said. As we
approached Dorracleugh, I began to feel more like myself.
After a little silence he said what I am going to set down;
I have gone over it again and again in my mind ; I know
I have added nothing, and I really think I write very
nearly exactly as he spoke it.

" ' When I had that strange escape with my life from the
Conway Castle,' he said, ' no man on earth was more
willing and less fit to die than I. I don't suppose there
was a more miserable man in England. I had disappointed my uncle by doing what seemed a very foolish
thing. I could not tell him my motive—no one knew it
—the secret was not mine—everything combined to em-
barrass and crush me. I had the hardest thing on earth
to endure—unmerited condemnation was my portion.
Some good people, whom, notwithstanding, I have learned
to respect, spoke of me to my face as if I had committed
a murder. My uncle understands me now, but he has
not yet forgiven me. When I was at Malory, I was in a
mood to shoot myself through the head ; I was desperate,
I was bitter, I was furious. Every unlucky thing that

could happen did happen there. The very people who
had judged me most cruelly turned up ; and among them
one who forced a quarrel on me, and compelled that miserable duel in which I wished at the time I had been killed.'

" I listened to all this with more interest than I allowed
him to see, as we walked on together side by side, I looking down on the path before us, and saying nothing.

" 'If it were not for one or two feelings left me, I
should not know myself for the shipwrecked man who
thanked his young hostess at Malory for her invaluable
hospitality,' he said ; 'there are some things one never
forgets. I often think of Malory—I have thought of it in
all kinds of distant, out-of-the-way, savage places ; it rises
before me as I saw it last. My life has all gone wrong.
While hope remains, we can bear anything—but my last
hope seems pretty near its setting—and, when it is out, I
hope, seeing I cross and return in all weathers, there is
drowning enough in that lake to give a poor fool, at least,
a cool head and a quiet heart.'

" Then, without any tragic pause, he turned to other
things lightly, and never looked towards me to discover
what effect his words were producing ; but he talked on,
and now very pleasantly. We loitered a little at the hall-
door. I did not want him to come into the drawing-room,
and establish himself there. Here were the open door, the
hall, the court-yard, the windows, all manner of possibili-
ties for listeners, and I felt I was protected from any em-
barrassment that an impetuous companion might please
to inflict if favoured by a *tete-à-tete.*

" I must, however, do him justice : he seemed very
anxious not to offend—very careful so to mask any disclosure of his feelings as to leave me quite free to 'ignore'
it, and, as it seemed to me, on the watch to catch any
evidence of my impatience.

" He is certainly very agreeable and odd ; and the time
passed very pleasantly while we loitered in the court-yard.

" Mr. Blount soon came up, and after a word or two I
left them, and ran up to my room.

CHAPTER LV.

MR. CARMEL TAKES HIS LEAVE.

ABOUT this time there was a sort of fête at Golden Friars. Three very pretty fountains were built by Sir Richard Mardykes and Sir Harry, at the upper end of the town, in which they both have property; and the opening of these was a sort of gala.

I did not care to go. Sir Harry Rokestone and Mr. Blount, were, of course, there; Mr. Marston went, instead, to his farm, at the other side; and I took a whim to go out on the lake, in a row-boat, in the direction of Golden Friars. My boatmen rowed me near enough to hear the music, which was very pretty; but we remained sufficiently far out, to prevent becoming mixed up with the other boats which lay near the shore.

It was a pleasant, clear day, with no wind stirring, and although we were now fairly in winter, the air was not too sharp, and with just a rug about one's feet, the weather was very pleasant. My journal speaks of this evening as follows:

"It was, I think, near four o'clock, when I told the men to row towards Dorracleugh. Before we reached it, the filmy haze of a winter's evening began to steal over the landscape, and a red sunset streamed through the break in the fells above the town with so lovely an effect that I told the men to slacken their speed. So we moved, with only a dip of the oar, now and then; and I looked up the mere, enjoying the magical effect.

"A boat had been coming, a little in our wake, along

the shore. I had observed it, but without the slightest
curiosity ; not even with a conjecture that Sir Harry and
Mr. Blount might be returning in it, for I knew that it
was arranged that they were to come back together in the
carriage.

"Voices from this boat caught my ear; and one suddenly that startled me, just as it neared us. It glided up.
I fancy about thirty yards were between the sides of the
two boats ; and the men, like those in my boat, had
been ordered merely to dip their oars, and were now
moving abreast of ours ; the drips from their oars sparkled
like drops of molten metal. What I heard—the only
thing I now heard—was the harsh nasal voice of Monsieur Droqville.

"There he was, in his black dress, standing in the stern
of the boat, looking round on the landscape, from point to
point. The light, as he looked this way and that, touched
his energetic bronzed features, the folds of his dress, and
the wet planks of the boat, with a fire that contrasted
with the grey shadows behind and about.

"I heard him say, pointing with his outstretched arm,
'And is that Dorracleugh ?' To which one of the people
in the boat made him an answer.

"I can't think of that question without terror. What
has brought that man down here ? What interest can he
have in seeking out Dorracleugh, except that it happens
to be my present place of abode ?

"I am sure he did not see me. When he looked in my
direction, the sun was in his eyes, and my face in shadow;
I don't think he can have seen me. But that matters
nothing if he has come down for any purpose connected
with me."

A sure instinct told me that Monsieur Droqville would
be directed inflexibly by the interests of his order, to consult which, at all times, unawed by consequences to himself or others, was his stern and narrow duty.

Here, in this beautiful and sequestered corner of the
world, how far, after all, I had been from quiet. Well
might I cry with Campbell's exile—

"Ah! cruel fate, wilt thon never replace me
In a mansion of peace where no perils can chase me?"

My terrors hung upon a secret I dared not disclose.
There was no one to help me; for I could consult no one.

The next day I was really ill. I remained in my room.
I thought Monsieur Droqville would come to claim an
interview; and perhaps would seek, by the power he possessed, to force me to become an instrument in forwarding
some of his plans, affecting either the faith or the property
of others. I was in an agony of suspense and fear.

Days passed; a week; and no sign of Monsieur Droqville. I began to breathe. He was not a man, I knew,
to waste weeks, or even days, in search of the picturesque,
in a semi-barbarous region like Golden Friars.

At length I summoned courage to speak to Rebecca
Torkill. I told her I had seen Monsieur Droqville, and
that I wanted her, without telling the servants at Dorracleugh, to make inquiry at the "George and Dragon,"
whether a person answering that description had been
there. No such person was there. So I might assume
he was gone. He had come with Sir Richard Mardykes,
I conjectured, from Carsbrook, where he often was. But
such a man was not likely to make even a pleasure excursion without an eye to business. He had, I supposed,
made inquiries; possibly, he had set a watch upon me.
Under the eye of such a master of strategy as Monsieur
Droqville I could not feel quite at ease.

Nevertheless, in a little time, such serenity as I had
enjoyed at Dorracleugh gradually returned; and I enjoyed
a routine life, the dulness of which would have been in
another state of my spirits insupportable, with very real
pleasure.

We were now deep in winter, and in its snowy shroud
how beautiful the landscape looked! Cold, but stimulating
and pleasant was the clear, dry air; and our frost-bound
world sparkled in the wintry sun.

Old Sir Harry Rokestone, a keen sportsman, proof as
granite against cold, was out by moonlight on the grey
down with his old-fashioned duck-guns, and, when the
lake was not frozen over, with two hardy men manœuvring
his boat for him. Town-bred, Mr. Blount contented
himself with his brisk walk, stick in hand, and a couple
of the dogs for companions to the town; and Mr. Marston

was away upon some mission, on which his uncle had
sent him, Mr. Blount said, to try whether he was "capable
of business and steady."

One night, at this time, as I sat alone in the drawing-
room, I was a little surprised to see old Rebecca Torkill
come in with her bonnet and cloak on, looking mysterious
and important. Shutting the door, she peeped cautiously
round.

"What do you think, miss? Wait—listen," she all
but whispered, with her hand raised as she trotted up to
my side. "Who do you think I saw, not three minutes
ago, at the lime-trees, near the lake?"

I was staring in her face, filled with shapeless alarms.

"I was coming home from Farmer Shenstone's, where
I went with some tea for that poor little boy that's ailing,
and just as I got over the stile, who should I see, as
plain as I see you now, but Mr. Carmel, just that minute
got out of his boat, and making as if he was going to
walk up to the house. He knew me the minute he saw
me—it is a very bright moon—and he asked me how I
was; and then how you were, most particular; and he
said he was only for a few hours in Golden Friars, and
took a boat on the chance of seeing you for a minute, but
that he did not know whether you would like it, and he
begged of me to find out and bring him word. If you do,
he's waiting down there, Miss Ethel, and what shall I
say?"

"Come with me," I said, getting up quickly; and,
putting on in a moment my seal-skin jacket and my hat,
without another thought or word, much to Rebecca's
amazement, I sallied out into the still night air. Turning
the corner of the old building, at the end of the court-
yard, I found myself treading with rapid steps the crisp
grass, under a dazzling moon, and before me the view of
the distant fells, throwing their snowy speaks high into
the air, with the solemn darkness of the lake, and its
silvery gleams below, and the shadowy gorge and great
lime-trees in the foreground. Down the gentle slope I
walked swiftly, leaving Rebecca Torkill a long way behind.

I was now under the towering lime-trees. I paused:
with a throbbing heart I held my breath. I heard hollow

steps coming up on the other side of the file of gigantic
stems. I passed between, and saw Mr. Carmel walking
slowly towards me. In a moment he was close to me,
and took my hand in his old kindly way.

"This is very kind; how can I thank you, Miss Ware?
I had hardly hoped to be allowed to call at the house; I
am going a long journey, and have not been quite so well
as I used to be, and I thought that if I lost this opportunity, in this uncertain world, I might never see my
pupil again. I could hardly bear that, without just saying
good-bye."

"And you are going?" I said, wringing his hand.

"Yes, indeed; the ocean will be between us soon, and
half the world, and I am not to return."

All his kindness rose up before me—his thoughtful
goodness, his fidelity—and I felt for a moment on the
point of crying.

He was muffled in furs, and was looking thin and ill,
and in the light of the moon the lines of his handsome
face were marked as if carved in ivory.

"You and your old tutor have had a great many
quarrels, and always made it up again; and now at last
we part, I am sure, good friends."

"You are going, and you're ill," was all I could say;
but I was conscious there was something of that wild tone
that real sorrow gives in my voice.

"How often I have thought of you, Miss Ethel—how
often I shall think of you, be my days many or few. How
often!"

"I am so sorry, Mr. Carmel—so awfully sorry!" I
repeated. I had not unclasped my hand; I was looking
in his thin, pale, smiling face with the saddest augury.

"I want you to remember me; it is folly, I know, but
it is a harmless folly; all human nature shares in it, and"
—there was a little tremble, and a momentary interruption—"and your old tutor, the sage who lectured you so
wisely, is, after all, no less a fool than the rest. Will you
keep this little cross? It belonged to my mother, and is,
by permission of my superiors, my own, so you may
accept it with a clear conscience." He smiled. "If you
wear it, or even let it lie on your table, it will sometimes"

—the same momentary interruption occurred again—"it may perhaps remind you of one who took a deep interest in you."

It was a beautiful little gold cross, with five brilliants in it.

"And oh, Ethel! let me look at you once again."

He led me—it was only a step or two—out of the shadow of the tree into the bright moonlight, and, still holding my hand, looked at me intently for a little time with a smile, to me, the saddest that ever mortal face wore.

"And now, here she stands, my wayward, generous, clever Ethel! How proud I was of my pupil! The heart knoweth its own bitterness," he said gently. "And oh! in the day when our Redeemer makes up his jewels, may you be precious among them! I have seen you; farewell!"

Suddenly he raised my hand, and kissed it gently, twice. Then he turned, and walked rapidly down to the water's edge, and stepped into the boat. The men dipped their oars, and the water rose like diamonds from the touch. I saw his dark figure standing, with arm extended, for a moment, in the stern, in his black cloak, pointing towards Golden Friars. The boat was now three lengths away; twenty—fifty; out on the bosom of the stirless water. The tears that I had restrained burst forth, and sobbing as if my heart would break I ran down to the margin of the lake, and stood upon the broad, flat stone, and waved my hand wildly and unseen towards my friend, whom I knew I was never to see again.

I stood there watching, till the shape of the boat and the sound of the oars were quite lost in the grey distance.

CHAPTER LVI.

"LOVE TOOK UP THE GLASS OF TIME."

EEKS glided by, and still the same clear, bright frost, and low, cold, cheerful suns. The dogs so wild with spirits, the distant sounds travelling so sharp to the ear—ruddy sunsets—early darkness—and the roaring fires at home.

Sir Harry Rokestone's voice, clear and kindly, often heard through the house, calls me from the hall; he wants to know whether "little Ethel" will come out for a ride; or, if she would like a drive with him into the town to see the skaters, for in the shallower parts the mere is frozen.

One day I came into Sir Harry's room, on some errand, I forget what. Mr. Blount was standing, leaning on the mantelpiece, and Sir Harry was withdrawing a large key from the door of an iron safe, which seemed to be built into the wall. Each paused in the attitude in which I had found him, with his eyes fixed on me, in silence. I saw that I was in their way, and said, a little flurried :

"I'll come again; it was nothing of any consequence," and I was drawing back, when Sir Harry said, beckoning to me with his finger :

"Stay, little Ethel—stay a minute—I see no reason, Blount, why we should not tell the lassie."

Mr. Blount nodded acquiescence.

"Come here, my bonny Ethel," said Sir Harry, and turning the key again in the lock, he pulled the door open. "Look in; ye see that shelf? Well, mind that's where I'll leave auld Harry Rokestone's will—ye'll remember where it lies ?"

Then he drew me very kindly to him, smoothed my hair gently with his hand, and said :

"God bless you, my bonny lass!" and kissed me on the forehead.

Then locking the door again, he said:

"Ye'll mind, it's this iron box, that's next the picture. That's all, lassie."

And thus dismissed, I took my departure.

In this retreat, time was stealing on with silent steps. Christmas was past. Mr. Marston had returned; he lived, at this season, more at our side of the lake, and the house was more cheerful.

Can I describe Mr. Marston with fidelity? Can I rely even upon my own recollection of him? What had I become? A dreamer of dreams—a dupe of magic. Everything had grown strangely interesting—the lonely place was lonely no more—the old castle of Dorracleugh was radiant with unearthly light. Unconsciously, I had become the captive of a magician. I had passed under a sweet and subtle mania, and was no longer myself. Little by little, hour by hour, it grew, until I was transformed. Well, behold me now, wildly in love with Richard Marston.

Looking back now on that period of my history, I see plainly enough that it was my inevitable fate. So much together, and surrounded by a solitude, we were the only young people in the little group which formed our society. Handsome and fascinating—wayward, and even wicked he might have been, but that I might hope was past—he was energetic, clever, passionate; and of his admiration he never allowed me to be doubtful.

My infatuation had been stealing upon me, but it was not until we had reached the month of May that it culminated in a scene that returns again and again in my solitary reveries, and always with the same tumult of sweet and bitter feelings.

One day before that explanation took place, my diary, from which I have often quoted, says thus:

"May 9th.—There was no letter, I am sure, by the early post from Mr. Marston; Sir Harry or Mr. Blount would have been sure to talk of it at breakfast. It is treating his uncle, I think, a little cavalierly.

"Sailed across the lake to-day, alone, to Clusted, and

walked about a quarter of a mile up the forest road. How beautiful everything is looking, but how melancholy! When last I saw this haunted wood, Sir Harry Rokestone and Mr. Marston were with me.

"It seems odd that Mr. Marston stays away so long, and hard to believe that if he tried he might not have returned sooner. He went on the 28th of April, and Mr. Blount thought he would be back again in a week: that would have been on the 5th of this month. I dare say he is glad to get away for a little time—I cannot blame him; I dare say he finds it often very dull, say what he will. I wonder what he meant, the other day, when he said he was ' born to be liked least where he loved most'? He seems very melancholy. I wonder whether there has been some old love and parting? Why, unless he liked some one else, should he have quarrelled with Sir Harry, rather than marry as he wished him? Sir Harry would not have chosen any one for him who was not young and good-looking. I heard him say something one morning that showed his opinion upon that point; and young men, who don't like any one in particular, are easily persuaded to marry. Well, perhaps his constancy will be rewarded; it is not likely that the young lady should have given him up.

"May 10th.—How shall I begin? What have I done? Heaven forgive me if I have done wrong! Oh! kind, true friend, Sir Harry, how have I requited you? It is too late now—the past is past. And yet, in spite of this, how happy I am!

"Let me collect my thoughts, and write down as briefly as I can an outline of the events of this happy, agitating day. No lovelier May day was ever seen. I was enjoying a lonely saunter, about one o'clock, under the boughs of Lynder Wood, here and there catching the gleam of the waters through the trees, and listening from time to time to the call of the cuckoo from the hollows of the forest. In that lonely region there is no more lonely path than this.

"On a sudden, I heard a step approaching fast from behind me on the path, and, looking back, I saw Mr. Marston coming on, with a very glad smile, to overtake me. I stopped; I felt myself blushing. He was speaking

as he approached: I was confused, and do not recollect
what he said; but hardly a moment passed till he was at
my side. He was smiling, but very pale. I suppose he
had made up his mind to speak. He did not immediately
talk of the point on which hung so much; he spoke of
other things—I can recollect nothing of them.

" He began at length to talk upon that other theme that
lay so near our hearts; our pace grew slower and slower
as he spoke on, until we came to a stand-still under the
great beech-tree, on whose bark our initials, now spread
by time and touched with lichen, but possibly still legible,
are carved.

" Well, he has spoken, and I have answered—I can't
remember our words; but we are betrothed in the sight of
Heaven by vows that nothing can ever cancel, till those
holier vows, plighted at the altar-steps, are made before
God himself, or until either shall die.

" Oh! Richard, my love, and is it true? Can it be
that you love your poor Ethel with a love so tender, so
deep, so desperate? He has loved me, he says, ever since
he first saw me, on the day after his escape, in the garden
at Malory!

"I liked him from the first. In spite of all their
warnings, I could not bring myself to condemn or distrust
him long. I never forgot him during the years we have
been separated; he has been all over the world since, and
often in danger, and I have suffered such great and unexpected changes of fortune—to think of our being brought
together at last! Has not Fate ordained it?

" The only thing that darkens the perfect sunshine of
to-day is that our attachment and engagement must be a
secret. He says so, and I am sure he knows best. He
says that Sir Harry has not half forgiven him yet, and
that he would peremptorily forbid our engagement. He
could unquestionably effect our separation, and make us
both inexpressibly miserable. But when I look at Sir
Harry's kind, melancholy face, and think of all he has
done for me, my heart upbraids me, and to-night I had to
turn hastily away, for my eyes filled suddenly with tears."

CHAPTER LVII.

AN AWKWARD PROPOSAL.

 WILL here make a few extracts more from my
diary, because they contain matters traced
there merely in outline, and of which it is
more convenient to present but a skeleton
account.

"May 11th.—Richard went early to his farm to-day.
I told him last night that I would come down to see him
off this morning. But he would not hear of it; and
again enjoined the strictest caution. I must do nothing
to induce the least suspicion of our engagement, or even
of our caring for each other. I must not tell Rebecca
Torkill a word about it, nor hint it to any one of the few
friends I correspond with. I am sure he is right; but
this secrecy is very painful. I feel so treacherous, and so
sad, when I see Sir Harry's kind face.

"Richard was back at three o'clock; we met by appointment, in the same path, in Lynder Wood. He has
told ever so much, of which I knew nothing before. Mr.
Blount told him, he says, that Sir Harry means to leave
me an annuity of two hundred a year. How kind and
generous! I feel more than ever the pain and meanness
of my reserve. He intends to leave Richard eight hundred
a year, and the farm at the other side of the lake.
Richard thinks, if he had not displeased him, he would
have done more for him. All this, that seems to me very
noble, depends, however, upon his continuing to like us,
as he does at present. Richard says that he will settle

everything he has in the world upon me. It hurts me, his thinking me so mercenary, and talking so soon upon the subject of money and settlements; I let him see this, for the idea of his adding to what my benefactor Sir Harry intended for me had not entered my mind.

" 'It is just, my darling, because you are so little calculating for yourself that I must look a little forward for you,' he said, and so tenderly. 'Whose business is it now to think of such things for you, if not mine? And you won't deny me the pleasure of telling you that I can prevent, thank Heaven, some of the dangers you were so willing to encounter for my sake.'

"Then he told me that the bulk of Sir Harry's property is to go to people not very nearly related to him, called Strafford; and he gave me a great charge not to tell a word of all this to a living creature, as it would involve him in a quarrel with Mr. Blount, who had told him Sir Harry's intentions under the seal of secrecy.

"I wish I had not so many secrets to keep; but his goodness to me makes me love Sir Harry better every day. I told him all about Sir Harry's little talk with me about his will. I can have no secrets now from Richard."

For weeks, for months, this kind of life went on, eventless, but full of its own hopes, misgivings, agitations. I loved Golden Friars for many reasons, if things so light as associations and sentiments can so be called—founded they were, however, in imagination and deep affection. One of these was and is that my darling mother is buried there; and the simple and sad inscription on her monument, in the pretty church, is legible on the wall opposite the Rokestone pew.

"That's a kind fellow, the vicar," said Sir Harry; "a bit too simple; but if other sirs were like him, there would be more folk in the church to hear the sermon!"

When Sir Harry made this speech, he and I were sitting in the boat, the light evening air hardly filled the sails, and we were tacking slowly back and forward on the mere, along the shore of Golden Friars. It was a beautiful evening in August, and the little speech and our loitering here were caused by the sweet music that pealed from the organ through the open church windows. The good old

vicar was a fine musician ; and often in the long summer
and autumn evenings, the lonely old man visited the
organ-loft and played those sweet and solemn melodies
that so well accorded with the dreamlike scene.

It was the music that recalled the vicar to Sir Harry's
thoughts—but his liking for him was not all founded upon
that, nor even upon his holy life and kindly ways.   It was
this : that when he read the service at mamma's funeral,
the white-haired vicar, who remembered her a beautiful
child, wept—and tears rolled down his old cheeks as with
upturned eyes he repeated the noble and pathetic farewell.

When it was over, Sir Harry, who had a quarrel with
the vicar before, came over and shook him by the hand,
heartily and long, speaking never a word—his heart was
too full. And from that time he liked him, and did not
know how to show it enough.

In these long, lazy tacks, sweeping slowly by the quaint
old town in silence, broken only by the ripple of the water
along the planks, and the sweet and distant swell of the
organ across the water, the time flew by. The sun went
down in red and golden vapours, and the curfew from the
ivied tower of Golden Friars sounded over the darkened
lake—the organ was heard no more—and the boat was
making her slow way back again to Dorracleugh.

Sir Harry looked at me very kindly, in silence, for
awhile. He arranged a rug about my feet, and looked
again in my face.

" Sometimes you look so like bonny Mabel—and
when you smile—ye mind her smile ? 'Twas very pretty."

Then came a silence.

" I must tell Renwick, when the shooting begins, to
send down a brace of birds every day to the vicar," said
Sir Harry. " I'll be away myself in a day or two, and I
shan't be back again for three weeks. I'll take a house in
London, lass—I won't have ye moping here too long—
you'd begin to pine for something to look at, and folks to
talk to, and sights to see."

I was alarmed, and instantly protested that I could
not imagine any life more delightful than this at Golden
Friars.

" No, no ; it won't do—you're a good lass to say so—

but it's not the fact—oh, no—it isn't natural—I can't
take you to balls, and all that, for I don't know the
people that give them—and all my great lady friends
that I knew when I was a younker, are off the hooks
by this time—but there's plenty of sights to see besides
—there's the waxworks, and the wild beasts, and the
players, and the pictures, and all the shows."

" But I assure you, I like Golden Friars, and my quiet
life at Dorraclengh, a thousand times better than all the
sights and wonders in the world," I protested.

If he had but known half the terror with which I contemplated the possibility of my removal from my then
place of abode, he would have given me credit for sincerity
in my objections to our proposed migration to the capital.

" No, I say, it won't do; you women can't bring your-
selves ever to say right out to us men what you think;
you mean well—you're a good little thing--you don't want
to put the auld man out of his way—but you'd like Lunnon
best, and Lunnon ye shall have. You shall have a house
you can see your auld acquaintance in, such, I mean, as
showed themselves good-natured when all went wrong wi'
ye. You shall show them ye can haud your head as high
as ever, and are not a jot down in the world. Never mind,
I have said it."

In vain I protested; Sir Harry continued firm. One
comfort was that he would not return to put his threat
into execution for, at least, three weeks. If anything was
wanting to complete my misery, it was Sir Harry's saying
after a little silence :

" And see, lass; don't you tell a word of it to Richard
Marston ; 'twould only make him fancy I'm going to take
him; and I'd as lief take the devil—so mind ye, it's a
secret."

I smiled as well as I could, and said something that
seemed to satisfy him, or he took it for granted, for he
went on and talked, being much more communicative this
evening than usual; while my mind was busy with the
thought of a miserable separation, and all the difficulties
of correspondence that accompany a secret engagement.

So great was the anguish of these anticipations that I
hazarded one more effort to induce him to abandon his

London plans, and to let me continue to enjoy my present
life at Dorracleugh.

He was, however, quite immovable; he laughed; he
told me, again and again, that it would not "put him out
of his way—not a bit;" and he added, "You're falling
into a moping, unnatural life, and you've grown to like it,
and the more you like it, the less it is fit for you; if you
lose your spirits, you can't keep your health long."

And when I still persisted, he looked in my face a little
darkly, on a sudden, as if a doubt as to my motive had
crossed his mind. That look frightened me. I felt that
matters might be worse.

Sir Harry had got it into his head, I found, that my
health would break down, unless he provided the sort of
change and amusement which he had decided on. I don't
know to which of the wiseacres of Golden Friars I was
obliged for this crotchet, which promised me such an
infinity of suffering, but I had reason to think, afterwards,
that old Miss Goulding of Wrybiggins was the friend who
originated these misgivings about my health and spirits.
She wished, I was told, to marry her niece to Richard
Marston, and thought, if I and Sir Harry were out of the
way, her plans would act more smoothly.

Richard was at home—it was our tea-time—I had not
an opportunity of saying a word to him unobserved. I
don't know whether he saw by my looks that I was unhappy.

CHAPTER LVIII.

DANGER.

SIR HARRY took his coffee with us, and read to me a little now and then from the papers which had come by the late mails. Mr. Blount had farming news to tell Richard. It was a dreadful tea-party.

I was only able that night to appoint with Richard to meet me, next day, at our accustomed trysting-place.

Three o'clock was our hour of meeting. The stupid, feverish day dragged on, and the time at length arrived. I got on my things quickly, and trembling lest I should be joined by Sir Harry or Mr. Blount, I betook myself through the orchard, and by the wicket in the hedge, to the lonely path through the thick woods where we had, a few months since, plighted our troth.

Richard appeared very soon; he was approaching by the path opposite to that by which I had come.

The foliage was thick and the boughs hang low in that place. You could have fancied him a figure walking in the narrow passage of a monastery, so dark and well-defined is the natural roofing of the pathway there. He raised his open hand, and shook his head as he drew near; he was not smiling; he looked very sombre.

He glanced back over his shoulder, and looked sharply down the path I had come by, and being now very near me, with another gloomy shake of the head, he said, with a tone and look of indescribable reproach and sorrow: "So Ethel has her secrets, and tells me but half her mind."

"What can you mean, Richard?"

"Ah! Ethel, I would not have treated you so," he continued.

"You distract me, Richard; what have I done?"

"I have heard it all by accident, I may say, from old Mr. Blount, who has been simpleton enough to tell me. You have asked my uncle to take you to London, and you are going."

"Asked him! I have all but implored of him to leave me here. I never heard a word of it till last night, as we returned together in the boat. Oh! Richard, how could you think such things? That is the very thing I have been so longing to talk to you about."

"Ethel, darling, are you opening your heart entirely to me now; is there no reserve? No; I am sure there is not; you need not answer."

"It is distracting news; is there nothing I can do to prevent it?" I said.

He looked miserable enough, as walking slowly along the path, and sometimes standing still, we talked it over.

"Yes," he said; "the danger is that you may lead him by resistance to look for some secret motive. If he should suspect our engagement, few worse misfortunes could befall us. Good heavens! shall I ever have a quiet home? Ethel, I know what will happen—you will go to London; I shall be forgotten. It will end in the ruin of all my hopes." So he raved on.

I wept, and upbraided, and vowed my old vows over again.

At length after this tempestuous scene had gone on for some time, we two walking side by side up and down the path, and sometimes stopping short, I crying, if you will, like a fool, he took my hand and looked in my face very sadly, and he said after a little:

"Only I know that he would show more anger, I should have thought that my uncle knew of our engagement, and was acting expressly to frustrate it. He has found work for me at his property near Hull, and from that I am to go to Warwickshire, so that I suppose I can't be here again before the middle of October, and long before then you will be at Brighton, where, Mr. Blount says, he means to take you first, and from that to London."

"But you are not to leave this immediately?" I said.

He smiled bitterly, and answered:

"He takes good care I shall. I am to leave this to-morrow morning."

I could not speak for a moment.

"Oh, Richard, Richard, how am I to live through this separation?" I cried wildly. "You must contrive some way to see me. I shall die unless you do."

"Come, Ethel, let us think it over; it seems to me that we have nothing for it, for the present, but submission. I am perfectly certain that our attachment is not suspected. If it were, far more cruel and effectual measures would be taken. We must, therefore, be cautious. Let us betray nothing of our feelings. You shall see me undergo the ordeal with the appearance of carelessness, and even cheerfulness, although my heart be bursting. You, darling, must do the same; one way or other I will manage to see you sometimes, and to correspond regularly. We are bound each to the other by promises we dare not break, and when I desert you, may God desert me! Ethel, will you say the same?"

"Yes, Richard," I repeated, vehemently, through sobs, "when I forsake you, may God forsake me! You know I could not live without you. Oh! Richard, darling, how shall I see you all this evening, knowing it to be the last? How can I look at you, or hear your voice, and yet no sign, and talk or listen just as usual, as if nothing had gone wrong? Richard, is there no way to escape? Do you think if we told your uncle? Might it not be the best thing after all? Could it possibly make matters worse?"

"Yes, it would, a great deal worse; that is not to be thought of," said Richard, with a thoughtful frown; "I know him better than you do. No; we have nothing for it but patience, and entire trust in one another. As for me, if I am away from you, the more solitary I am, the more bearable my lot. With you it will be different; you will soon be in the stream and whirl of your old life. I shall lose you, Ethel." He stamped on the ground, and struck his forehead with his open hand in sheer distraction. "As for me, I can enjoy nothing without you; I may have been violent, wicked, reckless, what you will; but selfish or fickle, no one ever called me."

I was interrupting him all the time with my passionate vows of fidelity, which he seemed hardly to hear; he was absorbed in his own thoughts. After a silence of a minute or two, he said, suddenly:

"Look here, Ethel; if you don't like your London life, you can't be as well there as here, and you can, if you will, satisfy my uncle that you are better, as well as happier, here at Golden Friars. You can do that, and that is the way to end it—the only way to end it that I see. You can write to me, Ethel, without danger. You will, I know, every day, just a line; and when you tell me how to address mine, you shall have an answer by every post. Don't go out in London, Ethel; you must promise that."

I did, vehemently and reproachfully. I wondered how he could suspect me of wishing to go out. But I could not resent the jealousy that proved his love.

It was, I think, just at this moment that I heard a sound that made my heart bound within me, and then sink with terror. It was the clear, deep voice of Sir Harry, so near that it seemed a step must bring him round the turn in the path, and full in view of us.

"Go, darling, quickly," said Richard, pressing me gently with one hand, and with the other pointing in the direction furthest from the voice that was so near a signal of danger. He himself turned, and walked quickly to meet Sir Harry, who was conferring with his ranger about thinning the timber.

I was out of sight in a moment, and, in agitation indescribable, made my way home.

CHAPTER LIX.

AN INTRUDER.

T was all true. Richard left Dorracleugh early next morning. Those who have experienced such a separation know its bitterness, and the heartache and apathy that follow.

I was going to be left quite alone, and mistress at Dorracleugh for three weeks at least; perhaps for twice as long. Mr. Blount was to leave next day for France, to pay a visit of a fortnight to Vichy. Sir Harry Rokestone, a few days later, was to leave Dorracleugh for Brighton.

Nothing could be kinder than Sir Harry. It was plain that he suspected nothing of the real situation.

"You'll be missing your hit of backgammon with Lemuel Blount," he said, "and your sail on the mere wi' myself, and our talk round the tea-table of an evening. 'Twill be dowly down here, lass; but ye'll be coming soon where you'll see sights and hear noise enough for a dozen. So think o' that, and when we are gone you munnon be glumpin' about the house, but chirp up, and think there are but a few weeks between you and Brighton and Lunnon."

How directly this kind consolation went to the source of my dejection you may suppose.

So the time came, and I was alone. Solitude was a relief. I could sit looking at the lake, watching the track where his boat used to come and go over the water, and thinking of him half the day. I could walk in the pathway, and sit under the old beech-tree, and murmur long talks with him in fancy, without fear of interruption; but oh ! the misgivings, the suspense, the dull, endless pain of separation !

Not a line reached me from Richard. He insisted that while I remained at Dorracleugh there should be no correspondence. In Golden Friars, and about the post-office, there were so many acute ears and curious eyes.

Sir Harry had been gone about three weeks, when he sent me a really exquisite little enamelled watch, set in brilliants ; it was brought to Dorracleugh by a Golden Friars neighbour whom he had met in his travels. Then, after a silence of a week, another letter came from Sir Harry. He was going up to London, he said, to see after the house, and to be sure that nothing was wanted to "make it smart."

Then some more days of silence followed, interrupted very oddly. I was out, taking my lonely walk in the afternoon, when a chaise with a portmanteau, a hat-box, and some other luggage on top, drove up to the hall-door ; the driver knocked and rang, and out jumped Richard Marston, who ran up the steps, and asked the servant, with an accustomed air of command, to take the luggage up to his room.

He had been some minutes in the hall before he inquired whether I was in the house. He sat down on a hall-chair, in his hat and great-coat, just as he had come out of the chaise, lost in deep thought. He seemed for a time undecided where to go ; he went to the foot of the stairs, and stopped short, with his hand on the banister, and turned back ; then he stood for a little while in the middle of the hall, looking down on his dusty boots, again in deep thought ; then he walked to the hall-door, stood on the steps in the same undecided state, and sauntered in again, and said to the servant :

"And Miss Ware, you say, is out walking ? Well, go you and tell the housekeeper that I have come, and shall be coming and going for a few days, till I hear from London."

The man departed to execute his message. Richard Marston had paid the vicar a visit of about five minutes, as he drove through the town of Golden Friars, and had had a very private and earnest talk with him. He seemed

very uncomfortable and fidgety. He took off his hat and laid
it down, and put it on again, and looked dark and agitated,
like a man in a sudden danger, who expects a struggle for
his life. He went again to the foot of the stairs, and
listened for a few seconds; and then, without much ado,
he walked over and turned the key that was in Sir Harry's
study-door, took it out, and went into the room, looking
very stern and nervous.

In a little more than five minutes Mrs. Shackleton, the
housekeeper, in her thick brown silk, knocked sharply at
the door.

"Come in," called Richard Marston's voice.

"I can't, sir."

"Can't? Why? What's the matter?"

"You've bolted it, please, on the inside," she answered,
very tartly.

"I? I haven't bolted it," Richard Marston answered,
with a quiet laugh. "Try again."

She did, a little fiercely; but the door opened, and disclosed Richard Marston sitting in his uncle's easy chair,
with one of the newspapers he had bought in his railway
carriage expanded on his knees. He looked up carelessly.

"Well, Mrs. Shackleton, what's the row?"

"No row, sir, please," she answered, sharply rustling
into the room, and looking round. She didn't like him.
"But the door was bolted, I assure you, sir, only a minute
before, when I tried it first; and my master, Sir Harry,
told me no one was to be allowed into this room while he's
away."

"So I should have thought; his letters lying about—
but I found the door open, and the key in the look—here
it is; so I thought it safer to take it out."

The old woman made a short curtsey as she took it,
dryly, from his fingers; and she stood, resolutely waiting.

"Oh! I suppose," he said, starting up, and stretching
himself, with a smile and a little yawn, "you want me to
turn out?"

"Yes, sir, please," said Mrs. Shackleton peremptorily.

The young gentleman cast a careless glance through the
far window, looked lazily round, as if to see that he had not
forgotten anything, and then said, with a smile:

2 A

"Mrs. Shackleton, happy the man who has such a lady to take care of his worldly goods."

"I'm no lady, sir; I'm not above my business," she said, with another hard little curtsey. "I tries to do my dooty accordin' to my conscience. Sorry to have to disturb you, sir."

"Not the least; no disturbance," he said, sauntering out of the room, with another yawn.

He was cudgelling his brains to think what civility he could do the old lady, or how he could please or make her friendly; but Mrs. Shackleton had her northern pride, he knew, which was easily ruffled, and he must approach her very cautiously.

CHAPTER LX.

SIR HARRY'S KEY.

P to his room he went; his things were all there
—he wished to get rid of the dust and smuts of
his railway journey.

He made his toilet rapidly; and just as he
was about to open his door, a knock came to it.

"What is it?" he asked.

"The vicar has called, sir, and wants to know if you
can see him."

"Certainly." Tell him I'll be down in a moment."

Mr. Marston had foreseen this pursuit with a prescience
of which he was proud. He went downstairs, and found
the white-haired vicar alone in the drawing-room.

"I am so delighted you have come," said Richard
Marston, advancing quickly, with an outstretched hand,
from the door, without giving him a moment to begin.
"I have only had time to dress since I arrived, and I
have made up my mind that it is better to replace this
key in your hand, without using it—and, in the meantime, it is better in your keeping than in mine. Don't
you think so?"

"Well, sir, said the good vicar, "I do. It is odd, but
the very same train of thought passed through my mind,
and, in fact, induced me to pay you this visit. You see
it was placed in my charge, and I think, until it is
formally required of me, I should not part with it."

"Just so," acquiesced the young man.

"We both acted, perhaps, a little too precipitately."

"So we did, sir," said Richard Marston, "but I take

2 A 2

the entire blame on myself. I'm too apt to be impulsive and foolish. I generally think too late; happily this time, however, I did reflect, and with your concurrence, I am now sure I was right."

The young man paused and thought, with his hand on the vicar's arm.

" One thing," he said, " I would stipulate, however; as we are a good deal in the dark, my reason for declining to take charge of the key would be but half answered, as I must be a great deal in this house, and there may be other keys that open it, and I can't possibly answer for servants, and other people who will be coming and going, unless you will kindly come into the next room with me for a moment."

The vicar consented; and Mr. Marston was eloquent. Mrs. Shackelton was sent for, and with less reluctance opened the door for the vicar, whom she loved. She did not leave it, however—they did not stay long. In a few minutes the party withdrew.

" Won't you have some luncheon ?" asked Richard, in the hall.

" No, thank you," said the vicar, " I am very much hurried. I am going to see that poor boy to whom Mr. Blount has been so kind, and who is, I fear, dying."

And with a few words more, and the key again in his keeping, he took his leave.

I was all this time in my favourite haunt, alone, little thinking that the hero of my dreams was near, when suddenly I saw him walking rapidly up the path. With a cry, I ran to meet him. He seemed delighted and radiant with love as he drew me to him, folded me for a moment in his arms, and kissed me passionately. He had ever so much to say; and yet, when I thought it over, there was nothing in it but one delightful promise; and that was that henceforward, he expected to see a great deal more of me than he had hitherto done.

There was a change in his manner, I thought—he spoke with something of the confidence and decision of a lover who had a right to command. He was not more earnest, but more demonstrative. I might have resented his passionate greeting, if I had been myself less surprised and happy at his sudden appearance. He was obliged to go down to the village, but would be back again, he said, very soon. It would not do to make people talk, which they would be sure to do, if he and I were not very cautious.

Therefore I let him go, without entreaty or remonstrance, although it cost me an indescribable pang to lose him, even for an hour, so soon after our long separation. He promised to be back in an hour, and although that was nearly impracticable, I believed him. "Lovers trample upon impossibilities."

By a different route I came home. He had said:

"When I return, I shall come straight to the drawing-room—will you be there?"

So to the drawing-room I went. I was afraid to leave it even for a moment, lest some accident should make him turn back, and he should find the room empty. There was to me a pleasure in obeying him, and I liked him to see it. How I longed for his return! How restless I was! How often I played his favourite airs on the piano; how often I sat at the window, looking down at the trees and the mere, in the direction from which I had so often seen his boat coming, you will easily guess.

All this time I had a secret misgiving. There was a change in Richard's manner, as I have said; there was confidence, security, carelessness—a kind of carelessness—not that he seemed to admire me less—but it was a change. There seemed something ominous about it.

As time wore on I became so restless that I could hardly remain quiet for a minute in any one place. I was perpetually holding the door open, and listening for the sound of horses' hoofs, or wheels, or footsteps. In vain.

An hour beyond the appointed time had passed; two hours. I was beginning to fancy all sorts of horrors. Was he drowned in the mere? Had his horse fallen and killed him? There was no catastrophe too improbable to be canvassed among the wild conjectures of my terror.

The sun was low, and I almost despairing, when the door opened, and Richard came in. I had heard no sound at the door, no step approaching, only he was there.

CHAPTER LXI.

A DISCOVERY.

 STARTED to my feet and was going to meet him, but he raised his hand, as I fancied to warn me that some one was coming. So I stopped short, and he approached.

"I shall be very busy for two or three days, dear Ethel; and," what he added was spoken very slowly, and dropped word by word, "you are such a rogue!"

I was very much astonished. Neither his voice nor look was playful. His face at the moment wore about the most disagreeable expression which human face can wear. That of a smile, not a genuine but a pretended smile, which, at the same time, the person who smiles affects to try to suppress. To me it looks cruel, cynical, mean. I was so amazed, as he looked into my eyes with this cunning, shabby smile, that I could not say a word, and stood stock-still looking in return, in stupid wonder, in his face.

At length I broke out, very pale, for I was shocked, "I can't understand! What is it? Oh, Richard, what can you mean?"

"Now don't be a little fool. I really believe you are going to cry. You are a great deal too clever, you lovely little rogue, to fancy that a girl's tears ever yet did any good. Listen to me; come!"

He walked away, still smiling that insulting smile, and he took my hand in his, and shook his finger at me, with the same cynical affectation of the playful. "What did I mean?"

" Yes, what can you mean ?" I stamped the emphasis on the floor, with tears in my eyes. " It is cruel, it is horrible, after our long separation."

" Well, I'll tell you what I mean," he said, and for a moment the smile almost degenerated to a sneer. " Look here ; come to the window."

I faltered ; I accompanied him to it, looking in his face in an agony of alarm and surprise. It seemed to me like the situation of a horrid dream.

" Do you know how I amused myself during the last twenty miles of my railway journey ?" he said. " Well, I'll tell you : I was reading all that time a curious criminal trial, in which a most respectable old gentleman, aged sixty-seven, has just been convicted of having poisoned a poor girl forty years ago, and is to be hanged for it before three weeks !"

" Well ?" said I, with an effort—I should not have known my own voice, and I felt a great ball in my throat.

" Well ?" he repeated ; " don't you see ?"

He paused with the same horrid smile ; this time, in the silence, he laughed a little ; it was no use trying to hide from myself the fact that I dimly suspected what he was driving at. I should have liked to die that moment, before he had time to complete another sentence.

" Now, you see, the misfortune of that sort of thing is that time neither heals nor hides the offence. There is a principle of law which says that no lapse of time bars the Crown. But I see this kind of conversation bores you."

I was near saying something very wild and foolish, but I did not.

" I won't keep you a moment," said he—"just come a little nearer the window ; I want you to look at something that may interest you."

I did go a little nearer. I was moving as he commanded, as if I had been mesmerised.

" You lost," he continued, " shortly before your illness, the only photograph you possessed of your sister Helen ? But why are you so put out by it ? Why should you tremble so violently ? It is only I, you know ; you need not mind. You dropped that on the floor of a jeweller's

shop one night, when I and Droqville happened to be there
together, and I picked it up; it represents you both
together. I want to restore it; here it is."

I extended my hand to take it. I don't know whether
I spoke, but the portrait faded suddenly from my sight,
and darkness covered everything. I heard his voice, like
that of a person talking in excitement, a long way off, at
the other side of a wall in another room—it was no more
than a hum, and even that was growing fainter. I forgot
everything, in utter unconsciousness, for some seconds.
When I opened my eyes, water was trickling down my
face and forehead, and the window was open. I sighed
deeply. I saw him looking over me with a countenance
of gloom and anxiety. In happy forgetfulness of all that
had passed, I smiled and said:

"Oh, Richard! Thank God!" and stretched my arms
to him.

"That's right—quite right," he said; "you may have
every confidence in me."

The dreadful recollection began to return.

"Don't get up yet," he said, earnestly, and even tenderly; "you're not equal to it. Don't think of leaving
me—you must have confidence in me. Why didn't you
trust me long ago?—trust me altogether? Fear nothing
while I am near you."

So he continued speaking, until my recollection had
quite returned.

"Why, darling, will you not trust me? Can you be
surprised at my being wounded by your reserve? How
have I deserved it? Forget the pain of this discovery,
and remember only that against all the world, to the last
hour of my life, with my last thought, the last drop of my
blood, I am your defender."

He kissed my hands passionately; he drew me towards
him, and kissed my lips. He murmured caresses and
vows of unalterable love—nothing could be more tender
and impassioned. I was relieved by a passionate burst of
tears.

"It's over now," he said—"it's all over; you'll forgive
me, won't you? I have more to forgive, darling, than
you—the hardest of all things to forgive in one whom we

idolise—a want of confidence in us. You ought to have told me all this before."

I told him, as well as I could between my sobs, that there was no need to tell any one of a madness which had nothing to do with waking thoughts or wishes, and was simply the extravagance of delirium—that I was then actually in fever, had been at the point of death, and that Mr. Carmel knew everything about it.

"Well, darling," he said, "you must trouble your mind no more. "Of course you are not accountable for it. If people in brain fever were not carefully watched and restrained, a day would not pass without some tragedy. But what care I, Ethel, if it had been a real crime of passion? Nothing. Do you fancy it would or could, for an instant, have shaken my desperate love for you? Don't you remember Moore's lines:

'I ask not, I care not, if guilt's in thy heart;
I but know that thou lov'st me, whatever thou art.'

That is my feeling, fixed as adamant; never suspect me. I can't I never can, tell you how I felt your suspicion of my love; how cruel I thought it. What had I done to deserve it? There, darling, take this—it is yours." He kissed the little photograph, he placed it in my hand, he kissed me again fervently. "Look here, Ethel, I came all this way, ever so much out of my way, to see you. I made an excuse of paying the vicar a visit on business—my real business was to see you. I must be this evening at Wrexham, but I shall be here again to-morrow, as early as possible. I am a mere slave at present, and business hurries me from point to point; but cost what it may, I shall be with you some time in the afternoon to-morrow."

" To stay?" I asked.

He smiled, and shook his head.

"I can't say that, darling," he said; he was going towards the door.

"But you'll be here early to-morrow; do you think before two?"

"No, not before two, I am afraid. I may be delayed, and it is a long way; but you may look out for me early in the evening."

Then came a leave-taking. He would not let me come with him to the hall-door—there were servants there, and I looked so ill. I stood at the window and saw him drive away. You may suppose I did feel miserable. I think I was near fainting again when he was gone.

In a little time I was sufficiently recovered to get up to my room, and then I rang for Rebecca Torkill.

I don't know how that long evening went by. The night came, and a miserable nervous night I passed, starting in frightful dreams from the short dozes I was able to snatch.

CHAPTER LXII.

SIR HARRY WITHDRAWS.

NEXT morning, when the grey light came, I was neither glad nor sorry. The shock of my yesterday's interview with the only man on earth I loved, remained. It was a shock, I think, never to be quite recovered from. I got up and dressed early. How ill and strange I looked out of the glass in my own face !

I did not go down. I remained in my room, loitering over the hours that were to pass before the arrival of Richard. I was haunted by his changed face. I tried to fix in my recollection the earnest look of love on which my eyes had opened from my swoon. But the other would take its place and remain ; and I could not get rid of the startled pain of my heart. I was haunted now, as I had been ever since that scene had taken place, with a vague misgiving of something dreadful going to happen.

I think it was between four and five in the evening that Rebecca Torkill came in, looking pale and excited.

"Oh, Miss Ethel, dear, what do you think has happened ?" she said, lifting up both hands and eyes as soon as she was in at the door.

"Good Heaven, Rebecca !" I said, starting up ; "is it anything bad ?"

I was on the point of saying " anything about Mr. Marston ?"

"Oh, miss ! what do you think ? Poor Sir Harry Rokestone is dead."

"Sir Harry dead !" I exclaimed.

"Dead, indeed, miss," said Rebecca. "Thomas Byres is just come up from the vicar's, and he's had a letter from Mr. Blount this morning, and the vicar's bin down at the church with Dick Mattox, the sexton, giving him directions about the vault. Little thought I, when I saw him going away—a fine man he was, six feet two, Adam Bell says, in his boots—little thought I, when I saw him walk down the steps, so tall and hearty, he'd be coming back so soon in his coffin, poor gentleman. But, miss, they say dead folk's past feeling, and what does it all matter now? One man's breath is another man's death. And so the world goes on, and all forgot before long.

> 'To the grave with the dead,
> And the quick to the bread.'

A rough gentleman he was, but kind—the tenants will be all sorry. They're all talking, the servants, downstairs. He was one that liked to see his tenants and his poor comfortable."

All this and a great deal more Rebecca discoursed. I could hardly believe her news. A letter, I thought, would have been sure to reach Dorracleugh, as soon as the vicar's house, at least.

Possibly this dismaying news would turn out to be mere rumour, I thought, and end in nothing worse than a sharp attack of gout in London. Surely we should have heard of his illness before it came to this catastrophe. Nevertheless I had to tear up my first note to the vicar—I was so flurried, and it was full of blunders—and I was obliged to write another. It was simply to entreat information in this horrible uncertainty, which had for the time superseded all my other troubles.

A mounted messenger was despatched forthwith to the vicar's house. But we soon found that the rumour was everywhere. for people were arriving from all quarters to inquire at the house. It was, it is true, so far as we could learn, mere report; but its being in so many places was worse than ominous.

The messenger had not been gone ten minutes, when Richard Marston arrived. From my room I saw the chaise come to the hall-door, and I ran down at once to the drawing-room. Richard had arrived half an hour before his time. He entered the room from the other door as I came in, and met me eagerly, looking tired and anxious, but very loving. Not a trace of the Richard whose smile had horrified me the day before.

Almost my first question to him was whether he had heard any such rumour. He was holding my hand in his as I asked the question—he laid his other on it, and looked sadly in my eyes as he answered, "It is only too true. I have lost the best friend that man ever had."

I was too much startled to speak for some seconds, then I burst into tears.

"No, no." he said, in answer to something I had said. "It is only too certain—there can be no doubt; look at this."

He took a telegraph paper from his pocket and showed it to me. It was from "Lemuel Blount, London." It announced the news in the usual shocking laconic manner, and said, "I write to you to Dykham."

"I shall get the letter this evening when I reach Dykham, and I'll tell you all that is in it to-morrow. The telegraph message had reached me yesterday, when I saw you, but I could not bear to tell you the dreadful news until I had confirmation, and that has come. The vicar has had a message, about which there can be no mistake. And now, darling, put on your things, and come out for a little walk—I have ever so many things to talk to you about."

Here was a new revolution in my troubled history. More or less of the horror of uncertainty again encompassed my future years. But grief, quite unselfish, predominated in my agitation. I had lost a benefactor. His kind face was before me, and the voice, always subdued to tenderness when he spoke to me, was in my ear. I was grieved to the heart.

I got on my hat and jacket, and with a heavy heart went out with Richard.

For many reasons the most secluded path was that best suited for our walk. Richard Marston had just told the servants the substance of the message he had received that morning from Mr. Blount, so that that they could have no difficulty about answering inquiries at the hall-door.

We soon found ourselves in the path that had witnessed so many of our meetings. I wondered what Richard intended talking about. He had been silent and thoughtful. He hardly uttered a word during our walk, until we had reached what I may call our trysting-tree, the grand old beech-tree, under which a huge log of timber, roughly squared, formed a seat.

Though little disposed myself to speak, his silence alarmed me.

" Ethel, darling," he said, suddenly, " have you formed any plans for the future ?"

" Plans !" I echoed. " I don't know—what do you mean, Richard ?"

" I mean," he continued, sadly, "have you considered how this misfortune may affect us ? Did Sir Harry ever tell you anything about his intentions—I mean what he thought of doing by his will ? Don't look so scared, darling," he added, with a melancholy smile ; " you will see just now what my reasons are. You can't suppose that a sordid thought ever entered my mind."

I was relieved.

" No ; he never said a word to me about his will, except what I told you," I answered.

" Because the people who knew him at Wrexham are talking. Suppose he has cut me off and provided for you, could I any longer in honour hold you to an engagement, to fulfil which I could contribute nothing ?"

" Oh, Richard, darling, how can you talk so ? Don't you know, whatever I possess on earth is yours."

" Then my little woman refuses to give me up, even if there were difficulties ?" he said, pressing my hands, and smiling down upon my face in a kind rapture.

" I could not give you up, Richard—you know I couldn't," I answered.

" My darling !" he exclaimed, softly, looking down upon me still with the same smile.

" Richard, how could you ever have dreamed such a thing ? You don't know how you wound me."

" I never thought it, I never believed it, darling. I

knew it was impossible; whatever difficulties might come
between us, I knew that I could not live without you ; and
I thought you loved me as well. Nothing then shall part
us—nothing. Don't you say so ? Say it, Ethel. I swear
it, nothing."

I gave him the promise; it was but repeating what I
had often said before. Never was vow uttered from a
more willing heart. Even now I am sure he reminded me,
and, after his manner, loved me with a vehement passion.

" But there are other people, Ethel," he resumed, " who
think that I shall be very well off, who think that I shall
inherit all my uncle's great fortune. But all may not go
smoothly, you see ; there may be great difficulties. Promise me, swear it once more, that you will suffer no ob-
stacles to separate us ; that we shall be united, be they
what they may; that you will never, so help you Heaven,
forsake me or marry another."

I did repeat the promise. We walked towards home;
I wondering what special difficulty he could be thinking
of now; but, restrained by a kind of fear, I did not ask
him.

" I'm obliged to go away again, immediately," said he,
after another short silence ; " but my business will be over
to-night, and I shall be here again in the morning, and
then I shall be my own master for a time, and have a
quiet day or two, and be able to open my heart to you,
Ethel."

We walked on again in silence. Suddenly he stopped,
laying his hand on my shoulder, and looking sharply into
my face, said :

" I'll leave you here—it is time, Ethel, that I should be
off." He held my hand in his, and his eyes were fixed
steadily upon mine. "Look here," he said, after another
pause, " I must make a bitter confession, Ethel; you know
me with all my faults—I have no principle of calculation
in me—equity and all that sort of thing, would stand a
poor chance with me against passion—I am all passion ;
it has been my undoing, and will yet I hope," and he
looked on me with a wild glow in his dark eyes, " be the
making of me, Ethel. No obstacle shall separate us, you
have sworn ; and mind, Ethel, I am a fellow that never

forgives, and as Heaven is my judge, if you give me up,
I'll not forgive you. But that will never be. God bless
you, darling—you shall see me early to-morrow. Go you
in that direction—let us keep our secret a day or two
longer. You look as if you thought me mad—I'm not
that—though I sometimes half think so myself. There
has been enough in my life to make a steadier brain than
mine crazy. Good-bye, Ethel, darling, till to-morrow.
God bless you!"

With these words he left me. His reckless language
had plainly a meaning in it. My heart sank as I thought
on the misfortune that had reduced me again to uncertainty, and perhaps to a miserable dependence. It was
by no means impossible that nothing had been provided
for either him or me by Sir Harry Rokestone. Men,
prompt and accurate in everything else, so often go on
postponing a will until "the door is shut to," and the
hour passed for ever. It was horrible allowing such
thoughts to intrude; but Richard's conversation was so
full of the subject, and my position was so critical and
dependent, that it did recur, not with sordid hopes, but in
the form of a great and reasonable fear.

When Richard was out of sight, as he quickly was
among the trees, I turned back, and sitting down again on
the rude bench under our own beech-tree, I had a long
and bitter cry, all to myself.

CHAPTER LXIII.

AT THE THREE NUNS.

HEN Richard Marston left me, his chaise stood at the door, with a team of four horses, quite necessary to pull a four-wheeled carriage over the fells, through whose gorges the road to the nearest railway-station is carried.

The pleasant setting sun flashed over the distant fells, and glimmered on the pebbles of the courtyard, and cast a long shadow of Richard Marston, as he stood upon the steps, looking down upon the yellow, worn flags, in dark thought.

"Here, put this in," he said, handing his only piece of luggage, a black leather travelling-bag, to one of the post-boys. "You know the town of Golden Friars?"

"Yes, sir."

"Well, stop at Mr. Jarlcot's house."

Away went the chaise, with its thin roll of dust, like the smoke of a hedge-fire, all along the road, till they pulled up at Mr. Jarlcot's house.

Out jumped Mr. Marston, and knocked a sharp summons with the brass knocker on the hall-door.

The maid opened the door, and stood on the step with a mysterious look of inquiry in Mr. Marston's face. The rumour that was already slowly spreading in Golden Friars had suddenly been made sure by a telegraphic message from Lemuel Blount to Mr. Jarlcot. His good wife had read it just five minutes before Mr. Marston's arrival.

" When is Mr. Jarlcot to be home again ?"

" Day after to-morrow, please, sir."

" Well, when he comes, don't forget to tell him I called. No, this is better," and he wrote in pencil on his card the date and the words, " Called twice—most anxious to see Mr. Jarlcot ;" and laid it on the table. " Can I see Mr. Spaight ?" he inquired.

Tall, stooping Mr. Spaight, the confidential man, with his bald head, spectacles, and long nose, emerged politely, with a pen behind his ear, at this question, from the door of the front room, which was Mr. Jarlcot's office.

" Oh! Mr. Spaight," said Richard Marston, " have you heard from Mr. Jarlcot to-day ?"

" A short letter, Mr. Marston, containing nothing of business—only a few items of news ; he's in London till to-morrow—he saw Mr. Blount there."

" Then he has heard, of course, of our misfortune ?"

" Yes, sir ; and we all sympathise with you, Mr. Marston, deeply, sir, in your affliction. Will you please to step in, sir, and look at the letter ?"

Mr. Marston accepted the invitation.

There were two or three sentences that interested him.

" I have had a conversation with Mr. Blount this morning. He fears very much that Sir Harry did not execute the will. I saw Messrs. Hutt and Babbage, who drafted the will ; but they can throw no light upon the matter, and say that the result of a search, only, can ; which Mr. Blount says won't take five minutes to make."

This was interesting ; but the rest was rubbish. Mr. Marston took his leave, got into the chaise again, and drove under the windows of the " George and Dragon," along the already deserted road that ascends the fells from the margin of the lake.

Richard Marston put his head from the window and looked back ; there was no living creature in his wake. Before him he saw nothing but the post-boys' stooping backs, and the horses with their four patient heads bobbing before him. The light was failing, still it would have served to read by for a little while ; and there was something he was very anxious to read. He was irresolute—there was a risk in it—he could not make up his mind.

He looked at his watch—it would take him nearly three hours to reach the station at the other side of the fells. Unlucky the delay at Dorracleugh!

The light failed. White mists began to crawl across the road, and were spreading and rising fantastically on the hill-sides. The moon came out. He was growing more impatient. In crossing a mountain the eye measures so little distance gained for the time expended. The journey seemed, to him, interminable.

At one of the zig-zag turns of the road, there rises a huge fragment of white stone, bearing a rude resemblance to a horseman; a highwayman, you might fancy him, awaiting the arrival of the travellers. In Richard's eye it took the shape of old Sir Harry Rokestone, as he used to sit, when he had reined in his tall iron-grey hunter, and was waiting to have a word with some one coming up.

He muttered something as he looked sternly ahead at this fantastic reminder. On they drove; the image resolved itself into its rude sides and angles, and was passed; and the pale image of Sir Harry no longer waylaid his nephew.

Slowly the highest point of the road was gained, and then begins the flying descent; and the well-known landmarks, as he consults his watch, from time to time, by the moonlight, assure him that they will reach the station in time to catch the train.

He is there. He pays his post-boys, and with his black travelling-bag in hand, runs out upon the gravelled front, from which the platform extends its length.

"The up-train not come yet?" inquired the young man, looking down the line eagerly.

"Not due for four minutes, Mr. Marston," said the station-master, with officious politeness, "and we shall hardly have it up till some minutes later. They are obliged to slacken speed in the Malwyn cutting at present. Your luggage all right, I hope? Shall I get your ticket for you, Mr. Marston?"

The extraordinary politeness of the official had, perhaps, some connection with the fact that the rumour of Sir

Harry's death was there already, and the Rokestone estates extended beyond the railway. Richard Marston was known to be the only nephew of the deceased baronet, and to those who knew nothing of the interior politics of the family, his succession appeared certain.

Mr. Marston thanked him, but would not give him the trouble; he fancied that the station-master, who was perfectly innocent of any treacherous design, wished to play the part of a detective, and find out all he could about his movements and belongings.

Richard Marston got away from him as quickly as he civilly could, without satisfying his curiosity on any point. The train was up, and the doors clapping a few minutes later; and he, with his bag, rug, and umbrella, got into his place with a thin, sour old lady in black, opposite; a nurse at one side, with two children in her charge, who were always jumping down on people's feet, or climbing up again, and running to the window, and bawling questions with incessant clamour; and at his other side, a mummy-coloured old gentleman with an olive-green cloth cap, the flaps of which were tied under his chin, and a cream-coloured muffler.

He had been hoping for a couple of hours' quiet—perhaps a tenantless carriage. This state of things for a man in search of meditation was disappointing.

They were now, at length, at Dykham. A porter in waiting, from the inn called the "Three Nuns," took Marston's bag and rug, and led the way to that house, only fifty yards off, where he took up his quarters for the night.

He found Mr. Blount's promised letter from London there. He did not wait for candles and his sitting-room. In his hat and overcoat, by the gas-light at the bar, he read it breathlessly. It said substantially what Mr. Jarlcot's letter had already told him, and nothing more. It was plain, then, that Sir Harry had left every one in the dark as to whether he had or had not executed the will.

In answer to the waiter's hospitable inquiries about supper, he said he had dined late. It was not true; but it was certain that he had no appetite.

He got a sitting-room to himself; he ordered a fire, for

he thought the night chilly. He had bought a couple of books, two or three magazines, and as many newspapers. He had his window-curtains drawn; and their agreeable smell of old tobacco smoke assured him that there would be no objection to his cigar.

"I'll ring when I want anything," he said; "and, in the meantime, let me be quiet."

It was here, when he had been negotiating for Sir Harry the renewal of certain leases to a firm in Dykham, that the telegraph had brought him the startling message, and Mr. Blount said in the same message that he was writing particulars by that day's post.

Mr. Marston had not allowed grass to grow under his feet, as you see; and he was now in the same quarters, about to put the case before himself, with a thorough command of its facts.

CHAPTER LXIV.

THE WILL.

ANDLES lighted, shutters closed, curtains drawn, and a small but cheerful fire flickering in the grate. The old-fashioned room looked pleasant; Richard Marston was nervous, and not like himself. He looked over the "deaths" in the papers, but Sir Harry's was not among them. He threw the papers one after the other on the table, and read nothing.

He got up and stood with his back to the fire. He looked like a man who had got a chill, whom nothing could warm, who was in for a fever. He was in a state he had not anticipated—he almost wished he had left undone the things he had done.

He bolted the door—he listened at it—he tried it with his hand. He had something in his possession that embarrassed and almost frightened him, as if it had been some damning relic of a murdered man.

He sat down and drew from his breastpocket a tolerably bulky paper, a law-paper with a piece of red tape about it, and a seal affixing the tape to the paper. The paper was endorsed in pencil, in Sir Harry's hand, with the words, "Witnessed by Darby Mayne and Hugh Fenwick," and the date followed.

A sudden thought struck him; he put the paper into his pocket again, and made a quiet search of the room, even opening and looking into the two old cupboards, and peeping behind the curtains to satisfy his nervous fancy that no one was concealed there.

Then again he took out the paper, cut the tape, broke the seal, unfolded the broad document, and holding it extended in both hands, read, "The last will and testament of Sir Harry Rokestone, of Dorracleugh, in the County of——, Baronet."

Here, then, was the great sacrilege. He stood there with the spoils of the dead in his hands. But there was no faltering now in his purpose.

He read on: "I, Harry Rokestone, etc., Baronet, of Dorracleugh, etc., being of sound mind, and in good health, do make this my last will," etc.

And on and on he read, his face darkening.

"Four trustees," he muttered, and read on for awhile, for he could not seize its effect as rapidly and easily as an expert would. "Well, yes, two thousand two hundred pounds sterling by way of annuity—annuity!—to be paid for the term of his natural life, in four equal sums, on the first of May, the first of August—yes, and so on—as a first charge upon all the said estates, and so forth. Well, what else ?"

And so he went on humming and humming over the paper, his head slowly turning from side to side as he read.

"And Blount to have two hundred a year! I guessed that old Methodist knew what he was about; and then there's the money. What about the money?" He read on as before. "Five thousand pounds. Five thousand for me. Upon my soul! out of one hundred and twenty thousand pounds in government stock. That's modest, all things considered, and an annuity just of two thousand two hundred a year for my life, the rental of the estates, as I happen to know, being nearly nine thousand." This he said with a sneering, uneasy chuckle. "And that is all !"

And he stood erect, holding the paper by the corner between his finger and thumb, and letting it lie against his knee.

"And everything else," he muttered, "land and money, without exception, goes to Miss Ethel Ware. She the lady of the fee; I a poor annuitant !"

Here he was half stifled with rage and mortification.

"I see now, I see what he means. I see the drift of the whole thing. I see my way. I musn't make a mistake, though—there can't be any. Nothing can be more distinct."

He folded up the will rapidly, and replaced it in his pocket,

Within the last half hour his forehead had darkened,
and his cheeks had hollowed. How strangely these subtle
muscular contractions correspond with the dominant
moral action of the moment!

He took out another paper, a very old one, worn at
the edges, and indorsed " Case on behalf of Richard
Rokestone Marston, Esquire." I suppose he had read it
at least twenty times that day, during his journey to
Dorracleugh. " No, nothing on earth can be clearer or
more positive," he thought. " The whole thing is as
plain as that two and two make four. It covers everything."

There were two witnesses to this will corresponding
with the indorsement, each had signed in presence of the
other; all was technically exact.

Mr. Marston had seen and talked with these witnesses
on his arrival at Dorracleugh, and learned enough to
assure him that nothing was to be apprehended from
them. They were persons in Sir Harry's employment,
and Sir Harry had called them up on the day that the
will was dated, and got them to witness in all about a
dozen different documents, which they believed to be
leases, but were not sure. Sir Harry had told them
nothing about the nature of the papers they were wit-
nessing, and had never mentioned a will to them.
Richard Marston had asked Mrs. Shackelton also, and she
had never heard Sir Harry speak of a will.

While the news of Sir Harry's death rested only upon
a telegraphic message, which might be forged or precipitate, he dared not break the seal and open the will. Mr.
Blount's and Mr. Jarlcot's letters, which he had read
this evening, took that event out of the possibility of
question.

He was safe also in resolving a problem that was now
before him. Should he rest content with his annuity and
five thousand pounds, or seize the entire property, by
simply destroying the will?"

If the will were allowed to stand he might count on my
fidelity, and secure possession of all it bequeathed by
marrying me. He had only to place the will somewhere
in Sir Harry's room, where it would be sure to be found,

and the affair would proceed in its natural course without more trouble to him.

But Mr. Blount was appointed, with very formidable powers, my guardian, and one of his duties was to see, in the event of my marrying, that suitable settlements were made, and that there was no reasonable objection to the candidate for my hand.

Mr. Blount was a quiet but very resolute man in all points of duty. Knowing what was Sir Harry's opinion of his nephew, would he, within the meaning of the will, accept him as a suitior against whom no reasonable objection lay? And even if this were got over, Mr. Blount would certainly sanction no settlement which did not give me as much as I gave. My preponderance of power, as created by the will, must therefore be maintained by the settlement. I had no voice in the matter; and thus it seems that in most respects, even by marriage, the operation of the will was inexorable. Why, then, should the will exist? and why, with such a fortune and liberty within his grasp, should he submit to conditions that would fetter him?

Even the pleasure of depriving Mr. Blount of his small annuity, ridiculous as such a consideration seemed, had its influence. He was keenly incensed with that officious and interested agent. The vicar, in their first conversation, had opened his eyes as to the action of that pretended friend.

"Mr. Blount told me, just before he left this," said the good vicar, "that he had been urging and even entreating Sir Harry for a long time to execute a will which he had by him, requiring nothing but his signature, but, as yet, without success, and that he feared he would never do it."

Now approached the moment of decision. He had read a trial in the newspapers long before, in which a curious case was proved. A man in the position of a gentleman had gone down to a deserted house that belonged to him, for the express purpose of there destroying a will which would have injuriously affected him.

He had made up his mind to destroy it, but he was haunted with the idea that, do it how he might in the village where he lived, one way or other the crime would be discovered. Accordingly he visited, with many precautions, this old house, which was surrounded closely by a thick wood. From one of the chimneys a boy, in search of jackdaws, saw one little puff of smoke escape, and his curiosity being excited, he climbed to the window of the room to which the chimney corresponded, and peeping in, he saw something flaming on the hob, and near it a man, who started, and hurriedly left the room on observing him.

Fancying pursuit, the detected man took his departure, without venturing to return to the room.

The end of the matter was that his journey to the old house was tracked, and not only did the boy identify him, but the charred pieces of burnt paper found on the hob, having been exposed to chemical action, had revealed the writing, a portion of which contained the signatures of the testator, and the witnesses, and these and other part thus rescued, identified it with the original draft in possession of the dead man's attorney. Thus the crime was proved, and the will set up and supplemented by what, I believe, is termed secondary evidence.

Who could be too cautious, then, it such a matter? It seemed as hard to hide away effectually all traces of a will destroyed as the relics of a murder.

Again he was tempted to spare the will, and rest content with an annuity and safety. It was but a temptation, however, and a passing one.

He unbolted the door softly, and rang the bell. The waiter found him extended on a sofa, apparently deep in his magazine.

He ordered tea—nothing else; he was precise in giving his order—he did not want the servant pottering about his room—he had reasons for choosing to be specially quiet.

The waiter returned with his tea-tray, and found him buried, as before, in his magazine.

"Is everything there?" inquired Richard Marston.

"Everything there? Yes, sir, everything."

"Well, then, you need not come again till I touch the bell."

The waiter withdrew.

Mr. Marston continued absorbed in his magazine for just three minutes. Then he rose softly, stepped lightly to the door, and listened. He bolted it again; tried it, and found it fast.

In a moment the will was in his hand. He gave one dark, searching look round the room, and then he placed the document in the very centre of the embers. He saw it smoke sullenly, and curl and slowly warp, and spring with a faint sound, that made him start more than ever cannon did, into sudden flame. That little flame seemed like a bale-fire to light up the broad sky of night with a vengeful flicker, and throw a pale glare over the wide parks and mosses, the forests, fells, and mere, of dead Sir Harry's great estate; and when the flame leaped up and died, it seemed that there was no light left in the room, and he could see nothing but the myriad little worms of fire wriggling all over the black flakes which he thrust, like struggling enemies, into the hollow of the fire.

Richard Marston was a man of redundant courage, and no scruple. But have all men some central fibre of fear that can be reached, and does the ghost of the conscience they have killed within them sometimes rise and over-shadow them with horror? Richard Marston, with his feet on the fender and the tongs in his hands, pressed down the coals upon the ashes of the will, and felt faint and dizzy, as he had done on the night of the shipwreck, when, with bleeding forehead, he had sat down for the first time in the steward's house at Malory.

An event as signal had happened now. After nearly ten minutes had passed, during which he had never taken his eyes off the spot where the ashes were glowing, he got up and took the candle down to see whether a black film of the paper had escaped from the grate. Then stealthily he opened the window to let out any smell of burnt paper.

He lighted his cigar, and smoked; and unbolted the door, rang the bell, and ordered brandy-and-water. The suspense was over, and the crisis past.

He was resolved to sit there till morning, to see that fire burnt out.

CHAPTER LXV.

THE SERPENT'S SMILE.

HERE came on a sudden a great quiet over Dorracleugh—the quiet of death.

There was no longer any doubt, all the country round, as to the fact that the old baronet was dead. Richard Marston had placed at all the gates notices to the effect that the funeral would not take place for a week, at soonest—that no day had yet been fixed for it, and that early notice should be given.

The slight fuss that had prevailed within doors, for the greater part of a day, had now quite subsided—and, quiet as it always was, Dorracleugh was now more silent and stirless than ever.

I could venture now to extend my walks anywhere about the place, without the risk of meeting any stranger.

If there is a melancholy there is also something sublime and consolatory in the character of the scenery that surrounds it. Every one has felt the influence of lofty mountains near. This region is all beautiful; but the very spirit of solitude and grandeur is over it.

I was just consulting with my maid about some simple provisional mourning, for which I was about to despatch her to the town, when our conference was arrested by the appearance of Richard Marston before the window.

I had my things on, for I thought it not impossible he might arrive earlier than he had the day before.

I told my maid to come again by-and-by; and I went out to meet him.

Well, we were now walking on the wild path, along the steep side of the cleugh, towards the lake. What kind of conversation is this going to be? His voice and manner are very gentle—but he looks pale and stern, like a man going into a battle. The signs are very slight, but dreadful. Oh! that the next half-hour was over! What am I about to hear?

We walked on for a time in silence.

The first thing he said was:

"You are to stay here at Dorracleugh—you must not go—but I'm afraid you will be vexed with me."

Then we advanced about twenty steps; we were walking slowly, and not a word was spoken during that time.

He began again:

"Though, after all, it need not make any real difference. There is no will, Ethel; the vicar can tell you that; he had the key, and has made search—no will; and you are left unprovided for—but that shan't affect you. I am heir-at-law, and nearest-of-kin. You know what that means. Everything he possessed, land or money, comes to me. But—I've put my foot into it; it is too late regretting. I can't marry."

There was an interval of silence—he was looking in my face.

"There! the murder's out. I knew you would be awfully vexed. So am I—miserable—but I can't. That is, perhaps, for many years."

There was another silence. I could no more have spoken than I could, by an effort of my will, have lifted the mountain at the other side of the lake from its foundation.

Perhaps he misinterpreted my silence.

"I ought to have been more frank with you, Ethel—I blame myself very much, I assure you. Can't you guess? Well, I was an awful fool—I'll tell you everything. I feel that I ought to have done so, long ago; but you know, one can't always make up one's mind to be quite frank, and tell a painful story. I am married. In an evil hour, I married a woman in every way unsuited to me—pity me. In a transitory illusion, I sacrificed my life—and, what is dearer, my love. I have not so much as seen her for years, and I am told she is not likely to live long. In the meantime I am yours only—yours entirely and irrevocably, your own. I can offer you safety here, and happiness, my own boundless devotion and

adoration, an asylum here, and all the authority and
rights of a wife. Ethel—dearest—you won't leave me?"

I looked up in his face, scared—a sudden look, quite
unexpected. I saw a cunning, selfish face gloating down
on me, with a gross, confident, wicked simper.

That odious smile vanished, his eye shrank; he looked
detected or disconcerted for a moment, but he rallied.

"I say, I look on myself, in the sight of heaven, as
married to you. You have pledged yourself to me by
every vow that can tie woman to man; you have sworn
that no obstacle shall keep us apart. That oath was not
without a meaning, and you know it wasn't; and, by
heaven! you shan't break my heart for nothing! Come,
Ethel, be a girl of sense—don't you see we are controlled
by fate? Look at the circumstances. Where's the good
in quarrelling with me? Don't you see the position I'm
placed in, about that miserable evidence? Don't you see
that I am able and anxious to do everything for you?
Could a girl in your situation do a better or a wiser thing
than unite her interests with mine, indissolubly? For
God's sake, where's the use of making me desperate?
What do you want to drive me to? Why should you
insist on making me your enemy? How do you think
it's all to end?"

Could I have dreamed that he could ever have looked
at me with such a countenance, and spoken to me in such
a tone? I felt myself growing colder and colder; I could
not move my eyes from him. His image seemed to swim
before me; his harsh, frightful tones grow confused. My
hands were to my temples, I could not speak; my answer
was one piteous scream.

I found myself hurrying along the wild path, towards
the house, with hardly a clear recollection, without one
clear thought. I don't know whether he tried to detain
me, or began to follow me. I remember, at the hall-door,
from habit, going up a step or two, in great excitement—
we act so nearly mechanically! A kind of horror seized
me at sight of the half-open door. I turned and hurried
down the avenue.

It was not until I had reached the "George and
Dragon"—at the sleepiest hour, luckily, of the tranquil

little town of Golden Friars—that I made a first effectual effort to collect my thoughts.

I was simply a fugitive. To return to Dorracleugh, where Richard Marston was now master, was out of the question. I was in a mood to accept all ill news as certain. It never entered my mind that he had intended to deceive me with respect to Sir Harry's will. Neither had he as to my actually unprovided state. Here then I stood a fugitive.

I walked up to Mr. Turnbull, the host of the "George and Dragon," whom I saw at the inn-door, and having heard his brief but genuine condolences, without half knowing what he was saying, I ordered a carriage to bring me to the railway station; and while I was waiting I wrote a note in the quiet little room, with a window looking across the lake, to the good vicar.

Mr. Turnbull was one of those heavy, comfortable persons who are willing to take everybody's business and reasons for granted. He therefore bored me with no surmises as to the reasons of my solitary excursion at so oddly chosen a time.

I think, now, that my wiser course would have been to go to the vicar, and explaining generally my objections to remaining at Dorracleugh, to have asked frankly for permission to place myself under his care until the arrival of Mr. Blount.

There were fifty other things I ought to have thought of, though I only wonder, considering the state in which my mind was at the moment, that I was able to write so coherently as I did to the vicar. I had my purse with me, containing fifty pounds, which poor Sir Harry had given me just before he left Dorracleugh. With no more than this, which I had fortunately brought down with me to the drawing-room, for the purpose of giving my maid a bank-note to take to the town to pay for my intended purchases, I was starting on my journey to London! Without luggage, or servant, or companion, or plan of any kind—inspired by the one instinct, to get as rapidly as possible out of sight and reach of Dorracleugh, and to earn my bread by my own exertions.

CHAPTER LXVI.

LAURA GREY.

YOU are to suppose my journey safely ended in London. The first thing I did after securing lodgings, and making some few purchases, was to go to the house where my great friend Sir Harry Rokestone, had died. But Mr. Blount, I found, had left London for Golden Friars, only a few hours before my arrival.

Another disappointment awaited me at Mr. Forrester's chambers—he was out of town, taking his holiday.

I began now to experience the consequences of my precipitation. It was too late, however, to reflect; and if the plunge was to be made, perhaps the sooner the better. I wrote to the vicar, to give him my address, also to Mr. Blount, telling him the course on which I had decided. I at once resolved to look for a situation, as governess to very young children. I framed an advertisement with a great deal of care, which I published in the *Times*; but no satisfactory result followed, and two or three days passed in like manner.

After paying for my journey, and my London purchases, there remained to me, of my fifty pounds, about thirty-two. My situation was not so frightful as it might have been. But with the strictest economy a limited time must see my store exhausted; and no one who has not been in such a situation can fancy the ever-recurridg panic of counting, day after day, the diminishing chances between you and the chasm to whose edge you are slowly sliding.

A few days brought me a letter from the good vicar. There occurred in it a passage which finally quieted the faint struggle of hope now and then reviving. He said, "I observe by your letter that you are already apprised of the disappointing result of my search for the will of the late Sir Harry Rokestone. He had informed several persons of the spot where, in the event of his executing one, which he always, I am told, treated as very doubtful, it would be found. He had placed the key of the safe along with some other things at his departure, but without alluding to his will. At the request of Mr. Marston I opened the safe, and the result was, I regret to say, that no will was found." I was now, then, in dread earnest to lay my account for a life of agitation and struggle.

At last a promising answer to my advertisement reached me. It said, "The Countess of Rillingdon will be in town till this day week, and will be happy to see L. Y. L. X., whose advertisement appeared in the *Times* of this morning, if possible to-day before two." The house was in Belgrave Square. It was now near twelve. I called immediately with a note, to say I would call at a quarter to two, and at that hour precisely I returned.

It was plain that this was but a flying visit of the patrician owners of the house. Some luggage, still in its shiny black casings, was in the hall; the lamps hung in bags; carpets had disappeared; curtains were pinned up; and servants seemed scanty, and more fussy than in the organized discipline of a household. I told the servant that I had called in consequence of a note from Lady Rillingdon, and he conducted me forthwith up the stairs. We passed on the way a young lady coming down, whom I conjectured to be on the same errand as myself. We exchanged stolen looks as we passed, each, I daresay, conjecturing the other's chances.

"Her ladyship will see you presently," he said, opening a door.

I entered, and whom should I see waiting in the room, in a chair, in her hat, with her parasol in her hand, but Laura Grey.

"Ethel!"

"Laura!"

2 d

"Darling !"

And each in a moment was locked in the other's embrace. With tears, with trembling laughter, and more kisses than I can remember, we signalized our meeting.

"How wonderful that I should have met you here, Laura !" said I; though what was the special wonder in meeting her there more than anywhere else, I could not easily have defined. "You must tell me, darling, if you are looking to come to Lady Rillingdon, for, if you are, I would not for the world think of it."

Laura laughed very merrily at this.

"Why, Ethel, what are you dreaming of? I'm Lady Rillingdon !"

Sometimes a mistake seizes upon us with an unaccountable obstinacy. Laura's claiming to be Lady Rillingdon seemed to me simply a jest of that poor kind which relies entirely on incongruity, without so much colour of possibility as to make it humorous.

I laughed, faintly enough, with Laura, from mere politeness, wondering when this poor joke would cease to amuse her; and the more she looked in my face, the more heartily she laughed, and the more melancholy became my endeavour to accompany her.

"What can I do to convince you, darling?" she exclaimed at length, half distracted.

She got up and touched the bell. I began to be a little puzzled. The servant appeared, and she asked:

"Is his lordship at home ?"

"I'll inquire, my lady," he answered, and retired

This indeed was demonstration; I could be incredulous no longer. We kissed again and again, and were once more laughing and gabbling together, when the servant returned with:

"Please, my lady, his lordship went out about half an hour ago."

"I'm so sorry," she said, turning to me, "but he'll be back very soon, I'm sure. I want so much to introduce him; I think you'll like him."

Luncheon soon interrupted us; and when that little interval was over, she took me to the same quiet room, and we talked and mutually questioned, and got out of each the whole history of the other.

There was only one little child of this marriage, which seemed, in every way but that, so happy—a daughter. Their second, a son, had died. This pretty little creature we had with us for a time, and then it went out with its nurse for a drive, and we, over our afternoon tea, resumed our confessions and inquiries. Laura had nearly as much to tell as I. In the midst of our talk Lord Rillingdon came in. I knew whom I was to meet. I was therefore not surprised when the very man whom I had seen faint and bleeding in the wood of Plas Ylwd, whom Richard Marston had shot, and whom I had seen but once since at Lady Mardykse' ball, stood before me. In a moment we were old friends.

He remained with us for about ten minutes, talked kindly and pleasantly, and drank his cup of tea.

These recollections, in my present situation, were agitating. The image of Richard Marston had re-appeared in the sinister shadow in which it had been early presented to me by the friends who had warned me so kindly, but in vain.

In a little time we talked on as before, and everything she told me added to the gloom and horror in which Marston was now shrouded in my sorrowful imagination.

As soon as the first delighted surprise of meeting Laura had a little subsided, my fears returned, and all I had to dread from the active malice of Richard Marston vaguely gathered on my stormy horizon again.

CHAPTER LXVII.

A CHAPTER OF EXPLANATIONS.

AURA'S long talk with me resulted in these facts. They cleared up her story.

She was the only daughter of Mr. Grey, of Halston Manor, of whom I had often heard. He had died in possession of a great estate, and of shares in the Great Central Bank worth two hundred thousand pounds. Within a few weeks after his death the bank failed, and the estate was drawn into the ruin. Of her brother there is no need to speak, for he died only a year after, and has no connection with my story.

Laura Grey would have been a suitable, and even a princely match for a man of rank and fortune, had it not been for this sudden and total reverse. Old Lord Rillingdon—Viscount Rillingdon, his son, had won his own position in the peerage by brilliant service—had wished to marry his son to the young lady. No formal overtures had been made; but Lord Rillingdon's house, Northcot Hall, was near, and the young people were permitted to improve their acquaintance into intimacy, and so an unavowed attachment was formed. The crash came, and Lord Rillingdon withdrew his son, Mr. Jennings, from the perilous neighbourhood.

A year elapsed before the exact state of Mr. Grey's affairs was ascertained. During that time Richard Marston, who had seen and admired Laura Grey, whose brother was an intimate friend of his, came to the neighbourhood and endeavoured to insinuate himself into her good graces. He had soon learned her ruined circumstances, and founded the cruellest hopes upon this melancholy knowledge.

To forward his plans he had conveyed scandalous falsehoods to Mr. Jennings, with the object of putting an end to his rivalry. These Mr. Jennings had refused to believe; but there were others no less calculated to excite his jealousy, and to alienate his affection. He had shown the effect of this latter influence by a momentary coldness, which roused Laura Grey's fiery spirit; for gentle as she was, she was proud.

She had written to tell Mr. Jennings that all was over between them, and that she would never see him more. He had replied in a letter which did not reach her till long after, in terms the most passionate and agonising, vowing that he held himself affianced to her while he lived, and would never marry any one but her.

In this state of things Miss Grey had come to us, resolved to support herself by her own exertions.

Lord Rillingdon, having reason to suspect his son's continued attachment to Laura Grey, and having learned accidentally that there was a lady of that name residing at Malory, made a visit to Cardyllion. He was the old gentleman in the chocolate-coloured coat, who had met us as we returned from church, and held a conversation with her, under the trees, on the mill-road.

His object was to exact a promise that she would hold no communication with his son for the future. His tone was insolent, dictatorial, and in the highest degree irritating. She repelled his insinuations with spirit, and peremptorily refused to make any reply whatever to demands urged in a temper so arrogant and insulting.

The result was that he parted from her highly incensed, and without having carried his point, leaving my dear sister and me in a fever of curiosity.

Richard Rokestone Marston was the only near relation of Sir Harry Rokestone. He had fallen under the baronet's just and high displeasure. After a course of wild and wicked extravagance, he had finally ruined himself in the opinion of Sir Harry by committing a fraud, which, indeed, would never have come to light had it not been for a combination of unlucky chances.

In consequence of this his uncle refused to see him ; but at Mr. Blount's intercession agreed to allow him a small annual sum, on the strict condition that he was to leave England. It was when actually on his way to London, which, for reason that, except in its result, has no connection with my story, he chose to reach through Bristol, that he had so nearly lost his life in the disaster of the Conway Castle.

Here was the first contact of my story with his.

His short stay at Malory was signalised by his then unaccountable suit to me, and by his collision with Mr. Jennings, who had come down there on some very vague information that Laura Grey was in the neighbourhood. He had succeeded in meeting her, and in renewing their engagement, and at last had persuaded her to consent to a secret marriage, which at first involved the anguish of a long separation, during which a dangerous illness threatened the life of her husband.

I am hurrying through this explanation, but I must relate a few more events and circumstances which throw a light upon some of the passages in the history I have been giving you of my life.

Why did Richard Marston conceive, in perfect good faith, a fixed purpose to marry a girl of whom he knew enough to be aware that she was without that which prudence would have insisted on as a first necessity in his circumstances—money.

Well, it turned out to have been by no means so imprudent a plan. I learned from Mr. Blount the particulars that explained it.

Mr. Blount, who took an interest in him, and had always cherished a belief that he was reclaimable, told him repeatedly that Sir Harry had often said that he would take one of Mabel Ware's daughters for his heiress. This threat he had secretly laughed at, knowing the hostility that subsisted between the families. He was, however, startled at last. Mr. Blount had shown him a letter in which Sir Harry distinctly stated that he had made up his mind to leave everything he possessed to me. This he showed him for the purpose of inducing a patient endeavour to regain his lost place in the old man's regard.

It effectually alarmed Richard Marston; and when a chance storm threw him at our door, the idea of averting that urgent danger, and restoring himself to his lost position, by an act of masterly strategy, occurred to him, and instantly bore fruit in action.

After his return, and his admission as an inmate at Dorracleugh, the danger appeared still more urgent, and his opportunities were endless.

He had succeeded, as I have told you, in binding me by an engagement. In that position he was safe, no matter what turned up. He had, however, now made his election; and how cruelly, you already know. Did he, according to his low standard, love me? I believe, so far as was consistent with his nature, he did. He was furious at my having escaped him, and would have pursued, and no doubt discovered me, had he been free at the moment to leave Dorracleugh.

His alleged marriage was, I believe, a fiction. But he could not bear, I think, to lose me; and had he obtained another interview, he would have held very different language. Mr. Blount thought that he had, perhaps, formed some scheme for a marriage of ambition, in favour of which I was to have been put aside. If so, however, I do not think that he would have purchased the enjoyment of such ambition at the price of losing me at once and for ever. I dare say you will laugh at the simplicity of this vanity in a woman who, in a case like this, could suppose such a thing. I do suppose it, notwithstanding. I am sure that, so far as his nature was capable of love, he did love me. With the sad evidences on which this faith was grounded, I will not weary you. Let those vain conclusions rest where they are, deep in my heart.

The important post which Lord Rillingdon had filled, in one of our greatest dependencies, and the skill, courage, and wisdom with which he had directed affairs during a very critical period, had opened a way for him to still higher things. He and Laura were going out in about six months to India, and she and he insisted that I should accompany them as their guest. This would have been too delightful under happier circumstances; but the sense of dependence, however disguised, is dreadful. We are so

constructed that for an average mind it is more painful to
share in idle dependence the stalled ox of a friend than to
work for one's own dinner of herbs.

They were going to Brighton, and I consented to make
them a visit there of three or four weeks; after which I
was to resume my search for a "situation." Laura entreated me at least to accept the care of her little child ;
but this, too, I resolutely declined. At first sight you will
charge me with folly; but if you, being of my sex, will
place yourself for a moment in my situation, you will
understand why I refused. I felt that I should have been
worse than useless. Laura would never have ordered me
about as a good mother would like to order the person in
charge of her only child. She would have been embarrassed
and unhappy, and I conscious of being in the way.

Two other circumstances need explanation. Laura told
me, long after, that she had received a farewell letter from
Mr. Carmel, who told her that he had written to warn me,
but with much precaution, as Sir Harry had a strong antipathy to persons of his profession, of a danger which he
was not then permitted to define. Monsieur Droqville,
whom Mr. Marston had courted, and sought to draw into
relations with him, had received a letter from that young
man, stating that he had made up his mind to leave America
by the next ship, and establish himself once more at
Dorracleugh. It was Mr. Carmel, then, who had written
the note that puzzled me so much, and conveyed it, by
another hand, to the post-office of Cardyllion.

Monsieur Droqville had no confidence in Richard
Marston. He had been informed, besides, of the exact
nature of Sir Harry's will, and of a provision that made
his bequest to me void, in case I should embrace the Roman
Catholic faith.

It was in consequence of that provision in the draft-will
of Sir Harry Rokestone, and from a consideration of the
impolicy of any action while Lady Lorrimer's death was
so recent, and my indignation so hot, that Droqville had
resolved that, for a time, at least, the attempt to gain me
to the Church of Rome should not be renewed.

Taking the clear, hard view they do of the office of the
Church upon earth, they are right to discriminate. In the

sight of Heaven, the souls of Dives and of Lazarus are equally precious. In electing which to convert, then, they discharge but a simple duty in choosing that proselyte who will most strengthen the influence and action of the Church upon earth. In that respect, considering the theories they hold, they do right. Common sense acquits them.

I have now ended my necessary chapter of explanation, and my story goes on its way.

CHAPTER LXVIII.

THE LAST OF THE ROKESTONES.

 SOLEMN low-voiced fuss was going on in the old house at Dorracleugh ; preparations and consultations were afoot ; a great deal was not being done, but there were the whispering and restlessness of expectation, and the few grisly arrangements for the reception of the coffined guest.

Old Mrs. Shackleton, the housekeeper, crept about the rooms, her handkerchief now and then to her eyes ; and the housemaid-in-chief, with her attendant women, was gliding about.

Sir Harry had, years before, left a letter in Mr. Blount's hands, that there might be no delay in searching for a will, directing all that concerned his funeral.

The coffin was to be placed in the great hall of the house, according to ancient custom, on tressels, under the broad span of the chimney. This arrangement is more than once alluded to in Pepys's Diary. He was to be followed to the grave by his tenantry, and such of the gentry, his neighbours, as might please to attend. There was to be ample repast for all comers, consisting of as much " meat and drink of the best as they could consume ;" what remained was to be distributed among the poor in the evening.

He was to be laid in the family vault adjoining the church of Golden Friars ; a stone with the family arms, and a short inscription, " but no flatteries," was to be set up in the church, on the south wall, next the vault, and near the other family monuments, and it was to mention that he died unmarried, and was the last of the old name of Rokestone, of Dorracleugh.

The funeral was to proceed to Golden Friars, not by the "mere road," but, as in the case of other family funerals, from Dorracleugh to Golden Friars, by the old high-road.

If he should die at home, at Dorracleugh, but not otherwise, he was to be "waked" in the same manner as his father and his grandfather had been.

There were other directions, presents to the sexton and parish-clerk, and details that would weary you.

About twelve o'clock the hearse arrived, and two or three minutes after Mr. Blount drove up in a chaise.

The almost gigantic coffin was carried up the steps, and placed under the broad canopy assigned to it at the upper end of the hall.

Mr. Blount, having given a few directions, inquired for Mr. Marston, and found that gentleman, in a suit of black, in the drawing-room.

He came forward; he did not intend it, but there was something in the gracious and stately melancholy of his reception, which seemed to indicate not only the chief mourner, but the master of the house.

"Altered circumstances—a great change," said Mr. Marston, taking his hand. "Many will feel his death deeply. He was to me—I have said it a thousand times —the best friend that ever man had."

"Yes, yes, sir; he did show wonderful patience and forbearance with you, considering his temper, which was proud and fiery, you know—poor gentleman!—poor Sir Harry!—but grandly generous, sir, grandly generous."

"It is a consolation to me, having lost a friend, and, I may say, a father, who was, in patience, forbearance, and generosity, all you describe, and all you know, that we were lately, thanks, my good friend, mainly to your kind offices, upon the happiest terms. He used to talk to me about that farm; he took such an interest in it—sit down, pray—won't you have some sherry and a biscuit—and such a growing interest in me."

"I think he really was coming gradually not to think

quite so ill of you as he did," said good Mr. Blount. "No
sherry, no biscuit—no, I shan't mind. I know, sir, that
under great and sudden temptation a man may do the
thing he ought not to have done, and repent from his
heart afterwards, and from very horror of his one great
lapse, may walk, all the rest of his life, not only more dis-
creetly, but more safely than a man who has never slipped
at all. But Sir Harry was sensitive and fiery. He had
thought that you were to represent the old house, and
perhaps to bear the name after his death; and that both
should be slurred by, if I may be allowed the expression, a
shabby crime . . . . "

" Once for all, Mr. Blount, you'll be good enough to
remember that such language is offensive and intolerable,"
interrupted Richard Marston, firmly and sharply. " My
uncle had a right to lecture me on the subject—you can
have none."

" Except as a friend," said Mr. Blount. " I shall,
however, for the future, observe your wishes upon that
subject. You got my letter about the funeral, I see."

" Yes, they are doing everything exactly as you said,"
said Marston, recovering his affability.

" Here is the letter," said Mr. Blount. " You should
run your eye over it."

" Ha! It is dated a long time ago," said Mr. Marston.
" It was no sudden presentiment, then. How well he
looked when I was leaving this!"

" We are always astonished when death gives no warning," said Mr. Blount; " it hardly ever does to the persons
most interested. Doctors, friends, they themselves, are
all in a conspiracy to conceal the thief who has got into
the bed-room. It matters very little that the survivors
have had warning."

Richard Marston shook his head and shrugged his
shoulders.

" Some day I must learn prudence," said he.

" Let it be the true prudence," said Mr. Blount. " It
is a short foresight that sees no further than the boundary
of this life."

Mr. Marston opened the letter, and the old gentleman
left him, to see after the preparations.

Some one at Golden Friars—I think it was the vicar—sent me the country paper, with a whole column in mourning, with a deep black edge, giving a full account of the funeral of Sir Harry Rokestone, of Dorracleugh. The ancient family whose name he bore was now extinct. I saw in the list the names of county people who had come in their carriages more than twenty miles to attend the funeral, and people who had come by rail hundreds of miles. It was a great county gathering mostly that followed the last of the Rokestones, of Dorracleugh, to the grave.

CHAPTER LXIX.

SEARCH FOR THE WILL.

THE funeral was over; but the old house of Dorracleugh was not quiet again till the night fell,
and there was no more to-ing and fro-ing in the
stable-yard, and the last tenant had swallowed
his last draught of beer, and mounted and ridden away
through the mist, over the fells, to his distant farm.

The moon shone peacefully over mere and fell, and on
the time-worn church of Golden Friars, and through the
window, bright, on the grey flags that lie over Sir Harry
Rokestone. Never did she keep serener watch over the
first night of a mortal's sleep in his last narrow bed.

Richard Marston saw this pure light, and musing,
looked from the window. It shone, he thought, over his
wide estate. Beyond the mere, all but Clusted, for many
a mile was his own. At this side, away in the direction
of distant Haworth, a broad principality of moss and
heath, with scattered stretches of thin arable and pasture,
ran side by side with the Mardykes estate, magnificent in
vastness, if not in rental.

His dreams were not of feudal hospitality and the hearty
old-world life. His thoughts were far away from this
grand scenery or lonely Dorracleugh. Ambition built his
castles in the air; nothing very noble. It was not even
the tawdry and tradesman-like ambition of modern times.
He had no taste for that particular form of meanness, nor
patience for its drudgery. He would subscribe to election
funds, place his county influence at the disposal of the

minister; spend money on getting and keeping a seat; be found in his place whenever a critical vote was impending; and by force of this, and of his county position, and the old name—for he would take the name of Rokestone, in spite of his uncle's awkward direction about his epitaph, and no one could question his relationship—by dint of all this, with, I daresay, the influence of a high marriage, he hoped to get on, not from place to place, but what would answer him as well, from title to title. First to revive the baronetage, and then, after some fifteen or twenty years more of faithful service, to become Baron Rokestone, of Dorracleugh.

It was not remorse, then, that kept the usurper's eyes wide open, as he lay that night in the dark in his bed, his brain in a fever. His conscience had no more life in it than the window-stone. It troubled him with no compunction. There was at his heart, on the contrary, a vindictive elation at having defeated with so much simplicity the unnatural will of his uncle.

Bright rose the sun next morning over Dorracleugh, a sun of good omen. Richard Marston had appointed three o'clock as the most convenient hour for all members of the conference, for a meeting and a formality. A mere formality, in truth, it was, a search for the will of Sir Harry Rokestone. Mr. Blount had slept at Dorracleugh. Mr. Jarlcot, a short, plump man, of five-and-fifty, with a grave face and a bullet head, covered with short, lank, black hair, accompanied by his confidential man, Mr. Spaight, arrived in his gig, just as the punctual clock of Dorracleugh struck three.

Very soon after the old vicar rode up, on his peaceable pony, and came into the drawing-room, where the little party were assembled, with sad, kind face, and gentle, old-fashioned ceremony, with a little powdering of dust in the wrinkles of his clerical costume.

It was with a sense of pleasant satire that Richard Marston had observed old Lemuel Blount ever since he had been assured that the expected will was not forthcoming. These holy men, how they love an annuity! Not that they like money, of course; that's Mammon; but because it lifts them above earthy cares, and gives them the power of relieving the wants of their fellow-Christians. How slyly the old gentleman had managed it! How thoughtful his appointing himself guardian to the young lady! What endless opportunities his powers over the settlements would present of making handsome terms for himself with an intending bridegroom!

On arriving, in full confidence that the will was safe in its iron repository, Christian could not have looked more comfortable when he enjoyed his famous prospect from the delectable mountains. But when it turned out that the will was nowhere, the same Christian, trudging on up the hill of difficulty in his old "burdened fashion," could not have looked more hang-dog and overpowered than he.

His low spirits, his sighs and ejaculations, amused Richard Marston extremely. When he heard him say to himself, when first he learned that the vicar had looked into the safe and found nothing, "How sad! How strange! How very sad!" as he stood at the window, with his head lowered, and his fingers raised, he was tempted to rebuke his audacity with some keen and cautious irony; but those who win may laugh—he could afford to be good-humoured, and a silent sneer contented him.

Mr. Blount, having, as I said, heard that the vicar had searched the "safe," and that Mr. Spaight, accompanied by Mr. Marston, and the housekeeper, had searched all the drawers, desks, boxes, presses, and other lock-up places in the house in vain, for any paper having even a resemblance to a will, said: "It is but a form; but as you propose it, be it so."

And now this form was to be complied with. Mr. Marston told the servant to send Mrs. Shackelton with the keys. Mr. Marston led the way, and four other gentlemen followed, attended by the housekeeper.

There was not much talking; a clatter of feet on uncarpeted floors, the tiny jingle of small keys, the opening of doors, and clapping of lids, and now and then Mrs. Shackelton's hard treble was heard in answer to an interrogatory.

This went on for more than twenty minutes up-stairs, and then the exploring party came down the stairs again,

Richard Marston talking to the vicar, Mr. Blount to Mr. Spaight, while Mr. Jarlcot, the attorney, listened to Mrs. Shackleton, the housekeeper.

Richard Marston led the party to Sir Harry's room. The carpet was still on the floor, the curtains hanging still, in gloomy folds, to the ground. Sir Harry's hat and stick lay on the small round table, where he had carelessly thrown them when he came in from his last walk about Dorracleugh, his slippers lay on the hearthrug before his easy-chair, and his pipe was on the mantelpiece.

The party stood in this long and rather gloomy room in straggling disarray, still talking.

"There's Pixie," said old Mr. Spaight, who had been a bit of a sportsman, and loved coursing in his youth, as he stopped before a portrait of a greyhound, poking his long nose and spectacles, with a faint smirk, close into the canvas. "Sir Harry's dog; fine dog, Pixie, won the cup twice on Doppleton Lea thirty-two years ago." But this was a murmured meditation, for he was a staid man of business now, and his liking for dogs and horses was incongruous, and no one in the room heard him. Mr. Jarlcot's voice recalled him.

"Mr. Marston was speaking to you, Mr. Spaight."

"Oh! I was just saying I think nothing could have been more careful," said Mr. Marston, "than the search you made upstairs, in the presence of me and Mrs. Shackleton, on Thursday last?"

"No, sir—certainly nothing—it could not possibly have escaped us," answered Mr. Spaight.

"And that is your opinion also?" asked Mr. Jarlcot of Richard Marston.

"Clearly," he answered.

"I'll make a note of that, if you'll allow me," said Mr. Jarlcot; and he made an entry, with Mr. Marston's concurrence, in his pocket-book.

"And now about this," said Mr. Jarlcot, with a clumsy bow to Mr. Marston, and touching the door of the safe with his open hand.

"You have got the key, sir?" said Marston to the good vicar with silver hair, who stood meekly by, distrait and melancholy, an effigy of saintly contemplation.

2 D

" Oh, yes," said the vicar wakening up. " Yes; the key, but—but you know there's nothing there."

He moved the key vaguely about as he looked from one to the other, as if inviting any one who pleased to try.

"I think, sir, perhaps it will be as well if you will kindly open it yourself," said Marston.

"Yes, surely—I suppose so—with all my heart," said the vicar.

The door of the safe opened easily, and displayed the black iron void, into which all looked.

Blessed are they who expect nothing, for they shall not be disappointed. Of course no one was surprised. But Mr. Blount shook his head, lifted up his hands, and groaned audibly, " I am very sorry."

Mr. Marston did not affect to hear him.

CHAPTER LXX.

A DISAPPOINTMENT.

"I THINK," said Mr. Jarlcot, "it will be desirable that I should take a note of any information which Mr. Marston and the vicar may be so good as to supply with respect to the former search in the same place. I think, sir," he continued, addressing the vicar, "you mentioned that the deceased, Sir Harry Rokestone, placed that key in your charge on the evening of his departure from this house for London ?"

"So it was, sir," said the vicar.

"Was it out of your possession for any time ?"

"For about three quarteas of an hour. I hand d it to Mr. Marston on his way to this house ; but as I was making a sick-call near this, I started not many minutes after he left me, and on the way it struck me that I might as well have back the key. I arrived here, I believe, almost as soon as he, and he quite agreed with me that I had better get the key again into——"

"Into your own custody," interposed Marston. "You may recollect that it was I who suggested it the moment you came."

"And the key was not out of your possession, Mr. Marston, during the interval ?" said Mr. Jarlcot.

"Not for one moment," answered Richard Marston, promptly.

"And you did not, I think you mentioned, open that safe ?"

"Certainly not. I made no use whatever of that key at any time. I never saw that safe open until the vicar

2 D 2

opened it in my presence, and we both saw that it contained nothing; so did Mrs. Shackleton, as intelligent a witness as any. And, I think, we can all—I know I can, for my part—depose, on oath, to the statements we have made."

Mr. Jarlcot raised his eyebrows solemnly, slowly shook his head, and having replaced his note-book in his pocket, drew a long breath in through his rounded lips, with a sound that almost amounted to a whistle.

" Nothing could be more distinct; it amounts to demonstration," he said, raising his head, putting his hands into his trousers-pockets, and looking slowly round the cornice. "Haven't you something to say?" he added, laying his hand gently on Mr. Blount's arm, and then turning a step or two away; while Marston, who could not comprehend what he fancied to be an almost affected disappointment at the failure to discover a will, thought he saw his eyes wander, when he thought no one was looking, curiously to the grate and the hobs; perhaps in search, as he suspected, of paper ashes.

" I am awfully sorry," exclaimed Mr. Blount, throwing himself into a chair in undisguised despondency. " The will, as it was drafted, would have provided splendidly for Miss Ethel Ware, and left you, Mr. Marston, an annuity of two thousand five hundred a year, and a sum of five thousand pounds. For two or three years I had been urging him to execute it; it is evident he never did. He has destroyed the draft, instead of executing it. That hope is quite gone—totally."

Mr. Blount stood up and said, laying his hand upon his forehead, " I am grieved—I am shocked—I am profoundly grieved."

Mr. Marston was strongly tempted to tell Mr. Blount what he thought of him. Jarlcot and he, no doubt, understood one another, and had intended making a nice thing of it.

He could not smile, nor even sneer, just then, but Mr. Marston fixed on Lemuel Blount a sidelong look of the sternest contempt.

" There is, then," said Mr. Blount, collecting himself, " no will."

" That seems pretty clear," said Mr. Marston, with, in

spite of himself, a cold scorn in his tone. "I think so; and I rather fancy you think so too."

"Except this," continued Mr. Blount, producing a paper from his pocket, at which he had been fumbling. "Mr. Jarlcot will hand you a copy. I urged him, God knows how earnestly, to revoke it. It was made at the period of his greatest displeasure with you; it leaves everything to Miss Ethel Ware, and gives you, I grieve to say, but an annuity of four hundred a year. It appoints me guardian to the young lady, in the same terms that the latter will would have done, and leaves me, besides, an annuity of five hundred a year, half of which I shall, if you don't object, make over to you."

"Oh! oh! a will! That's all right," said Marston, trying to smile with lips that had grown white; "I, of course, you—we all wish nothing but what is right and fair."

Mr. Jarlcot handed him a new neatly-folded paper, endorsed "Copy of the Will of the late Sir Harry Rokestone, Bart." Richard Marston took it with a hand that trembled, a hand that had not often trembled before.

"Then, I suppose, Mr. Blount, you will look in on me, by-and-by, to arrange about the steps to be taken about proving it," said Mr. Jarlcot.

"It's all right, I dare say," said Mr. Marston, vaguely, looking from man to man uncertainly. "I expected a will, of course: I don't suppose I have a friend among you, gentlemen, why should I? I am sure I have some enemies. I don't know what country attorneys, and nincompoops, and Golden Friars' bumpkins may think of it, but I know what the world will think, that I'm swindled by d—d conspiracy, and that that old man, who's in his grave, has behaved like a villain."

"Oh, Mr. Marston, your dead uncle!" said the good vicar, lifting his hand in deprecation, with gentle horror. "You wouldn't, you can't!"

"What the devil is it to you, sir?" cried Marston, with a look as if he could have struck him. "I say it's all influence, and d—d juggling—I'm not such a simpleton. No one expected, of course, that opportunities like those should not have been improved. The thing's transparent.

I wish you joy, Mr. Blount, of your five hundred a year, and you, Mr. Jarlcot; of your approaching management of the estates and the money. If you fancy a will like that, turning his own nephew adrift on the world in favour of methodists and attorneys, and a girl he never saw till the other day, is to pass unchallenged, you're very much mistaken; it's just the thing that always happens when an old man like that dies—there's a will of course—every one understands it. I'll have you all where you won't like."

Mrs. Shackleton, with her mouth pursed, her nose high in the air, and her brows knit over a vivid pair of eyes, was the only one of the group who seemed ready to explode in reply; Mr. Blount looked simply shocked and confounded; the vicar maintained his bewildered and appealing stare; Mr. Spaight's eyebrows were elevated above his spectacles, and his mouth opened, as he leaned forward his long nose; Mr. Jarlcot's brow looked thunderous, and his chops a little flushed; all were staring for some seconds in silence on Mr. Marston, whose concluding sentences had risen almost to a shriek, with a laugh running through it.

"I think, Mr. Marston," said Jarlcot, after a couple of efforts, "you would do well to—to consider, a little, the bearing of your language; I don't think you can quite see its force."

"I wish you could—I mean it; and I'm d—d but you shall feel it too! You shall hear of me sooner than you all think. I'm not a fellow to be pigeoned so simply."

With these words, he walked into the hall, and a few moments after they heard the door shut with a violent clang.

A solemn silence reigned in the room for a little time; these peaceable people seemed stunned by the explosion.

"Evasit, erupit," murmured the vicar, sadly, raising his hands, and shaking his head. "How very painful.

"I don't wonder—I make great allowances," said Mr. Blount, "I have been very unhappy myself, ever since it was ascertained that he had not executed the new will. I am afraid the young man will never consent to accept a part of my annuity—he is so spirited."

"Don't be uneasy on that point," said Mr. Jarlcot; "if

you lodge it, he'll draw it; not—but I think—you might do—better—with your money."

There was something in the tone, undefinable, that prompted a dark curiosity.

Mr. Blount turned on him a quick look of inquiry. Mr. Jarlcot lowered his eyes, and then turned them to the window, with the remark that the summer was making a long stay this year.

Mr. Blount looked down and slowly rubbed his forehead, thinking, and sighing deeply, as he said, "It's a wonderful world, this—may the Lord have mercy on us all!"

CHAPTER LXXI.

A WOMAN'S HEART.

WO or three notices, which, Mr. Jarleot said, would not cost five pounds, were served on behalf of Mr. Marston, and with these the faint echo of his thunders subsided. There was, in fact, no material for litigation.

"The notices," Mr. Jarleot said, "came from Marshall and Whitaker, the solicitors who had years before submitted the cases for him, upon his uncle's title, and upon the question of his own position as nearest of kin and heir-at-law. He was very carefully advised as to how exactly he should stand in the event of his uncle's dying intestate."

I was stunned when I heard of my enormous fortune, involving, as it did, his ruin. I would at once have taken measures to deal as generously with him as the other will, of which I then knew no more than that Sir Harry must have contemplated, at one time, the possibility at least of signing it.

When I left Golden Friars I did so with an unalterable resolution never to see Richard Marston again. But this was compatible with the spirit of my intention to provide more suitably for him. I took Mr. Blount into council; but I was disappointed. The will had been made during my father's lifetime, and in evident apprehension of his influence over me, and deprived me of the power of making any charge upon the property, whether land or money. I could do nothing but make him a yearly present of a part of my income, and even that was embarrassed by many ingenious conditions and difficulties.

It was about this time that a letter reached me from Richard Marston, the most extraordinary I had ever read —a mad letter in parts, and wicked—a letter, also, full of penitence and self-upbraiding. " I am a fiend. I have been all cruelty and falsehood, you all mercy and truth," it said. " I have heard of your noble wishes—I know how vain they are. You can do nothing that I would accept. I am well enough. Think no more of the wretch. I have found, too late, I cannot live without you. You shall hear of me no more; only forgive me."

There are parts of this strange letter that I never understood, that may bear many interpretations, no one distinctly.

When Mr. Blount spoke of him he never gave me his conclusions, and it was always in the sad form " Let us hope;" he never said exactly what he suspected. Mr. Jarlcot plainly had but one opinion of him, and that the worst.

I agreed, I think, with neither. I relied on instinct, which no one can analyse or define—the wild inspiration of nature—the saddest, and often the truest guide. Let me not condemn, then, lest I be condemned.

The good here are not without wickedness, nor the wicked without goodness. With death begins the defection. Each character will be sifted as wheat. The eternal Judge will reduce each, by the irresistible chemistry of his power and truth, to its basis, for neither hell nor heaven can receive a mixed character.

I did hear of Richard Marston again once more—it was about five months later, when the news of his death by fever, at Marseilles, reached Mr. Blount.

Since then my life has been a retrospect. Two years I passed in India with my beloved friend, Laura. But my melancholy grew deeper; the shadows lengthened—and an irrepressible yearning to revisit Golden Friars and Malory seized me. I returned to England.

I am possessed of fortune. I thank God for its immunities—I well know how great they are. For its pleasures, I have long ceased to care. To the poor, I try to make it useful—but I am quite conscious that in this there is no merit. I have no pleasure in money. I think I have none in flattery. I need deny myself nothing, and yet be in the eyes of those who measure charity arithmetically a princely Christian benefactress. I wish I were quite sure of having ever given a cup of cold water in the spirit that my Maker commends.

A few weeks after my return, Mr. Blount showed me a letter. The signature startled me. It was from Monsieur Droqville, and a very short one. It was chiefly upon some trifling business, and it said, near the end :

"You sometimes see Miss Ware, I believe ; she will be sorry to hear that her old friend, Mr. Carmel, died last summer at his missionary post in South America. A truer soldier of Christ never fell in the field of his labours. Requiescat!"

There was a tremble at my heart, and a swelling. I held the sentence before my eyes till they filled with tears.

My faithful, noble friend! At my side in every trouble. The one of all mortals I have met who strove with his whole heart to win me, according to his lights, to God. May God receive and for ever bless you for it, patient, gentle Edwyn Carmel! His griefs are over. To me there seems an angelic light around him—the pale enthusiast in the robe of his purity stands saint-like before me. I remember all your tender care. I better understand, too, the wide differences that separated us, now, than in my careless girlhood—but these do not dismay me. I know that "in my father's house are many mansions," and I hope that when the clouds that darken this life are passed, we may yet meet and thank and bless you, my noble-hearted friend, where, in one love and light, the redeemed shall walk for evermore.

At Golden Friars I lived again for a short time. But the associations of Dorracleugh were too new and harrowing. I left that place to the care of good Mr. Blount, who loves it better than any other. He pays me two or three visits every year at Malory, and advises me in all matters of business.

I do not affect the airs of an anchorite. But my life is, most people would think, intolerably monotonous and lonely. To me it is not only endurable, but the sweetest that, in my peculiar state of mind, I could have chosen.

With the flight of my years, and the slow approach of the hour when dust will return to dust, the love of solitude steals on me, and no regrets for the days I have lost, as my friends insist, and no yearnings for a return to an insincere and tawdry world, have ever troubled me. In girlhood I contracted my love of this simple rural solitude, and my premature experience of all that is disappointing and deplorable in life confirms it. But the spell of its power is in its recollections. It is a place, unlike Dorracleugh, sunny and cheerful, as well as beautiful, and this tones the melancholy of its visions, and prevents their sadness from becoming overpowering.

I wonder how many people are living, like me, altogether in the past, and in hourly communion with visionary companions?

Richard Marston, does a waking hour ever pass without, at some moment, recalling your image? I do not mistake you; I have used no measured language in describing you. I know you for the evil, fascinating, reckless man you were. Such a man as, had I never seen you, and only known the sum of his character, I ought to have hated. A man who, being such as he was, meditated against me a measureless wrong. I look into my heart, is there vengeance there against you? Is there judgment? Is there even alienation?

Oh! how is it that reason, justice, virtue, all cannot move you from a secret place in my inmost heart? Can any man who has once been an idol, such as you were, ever perish utterly in that mysterious shrine—a woman's heart? In solitary hours, as I, unseen, look along the sea, my cheeks are wet with tears; in the wide silence of the night my lonely sobs are heard. Is my grief for you mere madness? Why is it that man so differs from man? Why does he often so differ from the noble creature he might have been, and sometimes almost was?

Over an image partly dreamed and partly real, shivered utterly, but still in memory visible, I pour out the vainest of all sorrows.

In the wonderful working that subdues all things to itself—in all the changes of spirit, or the spaces of eternity, is there, shall there never be, from the first failure, evolved the nobler thing that might have been? I care for no other. I can love no other; and were I to live and keep my youth through eternity, I think I never could be interested or won again. Solitude has become dear to me, because he is in it. Am I giving this infinite true love in vain? I comfort myself with one vague hope. I cannot think that nature is so cynical. Does the loved phantom represent nothing? And is the fidelity that nature claims, but an infatuation and a waste?

London: SWIFT and Co., 1 to 5, Newton Street, High Holborn, W.C
21/3/76.

LaVergne, TN USA
05 October 2009
159880LV00002B/27/A